Wilder Stone

Wilder Stone

by JOHN LEGGETT

HARPER & BROTHERS
PUBLISHERS NEW YORK

WILDER STONE

Copyright © 1960 by John Leggett

FIRST EDITION
I–I

Library of Congress catalog card number: 60-5907

For Lee

Wilder Stone

1.

WILDER had awakened early, at six, and dawdled around his one-room apartment in Tudor City, devoting much time and care to the simplest acts—to drying and polishing his razor, to making up a laundry bundle, and to listing its contents in his broad, painstaking script.

He had become expert at the killing of time, at losing himself in these tiny tasks. He knew it for a vice and took the more pleasure from it and from the guilty shudder when at last he looked at the clock.

He breakfasted at the automat on Forty-second and read the *Times* aimlessly from back to front. He walked slowly down Park, stopping to observe a display of sculpture, the work of depositors, in a bank window and a dispute between a taxi driver and a pedestrian whom he had nearly run down.

It was ten minutes to ten when he stepped from the elevator onto the seventh floor of 430 Fourth Avenue. Helen Russo, the switchboard operator, smiled affectionately at Wilder. She held him in particular esteem. He was a good-looking, an aristocratic-looking man, with his ramrod back and the proud, straight nose. His small mouth tended toward a primness, a puckering when he was upset. His hair, which receded deeply, was thin at the back and lightly touched with gray. He wore a dark suit he had bought at Rogers Peet four years ago and a dark brown hat, very straight on his head, the brim turned up all around.

He lifted the hat to Helen Russo with elaborate, not mock, courtesy. He was invariably courteous to Helen Russo as he was to the elevator boys and strangers in a public conveyance, although he was sometimes abrupt with his associates—as though he were anxious to get away.

She held out some message slips and he read the names—Mrs. Newbold, Miss Winter. "Mrs. Newbold called twice. It's about the painters, Mr. Stone. She talked with Mr. Coe."

"I'll call her in a bit. Thank you." He started through the swing door.

"And, Mr. Stone," she called after him, an edge of urgency to her voice, "Mr. Lazarus wants to see you. Mr. Lazarus, Senior."

Wilder paused halfway through the door, reflected on what the summons indicated, assumed it was some unpleasantness. He looked for confirmation in Miss Russo's face and found it or thought he did in a gravity there. She would know. It was that kind of office.

"When?"

"He said to come in any time it's convenient, any time this morning."

"Thank you." Wilder proceeded toward his desk, which was located now in an enclosure between the ladies' room and Murray Kaufman's office, which had once been his own.

He shared this space with Harry Coe, a man five years his junior who assisted him in the management of M. A. Lazarus buildings. He was a short, stocky fellow with coarse red hair and the florid skin that gave the impression of an outdoor man. The impression was false. Harry was Brooklyn-raised and only lately had acknowledged the world beyond the five boroughs.

Harry greeted him with the sly grin of an accomplice. "Morning, Wilder," he said, and glanced at his watch.

Wilder replied with a waggle of his hat which he hung on the rack and, with a sigh, sat down at his desk.

Miss Kriendler had opened his mail and it lay before him now. From the letterheads he knew the contents—a superintendent's report from 125 East Ninetieth, a bill for the new uniforms at 412 Park Avenue, an insurance claim from a delivery boy who had fallen on the stairs at 24 East Eighty-sixth. He looked grimly at the cliffs of paper, each weighted with a nickel-plated casting—a bolt, the handle of a water tap, a hinge—which covered the yellow oaken surface of his desk. Here were the business forms, the invoices from painters, awning makers, plumbers, plasterers, electricians, and the correspondence, mostly in the nature of complaint from M. A. Lazarus and Co. tenants, and the fine print, an ocean of it, from the insurance companies.

"You look tired," Harry said.

Feeling a little worse for this advice, Wilder replied, "I didn't sleep well. The old complaint."

"Yeah?" Harry shook his head. "Well, I don't see why you don't do something about that, Wilder. There's things you can take."

"No. No pills, thanks." Wilder smiled. "I disapprove."

"How about one of these gyms you see advertised. Maybe you ought to go to one of them and get some exercise."

Wilder laughed. "You can't see me in a sweat suit, Harry. You know me too well."

Mildly offended, Harry shook his *Tribune* open to the financial page. "So stay awake."

"I'm afraid I'll have to," Wilder said. Turning, he looked

into Harry's face, so shining and resilient it often seemed a youth's, and was cheered by the sight of a man who did not take his troubles into bed. It was not a particularly handsome face with its snub nose and fleshy lips, but it had pleased Wilder from the first he had seen it thirteen years earlier. It had been in a lecture hall at Columbia, a night course in the School of General Studies.

While Wilder was initially repelled by Harry's person, by the toneless Flatbush speech and bright brown suit, the composite was a fountain of energy, of exuberance or occasionally bitterness, and to his astonishment he found the man attractive. When he had turned up looking for a job, it was Wilder who saw that he might serve him and M. A. Lazarus well.

"Why don't you come to dinner some night next week?" Harry asked. "Bernice is after me again to get you up."

"I appreciate that. I hope you'll tell her so, Harry." Looking up, Wilder saw that Margaret Kriendler had come to the little fence, her notebook and pencil in hand. "Do you want to do any letters, Mr. Stone? Mr. Moss won't need me until this afternoon."

"Thanks, Miss Kriendler." He nodded gratefully. "In about half an hour would be better if you're still free. I've got a couple of calls to make and I have to see Mr. Lazarus."

"Yes. I'll come back then."

"What night?" Harry resumed. "What night can you come?"

"I don't know. I'll have to see." He flipped the pages of his calendar. "There's the holiday on Monday, and I'll have to go out and see Mother one night. . . ."

Harry groaned. "Here we go. Putting it off." He pointed an accusing finger. "You know, it's over a year since you've been up to our place. Bernice thinks you don't like her cooking."

"Oh, but I do. I do want to come," Wilder protested. "It

seems there's never time for the things I'd like to do." Yet as he spoke he knew he wouldn't go, that he would submit some excuse. The prospect of dinner with the Coes in their small, immaculate apartment on Sixty-first Street depressed him. And that, he thought, was strange, for if he had a friend in the world it was Harry Coe. Nor did he dislike the intense, garrulous girl he had married. Yet he was uncomfortable with them, lonelier than being alone. Most particularly he didn't want to be cheered up.

"I'll let you know," Wilder said, and did not argue with the doubting smirk that Harry gave him as he turned to the market reports.

"And how do you feel the opening will be today?" Wilder assumed the mock-serious expression he wore for this phase of the daily ritual. "I've been meaning to ask you, Harry. What's your view of utilities these days. Man to man. Are they sound?"

"All right wise guy." Harry pushed the paper toward Wilder. "It's listed today, see?"

Over Harry's thumb in the curb listings Wilder saw the Quirido Oil. It was selling for a dollar a share, somewhat less than Harry had paid for it a year ago. He nodded gravely. "One of these days you're going to wake up and find yourself a very rich man."

"It might do something yet," Harry said. "I haven't given up hope. Why the hell should I? That's the way fortunes are made you know—on long shots like Quirido Oil." He smiled. "And wouldn't I just love to see your face when this stuff starts to climb."

"Maybe you ought to go down there—to Ecuador or wherever it is."

"Guatemala."

"Yes. I think the Quirido people make a great mistake not having you on the scene. I feel sure you'd find the oil. They're probably looking in the wrong place."

Harry, pleased and flattered by this foolishness, laughed, and it occurred to Wilder that these insanely speculative investments (there had been an unfortunate flirtation with a color film venture a few years back) were a reflection of the Coes' rather towering expectations and he wondered how much longer Harry would be content with his role at Lazarus.

Of late there had been some signs of discontent, mutterings against the firm, against its Jewishness, against its being family-owned, even against Wilder himself. Sometimes, it seemed, he was putting Wilder's loyalty to the test.

Wilder shuffled his phone messages. "Do you know what Mr. Lazarus wants?"

Harry looked at him vacantly. "What?"

"Mr. Lazarus wants to see me. Do you have any idea what it's about?"

He seemed consumed with thoughts of a soaring Quirido. "No. I don't know what he wants. How should I know."

Wilder's phone rang, and picking up the receiver he heard his mother's gentle voice. "Wilder? Is that you, dear?"

"Mother. Good morning." He gave the chair a quarter turn so that he faced the window, showing Harry his back. "How are you feeling?"

"Well, all right I suppose, for an old lady."

"I'm glad to hear that. The hand's better, I trust."

She sighed. "No. Not really. The aching does seem to persist. It was sharp as a needle this morning. You'd think they could do something for me with all these wonderful new discoveries."

"Did you take one of the white capsules?"

"Oh, those don't help at all, Wilder. Not a particle."

"Well, you must do something about it, Mother. I don't like to think of you suffering so patiently. There's no need. Won't you give Dr. Greenslet a ring?"

"Really, there's nothing he can do. I've been through it so many times."

"Well, we'll see. I'll have a talk with Lyddie first thing."

"You are coming out tonight, aren't you, dear? We're expecting you."

"Yes." He nodded gravely as though she were before him. "Of course."

"For supper? Will you be out in time for supper?"

"Yes. I plan to. I'm not sure what train. I have to go up to the Seventh Regiment to see Jimmy's drill. But I should be along directly after that."

"That will be lovely, dear." She hesitated. "Oh, Wilder, I know you'll think this is silly of me." She laughed in embarrassment, softly yet frivolously. "I've a yen for something, and I can't get it out of my mind. Do you know what it is? It's for some of those lemon cookies your father and I used to be so fond of. Do you remember?"

"Mother, of course," he said. "You shall have lemon cookies."

"I don't want you to go to any trouble. I just thought that if it were convenient . . ."

"It will be convenient, Mother. Now call Dr. Greenslet and look for me about half past seven or so."

"Yes, dearest. Do take care of yourself."

Wilder was searching on his desk for a slip of paper on which to write himself a reminder about the lemon cookies when Murray Kaufman emerged from his office. He was headed for the back but, seeing Wilder, paused. "Oh, Wilder, you're here." He began to look through the folder he carried.

"At last." Wilder supplied.

Murray Kaufman was thirty. He had worked at M. A. Lazarus for only four of those years, ten less than Wilder, and
although he was but an assistant to a department head, to
"Buddy," M. A. Lazarus, Jr., of Construction, he now occupied
the office that had once been Wilder's and commanded the
services of a secretary, the pretty Miss Hartshorne, throughout the whole of her eight-hour day.

Various economies and changes had been necessary in the
last five years, and most of them had affected Wilder ad-
versely. "We little fellows are caught," Mr. Lazarus would say
to Wilder each time some new privation was required of him.
"You understand, don't you, Wilder? So if you don't mind
sharing Miss Kriendler with Mr. Moss . . . if you don't mind
moving to the small office. Just temporary, of course. I'm sure
that next year . . ."

"I understand," Wilder would say affably, and he would
understand as he got up to go that he had let this man down,
had disappointed him, and that there was nothing he could
do about it.

Murray was short and slim with bright brown eyes and a
directness that was sometimes unfeeling, but on the whole a
pleasing, friendly fellow. His unusual success here was due
only in part to his humming vitality. Four years earlier, the
year following his graduation from the University of Pennsylvania, he had married Anne Lazarus.

"Oh yes," Murray said, "Did you ever give me back that
report on the water tank at 330 Wilder? It was a couple of
weeks ago. I wanted to know if it tallied with the super's. I
can't seem to find it anywhere."

"It's probably here," Wilder said. "I'll look for it."

Murray frowned at the papers on Wilder's desk. Every time

something was missing it turned up there. He had once spent a whole night looking for something that turned up there. "I wish you would, Wilder. I really do." And he stepped off smartly toward the back of the office.

Wilder began to look for the water-tank report but instead picked up the message from Mrs. Newbold. "What about Mrs. Newbold?" he asked Harry.

"The painters," Harry replied. "They didn't get the right blue in the dining room."

"If she wants it done over, she'll have to pay for it. Did you tell her that?"

"You'd better call her, Wilder. I told her you would as soon as you got in." He didn't look up from the report he was reading.

Wilder frowned, and as he picked up his telephone and waited for Miss Russo to get Mrs. Newbold he tore off yesterday's page on his desk calendar and confronted his plans for the day. There were only two notations, both at the bottom of the page. "four-thirty," he had written, "Jimmy, Father's Drill, Knickerbocker Greys," and below it simply, "Dinner, Greenfield."

"Hello, is this Mr. Stone?" It was Mrs. Newbold's voice, irritable and querulous from the real and imagined slights at the hands of blockhead landlords and incompetent artisans.

"Yes. Mrs. Newbold?"

"I've been trying to reach you since this time yesterday, Mr. Stone. Haven't they given you my messages?"

"I'm sorry," he said, his voice retreating. "I've been out a great deal."

There was a silence at the other end—Mrs. Newbold's way of saying that she knew he had been avoiding her and despite the fact she was three months in arrears needn't stand for that sort of treatment. In the same silence Wilder was reflecting that just a few years back the indignant Mrs. Newbolds were his extreme pleasure—a game at which he was an expert. He knew that even now, in a matter of minutes, he could make a placid pond of Mrs. Newbold's disposition. An attentive ear, a sympathetic cluck, a kind word for her patience, a threat to unionized labor—and it would be done. It would have made no great demands upon him, only some healthy interest in the game.

"Your men," she resumed, "have made a thorough botch of my apartment. They didn't seem to have the faintest notion about color. Don't you realize, Mr. Stone, that I have spent a great deal of money for a decorator's advice? That a plan was drawn for my apartment which co-ordinates the walls, the draperies, the rugs, the upholstery, everything. I explained it very carefully to your painter, and I left him a sample of the blue I wanted. I don't understand how he could go wrong. Do you, Mr. Stone?"

"Yes," Wilder said. "There are many ways."

"I came back from the country on Sunday night to find an absolutely incredible color—a blue that isn't remotely like mine. He's given me a blue with green in it. It's practically a peacock. I told him specifically there was no green in it. My blue is a blue blue. It won't do. It won't do at all. The dining room will have to be done over."

"I'm afraid it will prove rather expensive for you, Mrs. Newbold. It will run to a hundred dollars anyway."

"On the contrary. Expensive for you perhaps, or the painters. It's your mistake, not mine, Mr. Stone. And another thing. I shall want them finished with the repainting by next Wednesday. This apartment has been in a mess for a week, and I won't put up with much more of it."

"I'm afraid that isn't possible, Mrs. Newbold. The painters' work is scheduled for months in advance."

"Then get some different painters. I don't care what you do so long as you fulfill your responsibility of redecorating my apartment to my taste, not the painters'. It's in my lease, you know. I'm not asking for a favor."

"Mrs. Newbold . . ." Wilder began wearily.

"I think, perhaps, you'd better come up and look at this yourself."

"I'll try."

"No, no. I want a promise and a definite appointment. Or did you expect me to wait here at the door until you find the time. Can you come now—right away?"

"No."

"Sometime in the forenoon?"

"I'm sorry. I'm extremely busy this morning."

"At three then. I'll expect you."

Wilder groped for an excuse, found none. "All right." And for farewell he heard only the click of Mrs. Newbold's receiver. Another man would have cursed aloud.

Harry looked over at him expectantly and Wilder considered recounting Mrs. Newbold's half of the conversation, but he detected in Harry's zeal the danger. Harry had a way of repeating such things in a way that reflected on him.

"If anybody wants me," Wilder said, "I'll be in Mr. Lazarus' office."

He went out through the swing gate and, stopping by the water cooler, sipped from a paper cup. He listened to the industrious hum, the whirring of a calculator, the clicks and bells of the typewriters, a phone ringing, a humming of women's voices, a laugh. As he looked about this roomful of clerks and stenographers at their chores, it seemed to him that he saw a roomful of contented people. Oh, there were some grim faces, Mr. Rhau in the back seemed to have another one of his colds and Anna Ryan was a storm cloud this morning, but for the most part these people were getting pleasure out of being here—from the routine perhaps; routine was a comfort—or being together, or earning the money, or being able to leave at the big glass door in the lobby such troubles as they had acquired in the world outside.

He marveled briefly at the careless forces which led a man to a particular desk, sat him at it, and caused him to spin out the better part of his days there. And how was it that some men found some reason there in the pile of papers—some explanation? It wasn't the money or power they saw there, for here were these clerks whose meager incomes would grow by fives and tens at the annual Christmas raises until at fifty-five a man might hope for title to a shoe box of a house in the ranks that stood from Flushing to Floral Park and afford a new overcoat every third year.

Yet he took pleasure in none of these things. The money? Oh, yes, you had to have money, but he got no pleasure from its earning. It was scarcely enough (five thousand dollars a year, only, in salary and the insurance commissions, which came to another three thousand dollars) for a man to take pride in its making. Yet he didn't really care about more. He had simple tastes, ascetic tastes, took a pride in self-denial, in his sensible life with its bare minimum of indulgences.

The routine was no comfort to him now, but it seemed at least to have lulled him. The fourteen years he had worked here in this very office had slipped by as if they were as many days. He had gone from youth to middle age here, standing by the water cooler, trying not to acknowledge that some capacity, some vital juice, was drying up within him.

It took some effort now to recall just how he did first come here, but then painfully he could see himself on a late summer morning in 1945 reading the classifieds in the *Times* and finding the one that sent him here. He was twenty-six then and still full of the pride that had come from turning down the charitable offers of his mother's distant relatives to "find him something downtown."

He'd bought a new and expensive suit and a London hat at Brooks Brothers for the job hunting. He had taken great pride in his appearance then and dressed like a young man just down from New Haven. And now he recalled that first meeting with Mr. Lazarus. "Wilder," he had said when the interview was finished, "I think we need you here. I hope you'll come to work for us, and I also hope that in time you'll be a member of the firm."

Wilder was proud to bursting. What a compliment, and from the young president of a new and lively firm. At that moment, so filled with hope and direction, Wilder pledged his utmost to Milton Lazarus and fled into the street and onto the subway and the ferry and finally the little Erie train to tell them about it in Greenfield.

He threw the paper cone into the basket and walked rather slowly down the passageway between the desks of the auditing department toward Mr. Lazarus' office, and as he passed Margaret Kriendler's desk she looked up and smiled.

At the extreme rear of the office Buddy Lazarus was uncurling a roll of blueprints, spreading them on the wide table. He had taken off his jacket, and in the gleaming white shirt, with the sleeves rolled above thick, athletic forearms, he seemed agreeably out of place in this congregation of pencil-limbed clerks. He and the architect bent low over the drawing, following a conduit. Buddy pointed and the architect nodded. Seeing Wilder, Buddy smiled. It was wide open and affectionate. He raised a hand cupped about the stub of a cigarette in casual greeting, but then, before his gesture was complete and well before Wilder could return it, some new thought turned his face away toward the window and then, after a moment, back to the drawing on the table.

Wilder, alone among the office staff, habitually paused on the threshold of Mr. Lazarus' office and awaited an invitation to enter. He did so now, and Milton Lazarus, seeming grayer and more tired than ever before, said, "Come in, Wilder," and waved him to the chair beside his desk.

In his smile you saw the relation between this small, delicate man and the young lion outside at the drafting table. The smile opened like a door in his nervousness and preoccupation, revealing the gentleness and sympathy that was the man. He had been signing some letters, reading them carefully with the little dark horn-rims halfway down his nose, which gave him, when he looked over their tops as he did now, a misleading comic aspect. Even now, at sixty-three, when there was time for many things, there was no time for comedy in Milton Lazarus' life.

He pushed the letters back and turned with unmistakable gravity to Wilder. "Miss Kelly," he said, "would you leave us alone for a few minutes?"

Miss Kelly, a solid, severe woman, departed silently, closing the door after her. This unusual occurrence suggested to Wilder the gravity of the occasion. He faced up to the thought that Mr. Lazarus was about to fire him, and curiously he felt no panic. He felt an embarrassment for Mr. Lazarus—hoped it wouldn't be painful for him. He felt himself withdrawing some from the scene, taking up a position overhead, on the rim of the frosted ceiling fixture, where he wouldn't be involved but at the same time wouldn't miss anything. He was curious. But no anguish. Not yet anyway. Perhaps that would come later, like the big shocks that a man can only absorb slowly.

Mr. Lazarus swiveled toward Wilder and peered curiously at him. "How's your boy, Wilder? Getting along all right?"

Wilder nodded. "Fine, sir."

"Still up there at 312 with his grandmother?"

"Yes. At 312. He's everything to her. You can imagine. She does awfully well with him, better than I would certainly, and better than Mother and Lyddie, too. Mother's getting old. She's sixty-eight. And Lyddie. Well, you know Lyddie."

Mr. Lazarus brightened a bit. "You tell Lyddie that she did a good job for us up there at Eightieth Street and I"—he paused, not wanting to make a promise—"and I hope she'll work for us again . . . sometime." He ended rather lamely and, turning, looked out the window. He could see down Twenty-ninth Street to the East River, and a vessel moving slowly downstream absorbed his interest.

"That boy's going to be all right, Wilder. I saw him when he was in here the other day. He had on his little blue cap with the emblem on it. What's that emblem for?"

"Trinity. Trinity School. He's in the sixth grade up there."

"I passed him waiting there in the lobby for you, and when I said hello to him he said right back, 'Hello, Mr. Lazarus.' Didn't look away or mumble the way kids that age do. How old is he?"

"Twelve. He's just turned twelve."

"Smart? Like his old man?"

Wilder smiled at this facetiousness. "A good deal smarter than that I should think and I most certainly hope." He found Mr. Lazarus still looking at him inquiringly and realized the question was more than a politeness. "He gets average marks. B's and C's. He's not much of a mathematician at the moment, but he seems to have a feeling for languages. He seems to be happy there, and that's the main thing."

Mr. Lazarus nodded, though he did not agree. A string of A's on a report card of Buddy's or Anne's meant more to him than any other consideration. Home was the place to look for happiness. The schoolroom, like an office, was a place where business was done. His eyes strayed to the framed photographs on his desk.

In a pigskin frame Grace Lazarus, a frail, handsome woman in a white dress, shared a wrought-iron bench with Buddy, who looked about sixteen here, and his sister Anne, a lovely dark-eyed child of twelve. In the background there was a sizable brick house in the Norman style, the Lazarus home in Mamaroneck. In the other frame, a silver one, stood a grinning Buddy in cap and gown, holding his diploma. In the background were the steps and columns of the Columbia University library.

"You should be very proud of that boy," Milton Lazarus said.

"I'm afraid I can't take much credit."

He shook his head. "An infant must be cared for by a woman, but now he's growing up you're the great force. You are now. You will be more. It seems to me you've done awfully well. You've had some bad luck, Wilder." He spread his hands on the smooth, blue-stained surface of the desk. "I doubt I would have borne it so well. And here, I'm afraid, is some more."

Wilder sat up a little straighter. "What's that, Mr. Lazarus?"

"I've been talking to some of the agency men this week about the building insurance."

Wilder shifted uneasily, plucked at the button on his cuff. His mind scuttled among the possibilities, and he saw now the shape of what was coming. He felt no relief that Mr. Lazarus' news was not as bad as the worst he had prepared for. Indeed he knew a momentary regret that it was not the worst, which was not without its attraction.

"Which agency man?" Wilder asked.

"There's a fellow named Gordon."

"George Gordon? Maryland Mutual?"

"Yes. I suspect we'll go with him. I believe they're all about the same in terms." He opened his hands in a gesture of helplessness. "Well, you know, Wilder. It's a great deal cheaper. They'll write one mutual policy that will cover all buildings for liability and fire at a saving of several thousand dollars a year. I don't see how I can avoid it."

Wilder felt a weakness, as though the pins which had been holding him together at the joints had just been removed. "Nor do I," he said softly. "I've always known you could save that much in premiums. I think it will actually work out to around twelve hundred dollars. I thought you knew it. As a matter of fact, I told you that you could. I told you when the mutuals first came out, and I thought the reason you didn't take advantage of it was that you felt the commissions I made on insuring Lazarus buildings were part of my pay."

"That's true." He picked up his spectacles, held the lenses to the light for inspection, and then carefully put them on. "It may be we can make it up to you in some way when we review the salary schedule in the fall."

This last had a familiar, a just-temporary-of-course-I'm-sure-that-next-year ring to it, and Wilder felt very much the drowning man. "It's quite a sum to make up to me in salary. My commissions amount to around three thousand dollars."

"I didn't realize it was quite that much."

"I doubt I can live without it. It's not me, you know. I live very inexpensively, and I daresay could cut down even further, but there's Jimmy—his education in prospect—and the family in Greenfield. They don't have any other income."

"Your father left nothing?"

"Nothing."

Milton Lazarus made a wincing face and nodded.

"Do you mean—and I really must know—that in December you'll be making up to me something like three thousand dollars a year? You can't mean that. But if it's to be just a couple of hundred dollars I'm afraid . . ."

"We'll have to wait and see, Wilder." He looked thoughtfully at him. "Don't look so tragic. You're an intelligent fellow. You're still a young man."

From where he sat Wilder could read his own signature on one of the framed licenses of the New York Real Estate Board. It was the license from the year 1946, and he had signed it as Secretary of the Corporation, a position he had held, justifying Mr. Lazarus' original optimism, for the year prior to Catherine's death.

"I'm forty."

"That's young. That's a very young man today in America. You've got a whole life before you. Forty is still the beginning, the threshold of a man's career."

"Will you be frank with me, Mr. Lazarus?"

"Of course."

"I know it is hard. I find it impossible myself. But I also know it is the kindest thing to say it plainly so there can be no doubt. Am I being fired? Do you want me to go?"

"No, no, no. God forbid." He slapped the top of the desk gently, impatient with himself. "You must know that isn't so."

He spoke in a rapid monotone, through his nose, which gave his words a heartless recorded quality they did not deserve. "Now listen to me, for this is the important thing and everything else—what I say after it—is only conjecture, wondering, guessing, thinking about you. But this is fact. So long as I am in charge here, or Buddy for that matter, there is a place for you here. My God, Wilder, you must know that. You're as much a part of this firm as I am. Too much of you has gone into it ever to be otherwise."

"That helps a lot."

"But now, there's you." He looked at the photograph of Grace and the children on the lawn and seemed to become lost in it. "It's very hard to tell a man what you believe to be the truth about him—and it is almost always a mistake."

"Yes," Wilder said. "I think it probably is."

Mr. Lazarus raised an eyebrow. "Why?"

Wilder found the office oppressive, almost unbearable. He had the feeling that if the door were not opened in a moment he would suffocate here. "I don't want you to trouble," he stammered. He looked at the door, started to get up. "Just please don't trouble. It doesn't matter."

"It does matter." He held up his small hand. "Wait a minute."

Wilder sat down again stiffly, stared at a shoelace, untied it, tied it again.

"The trouble with you is you don't care as much as you should. Not as much as you used to."

"About my job?"

"About everything. Yes, your work but also yourself."

"Of course I care," Wilder said with a desperate shake of his head. "The job is everything to me. I can't do . . . I don't *know* anything else." He leaned forward eagerly. "I know

I've been no use lately. I've been feeling kind of rundown."
He managed a weak smile, scant reassurance. "But I'll come
around all right."

"Do you know why you care about this job?"

"Because of Jimmy and because of Greenfield—the family
—because of the people who depend on me."

"Well, I think that's wrong, Wilder, and I think you fail
them in that way. If you work simply to care for these wards
—a mother, a sister, a son—you will surely fail them. You
must somehow begin again to work for *you*." He made a wry
face. "Wilder, you don't hear me, do you? I'm telling you your
life is not over and you must not sit there in the ashes another
year."

"I know. I've had a lot of problems on my mind the last
year or so. But I'm pretty certain some of them will get settled
in the next couple of months."

"And when those are settled, there'll be new ones to replace
them. I wonder—and I'm not suggesting it, mind you, I'm just
interested in your reaction—about a change of job."

"I have thought of it." He pressed his hands between his
knees. "I don't think I could find another job."

"That's utter foolishness."

Wilder shrugged. "I've nothing to offer anyone. I'm a down-
at-heels middle-aged fellow with no college, without a pro-
fession, without even a skill. I know only one thing—the very
specialized job that I have made out of odds and ends here.
I'd be of no earthly use elsewhere."

"That isn't true. I think what you really mean is you are
familiar with things here and you don't want to have to adapt
yourself to new situations, new people."

"I'll think about it some more," Wilder said. "I might inquire around. But not now. I couldn't now."

"All right, Wilder," he said and, reaching for the letters across his desk, terminated the interview. "Would you ask Miss Kelly to come back in?"

"Yes, of course." Wilder paused in the doorway. "And you may make some salary adjustment . . . about the insurance?"

"I said we'd consider it. Don't count on it, Wilder. We're trying to run a business here, you know."

"I know." He started back toward his desk, dazed, forgetting to recall Miss Kelly.

He made another stop at the water cooler and, raising the cup to his lips, found his hand was trembling. The knowledge that he had disappointed was with him always—so familiar now that it could be thrust far back in the mind, nearly forgotten. But it stood beside him now, immense, the knowledge that at a dark hour of his journey he had lost some vital stuff, his heart, perhaps, that without it he was a fraud.

Returning, he saw Harry Coe catch sight of him and then pretend that he had not, and in this small, covert act Wilder sensed that Harry knew, had known all along, what business Mr. Lazarus had with him this morning.

Sitting down at his desk, Wilder saw a note impaled on the handle of his desk pen—"Did you find the 330 water-tank report? Murray"—and once more began to search his desk.

"So?" Harry asked.

"Hm?" Wilder looked up.

"Mr. L. What did he have to say?"

"Nothing much."

Oh, he knew. Harry knew! And Gordon. There was some link there. Harry and George Gordon. The realization cracked open before him.

Ironically it was Wilder who had known Gordon first, had given him some business a few years back and had, a year ago, introduced him to Harry, noting they were of an age, both married, childless, and living within a block of one another. Now he recalled he had seen them together recently, coming out of the Japanese place on Twenty-ninth. They had looked startled at the sight of him, and as he had stood with them for a moment on the corner of Fourth Avenue they had seemed uncomfortable. Now he knew why.

But turning to look at Harry going about his business in familiar fashion, jotting some figures on a yellow pad, reaching for the phone, leaning back, smiling as he spoke into the instrument, running his hand affectionately across the top of his head, Wilder found it increasingly hard to believe Harry capable of so black a conspiracy. He was his friend. He had proved it so many times it could not be otherwise.

He found himself recalling an April dusk of many years ago. He had been coming down the steps of Butler Library, arm in arm with Catherine, when Harry had appeared out of the light rain which was falling. He had introduced them, and Harry had said to Wilder, "You have all the luck." It was not a compliment but so clearly an honest expression of the admiration and envy he held for Wilder that no one laughed, and Catherine had simply said, "Thank you."

That was 1946, a year in which he had been happily in love and seeing all his plans take shape. Later in the spring he had found new pleasure in teaching Harry what he knew of M. A. Lazarus properties, of the tenements and lofts along Delancey and Houston Streets, of the walk-ups in Chelsea, the sooty brownstones off Amsterdam and Columbus, and the cliffs of marble and granite that looked into the rivers and the park. From the start it was apparent Harry had a talent for collecting rent from the reluctant, for keeping janitors and elevator boys anxious about the duration of their employment.

In June Harry had come down to Sea Girt for Wilder's wedding. He had come with Margaret Kriendler and the others from the office. If Charlie Rodman hadn't turned up, Wilder would have asked him to be his best man.

Then in the fall of 1947 Harry had done all a friend could. Each night he had come by Wilder's place at 21 Fifth Avenue to persuade him out for a walk. He was content to stroll along in silence through the dark Village streets. It was Harry too who had proposed the Mediterranean cruise which in the end *had* proved a restorative.

On that voyage, sharing a cabin on the *Excambion*, standing at the rail to see the white boulevard of their wake become a path and, miles astern, traceless, bottomless gray sea again, sitting side-by-side in the sight-seeing busses as they jostled along the cobbles of Marseilles and Naples, Wilder felt the closest thing to comradeship he had ever known.

As Harry hung up the phone he yawned, groped in his pockets and then turned to Wilder. "Got a cigarette on you?"

Wilder opened his desk drawer and found a half-empty package. He shook a cigarette out and held it toward Harry, who took it and rolled it thoughtfully between his fingers.

"Busy for lunch?" Wilder asked.

Harry shook his head.

"Let's have a sandwich downstairs. There's something I want to ask you."

In recent years they seldom lunched together, and Harry raised his eyebrows. "O.K.," he said and lit the cigarette. "Is there anything the matter?"

"Yes. There is."

At noon Harry and Wilder entered the luncheonette on the street floor of 430 Fourth Avenue and, taking the last available booth, ordered sandwiches and coffee.

As they waited, Wilder wondered how to begin. He could not bear to look at Harry and instead peered through the plate glass at the traffic passing by in the street.

"What's on your mind?" Harry asked.

"I've had a cut in my—my pay," Wilder said, turning to him. "That's what Mr. Lazarus was breaking to me this morning."

"Jesus," Harry wagged his head in sympathy. "That's tough luck, Wilder. I'm sure sorry to hear that."

The waitress set the sandwiches and coffee before them, and Wilder smiled at her gratefully as she punched his check.

"Listen, Wilder," Harry leaned across the table toward him confidentially. "I'm going to tell you something. It's about time both of us wised up to ourselves. I mean it." With his thumb he pointed upward. "It's a family affair. If your name isn't Buddy Lazarus or Murray Kaufman, you get so far and no farther. Isn't that true now?"

It was old talk and Wilder sighed. "It may be true, but it's beside the point. I'm talking about making a living."

"All right," Harry said. He took a bite of sandwich and chewed it rapidly, talking at the same time. "So am I. That's what we're all interested in and what I'm telling you, Wilder, is"—the thumb went upward again—"*wrong*. It's the wrong place for you and me. Now just for example I see this morning Buddy's still busy with the architects, even though we took a beating on new construction last year and costs have gone even higher."

"You can make a case for it," Wilder replied. "The demand for medium-priced housing in Manhattan is going to continue."

"Buddy wants to build. That's the real reason, and you

know it as well as I do." Harry sipped at his coffee. "Cut old Wilder back. He won't mind. And if he does, what the hell? The main thing is to keep Buddy and Murray happy. You really have to hand it to them. They know how to take care of their own."

"It's a family business," Wilder said just audibly. "There's no question about it."

"They use us. We're the front. Don't you see?" Harry said with increasing fervor. "We're the window dressing. Goyim to give the place a little class. But they're Jews and a Jew will use a gentile every time. They're using you, Wilder."

"That's not true," Wilder said. "If there's any using going on, and I suspect there is, I'm the one that's doing it. Milton Lazarus may be many terrible things—a family man, a business man, a Jewish man, but he's fair and honest. He's been very kind to me. He's an exceptional man, really. I couldn't ask for a better boss."

"But you've never worked any place else. You don't know. Look around." He shrugged. "We're up against a stone wall. You just can't see it is all."

"If you feel that way, why don't you get another job?"

"Maybe I will one of these days. I certainly will if they start fooling around with *my* pay check." Polishing off the end of his sandwich, Harry wiped his mouth. "But what the hell, I've got a stake in Lazarus too, you know. I don't want to do anything hasty."

Wilder smiled. "I understand that all right. I understand that point of view very well."

"You want anything else?" the waitress asked, gathering up their plates. "Any dessert?"

"Give me some of that apple pie," Harry said. "With ice cream on it. Vanilla ice cream."

"Just some more coffee, please," Wilder said.

They sat silently for a moment, and Wilder was stricken with the thought that he had come here to ask Harry his part in the placing of the policies with Maryland Mutual and that he had allowed himself to be diverted with this old argument. Now, Wilder said to himself, I must ask him. I must ask him if he did bring George Gordon in to see Milton Lazarus. And having so spoken to himself, he discovered that he could not. For the moment at least, his tongue rebelled from the accusation.

Harry had returned to thoughts of getting him up for dinner. "Now I tell you what, Wilder," he was saying. "You plan to come up on Thursday. How about that? How about Thursday night?"

"I don't honestly think I can Harry. I think they're expecting me in Greenfield on Thursday night. I do have to keep an eye on them out there."

"Greenfield? Couldn't you go another night?" He winked. "Oh come on, Wilder, you don't have to be like that with me. I'm not your minister."

Wilder looked away, out through the plate glass again.

The waitress arrived with the pie and coffee, and as she made an extra punch in his check, Harry looked at her accusingly as though about to tease her, but she left them quickly.

"Well, what about it?" Harry insisted. "Will you come and bring Bibi?"

"Thanks. I appreciate your asking. I'll have to see."

"Listen. If you're worried about Bernice and Bibi, don't."

"I'm not," Wilder said. "It's not that at all."

"You will come then? Next Thursday and bring Bibi?"

"I don't know. Don't count on it. I'll see."

"Oh God, Wilder, you're impossible."

Wilder refused one of Harry's cigarettes and sat, growing more tense each moment in the knowledge he could not bring himself to say it out to Harry. Why? Why can't I ask him? And then he realized he did not want to know—for with the knowledge of Harry's perfidy would come the necessity to renounce him. He would have to quit him and all the familiarities of their relationship.

Then another thought struck him—that even if Harry had played some part in the affair, had he done anything really reprehensible? After all, the mutual was a better plan, and if Lazarus took it, was anyone at fault—save perhaps Wilder Stone? Why blame Harry for what was probably a very minor role in something inevitable?

Leaving his coffee unfinished, Wilder got to his feet. "I've got to go," he said dazedly. "I've got to get back to the office."

"Wait a second, will you, for God's sake? I haven't even finished."

Wilder shook his head. "Can't," he said, and picking up his check, he took his place in the line at the cashier's.

Back on the seventh floor Wilder found another message that Miss Winter had called and tried to return it but found her out to lunch. At his desk he noted some new mail had arrived but left it unopened.

He heard the elevator door spring open, and he listened for Harry's returning footsteps. It wasn't he, but soon Harry would return, and Wilder would have to smile and pass the time and pretend the friendship. He looked at the empty chair with dread.

"Did you want to do any letters now, Mr. Stone?" He discovered Miss Kriendler at the edge of his desk. Shapeless and ugly, yet the prettiest sight of the day. He smiled and moved the chair for her.

"Yes," he said. "I should do a few of these things if you have a minute." He moved the papers about a bit and turned up the last of Murray's requests about the water-tank report. "I should find this thing for Murray."

"The tank at 330?" she asked, looking over his arm. "I gave it to Mr. Kaufman."

"Thanks," he said. "I don't know what I'd do without you."

She brightened but instantly resumed her sobriety—and it was more than that now. In recent years Wilder had the feeling that her respect for him had changed into a kind of compassion, that she had cast herself in the role of nurse for his final illnesses, and although it irritated him sometimes, at the moment it was a comfort.

"Miss Kriendler, do you remember George Gordon?"

"Yes," she said, and the compassionate expression deepened into one fit for a child's funeral. "He's been in here a couple of times this week. He was in with Mr. Lazarus yesterday afternoon."

"With Mr. Coe?"

"Yes." She was looking at the string of *o's* she was drawing into a spring across the top of her shorthand pad. "I think it's terrible their taking the insurance business away from you after all these years. It's not like Mr. Lazarus to do a thing like that."

Wilder leaned back in his chair. "No, it isn't like Mr. Lazarus to do anything mean, but he doesn't regard it as mean and I don't suppose I should either. What he is doing is letting me down easy, or more aptly"—he frowned—"letting me go easy."

Miss Kriendler's eyes widened. "Oh, that isn't so. You're needed here just as you've always been. There are people who seem to work against you at times, but everyone knows who they are and why they do it. Mr. Lazarus knows that."

"He suggested I look for another job."

"If I were you . . ." She looked up at him for permission to go on.

"Yes?"

"If I were you I *would* look around."

"Good Lord, Margaret," Wilder said. "I wouldn't know where to begin."

She looked at him obliquely. It was one of the very few times he had used her first name. "It wouldn't do any harm to try."

"The classifieds?" Wilder rubbed his eyes thoughtfully, then shook his head.

She did not look up from her pad. "People come to you for jobs every day. They call up. They write letters. You know how people get jobs in New York, Mr. Stone."

"Yes," Wilder said. "Thanks, Miss Kriendler. I'll give it some thought. Now I guess we'd better see to the mail."

When he had finished dictating, he tried Miss Winter again and this time reached her.

"Hello, hon," she said. This particular greeting jarred but did not displease him. She spoke rapidly as she generally did from the shop, where she was frequently under pressure. "Can I see you tonight?"

"I'd planned to go to Greenfield you know. They're expecting mc for dinner."

"Before, then. Can't you come by for a drink?"

"I'm going to the drill. Jimmy's Fathers' Drill at the Seventh Regiment."

"It's important. I wouldn't ask you if it weren't."

"All right," he said. "I'll try and stop by for a minute. It'll be about six, I should think."

It was nearly three when Wilder recalled his promise to Mrs. Newbold and, taking his hat and coat, went to look for Miss Kriendler. "I've got to go up to 67 East Eighty-fourth," he told her, "and I might not get back. I don't think there's anything that won't wait until morning, but if there is, you sign it."

Riding uptown in the bus, Wilder's thoughts returned to Margaret Kriendler's suggestion of looking around for another job and in turn to Harry Coe's detestable views on M. A. Lazarus management.

The truth was that, despite his loyalty to Milton Lazarus, whom he regarded as little short of a saint, and to the firm, which from the first day of his employ he had regarded as "his," he had never taken a wholehearted pride in the house for which he worked. Some men, those in the old Father Knickerbocker firms, did take pride in their corporate name as they might in a club, and Wilder had joined in joking about it, but he suspected he envied them a little too.

He still recalled the afternoon fourteen years ago when he had run up the steps in Greenfield to tell them the news of his job and accept the family's congratulations. Millicent Stone had said "Lazarus? Milton Lazarus? That's a strange name."

He looked out at a street sign and saw he had gone by his stop. Getting off, he found the sun had momentarily emerged from the gray scum of clouds under which it had hidden throughout the day, and now it dazzled on a crimson coat, a white hat, a Kelly green slicker.

He started back down Madison on foot, and arriving at Eighty-fourth Street, he found to his horror that it was twenty past three and Mrs. Newbold had already gone.

"You missed her by only a minute or two, Mr. Stone," Henry

the big doorman reported sadly.

"Thank you. You're looking well, Henry."

"It's the teeth, Mr. Stone. I've had all my teeth out." He glanced covertly into the lobby and opened his mouth revealing gleaming new dentures. "These here are not my own. These here are dental plates."

"They're very handsome, Henry."

He grinned happily. "I tell you the remarkable thing about these teeth. I feel so much better having 'em out. I don't like to speak ill of the departed. They had done me good service over the years, but they was old and they was putting a poison in my system."

Linstrom, the superintendent, arrived and shook Wilder's hand as though he were a relative just arrived from Sweden. "I'm sorry our Mrs. Newbold makes you so much trouble. She's a difficult woman."

"I'm afraid that in this case I'm the difficult one," and he followed Linstrom into the building to await Mrs. Newbold's return. But at five, although she had not appeared, Wilder felt he could delay no longer and started down Madison Avenue.

2.

HE arrived at the Seventh Regiment Armory to find the review already in progress, the entrance bustling with chauffeurs and governesses, little brothers and sisters in hand, while within the cavernous hall itself was still. All eyes were upon the youthful troops, lined up now in company streets awaiting some order.

"Are you a father?" a committee woman asked, bearing down on Wilder, and, when he nodded, directed him toward the reviewing stand already filled with men at the center of the south wall.

As he approached the stand, he saw that many of the men seemed acquainted, if not previously, at least through having sat in company thus far, and Wilder found the prospect of joining them now (there wasn't a familiar face) disturbing. He discovered an alternative in a nearly empty box at the back wall and took a seat there just as a thin alto voice sang out "Paaa-ahhs in Review!" It was a beautiful child's voice, a choirboy's voice, and it traveled into the girdered heights above and was lost as it was echoed by the other high, reedy commands of "Right face!" and "Forward . . . !", one of which Wilder realized with delight had been cried by Jimmy.

And with the command "March!" the parade began—the

tiny guidon bearers scuttling to the fore, their blue pennants streaming, the small, white-gloved hands swinging in time to the regimental band's "Under The Double Eagle," a skinny boy out of step, a round one, no more than eight, his rifle askew, waddling gamely, and all the baby faces screwed into such a resoluteness.

Wilder found Jimmy out in front of B Company, his blue ostrich plume fluttering, bringing the boys into a reasonably unwobbly line for the march past the reviewing stand. He saw Jimmy's saber flash in the air and heard Jimmy's voice calling out the "Eyees right!" and to his shame fancied he saw the disappointment in Jimmy's face as he searched the reviewing stand in vain and fancied he heard it in a doleful "Front!"

Wilder scanned the gallery for his mother-in-law, and when at last he spotted her in a new purple hat and coat just four boxes away, he made his way quietly over to her and sat down in the empty seat beside her.

"I was so afraid you wouldn't get here at all, Wilder," Alma Massee said sharply. "Why didn't you sit in the reviewing stand?"

"I was late."

"You missed the drill? The crack company drill?"

Wilder nodded.

"Oh, Wilder. Jimmy was in it. He was so proud. He'll be terribly disappointed. You'd better tell him you did see it."

"All right," Wilder said unhappily.

Across the hall the units were returning to a formation of company streets, and Wilder fastened his attention on Jimmy, watched him dress B Company's lines, and then step out in front of them to receive the final orders and ultimately dismissal.

The band embarked upon an inflexible rendering of "Vie-

ner Blut" as the Greys scattered to waiting families. Catching sight of Wilder, Jimmy had all he could do to keep from
running to him. His eyes shone with delight as he came
toward them.

Wilder felt the customary shock at seeing Jimmy. It seemed
to stop his heart. In the great brown eyes, the pale, translucent skin, the delicate lips, and the dark hair, he beheld the
girl he had married.

"You looked grand, Jimmy," Alma said as she planted a kiss
on his cheek. She was a small woman, no taller than Jimmy, so
imposing now in his plumage and jingling metal, and she no
longer had to bend to kiss her grandson.

Wilder, guessing that in his own case a kiss for a leader of
men was inappropriate, refrained. He shifted his hat nervously
from one hand to another. "My compliments, Captain," he
said. "A black day for our enemies I assure you."

"Daddy!" Jimmy cried. "You *did* come. Where were you?
I didn't see you."

"In a box over there. I had a fine view."

"Did you see the drill?"

"The crack company? It was first-rate. You looked like West
Pointers."

"Boy, wasn't that Inspection Arms something? The triggers
—that's the hard thing in Inspection Arms, you know—to pull
them all together, and if you're late you aren't supposed to
pull at all but there's always somebody. Last week Major said
he'd personally shoot anybody that pulled a late trigger and
you know what—darned if I didn't have one. I almost pulled
it, but I didn't. Whew, it was close." He dramatized this by
wiping some imaginary sweat from his brow and grinned,
bringing this rather breathless account to a close. He turned
from his father and grandmother and noted that the wiry,

much revered drillmaster had become the center of a crowd of Greys. He stood now, whacking at his boots with his swagger stick, shaking hands with fathers, giving a hearty, affectionate slap to the boys as he talked.

"Come on over and meet the Major, Dad," Jimmy said and, anticipating his father's resistance, took hold of his sleeve.

"Not now," Wilder said, freeing himself, "he's got a crowd over there."

"He's a neat guy, Dad. He's got a four-inch shrapnel wound in his left leg."

"I'm sure I'd like him, Jimmy." Wilder took note of the general movement in the direction of the huge door. "But some other time." He glanced at his watch and saw that it was already six. "As a matter of fact, I've got to be getting along."

"Oh, Wilder," Alma Massee said with asperity, "you aren't going off someplace now? We were counting on you so." She looked at her grandson. "I'm having early dinner and I was going to let Jimmy stay up." She looked her son-in-law directly and rather fiercely in the eye. "And I've asked Polly, though I don't suppose that's much of an inducement to you."

"Polly?"

"Polly Wilson."

Wilder fumbled with his hat, raised a hand helplessly. "I'm sorry Alma. I'm truly sorry, but I promised Mother. I thought I told you I had to go to Greenfield."

"I didn't know it was for dinner. I thought you were going afterwards."

"Daddy, please," Jimmy said forlornly. "Please come."

Wilder had the familiar and desperate feeling of being asked for more than he had. He studied the label inside his hat and then suddenly clapped it on his head. "If the Captain would care to get his cloak"—Wilder grasped both Alma's and Jimmy's elbows—"and if the Captain will permit, I should like to stand both him and his admirers a round of sodas at the nearest canteen."

"It'll spoil his appetite," Alma said, resisting. But then seeing the smile on Jimmy's face, she relented and allowed herself to be guided toward the door.

The Schrafft's at Sixty-seventh and Madison was noisy and crowded with Greys, but Wilder managed a table meant for two and sat, with Jimmy, squeezed against the telephone booth.

"Wouldn't a ginger ale do, darling?" Alma asked. "There's steak and blueberry pie for dinner, and with your father not there to help you'll need all your appetite."

"Steak and blueberry pie? Did you hear that, Daddy? Won't you come now?"

Although to Alma Wilder appeared indifferent, he was in truth tormented and felt he could not for another instant play the role of negligent parent here thrust upon him. Yet it did not occur to him that even now he might change his plans, call Greenfield, stay the night in town. He had promised, and he must strive to make it good. His behavior was habitual, shuffling backward in awkward farewell while they forever tried to keep him—Alma, his mother, Bi, Lyddie, all of them —as the clock hands moved on, leaving him hopelessly behind.

Noting the waitress' waning attention, he said to them, "What'll it be?"

"I'll have the ginger ale," Alma said.

"One ginger ale for Grandma. What's yours, Captain?"

"Can I have anything I want?" He addressed himself to the sugar bowl and took the resulting silence as an affirmative.

"A chocolate mint soda with coffee ice cream," he said defiantly.

"Oh Jimmy," Alma wailed in disappointment.

"A black-and-white soda for me," Wilder said.

"I bet they won't have steak and blueberry pie in Greenfield," Jimmy said.

"I bet they won't either," Wilder said. "I'll be lucky to get a little cold porridge."

"You know I've never understood why your sister doesn't cook at all. I can understand about your mother—that she'd consider it beneath her." In spite of Wilder's sharp look Alma continued without faltering. "But why Lyddie? I'd have thought she'd learn to cook out of boredom."

Wilder folded his hands across his waistcoat and smiled slyly. "Grandma, the only trouble with you is you're inclined to judge the world by your own gifts. Now the preparation of food, taking a chunk of meat and some vegetables and a pinch of this and that and turning out something pleasing to the palate is a gift—like the ability to compose music pleasing to the ear. Now if you were a composer and discovered my sister and mother could not write a note of music. . . ."

In spite of herself Alma laughed. "Bunk. Everybody's got to eat—three times a day."

"At least three times," Jimmy added, and all three laughed.

"Every woman should take some pride and pleasure in cooking. *Every* woman except a queen. And it wouldn't do the queen any harm either."

"It might," Wilder said, "if word got around. I don't think we'd want to have a queen who spent all her time looking up recipes and rattling pots around the palace kitchen while the ministers paced the great hall. How about it, Jimmy?"

Alma looked at Jimmy. "Your Little Mother," she said

solemnly, "was a good cook. She used to love to cook from the time she was a little girl. She was always happy in a kitchen."

Jimmy's head lowered. It embarrassed him when they spoke of her. There was always this lament for a loss he could not comprehend and the mystery of God who had taken her and whom he asked each night to watch over her. "God bless Little Mother, Amen," his prayer ended. But most of all he was embarrassed because they seemed to expect something when they looked at him and spoke of her . . . and he hadn't the least idea what it was.

"Yes," Wilder said, chastened, the smile gone now. "Yes, she was. She was good at everything." He looked up gratefully as the waitress set the ginger ale down in front of Alma. They sipped silently for a moment, watching the activity at the fountain.

"Is Bibi a good cook?" Alma asked.

Wilder gave her an angry glance.

"I'm curious," Alma insisted. "I'd really like to know."

"Yes," he replied quietly. "She's pretty good."

"That's what I would have guessed," Alma said. "Just pretty good."

"I've got the vanishing-handkerchief trick perfect now, Daddy. Would you like to see me do it?"

"Yes, I would. I'd like to see that."

"Tonight?"

"No. Not tonight. Some other time. As a matter of fact, I'm already—" He looked down at his watch again. "Good grief, it's six thirty." He pulled his wallet from his pocket, took out a dollar bill and some change. "Alma, I'm frightfully sorry to have to run off, but I've simply got to. Would you please pay the check for me?"

"I'll get it, Wilder," she said, pushing his money away while

Wilder continued to try to leave it with her. Together they heard the soft noise, the quick intake of breath from Jimmy and, turning, found him flushed and manfully but unsuccessfully trying to hold back the tears.

No sensible words, no gesture of comfort came to the stricken Wilder, and he sat for a moment, helpless, his own eyes misting, watching his son's heart break.

"Now, now," he recited, "you mustn't do that, Jimmy." He put a hand on the cadet's sleeve and kneaded his elbow. He looked across at Alma, pleading for assistance, and in answer she looked away, fumbled in her purse for the little perfumed handkerchief.

"Jimmy," Wilder said. "Would you want to come out to Greenfield?"

"When?" Jimmy choked. "Tonight?"

"No. You've got to go to Gran's party tonight. Tomorrow morning. I could come in for you." He looked at Alma again. "Would that be all right? Would you mind?"

She shrugged as though to say she did but what did that matter. "No."

Wilder released Jimmy's elbow, handed him his pocket handkerchief.

"Could we go bumming?" Jimmy asked with sudden enthusiasm. "Could we go bumming instead?"

"A little perhaps. On the way out."

"The trick store? Can we go to the trick store?"

"Maybe."

"Whoopee."

Wilder looked at Alma again. "Are you sure this doesn't upset any plans of yours, Gran?"

"We were going to Sea Girt in the morning . . . but that can wait. We needn't go until Sunday."

"You hear that, Jimmy? Sea Girt? Do you want to pass up Sea Girt for Greenfield? I'm afraid it'll be pretty stupid for you. Mowing the lawn and putting out the ash cans may be the most exciting event of the day."

"Can I mow the lawn?"

"Yes. I think so."

"I'll mow the lawn. I'll mow it all by myself."

"All right," Wilder said getting up. "But don't say I didn't warn you."

"When will you come for him?" Alma asked.

"I don't know." He slipped into his overcoat. "Around eleven I guess."

"Please be fairly prompt, Wilder."

"I'll try."

Jimmy, tearstained but radiant with expectations for tomorrow, still clutched Wilder's pocket handkerchief, and Wilder held out his hand for it.

"Can I keep it?" Jimmy asked.

"Haven't you got a handkerchief?"

Jimmy nodded. His face darkened. "But I want this one too." There was a hint in his voice that he had not exhausted his supply of tears.

"All right," Wilder said, pinching the crown of his hat. "If it makes you any happier."

"It does," Alma said.

Wilder put the hat on, tipped it to Alma, and touched the brim in a brisk salute. "Request the Captain's permission to make reconnaissance patrol, returning tomorrow by 1100 hours."

Jimmy, delighted, returned the salute. "Permission granted," he said and reverently watched his father pass through the revolving door.

When, minutes later, Bibi Winter opened the door of her Fifty-third Street apartment to Wilder he beheld a different woman from the overdressed, artificial one he had met at Alma Massee's six years earlier. Her hair, once dyed and elaborately waved, was now cut short in the loose Italian style, and she had made no attempt to camouflage an occasional strand of gray. The result lent some distinction to her rather plain, round face. For a woman of thirty-five who was both short and inclined to heaviness she had an excellent figure. At her ears were the little Danish silver clips he had given her at Christmas.

"Well, hello," Wilder said. Intending a peck at the corner of her mouth, he leaned toward her.

She saw the worry and fatigue like two companions. "Hello, yourself." Slipping her hands beneath his coat, she pulled him to her and kissed him solidly. "You look tired," she said.

"It's been a tiring day." He followed her into the small, masculine living room. It had cocoa walls hung with a Picasso reproduction and a dreadful painting of a lake shore done by an acquaintance. A book lay open in the seat of a tub chair. "It's been the kind of day where something went wrong hourly. It was so strong I could scent it—actually feel it coming."

"Bad luck?"

He shook his head. "It's too well planned to be luck. It's some system that organizes the dreads and herds them all in together."

She looked at him, considering, her hands folded. "Yes. I know," she said finally. "Nothing serious?"

He sat down on the sofa. "It's hard to say what's serious. I think I've lost my job."

"Oh, my God. You don't mean that, Wilder. You couldn't."
She sat down beside him quickly and took his left hand in hers.

"Well it amounts to that. They've taken the insurance business away. I can't make out on what's left of my salary."

"They didn't actually—"

"No."

"I'll make us a drink. And then tell me all about it. I'm sure
it isn't as bad as you say. It never is." She crossed the room and,
with a clatter, raised the Venetian blind, revealing the wall
kitchenette. She took glasses and whisky from the cupboard
and a tray of ice from the midget refrigerator and began to
empty the cubes into a bowl.

"Would you like some help?" Wilder asked. He picked up
the book and to his disappointment found it a detective novel
from the rental library at the corner.

"No," she said. "Relax. Take your coat off. At least take that
vest off. Nobody wears vests any more."

"They come with a suit. What can you do with a vest but
wear it?"

"You can throw it away. Someday I'll throw *all* your vests
away."

"All? I think I own three. Possibly four if you count one
with moth holes."

"That's four too many," she said, setting the tray on the
coffee table. Wilder put ice cubes carefully into each glass,
poured the whisky just so, and the water just so over it, then a
fastidious twist of lemon rind, and passed her the glass.

"Drink deep," she said, holding her glass aloft. "Hold your
nose and take a good gulp and everything'll be all right."

He took a gingerly sip and set his glass down. "The funny
part is that what's troubling me is Jimmy."

"What's the matter with Jimmy?"

"Nothing. The matter's with me." Wilder rubbed his knee unhappily. "Every time I see him I feel such a complete washout as a father."

"But you aren't, hon." She rested her hand on his sleeve. "You're so good to that boy."

"He's growing up into a stranger. I'm not with him enough. I never have been. And when I am, I'm shy and embarrassed. When I'm with him, I'm thinking about—getting away."

"That isn't so. You have wonderful times together. I've seen you. The three of us have wonderful times together." She took a cigarette from the pigskin box on the table, and he lighted it for her. She squinted as smoke drifted across her eyes. "It surprises me how well we three do get along, considering the conditioning Cousin Alma has done to that boy's mind."

"I'm talking about my own failure with Jimmy. God knows I've got no right to criticize anything Alma's done with him." He took another sip of his whisky. "She's done a superb job of bringing him up. Better, by far, than Mother at her age could do. And something I was . . . unable to do."

Wilder leaned back and closed his eyes.

"Wilder, you don't have to feel grateful to Cousin Alma. She'd have gone out of her mind without Jimmy to take care of." She watched him for some response, but he didn't stir. But for the taut muscles of his jaw he might have been asleep. "Cousin Alma's been unkind to me. Nobody knows that better than you do. But I'll give her her due. She's brought Jimmy up beautifully. I'll never underestimate Cousin Alma." She smoothed the skirt over her knees. "I saw her today."

Wilder opened an eye. "Alma? You've seen Alma?"

She nodded. "This morning."

"You couldn't have." He sat up, looked at her doubtfully.

"I left her not an hour ago. She didn't say anything about it."

"I'm not surprised."

"By accident? On the street?"

"I called on her. At 312."

"Why? What's all this about?"

She took some short, nervous puffs on her cigarette. "I want you to finish the drink."

He picked up his glass which was three-quarters full and drank it in one draught.

"Oh, Wilder. That's not good for you."

"Go on. Why were you seeing Alma? Why do I need the drink?"

She leaned back against the pillows. There was a crescendo of traffic noise from the street, a fugue of taxi horns, and her eyes went to the window where the curtains were drawn against the night.

"I don't know if what I have to tell you is bad news," she said. "It could be. It needn't be. But it is news, and coming as it does on a day in which, as you say, nothing has gone right, it can't help but upset you. And I don't want that. But I"—she turned to him, her hands upward, helplessly—"I've got to make a decision—and it depends on you."

He was sitting very straight now, listening, watching with grave apprehension. "Please tell me. Don't tease."

"I've been proposed to."

"Proposed to?"

"Yes." She smiled sadly. "A man has asked me to marry him. You find that so hard to believe?"

He was incredulous. He looked at her vacantly. "You're considering it?"

She nodded.

"Who? Who in the world?" He shook his head impatiently.

"Oh, damn it, I don't mean it that way. I just can't believe that I wouldn't know—that you and I could be so close and I not know that something of this sort could happen."

"It's Emil Braun."

"Braun? Mr. Braun?" He cocked his head doubtfully, allowed a smile. "Your Mr. Braun from the shop?" It was a joke with them—Bibi's other beau, a little gnome of a man, a kindly widower of sixty years, the head bookkeeper at Sophie's. Wilder's thoughts scurried crazily this way, that way, then, surer, he laughed. "You're joking."

"No, Wilder." She shook her head slowly, and her earnestness was clear. "He took me to dinner last night. He took me to Gaston's and proposed very formally and very sensibly. And I told him the truth. I told him I was in love with a man I'd proposed to many times, but who will probably never marry me. At least that's what my Mama tells me. And that maybe I've waited long enough. I told him I'd make up my mind in a week."

Stunned, Wilder folded his hands, rested his chin on them. "Yes," he said with a nod. "I see. That's fair enough."

"Another drink?"

"No. No, thanks."

"Will you fix me another?"

"Of course," he said. He looked at her intently as he took her glass, trying to see this woman afresh that he had come to know so well, had grown so accustomed to that she seemed his, whose little walk-up flat here in the East Fifties had become a kind of home and the only place in the wide world he had found any solace.

It was at Alma's, ironically enough, that Wilder had met Bibi. She was just back from California then, just back from writing off the disastrous love affair that had consumed her young womanhood.

And Wilder had but recently returned from the Mediterranean cruise he had taken with Harry Coe. He had dropped in at Alma's apartment toward the end of the afternoon to show Jimmy and Alma the snapshots just received from Eastman's.

Jimmy was sullen and brooding, brightening but slightly at the sight of his father astride a camel and the gully-gully man drawing a live baby chicken from his mouth. As it turned out, what troubled Jimmy was the rhinoceros-hide whip Wilder had brought him from Tangier. It was a riding crop actually—a short, flexible rod bound with the hide, a heavy braided handle, and a flap at the business end. It was not an appropriate present for a six-year-old, but Jimmy had requested a rhinoceros from Africa, and when the merchant in the bazaar described the whip as rhinoceros hide, it seemed for a moment the sensible compromise. He bought it and the misgivings had been swept away by Jimmy's delight in receiving it.

It was this same whip that Jimmy was now holding as he came to the doorway and stood staring, his eyes filling, his lips trembling. "Put that thing away, Jimmy," Alma said.

"It's mine," he said darkly. "Daddy gave it to me."

"I told you to put it away, Jimmy." She turned to Wilder. "I wish you'd never brought that to him."

"Why? What's the matter with it?"

"Nothing's the matter with it."

"Mom whipped me with it," Jimmy exploded, loosing the tears, and then he was pulling down his knee sock and showing his father what, though scarcely visible, he imagined to be welts.

Wilder held out his hand for the whip, and when Jimmy put it there he gave it an experimental waggle, noting its spring, and guessed that even a frail hand could deliver a painful stripe with it and, because of its special nature, a truly cruel one. He was suddenly furious with Alma, for surely there was something else at hand if the boy needed a spanking—a strap, a brush, whatever she generally used. She must have chosen this deliberately.

Jimmy was rubbing his eyes and awaiting some reaction from Wilder. It was quite silent in the room, and then Wilder reached out with the crop and flipped it playfully at the seat of Jimmy's short pants. "You know," he said, "it is quite a temptation."

And Jimmy turned away to hide the smile that began in a corner of his mouth, and the house phone rang and Alma went to answer it. When she came back she found them both going through the snapshots again quite happily.

"Wilder," she said, "there's a young woman coming up in the elevator to have tea. You're welcome to stay, though I don't think you'll enjoy it much."

Wilder got up instantly, glancing automatically at his watch. "Good heavens, I had no idea of the time. I've got to get along." He looked absently about for his hat and saw that Alma was already getting it out of the closet. This uncharacteristic gesture suggested she was anxious to have him on his way with the arrival of her guest, and he was just annoyed enough about the whip, just obstinate enough by nature, to balk.

"Why do you think I wouldn't enjoy your tea party, Gran?"

"Oh, I don't know," she said, seeing her error. "Just a hunch. Stay and find out if you like."

"Who is she?"

"The daughter of someone I used to know in Elmira. She's just back from California, and she has a job in a beauty parlor. She's a hairdresser."

"An Elmira girl? Did she know Catherine?"

"Scarcely. Certainly not well."

"What's her name?"

"Winter. Bibi, they call her. I haven't seen this girl in years, but as I remember she's stupid and not good-looking. At least I didn't think so."

Wilder looked into the crown of his hat. "After a sales talk like that, I'll stay. Just for a minute."

Wilder was astonished by Bibi Winter's appearance—by the watch-spring curls, the shiny icing of lipstick drawn to accentuate the cupid's bow of her mouth, the tight pastel sweater. She had been putting on weight then, and her natural voluptuousness was on the point of fat. Her slightly recessive chin and pouty cheeks made of her face a plump heart. He was speculating on what this woman admired that caused her to rig herself here like a UCLA coed and there like a chorus girl.

When Alma introduced them, Bibi held Wilder with her soft, artless eyes. "Catherine and I were chums," she said gravely. "What a terrible thing."

Her voice was not unpleasant and it too intrigued him, for like her appearance it was mostly borrowed. There was a nasal quality which he decided was western, and he detected the upstate flat *a* from which she departed when she thought of it to a broad, stagy one as startling as a raised pinky. It was particularly noticeable when she used the word *aunt* which was often, for she had prepared a list of questions about Elmira people, many of whom were known to Wilder, and she was claiming kinship with most of them, Alma included, whom she addressed to Alma's evident discomfort as Cousin Alma.

As Alma poured the tea, Bibi turned her entire exuberant attention on Wilder. Sensing he was sizing her up over the rim of his teacup and that he was a shy fellow by nature, she cheerfully undertook an account of life on "the Coast." She hinted an acquaintance (he guessed correctly that it was her professional one) with some minor motion picture actresses whose names she wrongly assumed were familiar to him. She spoke of the beneficent climate, the smart shops, the good life in Los Angeles (which she pronounced with a hard *g*), and forbade them to say "L.A.," which she explained was as distasteful to a true Angelino as "Frisco" to a true San Franciscan.

"And why did you come back East?" Alma inquired. She was making no effort now to conceal her irritation.

"I don't know," Bibi said uncertainly. "I needed a change, I guess. I think everybody needs a change now and then. Don't you, Cousin Alma?"

Alma sniffed and passed the tray of cupcakes.

"I quite agree," Wilder said.

Alma saw it coming, that Bibi and Wilder would leave together. Perhaps her horrified eyes saw more, the whole affair taking shape. She did what she could to prevent it, pleading with Bibi to stay on for supper, pointing out, for Wilder's benefit, how late it was getting. But they were firm. Wilder would drop her off at the Allerton House on his way downtown.

They did not speak in the cab. It was a humid spring evening, and crossing Fifty-seventh Street they looked out at other couples strolling. Bibi stole a glance at Wilder and marveled at the regularity of his profile, the strong chin, the fastidiousness of his mouth, his slender nose. In his stiff white collar fastened with the patterned, dark tie, the watch chain across his vest, in the careful, shy, well-bred way he spoke he had impressed her greatly. It seemed to her that he had some quality, a composure, some special knowledge that had been lacking in every man she had known.

"You don't stay up there with Cousin Alma?" she asked.

"No. I drop in as much as I can—a couple of times a week. But I don't live there. A man's mother-in-law, you know"—he smiled—"is never the best of companions."

"You live with your folks?"

"No. They're out in New Jersey. I have a little apartment here in town."

Bibi brightened. "You live there alone?"

"Quite alone."

"Oh, I'd love to have an apartment. I hate this tiny little hotel room. I like to have my own things around me. You know?"

"It's a little easier to get a small apartment nowadays. You'd want a one-room, I suppose."

"Oh, I'd adore a one-room apartment. Do you think there's any chance? It would have to be awfully cheap, I'm afraid."

"I'll keep an eye out," he said. "I'm in the real-estate business."

"Are you?" She turned to him, her eyes wide and glowing with admiration. "Well, don't I have all the luck."

Over his shoulder she saw they were approaching the Allerton House, and she weighed the possibility of seeing him again. She seriously doubted he would call her.

"Well, here we are," she said as they arrived at the awning.

Wilder got out and held the door for her, took her arm as she hopped with self-conscious nimbleness to the pavement.

"So nice meeting you," he was saying, "and if something turns up in a one-room I'll certainly get in touch. . . ."

"I'm going in there," she said, pointing out the hotel coffee shop. "I was going to ask you to stay and have a bite with me but . . . I don't expect Cousin Alma would like that much."

"Alma? What has Alma to do with it?"

"Well, I don't think she liked us. . . ." Here Bibi blushed becomingly and looked away. "I don't think she liked us going off together like this."

Wilder smiled. "I do believe you're right," he said, and paid the driver. "And we can't have Alma running our lives like that, can we?" It was a naughty notion, defying Alma in this way, and it delighted him. Harmless. He smiled again and looked up and down Fifty-seventh, thinking how to make it a gay sort of evening, the kind of evening Alma would want to thwart.

"What is it?" Bibi asked.

"I'm trying to think of a California restaurant. There's probably one around, but I don't know where."

"Oh, dear, I *have* been sounding like the chamber of commerce, haven't I? I'm sorry. I just talk. I won't do it again."

"Don't make any promises." He took her arm. "Do you mind Italian food?"

"Oh, I crave Italian food. We used to go to this terribly popular place in Santa Monica. . . ." She glanced at him and put a hand over her mouth and they both laughed.

It was six and Barbetta's had not yet begun to fill. In the first moments, while they ordered and looked around them, he was uneasy, but as Bibi began to chatter, saying what a nice place it was and how happy it made her, just being here, he found he was enjoying himself. She was so obviously making up to him. Of course it was a game at which she played. A girl like this, a small town girl, had a moral sense as strong, stronger even, than these proper-looking secretaries in their severe suits. She didn't mean what she seemed to be saying with her eyes and with the carmine-tipped fingers that reached across the table to touch him, that in the balcony of the Plaza Theater, where they went afterward to see *Mayerling*, reached for his hand and held it, stroking the hairs on his wrist. No, he thought, this is no invitation. It was the way she had been told, in California perhaps, in the beauty shop, to behave when a gentleman asked her to dinner.

He was thus confounded when at nearly midnight she asked if she could see where he lived. When she had looked around the small monastic room and looked out the narrow window into the court and looked at the books on the shelves, and accepted the glass of milk (it was all there was) he brought her from the kitchenette, and after a moment's silence in which Wilder began to fidget, she turned to him and smiled and said softly, "Aren't you even going to kiss me?"

"Yes," he said, "if you like," and embraced her rather clumsily, kissing her with his lips together as if afraid of germs.

She leaned back just far enough to look into his eyes. "You've forgotten, haven't you? You sweet man, you've forgotten how to kiss."

"Maybe I have."

She put her arms through his, pulled him to her, and he felt her hands in the small of his back, her breasts soft against him, and her mouth warm, pleading, enveloping his, and then the desire for her came of a sudden, sweeping aside the curiosity and the caution, the inhibition and the nervousness. He touched her hair, the tight curls at the nape of her neck, and he kissed her hard.

She put her lips very close to his ear—so close he could feel their touch. She whispered, "Would you like to go to bed?"

"Yes," he said hoarsely and cleared his throat. "Yes, very much."

Bibi was right in thinking he would be carrying a heavy load of remorse and guilt and would not call her again, and when two days had passed with no word she called him at the office, just before noon.

"Hey," she said cheerfully, "It's my painful duty to remind you of your manners. A girl likes to be called back by her date. Didn't anybody ever tell you that, Mr. Stone?"

"No," he said, "Nobody ever told me and it's a spendthrift plan if ever I heard one. It sounds like a tribal custom—very local—possibly southern California." He was pleased to hear from her, for his remorse was compounded by the thought that Alma might at some turn learn at first hand of his indiscretion. He had no clear idea of what confidences women traded. Thus he found her lightheartedness reassuring, and on the strength of it asked her to dinner once more on an evening in the following week.

And so the affair between them began. It was so unlikely, so insubstantial a relationship that each time they saw one another they both felt it was for the final time, and yet some emotional threads had passed between them and of these a few had been made fast.

Believing herself to be adaptable, able to take on the coloration of any man, Bibi Winter set out to become Wilder's woman. She sensed his dislike of pretense and felt her way eagerly, listening, observing him, asking his advice, noting what he admired in another woman. To his astonishment he began to hear in Bibi's voice the echo of his own, a turn of phrase, his own precise pronunciation. He had only to admire a plain gray flannel dress in Bonwit Teller's window for her to delight him by turning up in a similar one.

She undertook exercise—each morning and night, a half hour of bending and twisting—and a Spartan diet. Her body responded, her arms slimming, her stomach flattening (the legs, alas, were unaffected), but best of all the puffiness left her face, and in the dim light of a restaurant Wilder saw faint shadows in her cheeks and marveled that a lovely woman was emerging.

As he became aware that this extraordinary transformation was for his benefit, Wilder was flattered yet, not knowing how profound the change and thus his responsibility, uneasy.

And he found her generous, recklessly so. She gave unquestioningly all she had—her time, her thought, her body, her sentimental heart. If she had had money, she would have given that too.

As she got to know him better Bibi began to see in Wilder some alluring possibilities—primarily that of awakening him physically. She was thoroughly animal herself and doubted there was any other substantial relation between a man and woman. He had seemed in some puritan strait jacket which, she soon guessed, was put on along with the mufflers and galoshes by his mother. She felt she was making substantial progress.

Secondly, she sensed in Wilder an intelligence and insight that were going to waste, and she felt a first faint glimmer of ambition for him. She wondered what *she* could do. The two ideas joined in her mind. Perhaps at one stroke she could cut his ties to the past and bind him to herself. Then anything was possible.

Although they frequently spoke of doing so, they never left the city. In the fall they occupied themselves with finding Bibi an attractive apartment (Wilder was able to be of some assistance) and in fitting it out. They prowled the shops for fabrics, and Wilder found a painter to do the place inexpensively in bold colors. When it was complete, they turned to the city outside for amusement.

She was never demanding. Not then, at least, not at the start. She was content to walk in the park, to cook a meal, to spend an evening reading and listening to the radio. He persuaded her to read aloud from *War and Peace,* a book which Wilder had long felt obliged to try. They swapped it back and forth every few pages and managed just under a hundred of them.

She liked to go anyplace with him and, though left to herself she would have chosen a movie over an art gallery to pass a Sunday afternoon, for a few weeks she saw a lot of the Museum of Modern Art and the Whitney. Here Wilder sought to amuse her with fancies of what an abstractionist had in mind, and she tried to share his new and—he was the first to admit—superficial interest in painting, but she could not even pretend it.

They preferred the theater to any other sort of diversion and they went once a week. Customarily they had an inexpensive dinner in one of the little French restaurants in the West Forties and then went to second-balcony seats at a semipopular play. Wilder avoided hits—particularly farce and musical comedy which Bibi would have preferred. If one were available, Wilder would select a drama about some human problem, or a comedy based on a serious idea. Then afterward he liked to discuss it.

But Bibi was not good for much of such talk. Unless it related directly to herself, she wearied of it quickly. He would be amused and saddened to see her trying to pay attention.

For years Wilder had been subject to chronic blues, touched

off by some insignificant incident, a slight at the office, failure
to keep some promise to Jimmy, a tiff with Lyddie about the
Greenfield bills, but the attack would grow into something
like real sickness. During these blues, which might last several
days, he kept to himself, stumbling through his work at the
office, walking the streets at night, dreading the insomnia that
awaited him in his apartment. And Bibi worked some antidote. Wilder's blues became milder and less frequent.

But what most attracted Wilder to Bibi was that she wasn't
Catherine. He asked her once what she remembered of his
wife, and when she described a girl who was only vaguely
Catherine, he realized Alma was right. Bibi had known her
slightly if at all.

Catherine and Bibi might have come from different planets,
and Wilder found he could make a place in his heart for Bibi
without disturbing the chamber where Catherine lived.

Now, having prepared Bibi's drink as carefully as the first,
Wilder sat with it in his hands, looking around the apartment
he had helped her find, at familiar objects. He knew the history of every furnishing, the drapery fabric, the stone bud
vase, each book on the shelf. It was incredible that this place
which had so much of him in it could vanish—could be made
over to accommodate another.

"I'll have my drink, now," she said, reaching out for it,
"and whatever it is you're thinking."

Wilder handed her the glass. "I was wondering what you're
going to tell Mr. Braun at the end of the week."

"I don't know, Wilder. I was hoping you'd help me make
up my mind."

"Bi, I'll try. But I'm bewildered. I find it incredible that
you're taking Mr. Braun's proposal seriously. I can't believe

you have any feeling for him at all."

"I'm not in love with him, of course. But I'm not a school-girl, and I know that men I do love seem to lead me into trouble. They lead me away from the life I want to lead now. I'm not young. I have no particular talents or graces. I'm a middle-aged woman with, as you once pointed out, unusually fat legs. My choice is limited, Wilder."

"You're a young and attractive woman, Bi, and it's shocking you think of becoming a . . . whatever it is, to a man of sixty. A companion, I suppose, or a nurse."

"If you want to prevent that, I'll tell you how."

"Oh, Bi, we've been through all this before. You know I can't now. You know why. Perhaps it'll look better in September if I can get Mr. Lazarus to make some sizable salary adjustment. You've understood before. Why not now?"

She drank slowly, thinking, and then spoke quietly. "Because every day I learn something new about you. I learned quite a bit from Alma today."

"Alma? I had the impression you weren't speaking. You couldn't have asked *her* advice."

Bibi kicked off her shoes and tucked her feet beneath her. "I did."

"I could have told you what she'd say and saved you the trip."

"Cousin Alma knows you better than anybody. Better than I do. Better even than your mother."

"She's obsessed with the idea of breaking us up. She'd tell you any irresponsible tale."

"I went to her because I wanted her kind of advice. I wanted to be encouraged to leave you."

"I see," Wilder said. "That makes it quite final."

"That depends on you."

Wilder closed his eyes and massaged the bridge of his nose. "Bi, I earn little enough as it is and have the prospect of seeing that halved. I have a son who's going to have a good education, as good and extended as he is capable of. He'll have it if I must rob a bank."

"I wouldn't worry. Alma will see him through his education."

"He's my son."

"Yes, he is."

"And I have Greenfield. My sister and my mother totally dependent on me. They'd starve without me."

"They're not invalids. I sometimes think they'd be a lot better off if you let them alone."

"They're helpless. You've seen them. You know."

"I know they want you to *feel* they're helpless. They want you to think that if you ever stopped trotting out there to carry out the ashes and pay the bills for that ark the world would come to an end." She opened her hands. "Lyddie might have to go to work. It's no disgrace. A lot of people have to work."

Wilder got up and went to the window. "And this is Alma's idea? That Mother and Lyddie are not my responsibility? That I'd be doing them a service by letting the grocery stop their credit, the coalbin go empty, the house be sold for back taxes?"

"It's Cousin Alma's idea. And mine too."

"I'm using Mother and Lyddie as an excuse not to marry you? Is that it? Is that the sort of villain I am?"

"No. You're no villain. You're just confused. You seem to think you're running your life. You aren't and never have been. It's your mother."

Wilder considered. "Mother?" he said. "Mother is a gentle

old lady. She's nearly seventy, and frequently she believes Father is still alive. She sets a place for him at the table and is surprised when he doesn't come down to dinner. Yes, she runs my life just as Lyddie and Jimmy and you—all the people who are close to me—run my life. You all influence what I do."

Bibi looked at him sullenly. "I understand you're a hair-dresser, Miss Winter. What interesting work that must be." It was an inexpert but recognizable travesty of Millicent Stone's voice. " 'When I was a girl, we used to brush our hair five hundred strokes every evening. Julia, Mother's maid, used to brush it too if I were very nice to her. But I've never gone to anyone professional, nor has my daughter Lyddie.' What did she say, Wilder? How did she put it that I wasn't good enough?"

"I do recall you didn't get on."

"Didn't get on?" She laughed. "Well, I tried, Wilder. I tried to get on just as Catherine tried. And I failed just as Catherine failed. The only difference between Catherine and me is that I know when I'm licked. I'm not going to hang around and let her destroy me."

"Hush," Wilder said and walked to her. "Please hush."

"I'll not hush!" She spoke with sudden shrillness. "She destroyed your marriage. Before your very eyes. And you know what, Wilder? I think she destroyed Catherine, too—just as surely as if she had put a knife in her heart."

Wilder stood rigid before her. "Shut up, Bi! Shut up!" His hands reached toward her. He raised the right as if to strike at her.

"Go on, hit me. I dare you. You haven't got the—"

He swiped with the flat of his hand, but it was irresolute and struck weakly against her nose. It was painful if only in its clumsiness, and she looked up at him through tears.

"It's the truth, isn't it?"

"No. It isn't. And don't ever say it again."

"What? Say what again?"

He hesitated. "Catherine," he said.

"The name? I mustn't say her name?"

Wilder shook his head slightly. "No."

"Catherine! Catherine! Catherine!" Bibi cried. "She's dead, Wilder, and I'll say it as much as I like. Catherine! Do you hear me?"

He glanced once around the room as though trying to fix each object in his mind and then went to the closet and took down his hat and coat. He adjusted the hat very carefully on his head, slipped into the coat, and began struggling with the door latch.

Bibi groped for her shoes and slipped into them.

"Wilder!" she called after him, but he was out the door, walking fast across the landing. He paused halfway down the first flight, looked up at her and lifted his hat.

"Good-by," he said.

"Is that your answer? Shall I tell Emil Braun he can have me?"

But he was gone, rattling down the staircase. She stayed there, leaning on the banister until she heard the front door slam.

3.

IT was twenty minutes past seven by Cartier's clock, and Wilder started up toward the Independent subway entrance at Fifty-third Street.

He managed, for the moment at least, to thrust a recollection of the unpleasant half hour just past and the necessity for a decision about Bibi from his mind, and in their stead came thoughts of Catherine.

He dreamed of her often. Sometimes he dreamed of her alone as she sat beside him in a car or as he sought her in a huge dark house that suggested Greenfield, and sometimes she was mixed with Bibi. The woman he thought was Bibi walking ahead of him down the path would turn to speak to him and it would be Catherine's face—Catherine's great brown eyes and the little puckering at the corner of her mouth that meant something had struck her funny—and he would awake, crying out to her, and her name would die in his throat. He would struggle to separate them as his mind cleared, and until the dream itself had faded from his consciousness.

But although Catherine was much a creature of his sleep, she was seldom with him during his waking hours, and it was a strange sensation to feel that she was with him now, walking at his side past the American Express office with its gaudy display of midwinter vacations, past the stacks of Scotch sweaters in Peck & Peck's window, pausing to watch the pickets outside the Stork Club, before descending into the gray, mole world of rapid transit.

The year 1946 was a year of new peace, new hope and new love. Uniforms were packed away in trunks, and the once lonely personnel offices bustled with an activity familiar to a man just out of service—the tedious application form to be filled out, the lack of chairs, the apprehensive faces glancing up at the door each time it opened and, most of all, the waiting. And out beyond the subway lines the first of the new housing developments sprang in the fields.

Wilder, while hardly typical, was not without the new hope that year, and much of that hope was for new love. He was taking a course, Introduction to Business Management, in the School of General Studies at Columbia. It began at eight fifteen in the evening, and frequently he would leave the Lazarus office at five and take the subway up to 116th Street to stroll about the campus and read over his assignment. Sometimes he would get a bit of supper in the university neighborhood which he preferred to the commercial atmosphere of Twenty-ninth Street. There was something about these Morningside Heights that sometimes saddened, sometimes gladdened him, but made him feel so very alive.

It was in spite of Millicent, too.

"That's a lot of nonsense, going to school at night," she had said. "It's what butcher boys do."

"I want to know a little more, Mother," he had said. "I think it'll help me along. After all, I don't have college."

"But we never see you any more. You don't get home until all hours, and you're off again in the morning. I worry about you, you know, when you're not here at night, when you're in the city."

"What is there to worry about?"

"A great deal. All sorts of dreadful things can happen to a young man alone in a big city like New York, quite without your knowing it—until it's too late," she added. "Oh, I know, Wilder."

"Oh, Mother, you're worried that some wicked woman will find me." He laughed and hugged her. "And I'm worried that she won't."

"Wilder!"

"Now, Mother, really. I'm twenty-seven."

Millicent sighed. "You will be careful, Wilder. For a young man, for an attractive young man . . ."

"I'll be careful."

"And after this term—you will give it up? You won't be going in the summer surely?"

"You know it's possible to get a degree, a Columbia degree, just going nights. I was wondering if I oughtn't to make some sort of plan."

"Oh Wilder, that's not sensible. You'd just wear yourself out. You'd ruin your health. You mustn't think of it."

But he did think of it. He thought about drawing up some program that in time would lead to a Columbia degree—and also, in express disobedience of orders, he wished himself in love.

To Wilder there was no more moving sight than that of a Barnard girl in her tweed skirt and sweater, hugging a psychology text and a paperback Rilke or Kafka, her bright hair swept up in some knot or ponytail that gave a deceptive maturity to the young skin and eager eyes and the graceful body that was both a child's and a woman's. She was such a

bundle of his longings. She was so many desirable things
which he felt to be just beyond the grasp of an extension student. She was the real, the rightful, tenant of Morningside
Heights, and he the counterfeit.

Such feelings accompanied his first sight of Catherine
Massee. Wilder had come into the university bookstore to buy
the recommended collateral reading and was browsing his
way out of the shop. She was with another girl, selecting a tie
at the men's furnishing counter.

He was instantly and terribly attracted to her—to the confidence in the way she stood. It was so very straight, her feet
so very firm upon the floor beneath her. And there was an
intensity as she knotted the tie, said something to the girl
beside her, then laughed so sweetly, so femininely, and then,
holding the tie aloft like a prize trout, enhancing it, making
it by her touch the most desirable tie in the world. He stood
there, long after the clerk had wrapped the tie and the two
girls had fled happily into the street, mourning his loss.

For a week he carried her image in his mind, and as he
walked about the campus he found he was looking for her. A
dozen times an evening he would hurry after a dark-haired
girl, thinking that in the swing of a skirt, a tilt of the head, he
recognized her. And when it was not she, he was disappointed
and yet relieved, for he had no notion what he would do if he
found her.

One prematurely warm evening (it was, Catherine always
recalled, the evening of March twenty-first) he came face to
face with her in the middle of Broadway. She came out of the
116th Street subway station and crossed the street at a run.
She was carrying books and a clipboard, and she wore a tan
sweater with a collar and a gray flannel skirt. As she passed,
a foot away, she glanced at him, and it seemed that even in

her haste she had left him the suspicion of a smile.

To his own astonishment Wilder followed her, cautiously, for it was still daylight, and not at all sure he would go more than half a block, but then more rapidly, fearing he might lose her, as she turned into Barnard Hall.

In the lobby, still busy with student traffic, she continued into the north corridor, paused in front of the elevator to speak to another girl, and he bent to take a drink from a handy water fountain.

She went out through the north doors and entered the annex. She stopped in front of the lounge on the ground floor, looked at the girls assembled at the snack bar there, and then passed on up the stairs beyond.

Arriving at the second-floor corridor, he found it empty and he walked along, looking into the deserted classrooms.

She had thrown her books and clipboard on a table and was opening a file cabinet. On the glass door he read: THE BULLETIN. There were two other girls at desks. One, plump, with a pink square face and tight curls, was typing. The other, sallow and Punchlike, with straight hair that hung to her shoulders, sat smoking and staring into Claremont Avenue.

Wilder stepped back, leaned against a coiled fire hose. He looked back down the corridor and felt ridiculous and ashamed of himself. Supposing he were caught at this childishness. He had a momentary vision of Millicent's horrified face, and then he walked through the door into the *Bulletin* office and the three girls looked up at him.

The girl he had followed was at a third desk now. She had a pencil clamped between her teeth.

"Excuse me," he said to her. "Can I place an ad?"

She took the pencil from her mouth. "Sure," she said. It was a candid voice, from the Midwest, he thought, or upstate. She

was slim and she wore her dark hair short, so that it showed
her ears, so that it grew soft on her delicate neck like that of
a small boy in need of a haircut. Looking into her wide, dark
eyes, he was stunned to find this was no joke, for he saw there
a shape of things—of laughter, of mischief, of tenderness, and
of anguish—that he sought. He wondered if it was really there
or only a reflection of something in his own mind. He could
not tell, and it did not seem to matter.

"Are you from a store?" It was the square-faced girl with
the tight curls, and he turned reluctantly to her.

"A store?"

"Who do you represent?"

The Punchlike girl rested her chin in her hand. "What do
you want to advertise?"

"Oh." He turned back to the dark eyes. "I want to advertise
a typewriter. A second-hand Royal portable."

"Oh, a classified." The girl with the curls sighed and turned
to the copy on her desk. "We'll take it if you want. It's three
dollars an inch if you're a student. We only take classifieds
from students. You're a student?"

"Well, yes. Yes, I am. I'm not a Barnard student." He smiled
tentatively. "But I'm a university student."

"Graduate?"

"No."

"You're surely not an undergraduate?"

Glaring at her, Wilder reached into his hip pocket for his
wallet. "Someplace in here I have a bursar's receipt."

"Oh, forget it. I was just curious. You must be General
Studies."

"That's right."

"You can use this typewriter if you want." It was the girl
of the dark eyes speaking, and he turned to find her offering

him the desk beside hers.

"Thanks," he said, and sitting down, he put a sheet of paper into the roller and turned it. He stole a glance at the girl beside him. She was writing now. Then he became aware that, beyond, the Punchlike one had lit a fresh cigarette and was studying him carefully.

"Royal portable," he typed. "Like new. Will sacrifice. Fifty dollars. Inquire Wilder Stone." He leaned toward the girl beside him. "Can I use the *Bulletin* office for an address?"

She looked up. "I don't know. I'm kind of new. I'm just probationary staff. Phyllis—can he use the *Bulletin* for an address?"

"No," Phyllis replied, her eye still on the copy before her. "We don't have time to get out the paper as it is, let alone handling inquiries from classifieds. Not that I think you'll get any on a second-hand Royal for fifty bucks." She looked up. "Don't you have an address?"

"I have about a hundred addresses. But none of them are on the campus."

"Well, use one off campus."

The girl beside him stood up. "I've got a better idea." She pulled the sheet out of his typewriter and read it. "Come on with me."

He followed her out of the office, down the corridor and the stairs, back into the main lobby of Barnard Hall.

"Is she always so unpleasant?" he asked.

"Phyllis isn't so bad, really. She thought there was something fishy about it." Arriving back in the main lobby of Barnard Hall, she stopped before the bulletin board. Pinned to it, he saw a number of items being offered for sale, a fur coat, a ride to Dartmouth and several typewriters. "I think you'd better stick it up here with the others," she said. "What shall we put for an address?"

"An address?"

"Look, do you really have a typewriter for sale?"

"Yes. Yes, of course." He saw she had a pen ready to write it down. "Would a phone do?" He shook his head, as though answering his own question. He took the paper from her hands, folded it, and put it in his pocket. "You've been very kind. May I ask your name?"

"Catherine Massee."

"I'm Wilder Stone."

"Hello," Catherine said and smiled. "I remember you from the corner. I passed you outside the subway. You looked kind of dazed."

"I was remembering you from the bookstore. From a week ago. You were there buying a necktie."

"Oh? I didn't see you then."

"There's no typewriter."

"I figured. So did Phyllis."

"Can I buy you a Coke or something?"

She shook her head. "I've got to go back. I've got to finish here quick, and then I have to go to the library." She started to turn away.

"Some other time?" he asked.

She turned to face him. "What *are* you doing around here? Is it all right if I ask?"

"I work downtown."

"What do you do with a hundred addresses?"

"That was silly. I'm in the real estate business."

She smiled. "But here. Do you real-estate around here?"

"I just take a course here. In General Studies."

"What course."

"A business course."

"I thought it might be embalming."

"What?"

"You're so touchy about it."

"Am I? Am I that obvious?"

"Phyllis has a nose for tender spots."

He said, "I'll have to be more careful."

"When's your class over?"

"Ten."

"I'll be getting out of the library then. You can buy me coffee at the Chock."

"All right," he said. "I'll be there," and he watched her until she disappeared at the end of the hall.

In front of the Chock Full O'Nuts at 115th Street, Wilder hailed a cab on Broadway, and they rode down through the top of the park, aware of the couples walking slowly out of the darkness and the glittering lights in the park's black walls.

Wilder paid the driver in front of a large apartment house at Eighty-seventh Street and Central Park West and discovered to his relief that Catherine had not fled from him past the brass buttons of the doorman and the bronze and plate glass of the doors. She stood beside him, still embracing the books and clipboard.

"Well," he said, and put his hands in the pockets of his coat. "I guess I'd better say good night."

"All right," she said. "Thanks for the lift." She was already turning away when she said, "Unless you want to come up for a minute. I'll give you a glass of milk."

"Isn't it late? You probably have work to do."

"Yes, I do. You're such a *sensible* fellow."

"I'd love to come up," Wilder said, and he followed her into the lobby.

Seeing his professional interest in the furnishings, the equip-

ment of the elevator, she said, "Kirsten Flagstad lives here.
A lot of famous people like that." And Wilder nodded.

Catherine let herself into apartment 8B with a latchkey and
dropped the books and clipboard with a clatter onto the hall
table.

"Mother," she called down the hall, indicating by the tone
and volume she was not alone. A lamp with a blue silk Chinese
shade lit the hall dimly and drew attention to a brass tray
where Catherine's mail awaited her—a bill from Lord & Taylor, a subscription offer from *Time* magazine, and a letter in a
gray envelope. Wilder thought this last was from one of what
must be many admirers.

She studied the gray envelope's postmark and seemed about
to open it. He was scarcely a foot from her—close enough to
hear her breath, to see the tiny brown mole on the pale, fine
skin of her neck, the clean precise line of her upper lip at its
turning, the faint lavender shadows beneath her great dark
eyes that told of a succession of late nights and early morn-
ings. And he knew a fleeting sadness as she tucked the gray
envelope, unopened, into her belt.

"Mother," she called again, "Daddy," and started down the
hall past a tall, grandfather's clock, a bookcase, and some
ornate silver plates hung on the wall, turning on lights as she
went.

"Nobody home," Catherine said, and with a flip of the wall
switch, the living room was brilliant with light. There were
eleven separate lighting fixtures—table, floor, and wall lamps
—each fitted with a high-wattage bulb, and the effect was
dazzling. "Daddy likes it bright," she said. "And I guess I do,
too. I can't bear gloom."

The furnishings were, for the most part, expensive—a thick
Oriental rug, mahogany tables, a large sofa in peacock dam-

ask, which material also appeared in generous quantity at the windows where there was a view not of the park but the roofs of the low brownstones spreading westward to Broadway and the Drive. But there was no particular style nor even taste revealed here. The walls were unadorned save for a large gilt-framed mirror. But the room's center of interest, the grand piano spread with a white shawl embroidered with crimson flowers, displayed a score of picture frames, the nearest of which contained a photograph of a familiar-looking woman. It was autographed—a flourish of blue ink across the subject's white bodice.

"You don't have to have milk," Catherine said, pushing through the swing door into the kitchen. "There's beer—or even whisky if you like." She pointed to the glass doors of the china closet where liquor bottles could be seen but seemed not to be urging it.

"Milk is fine," he said.

He watched with surprise and pleasure the deftness with which she spread the napkin on the tray, filled the glasses, discovered a Camembert cheese, and added it, with a bowl of crackers, to the tray.

As they re-entered the living room, they heard the front door close and presently Alma Massee, a small nervous woman of forty, appeared. She had let her black sealskin coat slip off her shoulders, and now, glancing at Wilder, who had hopped to his feet, she made a frank appraisal.

"This is Wilder Stone, Mother. Isn't he nice?"

"Yes," Alma said, "I guess so." She met him in the middle of the room and shook his hand with a sort of solemnity.

"He's a self-made man," Catherine rattled on. "You'd hardly take him for that now, would you. And as if that weren't enough, he's taking courses at Columbia so he can make even more money. Isn't that so, Wilder?"

He grinned uncomfortably. "Well, no. It isn't so. It isn't so at all."

"Why don't you explain it to Mother then, while I get her a glass of milk."

He watched her exit into the kitchen and felt forsaken. He did not in the least like being left alone with Alma Massee. The relation between a man and a girl's mother had always seemed to him impossibly hostile. On the few occasions when he had found himself in this uneasy phase of a courtship, he had quailed, for he was certain no mother could regard him favorably as a possible son-in-law. He had neither wealth, nor dash, nor cleverness enough to satisfy the most modest of maternal ambitions. Mothers, he had found, reacted similarly, invariably pretending that the attraction between daughter and Wilder did not exist and, sometimes, as though Wilder did not exist. They might speak of their daughters' other beaux and the good times they had had with them, as though Wilder might rejoice to hear how dispensable he was.

No, no. It wasn't delicacy. He was certain of that. It was a pretense, born of the notion that if they did not recognize the attraction it would disappear. And more than likely it would. There was something peculiarly emasculating about a girl's mother.

Alma had settled on a straight chair across from him and was regarding him expectantly. "Well, I can't make a thing out of what Catherine said. You'll have to explain. Wilder? Is that right? Wilder?"

"That's right. It's a family name. My mother's. She was a Millicent Wilder." He looked for some sign of recognition in Alma's eyes, some encouragement, and, getting none, hurried on. "I sometimes wish I were Jim or Tom—but it makes Mother happy. She's very proud of the name. There's a Wilder Street downtown, you know, and she used to take me there as a little boy and tell me about an ancestor that used to have a farm there."

"A farm?" Alma said with real interest. "And you're with a bank now?"

"No. I'm in the real estate business. Lazarus & Company. We have some buildings up this way; 325, just up a block, is ours."

"And what's your job?" From the table behind her she picked up a half-knitted blue mitten that looked destined for Catherine and arranged the four steel needles.

"I'm in building management."

"What's that? Collecting the rent?"

He smiled. While he didn't enjoy the inquisition, she was surely not ignoring him. "That's the object. But you have to keep the tenants happy before they'll pay it. That's the hard part."

"They keep us happy here."

"It does seem well run. You can usually tell by the lobby— clean collars, the doorman at the door and not off having a smoke." He glanced again at the photographs on the piano and was surprised to see two women, arm in arm, dressed in identical, brief costumes and wearing roller skates. Both subjects had written across the picture.

Alma nodded. "We've been here four years now—since the building opened. Kirsten Flagstad, the opera star, lives here."

"Oh, Mother, you're not bragging about Kirsten Flagstad? I did too," Catherine said, arriving with Alma's glass of milk. Wilder noticed the letter was gone from her belt. "Did you find out about him, Mother? She's a marvelous detective. I'm thinking of letting Scotland Yard have her. They've been after me for years."

"Too soon," Alma said, preoccupied with counting the stitches on her needle. "You came back too soon, don't you see? I've only found out where he works and that his family used to have a farm downtown."

"A farm?"

"Well, it was some time ago," he said. "Six or seven generations at least."

"All the better," Catherine said. "They probably picked it up cheap from some Indians. I can see a talent for real estate runs in the family."

"I'm afraid not. As I understand it, Jeremy Wilder bought the farm from a clever Dutchman, and when he sold it, sometime in the late eighteenth century, he took a loss. He was very anxious to move away."

"Why?" Alma asked.

"He was something of an old crank and didn't like his road put to use as a lover's lane which it had become. Young people were coming from all over Manhattan Island to park their buggies in front of Jeremy's house. I can't imagine why."

"I can," Catherine said. "Necking's much more fun if there's someone around who disapproves, don't you think?"

Wilder, despite himself, blushed. He took a swallow of milk. "Yes," he said. "I guess that's it."

Alma broke the silence. "Is your father in real estate?"

"No." He tried to shake off the clumsiness which seemed to be growing on him like fatigue—hoping to think of something bright to say. "No, he's in insurance." He might have said that Everett, his father, despite many fine qualities, was an indifferent business man and because of a pervasive gentleness had failed at several careers—at mining and banking and selling securities and was only slightly less effective at the life insurance business which now occupied him. It would have been the truth, and might well have passed here for wit, but he could not say it and added lamely, "Life insurance, down on John Street."

"You live with your family?" Alma asked.

"Oh, Mother," Catherine protested, "have a heart." She had been spreading the soft Camembert onto the crackers, and she held one between her fingers toward her mother, who refused it with a shake of her head, and then toward Wilder. As he took it, his fingers touched hers for the first time and he felt the impulse—like a gentle and delicious shock, and he looked at her again, covertly, and felt a hopelessness.

"Yes," Wilder said, "in Greenfield. It's a little town in Jersey. It's not far from the Oranges. Father and I commute."

Alma looked up at the clock, saw it was nearly eleven, and gathered up her knitting. "I've got some letters to write," she said with a sigh and got up. Turning to Wilder, she said, "Don't you keep Catherine up too late. She's probably got two hours of studying to do, and I know for a fact she has an eight o'clock class in the morning."

"I'll be going right along, Mrs. Massee," Wilder said, standing, bowing a formal little good night.

"See you catch that train," Alma said with good humor. It was a sort of mock severity, as though she were playing at the role of Catherine's mother—and yet she meant it too. There was no doubt of that. With a final admonishing wave of her finger, she disappeared.

It struck him then, as it would frequently later on, that Alma could muster the gaiety to be one with Catherine, to be of an age with her. And yet it wasn't easy. You could see the

disenchantment in her eyes and with it a wistfulness. It was
the expression of a heavy loser who keeps hanging around the
game.

They were silent a moment, Wilder wondering if he ought
to leave now but not wanting to—feeling an incompleteness
to things, that if he left now he would not see her again. He
wondered what she would do if he tried to kiss her, but her
almost certain rejection was unthinkable. His hand, quite
unconsciously, touched the silver cigar box and he tilted the
lid slightly, caught a glimpse of plump Perfectos within.

"Have one?" Catherine said.

"No, thanks."

"You don't smoke?"

"A pipe now and again." He closed the lid. "Is your father at
home?"

"No." For a moment that seemed the end of it. She looked
out the window, following the blinking light of a plane moving
northward over the Palisades. She added, "He works late
nearly every night."

"Mind if I ask at what?"

Continuing to stare out the window, she pulled her feet up
and under her on the sofa. "I guess not. Between Mother and
me we've done a pretty thorough job on you." She looked
down at her nails. "He's an agent. An actor's agent. He goes
around to theaters and clubs—night clubs, places like that, to
see people."

It was a confession, clearly an embarrassment to her, and
he paused a moment before replying. "It sounds fascinating."

"I suppose it does." She looked at him. "Daddy was an
actor once when he was young. To hear him tell it he was
good. It was Broadway's loss that he never played anything

but stock."

"You?" he asked. "Theater in the blood?"

"I'm a parlor actress, not a stage one."

"Well, you'll probably come around."

"You know what? The smell of grease paint makes me sick to my stomach."

She spread her hand on the cushion between them and stared at it, and he thought of reaching out and taking it in his, and his heart began to beat fast, and then she took her hand away and it was too late.

"Do you have any brothers or sisters?" he asked. He had meant to ask her earlier and it came to him now automatically.

"No. Do you?"

"I have a sister—a younger sister. She's younger than I. She's twenty-three. But not so young as you. How old are you?"

"Nineteen."

"Good Lord."

"And you?"

"I'm twenty-seven," he said. "That must seem awfully old to you—like an old man, doesn't it?"

"No," she laughed. "It doesn't seem old at all. It seems a nice age."

"A nice ripe age."

"Now you mustn't, Wilder." It was the first time she had said his name, and it was sweet to hear. "It's an attractive age, an almost perfect age for a man. I'll spell it for you. At nineteen I find a man of twenty-seven more attractive than somebody my own age. There, do you have it?"

"Yes. That cheers me up no end."

"You're so sensitive about everything—like about the college. Why does that bother you?"

"It doesn't bother me."

"Oh, but it does. It plainly does. Now tell me why."

He smiled, realizing she was assuming the role of his senior. "I don't know," he replied, "except that I came very near to going."

Catherine leaned back, folded her arms. It was feminine and appealing, the graceful fingers spread across her arms just above the elbows, the arms now framing, now pulling the sweater tight across her small, round breasts. "Tell," she said. "Tell about it."

Wilder looked at his watch. "I'd better go," he said. "You've got lots of studying to do, and I did promise not to stay."

"You can't go until you tell about the college."

He drank the half inch of milk left in his glass and looked reflectively into its bottom, watching it clear. "When I finished high school we were out West—in Pueblo. We didn't have much money. Father had gone out there in a mining operation and it hadn't worked out as well as he'd hoped. But an uncle of Mother's, Uncle Robert, offered to pay my way through Princeton."

"And you didn't take him up on it?"

"Well, yes, I did. You see I wanted to go very much. I'd thought about going to Princeton since I was a little boy. I used to go to the games. Father didn't go to college, but all mother's family had gone to Princeton. And all the time we were West and I was in school in Colorado, I talked about coming back East to Princeton when it came time." He looked up into Catherine's eyes and found she was listening, watching him intently. "I had to tutor, to prepare for the college boards, and Uncle Robert agreed to pay for that too. I started off that winter—it was the winter of 1936—tutoring with an old tyrant, Heidrich." Wilder smiled. "George Heidrich. His house smelled of cabbage, and he wore a wig and had a terrible temper. He used to scream and beat the desk in a rage when I didn't know the trigonometry. I didn't think I was learning anything, and I used to come back from his house so shaken that finally I just quit."

"You didn't find another tutor?"

"No. It was nearly time for the exams anyway, so I put it off a year . . . and then another . . . and then it was too late."

"And there was no one—your father or mother or anyone—to tell you, you *had* to go back to the cabbage man or somebody else?"

He looked up at her for a moment. "No."

She shook her head. "Even so, I can't believe that if you wanted to go to college so badly you'd have let an irascible tutor stand in your way." She looked at him searchingly. "No. I know that. It was something else. Uncle Robert?"

"Perhaps," he said, in some awe of her perception.

There was a loud bang down the hall. The front door had slammed and they both looked up, startled.

A gnomish man with a high-domed bald head appeared quite suddenly across the room. He wore a brown coat with a velvet collar, and a gold-banded walking stick hung from the crook of his arm. Wilder felt the man's small, piercing eyes traverse him, practiced as the hands of a detective searching an outlaw, saw the straight lips twitch as though he had an itchy nose, and, as Wilder struggled to his feet, he had the impression that at the next instant the man would raise his cane over his head and come at him swinging.

"Daddy," Catherine murmured. "This is Wilder Stone."

But Joe Massee was already across the room. In three agile steps he came to Wilder and looked up at him. He smelled strongly of whisky and a spicy cologne. Wilder put out a hand tentatively.

"How do you do, sir," he mumbled, and to his great relief Joe Massee took his hand.

"Hello," he said. It was a sidewalks-of-New York voice, adenoidal and penetrating. "Want to have a drink with me? I'm going to have a drink."

"I've just been having a . . ." Wilder pointed down to his glass with the ring of milk in the bottom.

"My God," Joe Massee said. "What in the hell is that? Milk? It looks like milk." He pointed an accusing finger at his daughter. "Has she got you drinking milk?"

"I'm afraid so." Wilder teetered from one foot to the other.

"Milk is for babies." He tossed his stick onto a chair and still in his overcoat went toward the kitchen. "And listen. If a man drinks milk it will make a baby of him. It won't make him any younger." Pausing in the doorway he waggled a finger of warning. "You understand? No younger but a baby all the same. Now young man I prescribe whisky to counteract the effects of that stuff. How do you take it? Soda? Water?"

"I'd like to . . ." Wilder hesitated, glanced at Catherine.

"Oh, Daddy, don't make him. He's got to go. He's got to catch a train to New Jersey and I've got to do mountains of work. I promised Mother."

"You keep out of this, now," he said sharply. "I'm talking to the young man."

"I'm afraid Catherine's right, Mr. Massee. I really should be getting along."

He gave a grunt of disgust and stepped through into the kitchen, letting the door swing shut behind him, but instantly, and as Wilder sat down on the sofa again, his gleaming dome of a head reappeared through the door. "The best advice I can give you, young man, is never listen to a woman. If you do what you damn please, you'll be all right. Now, last chance. Drink?"

Wilder leaned forward, clasped his hands. "No, sir. I really don't."

Joe Massee disappeared but left the kitchen door open, and they could hear the opening of the closet, the clink of the bottles and ice. "Now, here's a good example," he called. "Tonight if I'd listened to the advice of a woman—and believe me I've got plenty of that—I wouldn't have gone into The Lambs for a hand of poker, and if I hadn't gone into The Lambs for a hand of poker I'd be fifty dollars poorer right now."

"You played poker? And you're home at this hour?" Catherine asked diffidently. "I don't get it."

"I cleaned 'em." Joe appeared in the doorway, examined the deep color of his drink approvingly, and smacked his nervous, active lips appreciatively. They were his most expressive feature, constantly in motion, a perceptible twitching at their center, always on the point of a grin or a grimace of disapproval. "I took their carfare. There was nothing left to do but come home." He had struck a pose in the doorway, ankles crossed, looking for all the world as though he were about to dance. "It's just my rotten lousy luck that on a night when I have the cards, nobody has a sou."

"At least you won," Catherine said. "And you got home early. You know if you could do that every night Mummy'd come along. And me too. We'd both take up poker."

Joe laughed and looked from his daughter to Wilder. "And the milk man here? Him too?"

Wilder blushed angrily.

"Sure," Catherine said tersely. "Him too."

Joe smiled and started slowly across the room. Pausing by the silver box he opened it, contemplated the row of cigars, drummed with his fingers on the table top.

"Daddy," Catherine cautioned. "How many have you had?"

"A hundred and two. Not enough, anyway." He turned as if it had occurred to him to offer the box to Wilder, who had sunk back in the sofa, disliking this little man with his whole heart. But thinking better of it, Joe selected a cigar, popped it into his mouth, closed the lid of the box, and, without so much as a backward glance, departed.

They were silent for a bit, and then Wilder stood up as though to go. "I didn't mean to offend him. I guess I should have taken the drink."

"No, you shouldn't. Not unless you wanted it." She frowned at the back of her hand. "Forget it. He's like that. He's an expert bullier."

She got up and led the way down the hall. He picked up his hat and coat from the chair, and she opened the door and stood leaning against it, unhappily. Overcome with sadness, feeling that what had appeared a beginning had turned inexplicably but surely into an ending, he stepped into the landing and pushed the button for the elevator. Then he looked into her face and saw the disappointment there, too.

"Well," he said. "I hope I'll see you around sometime."

"I hope so." Her eyes went up to the indicator over the doors, anticipating the elevator's arrival and the end.

"Will I find you at the *Bulletin* again some evening do you suppose?"

"It's not a very good place."

"Where then? Where do you suppose?"

The elevator arrived. The door swung open with a clatter.

There was the white-gloved hand, the shaft of light from the cab.

"Here would be the best place to look."

"Tomorrow?"

"No. Not tomorrow. I'm busy tomorrow."

Crushed, he looked into the sour face of the elevator man, then back to her. "But soon?"

"Sure."

"I'll call you sometime."

"Please." She said. "Please do," and closed the door softly.

In the days which followed Wilder, anxious, thoroughly uncertain of Catherine, called the Massee apartment several times without reaching her and when at last he succeeded was astonished that she accepted his invitation to the theater with enthusiasm.

He took her to an inexpensive French restaurant on Ninth Avenue and then to *The Voice of the Turtle,* and afterward they had a drink in a bar next to the theater and they talked excitedly of the play, their heads together, as though they had some part in its presentation.

"You weren't in the service, were you?" Catherine said, sitting back suddenly and contemplating the whole man.

"Well, yes I was. I was in the Navy for a few years. I was an enlisted man. I was a yeoman. That's a nautical term for clerk."

"Where were you?"

"My war story isn't much to brag about. Is it all right if I don't dwell on it?"

"Sure," she said. "Except now I'm curious."

"All right." He thought for a moment. "I'd like to tell you."

"Then do."

"We came East in 1937 and Mother rented the house in Greenfield."

"Mother?"

"Well, I mean she was the one that was enthusiastic about it. It reminded her of how Montclair had been. Father doesn't care where he lives. I don't think he knows a good deal of the time."

She nodded.

"I hadn't lost the idea of going to Princeton and I went down one day and walked around the campus. It was a fall day, and, oh golly, it was lovely, with the foliage turning and the excitement of the boys running around and the bells tolling. I saw a woman in the admissions office in Nassau Hall who encouraged me to think I could get by the Boards by studying hard on my own. I bought some course outlines, mathematics and history, in the Princeton bookstore, and I went back to Greenfield to find a job and earn some tuition money. You see, Father was not only broke but in debt and just starting a new job in New York." He made a signal to the bartender for another round, but it went unacknowledged.

"And I found a job in a machine shop in Rutherford run by a man named B. H. Hite." He smiled. It was an aside. "Mother didn't like it much."

"Why?"

"She has very strong feelings about overalls."

"But *you* liked it?"

"Lord, no. But I thought it was getting me into Princeton. The Spanish Civil War had been going a year, and there was a boom in airplane engines. I got sixty dollars a week for running a drill press. I studied in the morning and worked the four-to-midnight shift. When I went to Newark to take the College Boards I never wrote a word in those little green

books. I read a couple of questions and blotted my forehead
and sat there listening to the scratching of pens on paper all
around me. I didn't know enough. I didn't even understand
the questions. I got up and walked out."

He caught the bartender's eye now and held up his glass
and pointed to Catherine's. "The following year I decided to
try it again, this time with a cram school. I found one in New
York where they said they could get me by the Boards in six
months. But it wasn't a good year for studying. It was the
year Germany invaded Austria. There was talk of a draft. I
found the trip in to the tutoring school too much after eight
hours of the drill press. I thought about enlisting. I might
have, I think, if it hadn't been for the family."

"What about them?"

"I couldn't go off and leave them. Father wasn't well, really,
and he was having trouble keeping up with the rent and the
bills."

"And so you didn't?"

"I postponed it—all through 1939 and 1940. When the draft
came, I got a deferment because of my job. It was Hite Prod-
ucts now, and I was making ninety dollars a week. That was
more than Father was making, considerably more, and
Mother was depending on me." He bent the plastic mixing
stick, and it snapped, startling him. He dropped the two halves
into the ash tray.

The bartender brought the drinks on a small, round tray
and hovered, watching Catherine, until Wilder paid the
check, whereupon he departed without acknowledging his
generous tip. Wilder sighed. "Pearl Harbor changed things.
A week later I quit. Lord, that was a day."

"How?"

"The family. They felt I was doing more for the war there

in Rutherford than I would trying to learn how to be a warrior at that late date. And they needed my help. Father's job had gone sour. They felt I was being selfish."

"Selfish? Didn't they read the papers?"

Wilder laughed. "Not much actually. We never, so far as I can remember, have taken a newspaper regularly. Once in a great while Father would bring one home, and Mother and Lyddie and I might do the puzzles. I don't recall any of us ever reading the front page. The things that happened there didn't seem to have to do with us." He took a sip of his drink. "And they were probably right about my doing more good for the war where I was. I spent six weeks in boot camp at Great Lakes and two years at the supply depot in Norfolk. In the end I got to sea. On a tanker. The *Brazos*. The AO 61."

"Did you like that? You're smiling as though you miss it."

"Yes. I *did* like it. Not in the way I'd supposed. There wasn't much about a big old cow of a tanker to capture the imagination. I never saw a hair of a Japanese or even a task force. We were too slow." He shrugged. "It was a good time for me. Sometimes I think it was the very best time of my life. Where were you on V-J Day?"

"In a night club. Daddy took Mother and me to some place on Broadway. I think it was the Diamond Horseshoe. I re-member it was wild."

"I was in Cristobal—in the Canal Zone. And I was thinking of shipping over. I was thinking of being a peacetime sailor. I'd made first class, and the Executive Officer had encouraged me to think I might even get a commission someday. But Mother fell ill. She had a stroke actually, and the Red Cross got me some emergency leave. I came home, and in the end I got out before my enlistment was up. I got a hardship dis-charge." He opened his hands. "You see—not exactly bloodcurdling as a war memoir, is it?"

"It has its moments. I think you had a narrow escape at Mr. Hite's drill press."

For one terrible instant he thought she was making fun of him. "From what?"

She was silent and finally, looking away, said, "I don't know."

"Don't you really?"

"You feel more obligation to your family than most people. More than I. I think it's lucky you did what you wanted in the end. Better late than never. That's all I meant."

"You can't let your mother starve, you know."

"It's been done." She saw that this shocked him, and she smiled. "Don't look so glum. I'm not suggesting you do." She groped for the sleeves of the brown rabbit fur coat, which she had allowed to slip down behind her onto the seat. "We'd better go. I've got to be up at seven."

Taking her home on the subway, he felt depressed, as though he had revealed himself utterly to her and she had not liked (indeed how could she?) what she had seen. Tonight, surely, would be the last time.

His seniority which had intrigued and complimented her had vanished. Tonight in the bar they had become the same age. Indeed, due to some female clairvoyance she had occasionally assumed a greater maturity than his. Now she would return to her other young men. He saw them, a brigade of youths encamped in the rolling terrain across from 331 Central Park West, awaiting her return. He was certain that when he asked to see her again she would be quick to invent an excuse.

"It's late," Catherine said. "You hadn't better come up."

"Yes," he said, studying his watch. "I'll have to run."

To his surprise she took hold of the cuff button of his coat, a peculiarly tender gesture here at her door. Cocking her head, she looked at him, and to his delight he realized she wanted to be kissed. He leaned forward and her lips came up to meet his and they touched lightly, scarcely at all, but its effect was like thunder, and before he had quite recovered, she was disappearing through the doors.

He ran after her, a few quick steps. "When will I . . . ?"

"Tomorrow . . . call me." Raising her white glove, the fingers spread in farewell, she stepped into the elevator.

4.

ON a warmish early spring evening a week later they sat on the parapet below Grant's Tomb, smelling the damp earthiness that seemed to be stealing into the city and watching a tug with six loaded scows make slow progress against the current.

"Oh, I want to make the most of it," Catherine laughed. "I want to try everything—just a taste you know—and then choose. I'd like to go to Europe and ride in a gondola and climb the Jungfrau, and I'd like to stay here and get a job on *Life* and have an affair with a married man, and I'd like to be a nurse and a nun, and I'd like to dance all night at El Morocco, and I want to marry a nice young man with a brilliant future and raise a family of fourteen children out in Port Chester. I just don't want to miss anything."

"It'll take careful planning," Wilder said.

She leaned back, an elbow propped against the flat stone capital. She cradled her head in a hand and watched the first lights coming on in the increasing dusk—the bridge's festoon across the water, the first stars in the sky, a sign on a pier over on the Jersey side. "Yes, the planning. I'm planning all the time. I'm a planner. You've noticed that, haven't you?"

"No. I hadn't. You seem to me a nonplanner. A very impulsive young woman."

"Oh, no," she cried and sat up. "Impulsive women are invariably miserable. If you're a woman, you've got to have a plan."

"I don't believe it," he said. "If by an impulsive woman you mean someone like Carmen, I don't believe it for a minute. Carmen had a grand time. Everybody else was miserable—but not her."

Catherine sat back and drew her long, slim legs up under her and tucked the gray flannel skirt under her knees. "I mean Mother," she said soberly. "Oh, she's not miserable. It's not that. But it didn't work out as she'd hoped."

"What had she hoped?"

"She hoped to get away from Elmira. If you'd ever been in Elmira you'd understand that. Every Elmira girl with a grain of sense wants to escape."

Wilder laughed. "I note a tendency to exaggerate. I've lived in Pueblo, don't forget. I know what a small town is."

"I'm *not* exaggerating. I don't know about Pueblo but I do know Elmira. It's a coffin of a town. It's a *mean* little place."

"But she did get away. Here she is in New York."

"Yes, I know. But just getting away wasn't all she hoped for. Getting away was a means to the things she hoped for, and she didn't get half of them." She watched the lights of the traffic along the drive above them for a moment. "She was only sixteen, you know, when she first saw Daddy. She and some other girls had gone to this matinee. It was"—she paused and raised her eyes heavenward—"*Abie's Irish Rose.* And afterward they ran around to the stage door, and when Daddy came out he not only autographed their programs but took them into the coffee shop at the Bancroft Hotel and bought them beer. You can see him doing that, can't you?"

"Yes. He's very persuasive about that kind of thing."

"About anything. You won't believe this, seeing Mummy now, but a day later, just twenty-four hours after she asked him to autograph her program, she was home packing a bag to go off with him on the tour. They were going on to Syracuse and Erie and a lot of places she'd never heard of, but she didn't hesitate for a minute. She didn't hear my grandfather's pleas. She didn't see my grandmother's tears."

Wilder frowned. "He asked her to marry him?"

She smiled. "Oh, no. He thought—*thought,* mind you—he could get her a job as understudy."

"And he did?"

Catherine nodded. "Mother played in two performances. She was Mrs. Cohen in Duluth and Rose Mary Murphy in Cincinnati. I've got some pictures of them some place, pictures of them in the play. He had an idea they'd be Lunt and Fontanne. She says she was terrible, and Daddy doesn't deny it."

"But it sounds like such fun," he said. "It sounds the perfect kind of memory to have about the beginning of your life together."

She looked at the Sherwin Williams sign on the Jersey side, watched it twice drip its Mazda bucketload over the globe. "Yes, it does. It does sound that way, doesn't it?"

"And how does it come that a girl who was born in a stage trunk according to the best theatrical tradition isn't trying out for a part in the Barnard show instead of reporting the news?"

"I wasn't born in a stage trunk. I was born in Elmira. I was born at my grandmother's house on East Main Street."

"They came back to Elmira?"

"Not they, just Mother."

She meant, he realized, that they hadn't been married when

she was born, and his surprise and admiration of her frankness overcame his shock at the confession itself.

With a swift movement she swung her long legs clear of the balustrade and hopped down. "C'mon and take me home so I can change. I can't go to a dance, not even one of these crumby James Room things, in this outfit."

The dance, as Catherine had promised, was not pretentious. It was one of the monthly affairs, an opportunity to repay minor obligations, to examine dubious young men recommended by friends and relatives, and to expose a quantity of Columbia students to general survey.

A four-piece orchestra was playing "Laura" at one end of the rather cheerless pale green room, and at a table in front of the windows a man in a white coat was prepared to serve a lavender punch. There were already more men than women present. The boys, for the most part undergraduates, looked younger than Wilder had hoped. They were in some cases beardless and they huddled together, punch glass in hand, or danced mutely, wearing vacant expressions while performing intricate and strangely athletic steps that reminded Wilder unpleasantly of dance halls and roadhouses.

And there were still a few uniforms—a midshipman from the *Prairie State,* a marine lieutenant, and some army enlisted men.

As Wilder set out on the rather sticky floor, holding Catherine awkwardly, inches away from him, he felt himself resisting, the grim smile deepening on his face, the stiffness in his arms, the inability to speak. And in a moment he was out of this misery and plunged into another.

He felt a hand on his shoulder, and a round-cheeked, spiky-haired youth was separating him from Catherine, not even glancing at him, and dancing off with her, leaving him alone among strangers. He headed for the punch bowl, then the wall to watch Catherine as his fears of recent weeks took shape. The boy was intense, making dance-floor love to her, holding her tight and low, just above the waist, but leaning back, talking. He was telling her something, and she was flushed and excited by it. He was a good dancer, effortless and nimble, and Catherine's bright red slippers moved precisely with his gleaming loafers. They were one, and it was a painful sight to Wilder.

It occurred to him that he could cut back but that he ought to dance with someone else first, and dropping his glass on the window ledge, he approached a tall, outdoorsy-looking girl with her blond hair braided into two Rhine maiden discs behind her ears.

"Would you like to dance?" he asked, making a formal, dancing school bow.

She smiled at him wanly and shook her head. "I'm sorry," she said, pointing to the stairs. "I'm waiting for someone."

Turning, he confronted a small, round girl in black velvet who had, he thought, overheard. "Would you?" he asked. "Would you like to dance?"

"Oh, I'd love to," she said, revealing southern origin.

"I'm Lucy Clark," she continued, as they took their first experimental and not altogether reassuring steps. Beaming, she showed an abundance of very white teeth. "I'm from Birmingham, Alabama."

"How do you do." Wilder looked over her head for Catherine's black dress and red belt, spotted it at the far end of the room, and was somehow relieved to see she had changed partners. She was with a large blond boy in a brown jacket. "I'm Wilder Stone," he said to Lucy Clark.

"Hi. You from New York, Wilder?" She pronounced *new*

as though there were a *y* in it.

"Yes. You might say New York. Actually from New Jersey—Greenfield." Her hand was small and unpleasantly moist in his, and their feet were not going right. She was unconsciously trying to lead him.

"I don't know Greenfield. What's that near? Is it near Princeton? I know people in Princeton."

"No. It's near Newark. Newark and Jersey City. It's just across the river."

"Oh," she said, disappointed, her face flat and sallow, but brightening with a new thought. "Do you know anybody in Birmingham?"

"No," Wilder said, coming face to face with Catherine, who waved at him happily as she passed. "No. I don't know a soul in Birmingham."

"Oh," she said hollowly in temporary defeat. Then, "You at Columbia?"

"No," he said. "No. I'm not."

"I thought you weren't. You look older."

"Do I?" He was interested. "Much older?"

"Oh, heavens, I don't know. Not too much older, I guess. Like a graduate student or one of the teaching fellows or something. Maybe it's the suit."

"The suit?"

"I don't think I've seen anybody but my Daddy in a business suit in years."

"Oh," he said. "Well it's all right, you see. I'm in business."

"Oh," she said unhappily and then, remembering her manners, smiled. "What business?"

"Real estate."

"Oh."

The dance, it seemed, would never end, and only with that

happy circumstance could Wilder foresee an escape from his misery. She was too full of pride to find a pretext for leaving him, he too well-mannered to find one for leaving her, so despite the anguish they seemed destined to dance into eternity. Although pursuing their halting conversation propped against a window sill, punch glass in hand, had some appeal, it meant abandoning the slim hope that someone else would claim Lucy. Both aware of this, they plodded on, Wilder's unhappiness unlessened in noting the spiky-haired youth had returned to dance with Catherine. And she was flushed and happy, laughing as he spun her around, away from him, and then caught her again, deftly, about the waist.

When Catherine's eyes met Wilder's across a few feet of the floor and the tartan-covered shoulder of the spiky-haired young man, she bit her lower lip in sympathy and then smiled him some reassurance, but Wilder simply glared at her. Next time around she looked at him and shrugged helplessly. Wilder turned away.

"Well, what in the world could I do?" Catherine said, lagging behind him slightly as they descended the broad stone steps into the now darkened courtyard outside Barnard Hall. "You asked her to dance with you. I didn't."

Wilder made no reply. His coat collar turned up, his hands thrust into his pockets, he was a picture of the outraged male.

"I couldn't cut in on you," Catherine said.

"You could have asked somebody to," he said tersely. "You could have asked your friend with the horse-blanket coat. And I daresay you would have if you hadn't found him so appealing."

"Oh, Wilder, I don't find him appealing. I don't find him appealing at all."

They paused at the curb and a taxi slowed. Wilder shook

his head and it resumed speed. "There's no reason why you should deny it," he said. "It was apparent to everyone—to me, to Lucy Clark, to everyone at the dance."

"He's a good dancer. I enjoy dancing with Peter. Is there anything wrong in that?"

He turned to her. "You don't have to apologize, Catherine. I have no claim on you."

Her hand reached out to him, touched his sleeve, and he recoiled as if from a shock. He started rapidly down Broadway, feeling altogether a fool now but somehow obliged to play out this adolescent role. At 116th Street he paused and looked at the subway station looming out of the island in the middle of the street, a dim and dirty yellow light showing from the entrance. It was strangely quiet, and from where he stood he could hear the clack of a turnstile admitting some weary soul to the sour-smelling tunnels.

"Did you know him before?" he asked.

"Yes. He's been to a couple of the house dances—and he took me to a party."

"Lately?"

"Last week." She smiled at him plaintively. "I didn't have a good time. If that helps."

"Helps?" he repeated softly. "I don't need any help. I'm fine." He crossed 116th Street, Catherine at his heels, and entering Riker's, sat down at the nearly empty counter.

"I'm going to have a cup of coffee," he said. "What would you like?"

"The same."

As he gave the order to the counterman, Wilder saw the reflection of the electric clock in the mirror. It was midnight. Frowning, he reached for his wallet, put a dollar on the counter, and got up. "Drink mine for me, will you?"

She looked up at him, and for a moment he thought she was going to cry. "Why?"

He pointed to the clock. "I'm Cinderella."

"Oh, don't go, Wilder."

"I've got to. I don't want to spend the night in the Erie station."

"You could stay with us. There's a perfectly empty guest room."

"I couldn't. Your mother wouldn't want . . ."

"She'd love it. You can use a pair of Daddy's pajamas and I have a clean toothbrush."

He touched his chin.

"And Daddy's razor. He'll loan it to you, being a gentleman, though he won't to ladies for some reason, not even his relatives."

"My family would worry," Wilder said. "Mother would worry if I didn't turn up."

"Does she know when you get in—on the late train?"

"Yes. She doesn't sleep well."

"Call her." Catherine nodded toward the phone booths at the back.

"It's late. It's late to call."

"If it's not too late to worry, it's not too late to call."

He stood there irresolutely watching the clock while the minute hand moved to one minute past twelve, aware of the empty phone booths and Catherine looking up at him. With a simplicity that touched him she reached out and took his hand between both of hers. "You mustn't go," she said. "I don't want you to go."

The counterman set the coffee on the counter, picked up Wilder's dollar, and turned to his cash register, and Wilder sat down on the stool and with a flourish opened the top of the sugar bowl and passed it to Catherine.

"Aren't you going to call your mother?"

"Later," he said.

In the taxicab going down Central Park West they sat apart in silence. It seemed to Wilder that a great gulf of self-consciousness lay between them now. It was embarrassment over his behavior at the dance. It was the suspicion, generally confirmed, that when he needed it most, grace would fail him. It was the inability to let his physical self be the instrument of his emotions. His mind, busy with consequences, appearances, invited the paralysis.

He thought to touch her hand, to put his arm across the back of the seat and draw her to him, to kiss her. But it was Catherine who slipped her arm through his, pulling him toward her slightly, just as they turned into the park. He felt her head so lightly touch his shoulder and looking to see if it was really there found it was. Her hair made a dark fan on his chest, and the pale oval of her face tilted up, and her eyes, round and serious, searched his. And he knew that now it was the time. In a moment it would pass. He must now.

And yet with maddening perverseness his mind was busy with whether to call Millicent. It even presented him with a fleeting picture of her, seated in the little boudoir chair in her bedroom, the faded blue peignoir gathered about her, and every few minutes looking at the clock.

He was thinking that if he did call her now and say that he'd missed the last ferry, she would be prying and wheedling, wanting to know where he would stay—and it was just too much. He neither wanted to lie to her nor to get the wind up unnecessarily.

As he leaned now to kiss Catherine, these conflicting thoughts possessed his mind, and when he touched his lips to hers, it was gently, reverently, perhaps, and self-consciously, and he felt her mouth, so warm and eager against his, grow cold. She dropped her head back and looked at him.

"Well," he said ineptly. Country-clumsy. He felt embarrassment prickle around his collar and, in spite of himself, added, "Well, well."

She sat up straight, moved away a little, touched a lock of hair back off her forehead, and looked out the window.

Once inside the Massee apartment Catherine went in search of her mother. Although he seldom smoked, Wilder took a cigarette from the box on the table and lit it.

Presently Alma Massee appeared in a pink wrapper, her make-up on, carefully composed as though she had not yet retired.

"This is a terrible imposition," he said, rising.

"It isn't at all. It's no trouble. The bed's all made up. It would be silly of you to do anything else. Did you call home?"

"No. I didn't."

"The phone's right there."

"Thanks. I may. I haven't decided."

"Do you want something to eat, Wilder? Something to eat or drink?"

"No. I don't think so, thanks."

"The blue ones, Mother?" Catherine appeared at the end of the hall, holding up some folded pajamas.

"Yes," Alma said, turning to look. "Those are the ones."

"Gosh, I don't need . . ."

"Don't you worry." Alma smiled and gave him a reassuring pat. "Just have a good night's sleep. What do you want for breakfast?"

"Anything. Anything at all."

"Scrambled eggs and bacon?"

"That sounds grand."

"Good night," she said as Catherine reappeared and motioned him to follow her into the hall leading to the bedrooms. To the left he caught a glimpse of the master bedroom, the chaise longue where Alma had been listening to the radio and doing the puzzle in the Sunday *Times*. Turning to the right, he passed Catherine's room. He saw the books piled menacingly on the blue desk, childhood's tattered teddy bear on her pillow. The guest room was pleasant enough, with its own bath and twin beds, one of which had been turned down, and the blue pajamas lay folded there. There was even a dressing gown over the arm of a chair. In the bathroom he could see a toothbrush, razor, shaving cream.

"Good night," Catherine said abruptly and began to draw the door closed.

"Wait," he said.

She looked at him with curiosity and a perceptible sullenness as his hand touched hers on the doorknob. Taking her hand, holding it tightly, he put his other arm around her waist and tried to draw her to him, but to his surprise and confusion she resisted, backed off a step, and he released her.

"I've got to go," she said. "I've still got work to do," and with a thin smile she left him standing there by the neatly turned-down guest room bed as the weakness and shame simmered up in him like a fever.

Somewhere in the quiet apartment he heard a clock strike two. He had been aware of its single chime at one and at one thirty, and in between he had relived all of the evening's embarrassments and squirmed and turned in horror at the sight of himself. Oh why couldn't he have shut up about the dance . . . why must he open himself like a book to show his adolescent jealousy. Why couldn't he have taken her in his

arms in the taxi and kissed her with the passion that now in
phantasy, now in the darkness and solitude of this strange
room, was consuming him. It was *the* moment. He saw it
clearly now, and he had failed it. He had failed Catherine and
he had failed himself, and it would never come again. When
the clock struck half past two and he knew that he would not
sleep until dawn, the thought of confronting Catherine at
breakfast was more than he could bear, and he turned back
the bedcovers with the thought he would leave now, quietly,
a polite note of thanks propped on the bureau.

But as he swung his feet to the floor, another thought came
to him, that he might go now to see her, that now in this
moment when the night thoughts had swept away all the in-
hibitions when the desire for her and its frustration had
brought him to weeping, he must go to her, must not think
of consequences—that her door will be locked, that she will
not hear him knock, that he will wake instead Joe Massee,
that she might call an alarm or, perhaps, worst of all, simply
push him away again. No. He must not think these thoughts.
For it is now really, now or never. When the dawn breaks it
is too late, forever too late.

He groped for and found the dressing gown, closed the
window, looked out, and saw the moon and lights on in two
windows. Then, very quietly, he let himself into the hall where
a small night light cast a cartwheel shadow on the wall. He
moved cautiously toward it, looking ahead, eying the closed
door to the Massees' room, the open one, dark, this side.
Catherine's closed. He paused when he came abreast of it.
His heart, he felt, was making a noise to wake the Massees.
It seemed to thump even in the backs of his knees, and he
thought with sweet relief of turning back now, creeping back
to his room but saw the shame too, and then with a hand he

did not know for his own rapped softly on the door. In answer there was only the beating of his heart.

There was a noise, a click, down the hall in the direction of the Massees' door. His heart seemed to freeze for a full minute while he watched to see the figure appearing out of the darkness. But there was no figure. It was only the wind he decided or a radiator, a noise of the night.

Now the same hand, his hand that had rapped on Catherine's door, reached out and turned the knob. He opened the door a crack, then wider. He stepped into the darkened room, closing the door behind him. He stood flat against the wall, listening, and soon he could hear the ticking of a clock. It was quick, delicate, and feminine, a bedside clock, and then he heard her breathing, soft and regular. There was a sigh, almost a moan, and he heard the sheets rustle as she stirred in her sleep.

"Catherine?" he said.

She awoke. "What is it?" she asked drowsily, turning on the little lamp at the bed table. "What's the matter?"

Wilder crossed to the bed, looked down at her, astonished at how childlike she was in the white short-sleeved pajamas, her hair tousled, no lipstick.

"I couldn't sleep," he said.

"Oh," she said without surprise. She yawned, looked at him hazily, turned slightly in the bed as though to make room for him to sit on its edge.

He sat down. "I couldn't sleep on account of you. I'm miserable. I had to talk to you."

She smiled, still sleepy.

"I love you," he said. "I love you terribly." And he put his arms around her then, and when he kissed her pink, childlike lips and felt them warmly and drowsily accept his own, he sighed, and then he felt her hand caressing the back of his neck.

"You must be cold," she whispered into his ear. "There's a comforter at the foot of the bed."

He lay beside her and pulled the comforter over him and they kissed, the covers between them.

The noise came to him clearly and caused him to start. It was the click of a latch. A door someplace in the apartment had just closed. To his horror it was followed by rapid footsteps now muffled on a carpet, now ringing heels on bare floor.

"Who's that?" he asked hoarsely.

"It's Daddy. It's all right. He won't come in here."

"Are you sure?"

"Yes," she said. She reached out and turned off the lamp on the bed table. She touched her fingers lightly to his chin. "You're shivering," she said. "Are you cold?"

"More scared than cold," he whispered. "I'm trying to think what I'll say when your father comes in."

She laughed and they were silent, listening to Joe Massee's footsteps retreat up the hall. Another door closed, and then there was the sound of water drawn.

"My feet are cold though."

"They are?"

"Could I come in? Just long enough to warm them?"

"All right," she said. "Just that long."

Wilder got up then and slipped in between the covers and reaching out for her drew her to him, feeling every inch of her against him, her mouth against his, and his hand, the same strange hand, went to her breast, felt the swelling out from her arm and rib cage, and then her hand came up and very gently drew his away.

"I just had to be sure," he said, "that you aren't a little girl—a tiny little girl."

"Are you sure now?"

"Yes," he said and they kissed again.

5.

"I PROMISE you, Wilder, I did not sleep the whole night. I didn't close my eyes. Didn't you have a moment's thought for us—that we might be concerned about you? I hadn't the least notion of what had happened."

"I'd no idea, Mother. I thought you'd be asleep. I didn't want to wake you."

"And you stayed the night with them? With the Massees?"

"It was late. They have a guest room at the ready. Mrs. Massee assured me it wasn't putting them out."

"I don't quite understand how you met these people, Wilder. You seem to know them quite well. Are they business acquaintances?"

"I met Catherine at Columbia. She's a student there."

"Ah." Millicent was now fully alert, watching him.

"You'll like her, Mother. I promise you. She's an extremely nice girl."

"I'm sure. You say she's a classmate? She's also taking this course in business?"

Wilder laughed and, folding the newspaper he had been holding open in his lap, put it on the table. "Now, Mother, you mustn't be nosy." He arose and went to where she was standing in the entrance to the dining room. Smiling, he hugged her gently. "You must let me handle this in my own way. She's a Barnard freshman."

When he took his arm from around her shoulders, Millicent sighed and turned as though off to the kitchen, but she hesitated. "You sound quite serious, Wilder. Are you?"

"Now, Mother, you mustn't worry over such things. No. It's not serious. I rather like her. Not much more than that. And I assure you she's not serious about me."

"Oh? How do you know? My poor lamb—how could you possibly know?"

"I know." Wilder smiled, and as his mother started to leave again, he added, "Oh, she's asked Lyddie and me to a house party at some friends of hers in Darien, Connecticut. It's the last weekend of the month. I've told Lyddie, and she's dying to go."

"Oh? Is she? To a house party?"

"I'm delighted for Lyddie's sake," Wilder said, taking up his paper again. "It doesn't seem she's been having a very gay time lately."

"Yes." Millicent's eyes wandered out onto the front lawn where her husband was asleep in one of the raveling wicker chairs from the front porch. He had spread his overcoat like a blanket over his legs, and even from here he appeared painfully thin. She massaged her own right temple to mark the recurrence of her headache. "I'm afraid none of us have been having a very gay time lately."

"I'm so excited," Lyddie said. She was watching the squares in the station platform drift behind with increasing speed, and as she turned to him, Wilder saw that the anticipation had brought some new and subtle light to her eyes, a heightened color to her cheeks, and for a moment he saw his sister as other men might—and happily saw her a handsome girl.

Lyddie's features were delicate and yet strong. She had the same firm jaw as Wilder's but with a slight and becoming cleft at the chin. Her cheekbones were more prominent, as was the bridge of her nose, and the result was an interesting, a thoroughbred face which suggested she had borrowed heavily from some old Tory in the family, some fierce, proud seventeenth-century forebear.

She wore her black hair long, drawn back to a bun from a thin, true line of a part. It was an unusual, a severe style, for a girl of twenty-three and yet becoming. She wore no nail polish, no make-up save for an unobtrusive shade of lipstick. The impression she gave of being an English girl was heightened by the heather tweed suit, bought for the occasion at Best's, and the first major addition to her wardrobe in a year's time. In the rack overhead her mother's valise contained a borrowed evening dress for the promised country club dance.

"I hope you won't be disappointed," Wilder said. "They often fizzle, these things."

"I thought you hadn't been here before. I thought you scarcely knew these people."

"I scarcely do. I haven't." He tugged at the crease in his trousers. "I meant in general. I meant that the house parties one has hope for so often fizzle—so often disappoint."

"This one won't," she said earnestly. "You'll see. It's going to be lots of fun. Did you say the house is on the water?"

"Right on the Sound, I think. On a little inlet of the Sound."

"Will they have a boat?"

"I expect so. Why?"

"I don't know. I want them to have everything—boats, upstairs maids, and croquet on the lawn, with lots of tall young men in blazers."

Wilder laughed in delight. It was so unlike her. "I think there's only one unattached young man, and it's not likely he'll turn out in a blazer."

"What's he like?"

"I've never seen him. He's a neighbor, I think. And his last name is Hovey—Jim Hovey, as I recall it."

Lyddie nodded and looked about the crowded car. They were a younger, more prosperous lot of passengers than she was accustomed to on the Erie. The car itself, with its chrome and bright paint and fresh blue velour, was in itself a cheerful sight.

"It's much nicer, isn't it?" she mused and, turning her attention out the window, noted the first signs of Westchester County, the careful shrubberies and fieldstone of the parkways and the array of new motor cars at the New Rochelle station.

And Wilder went back to the copy of the *National Geographic* he had been reading or, more precisely, looking at— for he was planning a speech.

"Catherine," he meant to say. "I've known you just a few weeks. I know that's not long, and yet it seems like half my life. And I cannot conceive of the other half without you. I've never been in love before so I have no comparison, but I am so terribly in love with you Catherine that I know I can never love anyone else.

"I know I come along at the wrong time for you: that you want to see everything and go every place and above all not to be committed while you're still in your teens. I know how much college itself, finishing it, and all the good times ahead, mean to you. And there's not much I can offer that part of you—the curious, experience-hungry, not-wanting-to-miss-anything part of you—except that we'd have fun. I know that whatever we did it would be fun. If it was fitting out a little apartment in the Village . . . would you like to live in the Village? Or going on a trip, a long trip, to Scotland perhaps, a bicycle trip to Scotland. I've always wanted to do that. . . .

"But I have a lot to offer the woman part of you. The woman that I know and love and need I think knows and loves and needs me too. So, Catherine, I'm asking you to marry me— now, tonight, if it can be done or next week if that's a better time or after another year of college if you must, or even when you graduate if that's the only possible way. I'll wait until you're sixty and I'm seventy if I have to, but I'd prefer not to. I'd prefer tonight. Will you? Will you be my wife?"

And when Wilder had thus rehearsed his speech, he could visualize her lovely face turning toward him slowly. It was in some dark place out of doors, and there was a sound of music and people talking in the distance, and he would be watching her eagerly for some sign. Sometimes in Wilder's reverie Catherine would smile and hold up her face for a kiss and she would whisper, "Yes. Oh, yes, Wilder." And at other times she would cock her head slightly to one side and her eyes would be a little dazed and sad and she would try to look into his and find she couldn't, and then she would say, "I'm afraid you're right about it being the wrong time, Wilder. Time's against us, don't you see? Three years is too long to wait, and I mustn't ask you."

And when these fancies were done, Wilder would weigh very carefully in the scales of Catherine's mind the factors which would lead her to a decision. On the "no" side he put Joe Massee. In the few weeks of their acquaintance Joe and Wilder had built a tangible hostility that both deplored but were powerless to alter.

Joe had made an effort. He always made an effort for Catherine's beaux. He did so for Catherine, whom he loved and wanted to see happy above all things, and because he was just naturally a comradely spirit. He liked nothing better than boys around the house and he cherished the hope that the one who married Catherine would be his friend, his very good friend, and would understand, as a woman could not, his restless spirit—why he roamed the city at night, why he seldom came home before three.

But Wilder? Despite obvious effort the man could not suppress the bluenose in himself. He flinched when an arm was flung about his shoulders. He could never be counted upon for a well-told joke or a nightcap. He sipped at life. My God, here was no pal.

Catherine's devotion to Joe, no less than the passionate fealty of any girl for her father, was only increased by regular feats of forgiveness for the unhappiness he brought her mother. Yes, Joe Massee weighed heavily on the "no" side of Catherine's scales.

But now on the "yes" side he put Alma Massee, and instantly he saw the indulgent smile she had for him. He knew that he impressed her in many ways. She looked at him and saw stability. She had openly encouraged his courtship of Catherine. On the telephone she was a cheerful conspirator, making arrangements for their meetings, assuring Wilder he was welcome for dinner, making him feel at home. She even asked his advice on such matters as whether their old car (a three-year-old Buick used mainly at Sea Girt where they had a summer cottage) should be replaced and whether Catherine should be encouraged to go off to a camp on Lake Champlain where she had been offered a job as counselor.

Wilder was as pleased at this acceptance of Alma's (he felt he was plugging some hole in the boat which Joe had allowed to go unattended) as he was embarrassed by it. There was that indelicacy about Alma, that carrying of forthrightness to a fault: the way she would so obviously leave them alone, retiring hastily as though she would rather die than deter for one second the now-we-are-alone-together glance, the touch of hands, of lips, she felt to be coming. For one thing it had the reverse, an utterly inhibiting effect upon Wilder. In any case Alma brought the scales even, for Catherine's mind was Alma's doing.

And so perhaps it came to Catherine herself, Catherine alone, Catherine the girl, Catherine the woman. And what *did* a girl, a woman do? How could you predict the way she would act at this important moment of her life? Would she know what she really wanted? Could she overcome the untimeliness of his appearance or would she have to wait for a ripeness, until she had examined all the inviting baubles within her reach and found them unsatisfying.

But all this reasoning, this cause and effect, was of course to no avail. Women, Wilder had observed, did not behave according to laws. They were sprung on emotions. When the brain said yes, they were mute. It was only when their hearts or some other, less elevated, internal organ said yes, that their lips repeated it. And Catherine, all her protests about planning her life notwithstanding, would prove no exception. It was the internal voice, in a way not Catherine's at all, that would answer him, tell him if Catherine loved him or not. And what would it say?

Well, yes, there *were* some signs, the kind that women go by, and with their closer knowledge of the subject, reliable perhaps, if properly read. There was light and roundness in Catherine's eyes for him. Even he could recognize that. They lingered on him, those big, dark eyes of Catherine's. They turned away reluctantly, and she touched him now without embarrassment, unconsciously. Her hands, which were in constant motion when she talked, reached out, touched his for an instant, even when they were with others, and although she seemed not to know she was doing it, Wilder was thrilled, literally. Yet, being from a long line of *noli-me-tangere* people, it also distracted and embarrassed him.

And they kissed now when they felt no one was looking. Each night when they parted they clung to each other in the darkened hall. And invariably it was Catherine who turned the lights out. He kissed her soundly, still primly, but with his hands spread on her firm young back, feeling the strap of her brassière, the rise of its clasp through the silk of her blouse. And when he drew away and inhaled the smell of her skin and hair, she would whisper, "Do you love me?"

He would pause and swallow, embarrassed. "Yes," he would say hoarsely. "Yes. I do. More than . . . more than tongue can tell."

And she would smile at him—and at his quaint response, his valentine answer.

"And do you love me?" he would ask in a churchly whisper.

Catherine, the complete coquette, would shrug. "I don't know. Maybe." Then she would laugh and start him out the door with a peck on the cheek. "I'll keep you posted."

On the few occasions when they had been alone at Catherine's, really alone and without undue fear of surprise, they had sat, and ultimately stretched out side by side, on the blue damask sofa, where they kissed and fondled one another with a passion that left Wilder exhausted. And yet they did not sleep together. They had not, even on the first night of their corporal love in Catherine's bed, although it had occurred to Wilder that he could if he wanted, that at the right time and in the right place Catherine would give herself to him completely. But meantime he did nothing to bring it about.

Of course he wanted to sleep with her. He ached with desire for her, and he also sensed that in the act of temporarily possessing her body he would find her spirit his—and more durably.

Yet, curiously, he was always the one who stopped, the one who disciplined the fire of their love-making with a sudden chasteness, a buttoning of a cardigan sweater, hands now in hands, a prim cool kiss on the eyelids, a reluctant moving away, and a thought for the lateness of the hour, the soon-departing train, tomorrow.

With so much yearning for her and what was likely a pasteboard resistance from Catherine—the least genuflection to decorum—Wilder found it necessary to explain to himself why he had not tried. Well, they were not reasons that turned him back. No. They were faces, some indistinct, some not. There was the face of his Protestant upbringing which had given him the strong notion that to sleep with a nice girl was an evil act, that in the accomplishment of his venal purpose he would spoil her—for him, for her, for the whole world to see.

There was the face of fear. His was the kind of imagination that could borrow here and there from a book or motion picture and project with vividness a scene in which Catherine discovered she was pregnant, its anguished sequels in which they decided whether to marry, whether to tell Alma and Joe Massee, capped by a tragic finale at a clumsy abortionist in Brooklyn.

There was the face of the druggist. Wilder had never carried a contraceptive in his life—had once, in Denver, Colorado, walked for an hour in front of a drugstore trying vainly to raise the nerve to buy a package. To produce one from his vest pocket for Catherine, thus revealing his carnal thoughts of earlier in the day when he would have exchanged for it a dollar and a sly wink with the clerk—oh, no—unthinkable.

And there were the faces of the two women he had slept with in his life. Though it was two and a half years ago he could recall, sharply, her short, coppery hair, the way she kept combing it up the back with the widespread fingers of her chubby, childlike hand, the high cheekbones that had given her style, or seemed to, had at least set her off from the others; and most vividly he could recall his disgust when it was over, when she sat on the bed in her slip and he saw in her face how he had been cheated of his ten dollars.

He saw, less clearly, for it was more like ten years ago, the heart-shaped face of Diana Campbell, a girl from Pueblo who at eighteen had had her brief marriage annulled. She was a tiny doll-like girl with exquisite features and a perfectly pro- portioned body. The pocket Venus they had called her, and she seemed to make up for her smallness with an abundance of vitality; in the quickness of her speech, her bursts of laughter, the darting of her tiny hands, there was a visible tension.

In recalling Diana's face now he felt the anxiety again. They were on a porch glider. Her family was away someplace. She had turned to him suddenly in the darkness of the spring night, clung to him as with a thousand little hooks. She breathed heavily as she crushed her mouth to his, her small body shivering with a passion gone out of control.

It was out of curiosity that Wilder responded, feigning an ardor to meet hers, not revealing the faint revulsion when he felt the point of her tongue force through his lips nor his im- pulse to laugh when he felt it tracing the whorls of his ear.

"You're a virgin, aren't you?" she had whispered.

"Yes," Wilder had replied. His voice was thin with apprehension. But he was more curious. He still wanted to know.

"Come on, then," she had said. "I'll be good to you."

And so she was. Among the pink ruffles, in the narrow little girl's bed of her childhood, she overwhelmed him with her small, sinewy nakedness.

"So this is it. So *this* is what all the fuss is about," had gone round and round in his mind even at the very peak of their love-making, and when, so soon, it was over, he lay back on the pillow and felt the distaste rising inside him—at her hip against his, at her breast against his arm as she leaned toward him, at her teeth which bit gently, teasing at his ear lobe.

"You'll be all right," she had said then—reassuring. "All you need is some practice."

And in answer he had turned back the covers and hopped up, groping about now for his socks and shorts, fumbling into them, trying not to see her nakedness, trying not to think of himself here—feeling empty and a little frightened.

"Call me," she had said drowsily. "Please call me tomorrow."

"Sure," he had said as he left, but of course he hadn't—nor had he answered her calls. And, although he thought of going to a party she gave a month later, in the end he did not.

Lastly, there was the face of his mother. It was clearest of all, of course. It was only a matter of several hours since it had kissed him a tender farewell. Without effort he could see her gentle smile, the pale eyes absorbing him and loving him and the good soft hands extended toward him ready to soothe, to bandage the cut (not iodine—nothing that stings—some milder solution from the cabinet), to dry the tears, to stroke the neck gently, rubbing in a bit of Father's bay rum;

or when he had a cold, Vick's, the gentle, reassuring massaging of his chest, drifting him off to sleep, the slowly warming aroma of the ointment, the caressing of her soft fingers a lovely anesthetic.

Lyddie said, "You have such wonderful luck, Wilder, being in the city, meeting people, getting invited places."

Wilder closed the *National Geographic*. "You make me sound the ideal extra man. I'm not, you know. This kind of thing is unusual."

She looked at him without expression and then turned back to the window.

"Lyddie, you ought to come into town too."

"You know I can't, Wilder."

"Of course you can. You can if you want to."

"But what would I *do?* I'm a woman and I'm not trained for anything. I'm not about to be a salesclerk in the five-and-dime you know."

"Of course you aren't. You ought to get yourself some typing and shorthand."

"A typist?"

"Not necessarily. Stenography is basic for a woman who wants a job—even if you don't use it."

"I don't see why a girl has to spend six months and a lot of money learning something she isn't going to use."

"Don't worry about the money. I'll stake you."

She uttered a hopeless sort of sigh. "You're sweet, Wilder. I know you want to help, but it wouldn't work, my having a job. You know Mother."

"Oh, Lyddie, you could get around her. She'll accept it in the end if you're firm—if you really want to come in."

"I expect so. I wasn't thinking so much of whether she'd let me as whether I could—whether I have any right to leave her alone now." Her face turned mournful. She seemed to have caught a glimpse of forthcoming tragedy.

"Now?" he asked. "What about now? What's wrong with now?"

Lyddie put her chin in her hand and looked out the window moodily.

"What is it?" Wilder asked again. "Am I meant to know something—because I don't."

"Oh, you *do* know." She spoke softly, as though afraid of being overheard. "The house. That ark of a house. It's more than Mother can do alone."

"If you had a job you could afford a cleaning woman. And she'd probably do a great deal better in four hours than the two of you in a full day."

"You don't think Mother and I make a very good job of it, do you?"

Wilder opened the magazine again, riffled the pages. "Lyddie, I'm trying to help you get into town. I think it would be good for you. I think it would be good for all of us. I thought that was what you wanted."

"But don't you see that I can't? At least not for a job. Not with Father failing as he is—and needing more and more looking after."

"He's getting older. I don't necessarily see him as failing."

"Oh, Wilder, you must be blind."

They were silent for a moment—watching the countryside, glimpsing white houses through clumps of yellowing forsythia and thickets of young oak and suddenly, with breathtaking clarity, the harbor at Greenwich, already dotted with small boats, freshly painted, and, beyond, the Sound itself, a crisp royal blue in the spring sun.

"If a job isn't important enough—what is? Would you come in to take some courses?"

"Perhaps." She frowned, studying her hands which were small but with stubby, utilitarian fingers. "I've always thought I might do something with my singing."

"Nothing else? Nothing else interests you enough to get you away from Greenfield for a bit?"

"Oh, yes, Wilder." She looked at him slyly, smiling for the first time. "Oh, yes indeed. You know, because you're my brother I think you lose sight of the fact I'm a girl and not greatly different from other girls."

"A man, you mean?"

"The right one."

Wilder nodded. "But he may not come for you," he said gently, "all the way to Greenfield."

At the far end of the car the conductor opened the door. "Darien is the next station," he called.

"That's us," Wilder said and stood up to get his and Lyddie's suitcases down from the rack.

On the platform Wilder saw Catherine had come to meet them with the Wicks' dark green station wagon. She was standing before it in khaki shorts, a tartan shirt, and sneakers, looking every inch the Fairfield County resident.

"Well, hello there." Catherine's was a truly friendly smile and Lyddie, who did not take to people at once, nevertheless liked her instantly for it.

"Miss Massee." Wilder was clearly fussed. "Catherine. And this is my sister Lyddie."

Catherine directed Wilder to the tail gate with the luggage by pointing her finger, a gesture so simple it raised the thought in Lyddie's mind that Catherine knew her brother rather well. But as she drove away from the station, Catherine was still ignoring Wilder, drawing her into a knowledgeable feminine world of well-made arrangements, and Lyddie was feeling the contagion of Catherine's good humor.

"It's real relaxed," she was saying. "No special order of the day. There's a tennis court if you're ambitious."

"Oh, Wilder," Lyddie said reproachfully. "You didn't tell me. I don't have any tennis things."

"I didn't know," he replied, knowing Lyddie didn't play well and wouldn't step onto a tennis court with strangers for all the world.

"Don't worry. They'll outfit you. They've got an immense closet full of sneakers and shorts and things people have left behind. Oh, and the dance. There's the dance tomorrow night. You brought an evening dress, didn't you, Lyddie?"

Lyddie nodded. "A short one. That's all right, isn't it?"

"Perfect," she said, expertly passing a grocer's truck, and Wilder marveled again at Catherine's agility. It always surprised him, for he had supposed his real desire was for an indolent woman, a voluptuous, sleepy creature of darkness. The sun gleamed on the soft white skin of her neck and the wind blew a part in the dark curls, and Wilder yearned to have his arms around her, around the slim cage of her vitals, to touch the fair smooth skin, the fragrant hair, the firm muscles of her back, the swelling buttocks, the incredible softness of her breasts. And the yearning didn't sadden him. In his life he had not been so happy.

They were leaving Darien center, passing the tidy, colonial fronts of the shops and markets, the first barbered lawns and shrubbery.

"We're having dinner at the club tomorrow," Catherine said. "The Wicks, Mr. and Mrs. Wick, had to go away. They had to go to Chicago this morning, and they gave the cook the weekend off. We're sort of camping out. It's going to be wonderful fun. How are you on scrambling eggs, Lyddie?"

"Oh, dear. Not much more than that, I'm afraid. Not without guidance." Looking ahead down the road, she saw bright green countryside and she laughed aloud. "But I'll try. I can at least set the table. I'm sure I can do that."

Twenty hours later (it was the forenoon of a glorious April Saturday) Lyddie, Catherine, and Wilder were back at the Darien station.

"There's one in about fifteen minutes," Wilder said, returning from the ticket window. "You needn't wait."

Catherine, in a white tennis dress, clenched the steering wheel. "I'll wait." She spoke with noticeable economy.

Lyddie, pale and weary-looking, crept toward the door. "You mustn't wait," she said feebly. "I don't want to put you out further. You'll want to get back to the tennis."

"Stay here," Catherine said. "There's no good place for you to sit down."

Lyddie saw that this was true. The bench nearby was occupied by a colored woman and the child in her charge. Lyddie leaned back against the upholstery as Wilder took their valises from the rear of the station wagon and placed them side by side on the station platform. He looked up the track and then got back into the front seat beside Lyddie and folded his arms. They sat in silence, each one thinking with some remorse of the previous evening.

The departure of the senior Wicks and the cook had, as Catherine had predicted, added to the informality of the weekend plans and by sundown a party was under way.

The Wicks' retaining wall extended for fifty feet along the inlet, making a dry shelf at the water's edge, and here in the growing dusk a dozen young people in heavy sweaters were preparing a cookout. The tide was out and the black mud speckled with clamshells released a penetrating, briny odor. The fire which had been built inside a ring of stones was still too high, but someone had put on the first batch of hamburgers, and as they seared they sputtered appetizingly.

Lyddie, sitting on the low wall, looking across the water, was startled to find Jim Hovey had come up. He was a stocky, muscular fellow, and he put a foot on the wall beside her and leaned lazily on his knee. In one hand was a can of beer and he drank from it, tilting his head back. There was a toughness and agility about him. He was surely a good athlete.

"Don't you want some beer?" he asked.

"No. No, thanks." She felt the importance of the moment. There was a fluttering panic in her chest, and she tried to master it.

"Don't you drink?" He smiled and scratched his back with a thumb. "You a Moslem or something?"

She returned the smile but felt instantly that it had only exposed her nervousness, that it looked more a twitch than a smile. "I've never liked beer much. Particularly out of a can. It always seems to give it a metallic taste." Oh, why did I say that, she thought. "I'm sure it's just my imagination."

"I think we can get you a glass."

"Oh no, please." By the fire she glimpsed Catherine Massee watching them and was further humiliated to realize she had sent him over. She felt herself blush and hoped it was dark enough for him not to notice.

"Hamburger? The hamburgers are almost done."

"You mustn't worry about me because I'm here alone. It's all right. Really it is. I like it." And to prove it she looked with some rapture at the sky, which was darkening overhead but still pale and silvery at its western reaches. The wind was still. There was the sound of water, the cry of a gull overhead.

When she turned back he was gone. She saw him a few feet away talking to a girl in a pink sweat shirt with the word ISLANDER spelled across its front in block letters.

With relief she saw that darkness was enveloping her. She took a sandwich and a bottle of ginger ale and moved farther down the wall, into the shadows, and it was from there she saw that Catherine Massee, who was standing at the other side of the fire, beside Wilder, had taken his hand. Lyddie shivered and buttoned her jacket.

Lyddie saw the lights come on in the houses across the inlet. To the north there was already a scattering of tiny stars. Overhead the last moment of day lingered on the fields of gray cloud. She went toward the firelight, peering among the silhouettes, but she found only strangers.

Crossing the terrace, she looked up the path and through it saw the lights of the house above. There was music playing, a radio she thought. It had the thin, scratchy voice of a portable set. She saw figures on the lawn—moving away. She was, of a sudden, stricken with a loneliness that forced the cry from her on a note of real terror.

"Wilder!"

On the terrace below they had stopped talking and all that could be heard was the voice of the little radio above. And in the stillness, she called again, up toward the house, louder this time, shrill, she called for help.

"Wilder!"

The answer came, not from the lawn above as she had expected but from close at hand. It was Wilder's voice. "Lyddie. What is it?"

Following the sound of it, she saw that a path, a narrow

one, led through the brush and wood toward the boathouse, now a dark shape against the shore below her. She started along it quickly, and as she came into the clearing, she halted and caught her breath, seeing, as she knew she would, their shadows.

Catherine was sitting on the edge of the wooden ramp, leaning against a corner of the house. Wilder stood only a few feet from her. "What's the matter, Lyddie?" he asked. "Is anything the matter?"

"I think I'm getting ill," she said.

Catherine stood up. "Ill? In what way, Lyddie?"

"I want to go, Wilder," Lyddie said. "I want to go home."

"Now?" Wilder asked. "Surely not tonight. It can't be that bad."

"Do you have a temperature?" Catherine took a step toward her with the intention of feeling her brow.

"No. Please." Lyddie said. "It's a chill. A chill and a rather peculiar sensation in my—stomach."

"Can I get you something?" Catherine asked.

"No." Lyddie shivered miserably.

"Perhaps you'd feel better if you went up to the house and lay down for a bit," Wilder suggested. "Do you want to do that?"

"I don't know," she cried, tears rising in her voice. "I don't know, Wilder." Running to him, she grasped his arm, and her fingers dug convulsively into its flesh. "Please, please let's go."

Lyddie was alone in the room lying on top of the covers, her head and shoulders propped against the pillows. She gave him a wan, grateful glance for coming and then turned her head away toward the wall, her slender fingers stroking its surface. "Don't bother about me," she said weakly. "I'll be all right."

"Are you still cold?" he asked. Seeing a blanket at the foot of the bed, he unfolded it, placed it carefully across her legs, and tucked it in beneath them.

"Thanks, Boo," she murmured, using the baby name that hadn't occurred to her in years. "Now run along and have a good time."

"Won't you come down for a bit? It's awfully close in here." And it seemed to him that it was. "Catherine's offered to make you comfortable on the porch. There's an elegant chaise longue."

Her lips tight together, Lyddie shook her head. "If I'm to be ill," she said grimly, "it won't be in public. I don't like to make a spectacle of myself." She looked at him significantly.

"But you're not going to be ill. And you won't be cold. We'll bundle you up in some blankets."

She shook her head, and they were both silent. He knew his sister's moods, for they were his own, or nearly so; and he read now—in the furrow between her eyebrows, the tautness at the corners of her mouth, the somewhat higher pitch of her voice—a danger signal.

"Go away," Lyddie said. "I really feel awful. And don't let *anyone* come up here."

On the porch he found Catherine sitting on the railing. She looked at him and took short nervous puffs on a cigarette.

"Lyddie doesn't want to come down," he told her. "But I think she'll be all right. I don't think it's anything serious."

Catherine flipped the cigarette away. "I'll go see if there's anything I can do."

"No." Wilder reached to prevent her. "She wants to be left alone. Really."

Catherine paused halfway through the screen door. "Oh? I'm not so sure. I'll see." And she was gone, across the hall.

"Catherine!" he called after her, but she continued determinedly up the stairs.

Catherine reappeared moments later, looking, he thought, somewhat shaken. "Lyddie doesn't want a doctor," she announced. "But I'm going to call one anyway. She's been ill."

A doctor, summoned, arrived at nine o'clock but departed a half hour later without seeing his patient, who had locked herself in her room and refused him, along with everyone else, admittance.

In the hall outside Wilder had knocked and pleaded to no avail. In answer came only the sound of Lyddie's weeping—a soft, convulsive whimper, endlessly repeated.

The party broke up early. It was scarcely eleven, and the house was quiet. The girl with whom Lyddie shared her room had to borrow pajamas and sleep in the Wicks' big double bed.

On the far track a Boston-bound express train thundered by, and then it was still again.

"I hate to spoil it all for you," Lyddie said. "I'm terribly sorry."

And after a moment Wilder said, "I hope you'll have a good time at the dance. We'll both feel very badly if you don't."

"I don't care about the dance. It's just a dance." She looked across Lyddie at him. "Oh, hell."

Wilder sprang from the car. "Come with me," he said to Catherine, and walking around the front, he opened her door and helped her out. On the platform he saw an empty baggage wagon and steered her toward it.

"You mustn't look unhappy," he said to her. "It can't be helped."

"I know," she said beside him. "It's all right. A lot of things collapse."

He leaned against the wagon and took her hand. "You know

what I was going to do this weekend?" He looked up the
track.

"No."

"I was going to wait until the right time, the right place—
along towards the end. I'd prepared a treatise—all the argu-
ments, all sides of the question." He smiled at her. "I was
going to ask you to marry me."

She looked down at the toes of her bright, white sneakers,
then up at him, curiously. "You were?"

He nodded unhappily.

She laughed softly. "Well, if you were to ask—I will."

And in spite of Lyddie watching like a sentry from the car,
Wilder reached out to touch Catherine, and then he kissed
her and took her in his arms.

6.

EMERGING from the subway into a deserted Chambers Street, Wilder trotted the block down to Cortlandt, paused in front of the entrance to the tubes, saw from the clock in the Western Union office that if the ferry departed punctually he had slightly over three minutes to make it—not enough by a minute. The tube, although it ran irregularly at this hour, was a better bet by far. Yet out of a perversity he himself acknowledged, he started off down Cortlandt toward the ferryhouse at a run, his footsteps echoing like a fugitive's past the dark fronts of the cut-rate hardware and electrical shops, the shuttered fruit stands and lunch counters.

At West Street he paused, teetering on the curb, taking the measure of a huge trailer truck rumbling into Washington Market. He let it pass, then darted behind it under the West Side Highway, and then he heard the warning whistle. It was a familiar sound, an old friend, yet stern, remorseless. Wilder sprinted across the plaza, through the doors and into the ferryhouse. Ahead lay the brass-railed passenger entrances— now chained, their ticket receptacles hooded. Although he was still inside, locking his cash drawer, the agent had closed the window of the ticket booth.

Wilder tapped on the window. "Can I make it?" he called. "Can I try for it?"

The agent turned, frowning. "It's too late. Ferry's gone."

"It's not. It's still here." Wilder pointed into the gloom behind where the *Pocono's* stern was visible in the slip, the rear end of a silvery milk truck looming above its rail. Then, dimly, Wilder heard the sound of the chain and saw a man beginning to tug at the tall iron gate.

"You can try if you want," the agent said and released the turnstile. Wilder burst across the waiting room toward the gate, half of which was now closed. The attendant was pulling the other half to meet it, and as he saw Wilder heading for the narrow opening which remained, he put up a hand.

"It's still there," Wilder cried. "It hasn't gone."

But as the attendant turned to look—the milk truck, the rail, the little shelf of top deck, shuddered slightly, as though with a chill, and crept out of sight.

Wilder, panting, the heat prickly under his shirt, heart thudding against his ribs, felt a rage at the attendant who had closed the gate, snapped its lock, and, turning his back, walked away.

"Dammit!" Wilder cried after him. "Dammit to hell!"

He went into the phone booth and called Greenfield.

"Oh you haven't, Wilder," Lyddie said. "You haven't missed it."

"I'm sorry. I didn't realize how late it had gotten."

"Mother, he's missed it," he heard Lyddie say. "He's missed the ferry." And after a moment Millicent Stone's voice came onto the phone—tremulous, gentle yet firm, and from its first word, which was simply "Wilder," he felt better. He felt the anger and frustration draining away. Looking out at the closed gate, the empty ferry slip, he smiled at the ridiculous spectacle he had made there a few moments ago.

"What a shame. We'd counted so much on seeing you, dear. Well, it can't be helped. You mustn't fret about it. Where are you now?"

"At the ferryhouse."

"And the next train's not for hours. Well, you may as well stay in town now. Get a good night's rest and come along in the morning."

"Yes, Mother. That's exactly what I had in mind."

"Promise me, Wilder, that you'll go straight to bed and not sit up reading. I thought you looked rather tired last week. . . ." She paused. "Or was it the week before when you were home last?"

"Last week. A week ago today."

"An eternity in any case."

"Yes, Mother," he laughed. "An eternity."

"Well it is, you know . . . for us out here. We're always thinking of you."

"I know," he said, sobered, and there was a silence between them, broken when he resumed brightly, "Oh, I'll be bringing Jimmy tomorrow."

"What a lovely idea, Wilder. It's been ages since we've seen him." He heard her reporting this news to Lyddie. "We'll have a nice luncheon for you both. Is there anything that he especially likes? I never can recall."

"No," he said. "Just the ordinary things. Please don't go to any fuss."

"Jimmy?" Lyddie said, and it seemed to Wilder she had snatched the telephone from his mother's hands. "You're bringing Jimmy?"

"Yes," he said. "I hope so."

"Oh, that's nifty, Wilder." Her enthusiasm was girlish and

real. "That's the best news of the week. What time will you get here?"

"I don't know. Early, I hope. I was going to get him at eleven but I'll call. . . . I'll call at nine and see if we can't step things up a bit. There's a ten-something train. We'll try and make that."

"A roast," Lyddie said. "I'll buy a roast. And some potatoes. What kind of potatoes does he like?"

"I don't know, Lyddie. Any kind. Any way you want to do them. Now, no fuss, Lyddie. Do you understand? Is Mother still there? Let me say good night."

"I am going to get a roast."

"Fine," he said. "Do put Mother on."

"Okey-dokey," she said, suddenly bright, kittenish.

"Is it all right?" Millicent Stone asked. "Is everything all right?"

"Yes, Mother. I just wanted to say good night."

"Good night, dearest."

"Yes. See you in the morning."

"Sleep well."

"I will," he said and hung up.

Leaning back in the booth, he sighed. It was faintly stuffy and he opened the door a crack, but he made no effort to leave. He felt better. Some kind of tension had left him here in this narrow box. Everything was all right now, better really than if he had caught the ferry since he would have had to return first thing in the morning. Now he would have the day with them *and* with Jimmy.

Looking out now into the cavernous waiting room, he saw that the lights were being turned out, the new fluorescent tubes that shed an unreal, a five-and-dime, brightness over the gleaming tin façade of the newsstand, the shabby old benches and the worn linoleum. Opening the door all the way, he stood up and started toward the street.

On the platform of the Chambers Street station there was a drunk with his head in his hands and a stoical colored woman staring straight ahead at nothing and some boys laughing. As he stood there with them waiting for the local train, Wilder felt the full weariness of the day, and with it the tension returned—a firm knot in his stomach that would give him no peace.

It was Wilder's intention to follow his mother's advice to the letter. He expected to alight at Forty-second Street and take the crosstown bus to Tudor City. Or he might walk. He liked walking the city at night. There was a serenity to it then, with the frenzies of daylight spent, the sidewalks empty. There was room now in the cafeterias, in the buses and subways, and on the avenues where taxis prowled for a fare.

But when the train reached Times Square, Wilder sat looking at the door, momentarily open to the platform, knowing that he ought to dart through it directly, saying to himself that at any moment, the last moment, he would, not admitting that on some lower level of his consciousness a contrary decision had been made. The door closed and the train moved out of the station, carrying him uptown, and Wilder, irresolute, queasy with guilt, wishing he had got off and gone home, stared at a legend in bright orange letters—CURE CALLUSES INSTANTLY.

Standing across from Bibi's apartment, he looked up at her third floor, saw that the living room windows were dark. With both blinds and curtains drawn, as she generally kept them, this was not significant, but the window in the bedroom was open slightly and through it he could see a dim light—possibly from the bed lamp, possibly coming through the door from the living room.

He stood there on the curb angered at his feebleness, his inability to make some decision about her. He couldn't even apply his mind to it. He shuddered at the thought of himself here skulking like a schoolboy, unable to want her enough to thrust the doubts aside and take her, yet unable to let her go.

"Beat it," he whispered to himself. "Go on home." And at the same time he was looking up at the drawn shades, wondering what she had done when, slightly over an hour ago, he had left her. Had she taken the badly aimed slap, his brusque departure as the final appalling scene of their affair and called Braun? Had she given him then, on the high tide of her bitterness, the answer he wanted? If that were the case—and it seemed likely as he considered it—she would not be alone now. Braun would have come to her from wherever he lived, in Queens probably. He would be there now. Or he would have taken her out somewhere, to some bar in the neighborhood. He walked across the street, entered the vestibule, and rang Bibi Winter's bell.

There was a long wait, so long Wilder was convinced no one was in the apartment. He rang again, and then he heard Bibi's voice from the wall speaker.

"Who is it?" Her voice was sharp, frightened.

"Wilder."

"Oh. What happened? I thought you were going to Greenfield."

"I missed the ferry."

"Oh," she said again.

He waited, thinking that now she would press the door release and his eyes went to the heavy brass plate on the front door. He waited for the click-click that would pass him through, but it did not come, and the certainty grew that

Braun was upstairs.

"I came back," Wilder said, "to apologize. I don't know what got into me. It was the day I guess—so many things. So many slings and arrows."

"Yes," she said. "I guess that was it."

"Had you gone to bed? Did I wake you?"

"I was in bed but not asleep. I was reading."

"I guess you'd rather I didn't come up."

"Do you want to?"

"May I? Just for a moment."

The release clicked, and he lunged for the doorknob.

He stood on the third-floor landing, getting his breath, wondering what he would say to her. Without his ringing Bibi opened the door of her apartment. She wore a blue nightgown and a Viyella wrapper. It had small yellow rosebuds on a white background, and he had given it to her for her birthday a year ago.

He looked at her, puzzled at the expression of her face. In the dim light of the hall he could see she had taken off her make-up, and she now had a plump, childish appearance— lips, cheeks, forehead, uniformly pale with an illusion of translucence. Yet there was an unaccustomed gravity to her face. There was something new, and he gazed at her, trying to comprehend it.

"You'd better come in," she said.

"Yes." He walked by her into the apartment, glancing around quickly, expecting to see another guest rising from the sofa to greet him. But there was no one here, nor had there been. He knew it instinctively. He could have scented any other presence. Relieved, he turned and saw that she was still standing by the door watching him and in the light of the table lamp that her eyelids were pink and swollen, and now he knew how she had spent the hour they had been apart. He felt the tears start to his own eyes.

"Oh, hell," he said.

"You're back." She shrugged her shoulders. "You came back. What does it mean?"

He shook his head. "I don't know." He smiled. "It means I missed the ferry."

"I don't mean that."

"I know."

She gave him a cross look. "And what did it mean when you left?"

"I don't know, Bi," he said forlornly. "I really don't."

"Why did you strike me?" Her voice quavered. Her hand crept to her face, trembling over her cheekbone and nose as though there were a wound. "Why did you leave like that?"

"I don't know, Bi. I swear I don't. If I knew . . ."

"But what am I to do, darling?" The tears welled into her eyes, glistening. She sat down on the sofa. Leaning forward, she covered her face with her hands and cried like a child.

Wilder sat beside her and after a moment put his arm about her waist. They were so until at last her sobbing abated, and quite suddenly she turned her face up to his. There in her inflamed eyes he saw everything she felt for him—hatred and love, loathing and desire—and he had never wanted her more.

Embracing her, he brought her mouth to his, felt the heat of her skin, the wetness of her tears.

"Bi," he whispered. "Bi, Bi."

In answer she kissed him, a whimper dying in her throat, and lying back into the pillows they made love with a desperate fury—as though the end of the world were upon them.

7.

"YOU look tired, Wilder," Alma Massee said. "Are you getting enough sleep?"

"Yes. It isn't that." He frowned, looked away from her searching gaze. "I might be catching a cold. I've got that kind of feeling at the back of my throat."

"Wait a minute, then. Take off your coat. Let me give you something for it."

"No. It's all right." He looked at Jimmy, who stood beside him in new gray flannel, the blue cap with its school emblem set square on his head. "We'll have to hustle to make the ferry."

"Can we go bumming?" Jimmy asked and seizing his father's hand started him down the hall toward the front door.

"You go on and ring for the elevator," Alma said. "I'll bring you some aspirin, anyway."

"Don't bother, Gran," Wilder called.

"Can we, Daddy?"

"Not much, I'm afraid," Wilder said. He went out into the landing and pressed the bell. Jimmy, following, let the door slam behind him. The elevator, which had been descending with a passenger, came promptly, but as they stepped into it they heard the apartment door open.

"Wait," Alma called, and appeared with a small envelope which she handed to Wilder.

"Thanks, Gran," he said.

"Two aspirins," she said. "Take them when you can get a cup of water someplace." Alma looked around the cab, at the operator, the stranger, and then Jimmy, toward whom she bobbed quickly, intending to place a farewell kiss on his cheek.

"Don't, Mom," Jimmy said and shied away toward his father. Then seeing the hurt and surprise on her face, he added, "We're late. Don't you know we're late?"

Alma stepped back onto the landing, and as she did so the nervous energy that made her seem so young drained away. It appeared to be an old and forsaken woman who now said, "Of course you are. Have a good time."

It was a clear day with high clouds but cool for Decoration Day, and they walked along Fifty-seventh Street briskly toward the subway entrance at Columbus Circle. They did not speak. The sight of Alma Massee as the elevator door closed upon her stayed with them, troubling them and silencing them.

They stood together awkwardly watching the groups of school children off on various holiday excursions, looking down the track to see if the train were coming.

"It's just for the day, for crying out loud," Jimmy said at last. "Gee, the way she carries on you'd think we were going to Africa or something."

Wilder smiled, and in an unusual gesture put an arm around him, gave his far shoulder a comradely squeeze.

"Ladies are different, Jim," he said. "They like that stuff— fond farewells and all, even if it's only for a couple of minutes. I can't tell you why."

"Yeah, well *I* don't like it much."

"Most men don't. But most men do it just the same."

Jimmy thought for a bit but did not reveal what decision he had reached. Then he looked down the track again. "Here it comes," he announced jubilantly.

They sat side by side gazing at the car cards as the train moved out of the station. Wilder stole a glance at his son.

"Shall we see how many *e's* we can get?" Jimmy asked.

"Jimmy," Wilder said. "Do you know how much you mean to Gran?"

Jimmy looked up at his father, puzzled.

"No. You couldn't. But I'll try to tell you. I'll try to give you some idea." Wilder rubbed the palms of his hands back and forth on his knees. "A good-by kiss from you means as much to her as . . . a string of pearls."

Jimmy looked away, up at the car cards again. "I know," he said.

Wilder nodded and wondered if he did—if anyone ever did. "Perhaps you do," he said, and after a minute put his arm through Jimmy's.

"I've got a better game than the letters game." Wilder glanced along the seat opposite and then spoke into Jimmy's ear. "Sherlock Holmes, it's called, and you play it with people. You look at them, at every detail of their clothing, hands, faces, what they're carrying or reading, and then try to guess what sort of person they are. You're meant to tell where they live, what they do for a living—everything about them just from what you can see. Supposing we start with that man at the end, the man with the high black shoes. I wonder why a man would have such shiny black shoes while the rest of his clothes are so mussed and untidy."

Jimmy, delighted with this new game, insisted that his

father continue to invent backgrounds for their fellow passengers until long after Wilder, who was feeling worse as the day progressed, had tired of it. It was only when they had climbed the stairs of the ferry and at Jimmy's insistence gone out onto the top deck that he could be diverted. They stood looking down the slip, its great black timbers heavy with slime, and out onto the surface of the river beyond.

"Just supposing," Wilder said, turning to look and thereby directing Jimmy's attention toward the wheelhouse where the helmsman could be seen reading a newspaper, "supposing we were sailing for some port in the Mediterranean—Marseilles or Genoa." He leaned out over the *Pocono's* rail and shaded his eyes. "Our trunks have come aboard—lifted up from the pier in that big cargo net and nestled safely in the hold. The hand luggage with all that we'll need for the voyage and the first few days ashore in—Marseilles, is it?"

Jimmy nodded vigorously. "Yes. Marseilles."

"The hand luggage, stowed away in our stateroom down on C Deck. It's an inside stateroom. We'll be out of it except when we're sleeping, and we may as well spend our money on something we'll enjoy more than a porthole."

"Yes," Jimmy said. "We could buy a camera and take pictures."

"Of course. We'll need a camera." Wilder peered forward, toward the end of the slip. "You might want to take a picture of the people down there on the dock seeing us off. There's Gran now. See her? She's waving. Give her a wave, Jimmy."

Jimmy, who had been concentrating on the last piling, turned to his father tentatively, grinned, and then waved, as Wilder did.

"We'd better remember to send her postcards. We'll send her a postcard from every place we go," Wilder said.

"We'll get her a present. We'll bring her back a"—Jimmy hesitated over the selection—"a mirror."

"Perhaps," Wilder said, wondering just how appropriate that would be. "We'll find something. Something fine."

At that moment the *Pocono's* whistle blew—splendidly, authoritatively. There was a clank of chains, the trembling of the deck. Without a word Wilder and Jimmy waved once again, watched the planks as they began to move astern, then looked ahead where more and more of the swelling river was coming into their view—slick and blue-black and beckoning.

"How about a turn around deck," Wilder said, and slipping an arm through Jimmy's led him aft, keeping pace for a moment with the mouth of the slip. "This is going to be one of our principal pastimes, you know. People on a ship walk— arm in arm, round and round. All the day and most the night."

"Why?"

"So they won't miss anything that's happening on the other side. And I suppose because there's much pleasure to walking when it's round and round like that and you don't have to think where you're going. But most of all it's to work up an appetite. You'll see why when we get into the dining saloon there." Wilder paused, pointed into the forlorn aftercabin of the *Pocono's* upper deck where a handful of passengers dozed on the straight-backed, dirty benches. "That's our table there where the steward is laying the cloth. Wait until you see the menu. Long as your arm and *everything* on it, everything you've ever dreamed of—oysters and clams and shrimps and seventeen kinds of soup and steak and roast beef and every kind of dessert you can imagine." Wilder pretended to examine the menu. "Now to prove my point you imagine a dessert and I'll tell you whether it's on here."

Jimmy put a finger to his temple, thought. "Strawberry shortcake."

"Three kinds. Old-fashioned, new-fashioned, and with waffles."

"What kind of ice cream do they have?"

"Thirty-two different flavors, including pistachio and pinora—that's pineapple and orange mixed. I also note that in addition to parfaits and melbas they have baked Alaska. Ever had any baked Alaska?"

Jimmy, hypnotized, shook his head.

"It's ice cream covered with cake and meringue, browned in the oven. So you can see"—Wilder urged Jimmy off again on their promenade—"why we must walk."

"Yes," Jimmy said, lagging, still seeing magic through the *Pocono's* dirty windows.

Rounding the starboard side, Wilder was pleased to find some river traffic, and they paused to lean on the rail. A Moran tug was towing a bargeload of boxcars to Hoboken. A man in a peacoat, leaning against the engine room door, appeared to be looking at them. Jimmy waved and to Wilder's surprise the man waved back.

Beyond, a modern ship with gleaming white sides was moving away from the Norwegian Line pier at Christopher Street. They saw and then heard the long blast of her whistle, the answer from the tug whose padded nose promptly left off nudging at the white ship's stern and stood off.

"Norway," Wilder said. "Would you like to go to Norway?"

"Yes," Jimmy said. "I sure would."

The white ship, now gliding gently into the stream, looked for a moment as if it might pass before them, a thought which must have occurred to the ferry captain, for the trembling ceased and they too moved silently in the water. But with a ding-ding the engines turned again, and the *Pocono* crossed the white ship's bow close enough so they could read her name there—*Bergensfjord*—and see a blond sailor dogging down a hatch cover and on the bridge an officer with a black beard and on deck passengers, arm in arm, already busy with the promenade.

"There are so many wonderful places to go," Wilder sighed. Taking Jimmy's arm, he pried him gently from a last precious glimpse of new love.

"When, Daddy?" Jimmy tugged at Wilder's sleeve. "When can we go?"

"Someday," Wilder said, persuading him forward. "Someday soon."

"But when? Could we go this summer?"

Wilder shook his head. "Not so soon, I'm afraid. It takes planning." He frowned. "I'd have to arrange to get away from the office. And the money. Even a modest trip takes a great deal of money." They had reached the forward part of the deck again and looked ahead to the dismal docksides of the Jersey shore. "Can you find our slip?" he asked.

"No," Jimmy said sadly. He was looking over his shoulder at the white *Bergensfjord*, small now—he could cover it with the tip of his little finger—just clearing the Battery and standing out to sea.

"Look now," Wilder said. "It's there by the big tank. Do you see the Erie sign? It's way below where we're pointing. Do you suppose the captain's gone to sleep?"

Jimmy, interested at last, looked where his father pointed, saw that they were indeed heading for a point miles from their destination. Turning to the wheelhouse, he saw the helmsman, alert enough, hands on the wheel.

"Maybe we're going someplace else," Jimmy suggested

hopefully. "Maybe he's going to some other dock."

"No, I don't think so," Wilder said. "I think he's just compensating for the current. The river's carrying us downstream. Watch and see. The point where we're heading will move down the shore and become, just as we reach it, the Erie ferry slip."

And Jimmy was intrigued to see Wilder's prediction fulfilled. He turned but once to seek a last glimpse of the *Bergensfjord*. She was gone.

Walking down the ramp into the dark cavern of the ferryhouse, Wilder entertained the unpleasant thought that he and his son were passing, indeed stepping on, the exact spot where his father had died. He had not actually died there. He had died in a hospital ward in Newark, but it was here on that very timber that he had fallen from the ranks of the commuters when his heart had failed him. Hurrying home with half a dozen blueberry muffins in a bakery box. (Wilder was reminded of his mother's request for the lemon cookies which had, of course, slipped his mind.)

Glancing again at the timber—it was part of the huge ramp, centrally for vehicles with side passages for pedestrians which led from ferry to ferryhouse—he saw his father stricken there, his frail, tottering dignity asprawl, along with the yellowing Panama hat, the umbrella, the little bakery box still attached by white twine to a brittle finger.

And he saw the others, the stampede that a few years back used to funnel through here of an evening, stepping over him. They came upon him so quickly there was no other way. It was a mercy he wasn't trampled. Some few paused, trying to think what to do, but then, knowing it was someone else's job, hurried on to their trains. And he saw too his father's pale gray eyes looking up at them, filled with fear, not thinking they might help him for they never had. He was dreading, not death itself, but the vulgar way in which, it seemed, he was to meet it.

Turning, Wilder looked at his son, who was happily absorbed in examining the chain drive of a Mack truck as it labored onto the oil-soaked planks ahead.

"We'll go," Wilder said fervently. "We really will."

Jimmy looked up questioningly.

"To Europe," Wilder said. "For a long time. Not just a couple of weeks. That's a waste, I think."

"You always say . . ." Jimmy began doubtfully.

Wilder, taking his elbow, gave it a squeeze and set a course through the shed toward the Erie tracks. "I mean it, Jimmy. We'll really go. Perhaps to England. Your mother and I were going to go to England."

"When though?" Jimmy insisted.

They came through the gate and beheld the pitiful Greenfield train—two antiquated coaches and a steam locomotive.

"Soon," Wilder said, boosting Jimmy ahead of him up the steps. "But not right away. After all, you can't pick up right in the middle of school, you know—not for a long trip. Not for a year."

"But when?" Jimmy asked. He slid into the old green plush seat and with the heel of his fist tried to rub a peephole in the window's grime. "I won't believe you until you tell me when."

"Well," Wilder said. He took off his coat, folded it carefully, and put it on the rack with his hat. Feeling flushed and the least bit dizzy, he wondered how unwise it had been to cross the river on the *Pocono's* open deck. He sat down beside Jimmy. "Well, I suppose the ideal time would be when you finish school. Maybe we can take a year between the time you finish school and go on to college."

"Oh no," Jimmy wailed. "Holy smokes, that's six years from now."

"Well," Wilder said vaguely, "we'll see."

The distance from the Erie depot at Jersey City to Greenfield was scarcely a dozen miles, and the route offered as scenery some of the most cheerless in the nation—the tangled pipes of a petroleum dump, an auto graveyard, piled with the rusting skin and battered bones of bygone splendor, the Meadows, with its foul-smelling pigsties, shantytown, and, between mud banks, a stream of surely lethal black water streaked with green.

Emerging from a narrow defile, the train slowed to make the first of its ten stops in Union and Essex counties. Here was no town at all but a section of sprawling industrial New Jersey—that forest of rooming houses, lunch wagons, and gasoline stations. Everyone used the bus now. It was quicker and easier. There was one every hour. Soon the last of the trains would go, but Wilder vastly preferred this old-fashioned way to Greenfield.

As the train proceeded toward the Orange Mountains, there was improvement in the landscape. It became less an industrial wasteland, more suburban, but a stranger was in no way prepared for Greenfield, the fifth stop.

Wilder and Jimmy were the only passengers to alight at the little station, long unattended, boarded-up, pasted with the handbills of a forgotten election for alderman. As the train rattled off on its single track, Wilder had the impression, as he always did here, that he had just completed a long journey, not in space, but in time—backward, by many decades.

There was a thick stillness. A dog barked blocks away, and

it was the only sound. As they started up the hill, their heels rang on the slate, echoed from the empty porches. They were big, these houses. Some were empty, humiliated by a for-sale sign. Their lawns were broad, though frequently high and gone to seed. The sad smell of burning leaves was on the air, and they saw a tall, bald man raking a fire in front of a garage. He looked up at them and then back at his work. Save for a derelict baby buggy, there was no sign of a child anywhere.

As they turned into the rutted, weed-grown driveway the first impression the house gave was of a rambling, rather elaborate, turn-of-the-century summer cottage. The dormers and bowings gave it a plumpness, an aspect of comfortable middle age. While it was in need of a fresh coat of the dark green paint which was checking and in several patches revealed the gray beneath, it was no worse off than others on the street, where a degree of shabbiness was the rule.

The first whiff of the special aroma which Jimmy had come to identify with his infrequent visits here reached them as they climbed the porch steps and stomped to annouce their arrival. It was a fetid smell and made him think of night, of narrow places where light never came.

No face appeared. Wilder looked in at the vestibule window, saw no one, tried the massive Dutch door, and found it locked, banged the knocker, a large brass one blackened with weather.

Jimmy, stepping forward, pressed the doorbell.

"It doesn't work," Wilder laughed.

"That's right," Jimmy said. "I remember now."

"Most things don't here." Wilder knocked again, louder.

"Maybe they're out," Jimmy suggested.

Wilder smiled, shook his head.

Within, they heard the sound of running on the stairs, then in the hall, and a clatter of latches pulled and turned, and finally the top of the Dutch door flew open, revealing a flushed, breathless Lyddie.

"It's the boys, Mother," she cried over her shoulder. "They're here."

She gave Wilder an enthusiastic embrace and pecked at his cheek. Then, opening the bottom half of the door, she turned to Jimmy. "May I have a hug from Jimmy, too?"

Jimmy, bewildered, did not retreat when she clutched him and placed a kiss, faintly damp with the perspiration of her upper lip, smelling of Ivory soap, upon his cheek.

She was dressed like a dowdy schoolgirl—sweater and skirt, a worn leather jacket, bobby sox, and rubber-soled shoes. She wore no make-up, and her skin seemed very pale, the nose thin, emphatically aquiline, and her hair, which she still wore done up in a bun, raveled in a dozen undirected wisps of which she now became aware.

"My hair," she cried, poking at it ineffectively, "must look a sight. I was asleep when you came. I woke to the sound of the door knocker, and I couldn't for the life of me think who it was for a second. I just leaped up and came running down. Isn't it lucky you weren't the Reverend Mr. Wiley?" She released a girlish peal of laughter at the thought. "Well, come on in. Mother's bursting to see you both. Didn't you bring anything? Don't you have a valise? Aren't you staying the night?"

"No," Wilder said, walking into the vestibule and noticing at once how cold and damp it was inside the house. "We both have to get back to town tonight."

"Oh, blast," she said. "Well, we'll have a good time today

anyhow. Won't we?" She turned to Jimmy and he nodded tentatively.

Millicent Stone, a small, round woman with twinkling, jolly little eyes, appeared in the doorway to the library. She wore a heart-shaped smile. Her stubby hands, folded at her waist, opened to accept her son's embrace.

"Oh, Wilder dear," she exclaimed. "It's you at last. We thought you'd never come."

"Hello, Mother." Wilder touched her gently as he leaned to kiss her, and through the thin folds of lavender voile which made up her Sunday best he could feel the chill of her flesh.

"Aren't you cold, Mother?" he asked at once. "It's cool in here."

"A bit, perhaps. But I don't mind." She turned to Jimmy. "And here's Jim. My, what a big boy."

Jimmy, pained at the thought of yet another kissing (the day was ridden with them), hung behind his father and Millicent Stone, never overly fond of affectionate displays herself, made no attempt upon him.

"Hello, Mrs. Stone," Jimmy said, and Wilder, noting the snap of his mother's eyelashes, resolved again to ask Jimmy if he would mind calling his grandmother "Grandma," in any case something less formal than Mrs. Stone.

From the door of the hall closet a cat, a gray tom, sprang and landed deftly on the cushion of a ladder-back chair. It turned and spat at a smaller, striped cat, which pursued it to the chair's leg where it crouched, ready to spring.

Lyddie, startled, cried out, then laughed, and snatching up the tom in her arms urged the striped cat back into the closet and closed the door. Leaning against it, she nuzzled the gray cat, rocked him in her arms.

"Hallett," she crooned. "Were you teasing Hopie? I'll bet you were. You're such a terrible old tease. You mustn't tease Hopie."

"Oh, Lyddie," Millicent Stone laughed and fluttered her small hands helplessly.

Kneeling, Lyddie pointed Hallett's wide, blinking eyes at Jimmy. "Here's your cousin," she went on, "come out to see us from the city. Isn't he a fine boy? I hope he likes his country cousins, don't you?"

Hallett blinked, switched his tail.

"That's Hallett," Wilder explained. "In case you haven't met him before. He's more or less a member of the family."

"More or *less*." Lyddie took exaggerated offense. "What a dreadful thing to say. Isn't it, Hallett? Why, you *are* a member of the family." To Jimmy she said, "He's named for your great-grandfather, you know. Hallett Wilder."

Jimmy nodded and Lyddie, opening the closet door, narrowly prevented Hopie's exit with her foot as she dropped Hallett inside, closed it again. There was a commotion within.

"Now stop that, Hallett," she said sharply, and all was silent.

Wilder, peering at the thermostat, noted that although it called for eighty, the thermometer registered an actual fifty-nine degrees.

"Good Lord, it's only fifty-nine in here," he said. "It's warmer outside. The furnace must be out." He saw the smudge on his mother's forehead and guessed this was not news to her.

"Perhaps it is, Wilder," Millicent replied. "I don't really know."

"It's such a spiteful old thing," Lyddie pouted. "We ought to have an oil burner. Everybody in the world has an oil burner, except for us."

"I'll go down and have a look," Wilder said. He touched his mother's hands, squeezed them affectionately. "You are cold, Mother."

Millicent smiled. "I hadn't noticed."

"If you're going down there I'll have to clear the coast," Lyddie cried and flew ahead of Wilder—through the dining room toward the cellar door in the pantry.

Jimmy, not wanting to be left alone, trailed after them and saw his aunt slip through the cellar door, close it quickly after her.

"Cats," Wilder explained and leaned against the pantry table. His eye fell upon the makings of the dinner. The roast, still amidst the butcher's wrappings, would, he guessed, require several hours in the oven. There was a saucepan of new potatoes, only two of which had been prepared, and their thick, inexpert parings were scattered on the counter. Piled in the old-fashioned sink he saw, with mounting disgust, a stack of dirty dishes and silver. Beneath it, he knew, the garbage container would be overflowing. He looked and it was.

"What about the cats?" Jimmy asked. He was looking with mild apprehension at the cellar door.

"She's going to shut them up, I think. She lets them run around loose down there."

"I'm not afraid of a few old cats."

Wilder shook his head. "It isn't that. Lyddie doesn't want a census. I suspect the population is growing, and she doesn't want the figures made public."

The cellar door opened and Lyddie smiled at them radiantly. "Coast is clear, now. Come ahead."

The smell, the dark smell, floated up to them from the

cellar with unusual pungency, and Wilder's stomach turned.
He felt worse than he had all day. A weakness was overcom-
ing him, and he felt that if he were to close his eyes he would
go to sleep right here.

"Hadn't you better get that roast in the oven?" he said.
"It's eleven thirty."

"I want to see you boys for a minute first," she said and
following them down the stairs sat on the third step. Pulling
the skirt tight over her knees she rested her chin on them,
tilted her head coquettishly and smiled at them both. "Goodness, I haven't seen either of you in *so* long."

The single bulb shed baleful light on the black iron mon-
ster, a scattering of coal at its open mouth, its many arms
disappearing into the blackness overhead. The floor was
littered with newspapers, some shredded and crumpled. The
odor was overpowering.

Wilder peered through the furnace door. Then he took
off his coat, hung it on a nail, and rolled up his sleeves. "No
reason for you to stay," he said to Jimmy. "It'll take me a
while and it's a dirty job—not much fun, I'm afraid."

"I'd like to watch," Jimmy said.

Wilder nodded and set to work silently—shoveling out
the clinkers, emptying the ash dump (onto the floor to be
cleaned up later as the ashcans were heaping), and building
at last a crackling wood fire.

"Good Lord, Lyddie," he said, turning from the coal bin.
"There's hardly any coal. There's not two days' worth here.
What's become of it?"

"I don't know," she said evasively. "I don't like to order any
more, owing them as we do."

Wilder leaned on his shovel. "Owing them? What do you
mean *owing* them? I paid the coal bill last month."

"Did you? I'd forgotten. We owed them for such a long time."

"We needn't have if you'd told me. I may balk at cases of cat food and condensed milk—but never at coal bills. I don't want Mother to be cold. Do try and remember that, Lyddie."

Lyddie arose and took a few quick steps up the stairs. "If you don't want Mothy to be cold, you'd better do something about that old furnace. I don't know how you can expect two frail women to stoke that wretched thing. We're not coal heavers you know."

Wilder threw a shovelful of coal onto the fire. "It takes a couple of those a day. That's all. You just have to remember."

"With an oil burner you don't have to remember anything. There are no ashes to carry out—no dirty old coal men."

Wilder laughed. "Ah, now we're getting to it. It's the coal men we don't like. The coal men who disturb the cats. The coal men who put coal in the cat bin. Well, I'm sorry to say we're going to have to make do with this. An oil burner costs a thousand dollars, and I don't have it."

Lyddie went up two more steps, her head and shoulders disappearing, then, thinking better, knelt so she could still be seen. "That's fine for you, isn't it?" she called. "In your dandy little flat in town. Hot water and steam heat at the press of a button. You might think of us out here once in a while—but you never do." She sprang up and was gone. They heard the cellar door slam hard behind her.

"I'm sorry," Wilder said to Jimmy. "We oughtn't to do that. It doesn't do anybody any good. I apologize."

"I don't mind," Jimmy said.

Wilder grinned. "Good," he said putting on his coat. "I'm glad you don't."

Emerging from the cellar, Wilder found no change in the

preparations for the meal. "Well," he said. "What would you like to do? I'll see if I can't get the lunch going somehow—but meantime you'll want a project. Do you really want a crack at the lawn? You could go out and see if the lawn-mower's in any kind of shape. It's in the garage."

"Yes," Jimmy said with real enthusiasm. "I do want to mow the lawn. May I?"

"Sure thing. And we can go for a walk. There's a pond with some ducks if I remember correctly. I feel kind of punk now, but perhaps later I'll be up to it. And about ten minutes before luncheon is ready you can go down and get the ice cream. You remember where the drugstore is?"

Jimmy nodded. "Pinora? Can I get pinora?"

"Any kind you like. I wouldn't count on their having pinora."

Jimmy started out the back door but hesitated. "Isn't there any way of going sooner?"

"You can go now, but it'll melt. We haven't any freezer."

"I mean on the trip—abroad."

"Yes," Wilder said. "Perhaps there is. I'll think about it." He watched Jimmy walk slowly, thoughtfully out the path toward the garage, and then he went off in search of his mother.

Millicent Stone was alone in the living room. She sat erect in a high-backed chair, looking reflectively through the window. Glancing up as though startled at Wilder's step, she smiled and reached out her small hand to him.

"Oh Wilder dearest, come look. Come see how the light falls on the rhododendron leaves here. It's too pretty."

Wilder bent by his mother's chair, looked out, and noted that the shrubbery which his mother so much admired was in dire need of pruning. "Yes," he said. "It's very nice."

"I can sit here by the hour, Wilder, and get such pleasure. There's a little nest there. Do you see the little nest—there in the eaves? There are little baby birds and mother comes and brings all sorts of things. Sit down, Wilder." She pointed to the footstool. "Sit down here by me for a bit. Let me look at you, dear."

"In just a minute, Mother. Where's Lyddie?"

Millicent's sunny countenance clouded momentarily. "I think"—she turned to look out at the bush again—"I think she's gone upstairs."

Wilder looked out into the hall where he could make out dimly the stairway and the landing at its head. "In her room? Was she in a pet?"

Millicent's hands fluttered. "She did seem a bit upset. Oh, Wilder dear, you mustn't pique one another. You mustn't spoil this lovely day."

"I'm sorry, Mother." He patted her folded hands. "We'll do our best."

"I know you will."

"Lyddie hasn't put the roast in the oven yet, and it's nearly noon." He looked at his watch to confirm this. "What time are you planning luncheon?"

"Heavens, Wilder, you mustn't worry about luncheon. I'll have things started in just a moment."

"I'll be glad to do it if you tell me what. Do you want me to light the oven?"

"No, no, no." She laughed, protesting. "I want you to sit down here for just a moment. Don't you understand, dear? I want to see my boy."

Smiling, Wilder sat upon the footstool, and Millicent's

fingers touched his cheek, traced his lips, his temple where the hair was gray. "Yes, dear. I thought so. You're tired."

Wilder nodded. "I am. I'm feeling pretty played out. It's a great many things."

"What things? Tell me, dear."

"Oh. Things at the office. Not now, Mother."

As he started to get up, Millicent caught his sleeve. "If you don't want to tell me about it now, will you later?"

"Yes. Later."

"Couldn't you stay the night and have a good rest?"

"No. I don't think so."

Millicent laid her hand gently on Wilder's forehead. "Goodness," she cried, "you have a fever. I knew it. I could tell by your eyes."

"I have a cold coming on. It's nothing to worry about. Come to think of it, I've got some aspirin here." Reaching into his pocket, he produced the little envelope Alma Massee had given him. "I'll get a glass of water."

Millicent arose, all her senses quickening. "Come along up to your room, Wilder, and have a little rest before luncheon. It'll do you a world of good and I'll make you some nice hot cambric tea."

Wilder, who had it in mind to protest further about luncheon, now did feel really ill. His head throbbed. The back of his throat felt raw and prickly, and his bones were hollow with weariness. His mother took his hand, and he offered no resistance as she led him up the stairs to his room.

At her insistence he got out of his clothes and into clean pajamas. Once in bed he did feel immeasurably better. With a smile he watched Millicent putting his suit on a hanger, giving it an appraisal and a touch here and there with the clothesbrush. Outside he heard the reassuring, summery clop-

clop of the lawn-mower, and he closed his eyes. The pillow was cool beneath his cheek, and he allowed himself to sink into the blissful shallows.

"Now you rest, dear," Millicent said softly. "I'll go down and get luncheon under way and make your tea."

8.

AND he was thinking of Catherine again. Perhaps it was that last glimpse of his mother, the familiar click of the latch. He was thinking of the time that Catherine had stayed in this house. It was in the little corner room, the room they called the sewing room, the room that Lyddie sometimes spoke wistfully of fixing up as "Jimmy's room."

Looking across at his bureau, Wilder could see Catherine's photograph. She wore the dress, the blue-green dress that he remembered so well, loved so well and was now, he recognized, out of fashion. But she had looked like that, and she had been very much in fashion in the spring of 1946 when he had brought her here to meet his family.

Lyddie had walked down to meet them at the train and been cordial enough as they all three walked up the hill to the house. She had even joked about her unusual behavior of ten days earlier, and yet there was a noticeable hostility in her endless apologies.

"I'm afraid we'll seem awfully dowdy to you," Lyddie had said. "We're not at all Connecticut. We're plain old run-down Jersey. I hope it won't be too miserable for you."

"Oh, Lyddie," Catherine had exclaimed, "it's absolutely lovely here. I had no idea Greenfield would be so tranquil.

I can't believe we're so close to New York."

Catherine was game. She had given but casual regard to Wilder's warning that she might expect a certain coolness in Greenfield, dismissing it as further evidence of Wilder's lamentable tendency to pessimism. She would attend to that in time. Meanwhile she was reasonably certain of a quick and easy conquest of Wilder's family. It was now, as always, simply a matter of being herself.

She had assumed, wrongly, that by now Wilder would have announced to Lyddie and his parents that he was engaged —had indeed spent a glorious afternoon shopping Fifth Avenue for a diamond ring.

And expecting real grandeur of some sort, Catherine had unwisely chosen to dress up to that—borrowing her mother's mink jacket, wearing a magnificently becoming little feather hat, and a simple black dress with a rather daring slash down its front. Catherine knew it for a mistake with her first glance at Lyddie in her shapeless tweed skirt and sweater, stout shoes, the determinedly mussy hair, and the complete lack of make-up—not a trace, not even lipstick.

As he recalled the incidents of that visit he saw that in a way they were slight, possibly laughable but for the way things turned out. As it was he felt the anguish again, undiminished by the thirteen years that had passed.

The gift—the "hostess present"—that was the first thing. As they stood awkwardly in the drawing room, his mother in flowered chiffon, Father stiff and formal in high starched collar and little butterfly tie, bowing like a chancellor, Wilder had the unhappy feeling he was presenting Catherine at court—that it wasn't fair and he had failed her here.

In the midst of the silence, fidgeting, grasping for some word to tide them over, Catherine produced the box she had been carrying under her arm. It was green and tied with a great rosette of gold ribbon and bore the name of a gift shop in the East Fifties.

Millicent, taking the thing from its nest of tissue paper, fingered it gingerly. "Isn't it nice," she said absently and, noting the marble, the little brass balls of the pedestal, the fine wood, and precisely fitted *découpage* of the shaft, guessed its costliness. She looked at Wilder (not Catherine) for help.

"I don't know," Wilder said. "May I look?" Turning it over in his hands appreciatively, he added, "Whatever it is it's magnificent."

"It's an obelisk, dopey," Catherine had laughed. It was wrong, too sudden, the sobriquet, and she knew it instantly.

"Of course," Wilder said, "Cleopatra's Needle in Central Park. And in Paris. Place Vendôme, is it? Surely you know about obelisks, Mother?" He was joking, the way they did sometimes, gently, hoping Millicent would respond. He handed the obelisk on to Lyddie, who glanced at it and returned it without comment to her mother.

"It doesn't *do* anything," Catherine said. "I mean it's not a cigarette lighter or anything. It's just a decoration. I saw it in this shop and I couldn't resist it. They're Egyptian originally, I guess."

"It's very nice," Millicent said and returned the obelisk to its box on the table where it seemed to glow too richly, as though with a light of its own, in this threadbare room.

Wilder knew now that it would not go well, that it had been foolish of him to hope otherwise. He saw his mother's swelling ire. He heard her gasp when, as they stood on the porch just before going into luncheon, Catherine put her hand in his and again as they sat at table and Catherine, not realizing the saying of grace was a custom here, had begun to chatter with Lyddie about college just as Everett Stone had bowed his head.

"For these and all . . ." Everett had said, then paused, looked up, smiling.

"Miss Massee," Millicent had said in an ecclesiastic whisper that might have heralded a bishop, "my husband is about to say grace."

"Oh, I'm sorry," Catherine had said fervently.

Catherine was trying so hard now that perversely everything she said, however innocent, seemed to turn or be turned against her.

"What interesting spoons," she had announced, examining her own, noticing that its bowl ended in bluntness rather than a point. A glance around the table revealed that all were alike. "I've never seen spoons like these." She looked at Millicent for some explanation, but it was Wilder who supplied it.

"They're worn," he said. "They were like anybody else's spoons to begin with. Here you see the result of generations of zealous plate scraping."

"How marvelous," Catherine said.

"You're kind," Lyddie said darkly.

"But I mean it. Just imagine having such old silver. It must have been in your family for years and years."

She was rewarded by a polite smile from Millicent. "It was my great-grandmother's. She brought it here from England, just before the war."

"The Civil War," Wilder supplied, smiling, leaning back in his chair, trying once again. "That's Mother's war."

Everett Stone, who since the saying of grace had been silent, blinking like an owl from the head of the table, cocking an ear to whoever spoke, nodding, returning with a diligent concentration to his plate, now dabbed at his lips with his napkin and cleared his throat, an indication he judged the occasion festive enough for one of his half-dozen stories.

These stories of Wilder's father were an ordeal which over the years had come to be accepted as an important part of the rituals of their existence. Although Everett Stone fancied himself a raconteur of great ability and thus permitted himself all sorts of embellishments and digressions in the course of a tale, he had in fact no feeling for a story at all, never had had, and now as he grew old he was impossible.

Everett began now by being reminded (how it was not clear) of a lady in Boulder, Colorado, whose postman complained about the barking of her dog. This was instantly recognizable to the Stone family as the one about the patent medicine salesman whose elixir is "meant for *her*, not the dog," and they settled back with their own thoughts for the ten minutes or so he would require, holding the appreciative laughter for the final line.

Only Catherine attempted to follow the errant thread of his thought, and in finding him hopelessly adrift decided he was not telling a story at all but out of kindness trying to make conversation with her. As he paused, bewildered by some crossroads in his yarn, Catherine, to everyone's dismay, began to tell him with some enthusiasm of a man, a trainer, who could bring a whole kennel of barking dogs to silence simply by saying, "Quiet, please."

"Miss Massee," Millicent had said quietly, "my husband hasn't finished his story."

"Oh, I'm sorry," Catherine cried, looking to Wilder, "I didn't know."

"It's all right," he said. "Father's inclined to longish stories. I've been thinking they needed a bit of editing. How about it, Father?"

"Pardon?" said Everett Stone, who had happily returned his attention to his plate.

"I thought it was a swell story," Catherine said in some confusion. "I just thought it was over, that's all. Oh, dear."

"Do go on and finish, Everett," Millicent said. "You have the floor now."

"No, no," he had said with a little protesting gesture, a smile for Catherine which confused her. "Miss Massee is quite right. I had finished."

"You hadn't at all, Father," Lyddie said. "You know you hadn't."

Millicent sighed, and silence descended upon them all, broken only by the clink of the worn silver as it blunted itself further on the blue-rimmed plates where, despite the chips and cracks of half a century's service, the arms of the Wilder family were still discernible.

"You're from New York, Miss Massee?" Millicent asked at last.

"Yes. Central Park West."

"Your family, I mean."

"Oh, you mean where do we come from. We're from Elmira originally. At least Mother's family is."

"Elmira? Where is that?"

"Surely you know where Elmira is, Mother," Wilder said. "It's in upstate New York."

"Near Cooperstown, is it?" Millicent asked. "A cousin of ours lived in Cooperstown. I went there once as a girl."

"No," Catherine said. "It's over a hundred miles from Cooperstown."

"Your father's family? Are they New Yorkers?"

"My father's in the theater," she said. Wilder saw Catherine's jaw set, the angry flash of her eyelashes, and although he had been dreading this—he rejoiced. "He used to be an actor. He was born, I think, in Philadelphia, but actors are not from any place, really, except the theater."

"Oh?" Millicent said, watching Catherine carefully, sensing the growing danger there. "I see."

"My mother's father was a policeman," Catherine continued. "My father's father never did anything long enough to be identified with it. As near as I can make out he was a sort of professional Irishman."

"Wasn't your grandfather mayor of Elmira?" Wilder asked.

"For a year. And thirty years a policeman. I think it's fairer to say he was a policeman. And anyway I prefer it. I'd rather be the granddaughter of a cop than of a mayor." She looked defiantly at Millicent, waited to see if she would rise to the challenge.

Millicent reached out for the bowl of sliced peaches. "Yes," she said mildly. "I can see how you might."

"And it's funny, you know," Catherine said, leaning back in her chair, addressing the whole table but looking finally at Wilder, "I've never been sure of that until right now—until this very moment."

Wilder nodded.

"Would anyone care for more peaches?" Millicent asked, "Miss Massee?" thereby ending a contest in which, Wilder suddenly realized, there was some doubt of her victory.

One thing had been spared Catherine so far—the knowledge that despite the kindnesses she had shown Lyddie, Lyddie was no ally. But over the coffee which Wilder brought into the drawing room, Lyddie left no doubt.

"I was uncomfortable the whole time," she said in answer to Catherine's question about the weekend in Connecticut. "I had no idea we weren't to be chaperoned."

"And I would never have let you go, Lyddie. I thought it very strange there was no letter," Millicent said. "Sugar, Miss Massee?"

"Black, please."

"I don't know what's come over young people nowadays," she sighed, offering Catherine the cup. "Or their parents either for that matter. It's appalling."

"I don't know what you mean," Catherine said. "We were guests of the Wicks—a brother and sister."

"A brother and sister, particularly if they are of an age with their guests, are hardly chaperons," Millicent said, filling her husband's cup and adding cream. "Perhaps with some people these things are not important any more. I daresay there are places where young people are given complete license . . . where they do as they choose."

"Mrs. Wick went off at the last minute. She knew all about our being there," Catherine said. "There wasn't anything sneaky about it. Lyddie, did you think there was anything sneaky about it?"

In answer, Lyddie tightened her lips, looked down at the coffee cup which she held balanced on her knees, and began to stir it vigorously.

"Apparently you did," Catherine said. "Well, what, Lyddie? You must think something 'went on.' What do you think 'went on'?"

"I'm not a snoop," Lyddie replied.

"But you must suspect someone. They're my friends. Tell me. I'd like to know."

"More coffee, anyone?" Millicent asked.

"I'd really like to know, Lyddie," Catherine insisted.

"Lyddie, would you take the tray out to the pantry," Millicent said, getting up and moving toward the dining room.

"We'll tidy up out here."

"May I help?" Catherine asked, gulping the remainder of her coffee and hopping up.

"No, no," Millicent said firmly. "Lyddie and I will manage."

And there was a final humiliation in store. By ten o'clock it was clear there was no more to say. Like a machine out of fuel that has been clanging along on impetus, the conversation stopped with a murmur and a wheeze. Catherine, slumped in her chair, stared incredulously from Lyddie to Millicent. She watched with interest as Everett mumbled apologies for his fatigue, examined the face of the mantel clock, compared it with his pocket watch and, with a bow in her direction, tottered up the stairs.

He was followed promptly by a mute, a grim-lipped, Lyddie. Millicent on the other hand was rooted to her chair. Stiff-backed, sentry-eyed, fussing with some long-abandoned embroidery, she seemed bent on making up tonight for any previous omissions of proper chaperonage. So Catherine went too, murmuring a good night as she left the drawing-room.

"Good night, Miss Massee," Millicent called after her.

But there was no sound from Wilder, and she paused on the stairs and looking back saw Millicent bending to her sewing basket, replacing the embroidery hoop, while Wilder, his hands folded between his knees, leaned toward the fire whose light, flickering, revealed a face stunned by disappointment.

She took a step down the stairs, toward him, and as she did so, Millicent, sensing that significant motion, glanced up, looked at her questioningly, halted her on the bottom step.

"Wilder," Catherine said.

He turned, opened his hands in a little gesture of resignation, clapped them back on his knees, and smiled sadly. "Yes?"

"Aren't you coming up . . . to bed?" she asked.

A sound emerged from Millicent Stone's throat. It was a sudden intake of breath, half gasp, half cry, appropriate for a polite lady on being stabbed with a narrow blade.

Wilder looked at his mother, then back at Catherine whose eyes were slowly widening. "Yes, soon," he said.

"Oh, Lord!" Catherine said and fled up the stairs.

An hour later Wilder got into bed and turned out the light. He saw with certainty there was no easy way out, that he had already made Catherine miserable as well as his mother, and that this was only the beginning. The knowledge was breaking his heart.

The door into the hall opened admitting a crack of light, someone's shadow, and his first and exciting thought, one that made him sit up straight, was that it was Catherine.

"Wilder?" It was Millicent Stone's gentle voice. "You're not asleep?"

"No," he said unhappily and dropped back into his pillow.

She came softly around his bed, sat down in the chair by its side and after a moment reached out to take his hand. He took it away from her and turned on his side, his back to her.

"Oh, Mother," he said in despair. "Mother, give her a chance."

"Wilder dear, trust your mother. You must believe me when I tell you that this young woman, this Miss Massee. . . ."

"This Catherine."

"Yes. She's what I feared all along"—Millicent paused as though to catch her breath—"might happen to you."

"What do you mean?" Turning, he could not see his mother's face. The shaft from the door fell upon a hand pressed to her side.

"She . . . oh, Wilder dear, I can't expect you to see, but she hasn't the qualities you have. She won't ever. Never in a thousand years. I see it all so clearly—even in the little things. The little things that tell so much."

"What little things?"

"The little rudenesses. Interrupting your father. That hurt us all very much."

"Oh, Mother. . . ."

"Manners tell, Wilder. They always tell about what's inside a person."

"Oh for heaven's sake, Mother. Catherine wasn't rude. She's just not familiar with our silly crotchets. She's nineteen. Four years younger than Lyddie. What did you expect?"

Millicent answered with a little cry of pain.

"What's the matter?" he asked. Reaching for the light, he turned it on, and by it saw his mother had closed her eyes and was leaning back against the headrest of the chair. Her lips were tight together.

"It's the stitch," she said, gasping a little. "I'll be all right in a moment."

She did look pale, and swinging out of bed, he reached for his robe which hung over the footboard. "Can I get you something? A glass of water?"

"No, Wilder dear. It'll go away. It comes when I'm upset. I'll be all right in a moment. Do cover yourself. It's chilly in here." She sighed. "There. It's going away now."

"Sure?"

"Yes."

He turned out the light and got under the bedcovers, and he felt her hands smoothing them, pulling them tight over his chest, securing them under the mattress.

"What does the doctor say—about that stitch? I'm sure he doesn't call it that."

"It's nothing, Wilder. Nothing at all."

"Did you ask him, Mother?"

"I think so. A year or so ago."

"And what did he say?"

"I don't recall. But it's not worth anyone's troubling about. It's old age. That's all. There are many such things."

"That doesn't really satisfy me, Mother. I do wish you'd ask the doctor again. I want to be sure it's nothing to be alarmed about."

"Perhaps. Perhaps I will."

"Will you promise?"

"Yes. Sometime."

He waited a moment and then resumed. "I have a feeling that what's put you off about Catherine is that she speaks her mind."

"That's not such a virtue as it's made out. You should be grateful I didn't speak mine tonight."

"Mother, she's just a girl."

"Yes. So you said earlier. But her age in years is unimportant. In experience she would seem to be as old as time."

"Mother, that's New York. It's any big city today. The girls all dress and fix their hair and wear the same shade of lipstick as their mothers and look about the same age. You just don't see that here in Greenfield."

"There's much we don't see here in Greenfield, Wilder. There's much I don't know about—much I don't want to know about. But one thing I do know about is the difference between quality and commonness in a person."

"Mother. . . ."

"No, please. You must listen to me. You must hear me out. You cannot, Wilder dear. As a man, as *the* man, you cannot see when a woman as clever as this one has set out to . . . to get you. Your eyes deceive you. What you see, what you believe you see, is what she wants you to see in her—not what is really there."

"Mother, I'm not such a fool."

"Aren't you? I hope not. I truly do. But surely you are a little foolish if you believe this young woman's . . ."

"This Catherine's."

"This Catherine's," she conceded, "this Catherine's behavior is—proper. *I* can't, Wilder. I cannot believe that a nice girl, from New York City or any place else, the sort of girl you'll marry one day, will go off on a party such as this one in Connecticut, will paint her face, will wear a dress that so displays her . . . her wares."

"Mother," Wilder cried, sitting up in bed, "you mustn't. You mustn't say . . ." He broke off, for the shaft of light from the hall now fell upon his mother's face, and he saw her tears. She was crying silently. Leaning on an elbow, he reached out and patted her hands. "No more now. When you know Catherine better, Mother. Just give her some time. She's nice. You'll see."

They were silent together for a time. A breeze stirred the young leaves just outside the window, and from somewhere in the house came a sound of running water. Lyddie, he decided, taking a bath. She kept odd hours.

"Yes I am old-fashioned," Millicent said at last. "I'm afraid I must stay so, Wilder dear." She winced slightly, whether from some physical pain or for what she was about to say he could not tell. "If you must see Catherine again, that's your affair. I hope you won't, of course, but it's up to you. You're over twenty-one, dearest. However, for your father's sake, your sister's, and mine too, I am going to ask you not to bring her here again."

Rising, she bent quickly to kiss him on the brow and then left. The door closed behind her leaving him in darkness, and the soft click of the latch echoed in the stillness of the room.

Through the long dark hours which remained of that night Wilder did not sleep. Wide-eyed he followed the slender, idly moving fingers which a pale light from the street drew upon the ceiling. His mind reeled again over the conversation with his mother and over every incident of his courtship of Catherine, searching for the thoughts and words that would strengthen his defiance of his mother. Yet they eluded him. They would not make the pattern he sought.

And then he found that even as he denied his mother's contentions he was accepting the possibility that in some way he had been deceived by Catherine, that it was she who had perceived his virtues and thus set her cap. He considered, as Millicent proposed he should, the willing lips, the soft breasts so available to his touch, the admission—a very ready one, come to think of it—to that narrow, little girl's bed.

As the ceiling whitened above him and the threatening shadows became bureau, chair and closet door ajar, he began to wonder if Catherine had slept with any man? with many? and where? and when? and why? Giving full scope to his pessimism, he was assuming the most distressing answers to these questions and wondering how he might put his mind at rest when he heard footsteps on the stairs.

They were light, a woman's. Quick, a young woman's. Firm, determined, not Lyddie's. Catherine's! He looked at his watch. It was six. The steps again—tap, tap, tap across the hall. He raised himself on one elbow, alert. Then the latch, the turning of the bolt, the squeak of the big Dutch door as it swung open. *Slam,* and it seemed the whole house shook.

Leaping from the bed, he ran to the window and peered down. The footsteps—tap, tap, tap across the porch, down the steps, and then she appeared in the path, dressed, valise in hand, skirt and hair aswirl in her haste.

"Catherine!" he called hoarsely.

She paused, hearing him and looked up, searching the front of the house to find the window where he stood.

"Here," he said waving, and when she found him he saw across the thirty feet that separated them the fury in her eyes. "Now don't be foolish, Catherine. You mustn't run off."

She simply stared at him.

"It'll just make everything so much worse, don't you see? Hold on. I'll get dressed and we'll have breakfast. Then if you like we'll both go into town."

She continued to stare up at him, and when at last she spoke the words seemed to come from the very soles of her feet. "I hate you," she said. "You . . . baboon." Whereupon she resumed her way down the path to the driveway.

Seeing her hesitate at the sidewalk, then turn up, retracing their steps from the station, he flew to the closet, grabbed at the nearest clothes, sneakers, khaki trousers, checked wool shirt, sweater, and dressed hurriedly. He snatched handkerchief, wallet, change, ran the brush across his hair. In the hall he paused, hearing his mother's voice, and found her standing just outside her own door, sleepily drawing the wrapper about her, touching nervously at its collar.

"Is anything the matter, Wilder?"

"No, Mother, it's all right," he said and went by her down the stairs. "I'll be right back."

"Where are you going?"

"Out," he said.

"Wilder," she called after him.

But he did not answer. He closed the front door softly behind him and started off down the driveway at a jog. From the top of the hill he could see all the way to the grade crossing, but there was no sight of Catherine. As he continued he was thinking what he would do if she weren't there, how he might predict and pick up her trail, but in rounding the corner of the little depot he was relieved to find her on the bench reading a day-old *World-Telegram* plucked from the trash can beside her.

"Catherine, do be reasonable," he said. "Come back to the house while I get dressed and have some breakfast. Then we can go in together."

She did not reply.

"It's a waste of time sitting here. The first train isn't until eight. That's an hour and three-quarters from now."

She turned the page of the newspaper, scanning it for something of interest, seemed to find it, and began to read. With a sigh Wilder sat down beside her, stretched out his legs, and looked up at the sky which was gray and held the promise of rain.

"There's a bus," he said. "There's a bus that goes about every half hour into Journal Square. If you're in such a blooming hurry we can take the bus, but you've got to let me get dressed first. I can't go in like this. I haven't shaved." He pointed to his bare ankles. "No socks."

She turned another page.

"Will you come back with me while I change? It will take me a quarter of an hour—no more." He watched her face in vain for some reaction. "Hey," he said and tugged at the furry sleeve.

She snatched it away with such violence that the newspaper fell from her lap. "Don't *touch* me!"

"O.K. Sorry."

They were silent then. There was a rustling of leaves above them and the sound of an approaching vehicle. It proved to be a milk truck which crossed the tracks with a rattle of bottles and disappeared down the hill.

"All right, will you wait here? Will you wait right here while I go home and change? Will you promise me you won't disappear?"

The ensuing quiet was broken by the unmistakable sound of a locomotive whistling to a crossing. Wilder frowned and went over to look down the track. "It can't be," he muttered, but even as he did he heard the familiar rumble. Folding the newspaper, Catherine tucked it under her arm and carried her valise across the platform, setting it down confidently near the edge.

A slow smile spread across Wilder's face, and turning he saw the train approaching—but from the other direction. It was coming from the city.

"This won't do you, I'm afraid," he said. "It's going the wrong way."

The train slowed and stopped. Catherine, valise in hand, mounted the steps as the conductor alighted. She entered the coach, and the door slammed behind her. The conductor looked at Wilder, then, raising a hand, signaled the engineer, and the train began to move.

With a final distressed glance at his sneakers Wilder started down the platform, but as he reached out to grasp the handle with which he hoped to pull himself aboard, the voice of the conductor ordered him sharply, "Don't do that."

Looking up, Wilder saw the man shaking a stern finger at

him but continued to trot along the platform until with a grimace the conductor reached overhead and pulled the emergency cord, bringing the train to a fitful halt.

Within, he found her sharing the close, foul air with half a dozen dozing railroad workmen and sat down beside her. From the conductor she bought a ticket to Newark, the train's destination. Then she produced a little gold pencil from her purse, opened the paper to the crossword puzzle, and began to solve it.

"I'll carry it," she said as he reached for the valise in the luggage rack. And so she did—into the Erie station and out onto the street which they found to be deserted. It was not yet seven o'clock.

"Do you know where you're going?" he asked.

"I'm going to the Pennsylvania Station if I can find a cab."

"It's only a couple of blocks. We can walk it."

"Which way?"

"Carry your bag?"

She reflected, then put it down for him, and together they set off down the street.

The waiting room of the familiar Newark terminal of the Pennsylvania Railroad was active. The departure of a train to the South was being announced, and there was a cheerful bustle about the place. Catherine seemed to gather confidence and purpose, while Wilder with growing consciousness of his attire trailed her in humiliation. Stopping at the window, she bought a ticket to uptown New York and ran up the stairs to the platform just as a long train of sleeping cars arrived from the West.

"No, ma-am," the porter said. "No local passengers. This here's the Broadway Limited."

Catherine walked backward rapidly, found no one at the

next vestibule, and stepped into it.

"You can't," Wilder said.

Catherine held out her hand for the valise, and he stepped aboard as the train began to move. Reluctantly he followed her into the Pullman and the first empty compartment. To his surprise they were undisturbed on their mute, brief journey into New York. On his several trips past the door the porter took no notice of them, murmured an undismayed, "Thank you, sir" for Wilder's half dollar as they took their leave.

She led him rapidly up the escalator, along the great hangar of a concourse, and onto the Eighth Avenue entrance.

"Thanks," she said, holding out her hand for the valise. "I'm taking the subway home. Thanks for everything."

"Oh no," he said, gripping the valise handle with both hands. "You're not going home until we've had a sensible talk."

"Talk? There's nothing to say."

"There's a lot."

"For instance?"

"That I'm sorry."

"Oh? You didn't seem sorry last night. You sat there like a stick while they clobbered me."

"It won't happen again."

"You're darned right it won't."

"All right, we're agreed on that." He took her arm and tried to start her down the steps but she would not move.

"Where?" she asked. "Where do you want to go?"

"Schrafft's." He pointed across Eighth Avenue. "For some breakfast. If they'll let me in looking like this."

Relenting, she allowed him to guide her down the steps and across the street.

"I don't understand it," she said when they had ordered.

"I don't understand what they were trying to do to me. I don't understand what you were trying to do to me. Didn't you know it would be like that?"

"No."

"You must have suspected."

He shrugged. "But I also hoped."

"What did you tell your mother about me?"

"Very little."

"You didn't tell her we were engaged?"

"No."

She shook her head in bewilderment. "Why?"

"I wanted to go about it gradually. I wanted her to like the idea first. I knew it wouldn't do to confront her with it."

"But what about me? If you couldn't prepare her, you could have prepared me. You could have given me some hint I was walking barefoot into the snake pit."

He picked at the paper doily with his fork. "I didn't know it would be so difficult."

"Difficult? Impossible. You know me. You know your mother. You knew she was going to hate my guts on sight. No. Before sight. Before she even saw me."

"That's not true."

"It is true. She never gave me a chance."

"And you're not giving her one."

"Oh, Wilder."

"She's strait-laced and provincial and opinionated some-times. But she's not mean, Catherine. She doesn't hate you. She doesn't hate anyone. I suppose she fears you—fears you'll take me away."

Catherine laughed. "Not a chance."

"Don't say that."

"Why not?"

"It would be pretty stupid to let the behavior of my family"
—he smiled at her—"my eccentric family, influence us,
change any plans of ours. After all it's me you plan to marry
—not Mother."

Catherine took a sip of orange juice and leaned back in her
chair, looking at him intently, as though trying to project him
on some screen of her mind. "Wouldn't I though?"

"Wouldn't you what?"

"Be marrying your mother. Don't you two come in one
package? A special introductory offer?"

Wilder smiled, nodded. "I see what you mean." He spread
an English muffin with marmalade and took a bite. "But
doesn't everyone? Don't you come fully equipped too? Aren't
I marrying your . . . father say?"

Catherine put a lump of sugar in her spoon, lowered it into
the coffee slowly, watching it dissolve. "Well, no. With a girl
—with me anyway—the man I marry will be number one—
everything."

"How do you know?"

"I know," she laughed, "what every woman knows."

Watching her now, still smiling, thinking about what she
had just said, Wilder was deeply touched. Here in this plain
restaurant flooded with cold, gray morning light, he had had
a revelation. It was the thought of her as woman, not girl—
that she held for some one man, for him there was still good
reason to hope, the key to untold feminine mysteries and
tenderness. She was all desirable. The fleeting doubts of the
dawn were but ugly night thoughts. All he would ever need
to know was what came to him now with shattering clarity—
that he loved her so completely he would give his life for her.

He wanted to take her in his arms and he looked around
with the intention to do just that, but seeing a businessman

frowning over his newspaper, the prim, watchful waitress, he sensed the spectacle and compromised by reaching for her hand, taking it in his across the table. He felt her return the pressure slightly.

"Same here," he said in a tremulous voice. "Only you."

Slowly Catherine withdrew her hand from his. Her face was serious now. "But I was alone last night. I felt so all alone."

"What could I do? I kept thinking."

"I don't know," she replied miserably. "I don't know."

"May I have your hand again," he asked. "It helps."

"Yes," she said.

He took it between both of his and stroked the back of it gently. "I wish my family—my mother, were not as she is. I wish for your sake I could change her in some way, make her more like your mother, but I can't. It's beyond my power. Mother's good and kind, Catherine. In the end you'll come to be fond of one another. I'm certain of that. But it's not important. It's you that's important. Only you. And if you want, you needn't see Mother again. Mother, Lyddie, Father, any of them—never again."

Catherine put her other hand on his. "That wouldn't be very nice for you."

"It would be nicer," he said, "than never seeing you again."

She looked at him, a slow smile spreading on her lips, her eyes filling, and then he did kiss her. He sat down beside her on the banquette and kissed her quickly. Looking up he saw the cashier and two ladies at a nearby table watching. He laughed and kissed her again. "Come on," he said. "We've got to get out of here."

Waiting for the uptown subway, her hand went up and touched his chin. "You do. You need a shave."

"I'm going home to get one. And change my clothes. But I'll be right back—almost before I've gone."

An uptown express drew in and opened its doors on nearly empty cars. She stepped into one and turned to face him.

"Dinner?" he asked.

She nodded.

"I'll come by for you about six?"

She nodded again. "As soon as you can."

The door closed between them, and as the train moved out of the Thirty-fourth Street station, she blew him yet another kiss.

9.

CATHERINE'S visit to Greenfield was early in May of 1946, and in the week which followed it Wilder Stone made some decisions that had immediate and far-reaching effects on nearly everyone who knew and cared about him.

In Greenfield he went about it quietly, for he so dreaded the scene with his mother. With the knowledge that he might well be leaving for good he went up to the attic and raising the shade sat upon the edge of his steamer trunk. Here in this corner which he had reserved for his own things there was some order in the midst of chaos. Beyond he could see the tipsy dress form, the stained, mouse-chewed mattress, a helter-skelter of hatboxes, crates of broken, useless things.

But before him was the sleeping bag, still neatly rolled; against the wall, a fly rod and a .22 target rifle, each in its canvas case. He regarded them, the urban man, with faint disappointment. He'd been fond of the outdoors. Wilderness had always appealed. He had never been an expert woodsman, though he had hoped when he had acquired each of these articles that he would prove to be.

With a cloth he carefully dusted the expensive leather suitcase. He'd bought it in Denver to come East. It had cost him forty-five dollars in 1937, and it was still good. He rubbed the

leather appreciatively, promised it some saddle soap soon.
Here was confirmation of the belief that if you had to have
something, if it was a necessity, it was wise to buy the best
you could get.

Opening it, he found it contained an assortment of half-
forgotten articles and he began putting them into a pile to be
discarded. He came upon a catalog from Princeton University
with an application for admission partially filled out protrud-
ing from the leaves. There were two loose-leaf binders with
his lecture notes from the Whitfield Tutoring School in New
York. He flipped the pages of one and to his surprise remembered writing them—the significance of Shays' Rebellion. As
he put them aside he was recalling the arduous days at Whitfield's and for some reason Locke, Robert Locke, the blond
fellow who had sat beside him and whom he had grown to
like. He wondered if Locke had passed the Boards and got
into Dartmouth as he'd planned.

And here was a slim, silver cigarette case. It was black with
tarnish, but it had once gleamed. He'd bought it, although he
seldom smoked, because it did not bulge inside his Navy
jumper, and it seemed to him at the time an antidote to the
anonymousness of that uniform. A splendid example, he
realized, of the folly of buying anything you don't need. But
then it struck him he might shine it up and give it to Catherine,
that it might please her. And with that happy thought he
dropped it into his pocket.

Now some postcards and letters. There were a number from
a girl named Alice Carling in Pueblo of whom nine years ago
he was fond. He could not now recall much more than that
she had been handsome and he had kissed her good-by when
he left, promising to write her and apparently had. There
were odd letters from other friends—from Al Moore, from

Charlie Rodney, who had wanted him to go on a bicycle trip to Scotland and who had written him about it from Pueblo and called him when he came through New York and sent him a postcard (here it was) from Edinburgh.

Here was his photograph album with snapshots glued in for a few pages and the rest of them loose. A camping trip in the Rocky Mountains. Three frowzy boys (Charlie Rodney there) cooking by a stream bed. The football game with Boulder. Indoor pictures of a party, his own face turning up from time to time—once with his arm about a girl whose name he could not recall.

Clipped together was some official correspondence from the recruiting office of the Royal Canadian Air Force in Toronto. He'd forgotten about that. In 1939, when he was twenty, he had thought about volunteering and had written to ask particulars, but it had been too complicated and difficult, and soon afterward he'd gone in to talk to the American Field Service people and in the end been convinced that Millicent was right—doing his job at B. H. Hite's in Rutherford was the most telling blow he could strike at Adolf Hitler. And it probably was.

He came upon his high school year book and flipped through it, pausing at his own picture. He looked incredibly young to himself, with startling plump cheeks and that bush of hair. He wondered if he had aged a great deal.

Beneath his picture he read: "Wiley," "Stoney," "Stonewall" Wilder Stone is a case of still waters running deep. He is President of The Debating Society and has been on the honor roll twice. He was Class Treasurer in his sophomore year. Which doesn't mean he was neglecting sports either. He was a member of the cross country team and, before an illness forced his retirement, the championship basketball squad.

Always popular with his classmates of both sexes, he was voted in the Class Election, "Shyest Boy," and he placed third for "Handsomest Boy." Be careful of those eastern gals, "Stoney," we're expecting great things of you at Princeton next year.

"Good Lord," Wilder said aloud and tossed the yearbook onto the discard pile.

Finally the suitcase contained a wad of clippings from *The Greenfield Advocate,* the local weekly. He had written them himself in the summer of 1938 when he had worked there, thinking he might make a career as a newspaperman. He had read Lincoln Steffens that year and fancied himself as a crusader from some city room or perhaps a foreign correspondent filing a story from Barcelona where Americans were fighting alongside the rebels at the Ebro River or from Vienna where Germany had just annexed all Austria.

He set his suitcase by the door and then opened the trunk from which he removed his navy uniform—blues and whites —with the first class yeoman's insignia on the sleeves. To these he added a pair of moth-eaten flannels and a blazer too small for him. In a box he found a ship model, his own work, assembled from a kit but good-sized, carefully detailed and painted. He saved this out, along with an Indian rug he had bought at a souvenir shop near the Grand Canyon, thinking they would add a proper touch to bachelor quarters and, if Catherine approved, those of a married man.

At the bottom were some books, Sumner Welles' *Time For Decision* and Spyckman's *America's Strategy in World Politics.* He frowned, recalling an old resolve to be more knowledgeable on such matters, and picked them up. He was trying to remember some fact learned here, if indeed he had read far in either volume, when the attic door opened and he looked up into his mother's eyes.

"Wilder," she asked, a little amused, "what on earth are you up to?"

"I'm moving some things into town, Mother. I'm emptying my suitcase and trunk."

"Moving things into town?"

"Mostly clothes. I find I won't be needing much of the memorabilia here. I'll cover it with some newspapers. You can throw it out if it's in your way."

She knelt and touched the pile he had made. "Your yearbook? Your photograph album?"

"Yes. I'm suddenly and exclusively interested in the future. The future seems to hold great promise today. The past is for burning. If I get time"—he glanced at his watch—"I might do just that."

Millicent retrieved the album and yearbook so quickly it seemed she saw the flames already licking at them. "If you don't want these I most certainly do."

"You're welcome to them." He slammed the trunk shut and dragged it to the door. "I plan to pack this and leave it in the hall for the expressman. I'll send for it when I know where I'll be staying."

"Staying?" she asked sweetly. "Are you going on a trip of some sort, Wilder?"

"I'm moving into town, Mother."

She gasped, as though from a sharp pain, and her hand indeed went to her side. She swayed slightly, her eyes upon him, round with surprise and hurt. She reached out for the support of an iron bedstead and lowered herself slowly onto its rusting mesh of spring. She put the two books down beside her.

"Wilder," she whispered so faintly he could scarcely hear

her. "We can't do without you."

He picked up the rag and began to dust the trunk vigorously. "Yes. I've been worrying about that. I'll continue to help all I can."

"I don't mean the money."

"I do. I'll be able to send you quite a bit at first. My place won't be expensive. I think I can get servants' quarters in one of our buildings, and I'll be saving on the commutation. But soon, perhaps very soon, I may not be able to do so well. And I think Lyddie should look for a job. At once. I mean on Monday."

"Lyddie? But she isn't equipped for any sort of job."

"She has two hands, two eyes. That will have to do her. It's too late now to get her a doctor's degree."

"You'd have your sister work at some grocer's? You'd have her wrapping a pound of butter for . . . any dreadful person that comes into the shop?"

"Mother, she's got to do something. It needn't be in a shop. I'm sure she can find a job in an office, but it must be something useful, something she'll get paid for. She has got to help support the family. You see I've asked Catherine to marry me, and though it's hard for me to believe, she tells me she will."

Millicent passed a hand across her eyes and then gazed up at him with a saddening smile.

"Well," he said, "aren't you going to congratulate me?"

"No. I think that would be rather hypocritical of me."

"Not even for harmony's sake?"

She shook her head. "It would be foolish to encourage you to do something of which I so thoroughly disapprove for the sake of a little harmony."

"Mother, it's all decided. There's nothing more you can do.

Don't you understand? I love her very much."

"I can't believe that."

"Perhaps you will, perhaps it will make it clearer if I tell you that as long as I live I'll never forget your rudeness, yours and Lyddie's, to Catherine here last night. I'll never forget . . . nor forgive it."

Millicent sighed, frowned at the flaking enamel of the bedstead, and then gripping it firmly, pulled herself to her feet and walked to the door.

"I'm sorry, Mother. I'm sorry to thwart you."

In the doorway she turned and looked at her son. "Wilder my dear, you don't understand. It's not me. I don't count. I live only for you—only for your happiness. It's always been that way and always will. I don't see how this very ordinary girl can make you happy. I'm sure you'll find I'm right and I pray it will be in time." And she descended the attic stairs with a sure tread, one hand on the rail, the other holding up the skirt of her wrapper.

An hour later Wilder stood in the foyer dressed for town, the bulging suitcase, the box with the ship model in hand. The trunk, packed and tagged, stood by the door.

"I'm taking a place in town, Father," he explained. "In one of the buildings, I hope. It will make it a lot easier for me."

"Yes, of course," Everett Stone said, peering intently at his son, not sure he was getting the drift. "That's sensible enough. You'll just be coming out weekends?"

"Perhaps. I'm not sure. We'll see how it works out." He turned to see Lyddie descending the stairs at a run, her face squinting with concern. Grasping the banister, she leaned across it.

"Wilder, you can't do this to Mothy." Her voice was high and taut. "I won't let you."

"So long, Lyddie," he said.

She glanced up at her mother's closed bedroom door. "Mothy's up there crying. You can't leave like this."

"Watch me." He took his father's hand and shook it warmly, then did something he hadn't done since he was a boy. Leaning toward him, he kissed him upon the cheek. He opened the door, carried his suitcase and box onto the porch, waved, pulled the door shut and was gone.

It was a heady, dizzying week, and it seemed to Wilder that the earth had become enchanted, a place where all things were possible for the wishing. The servants' room he hoped for proved to be two small connecting rooms on the roof of the twelve-story Lazarus building at Tenth Street and Fifth Avenue. For a previous tenant, one had been fitted with a tiny electric refrigerator and a pair of gas rings. The bath and lavatory were communal and down the hall, but since living-in maids had all but disappeared from the lower Fifth Avenue scene he would share it with only a bachelor professor from New York University.

But the happiest feature was the broad terrace outside, and here, on the warm, early May night that he moved in, he held Catherine in his arms and they looked out across the rooftops of Greenwich Village, delighting in the crooked chimney trunks, the thicket of antennae, the golden squares of light that were a thousand neighbors, the twinkling reds and blues and greens that marked the bars and restaurants and tiny theaters, scattered like jewels from Washington Square to Sheridan.

And they smelled the many smokes and something delicious cooked in olive oil and heard a tangle of music, jazz from a night club, piano from a bar, a string quartette from a record and through open windows the voices of half a dozen radios, and it mingled with the sound of tires on the street and the sigh of air brakes and the soft bleat of taxi horns and the murmur of people. It was glorious, having the city thus about them, and soon they went into Wilder's bedroom where the blue chintz curtains Catherine had brought down were not yet hung and they lay down upon the freshly made bed and made love of their furious joy.

The place would do, they decided, for them both, not permanently, but for the first few months after they were married and Catherine, aided by Alma Massee, gave thought to its furnishing. A three-quarter bed, a tiny chest of drawers, two lamps, and some basic kitchen equipment were borrowed to supplement Wilder's Indian rug, which Catherine viewed with doubtful tolerance, and the ship model with which she was delighted. Indeed she proposed it as their eternal symbol of home.

Alma Massee, so admirably suited to it she might already have married off a dozen daughters, took command of the wedding preparations with a firm authority.

"Catherine's set on a church wedding," she told Wilder at dinner on Tuesday, "and Sea Girt seems the best place. It'll be much more difficult here in the city. Catherine won't know where to stop with her college friends for one thing."

"What's wrong with that?" Joe Massee asked. "If you're going to have the thing at all, you might as well do it up right."

"We are going to do it up right," she said patiently. "We can do it up righter at Sea Girt. We can have just the people we want. It's a darling little church and that's where Catherine wants to be married."

"Where's the party going to be?" Joe inquired.

"At the Stockton."

"The Stockton? What's wrong with the Monmouth Grill? They've got a band there and a decent place to dance."

"Now, Joe," Alma said, "you're interfering."

"If it's a matter of expense—I've got one daughter and I want her to have the best wedding money can buy."

"It's not the expense, Joe, and you may as well know now that you aren't going to have the least thing to say about this wedding. It's Catherine's and it's going to be just the way we want it."

Joe laughed heartily and winked at Wilder. "You heard that didn't you? The way *we* want it."

"Well it is," Alma insisted. "A wedding is entirely a woman's affair. You men are just so much excess baggage."

Still laughing, Joe raised his third Scotch highball of the evening to Wilder. "Here's to us, the excess baggage."

"To us," Wilder replied, touching the rim of his glass to Joe's. "Why don't we just not go."

"That's the idea," Joe cried. "We'll go to Havana. You just let us know when it's over, Alma—so we can come back."

"Now seriously," Alma resumed. "We've got to decide on a date. Catherine and I can't think of any reason to put it off until fall, and I do think June is *the* lovely month to marry in. Do you think it's too soon?"

"Who, me?" Joe said. "I thought you didn't want any help from us."

"Will you be serious, please?"

"It's not too soon for me. How about you, young fella?" He turned in mock seriousness to Wilder. "Rushing you at all?" Then he laughed until he had to wipe his eyes.

"Oh *Daddy*," Catherine said.

"Late June." Alma produced a pocket calendar. "Let's say Saturday the twenty-ninth. That will give us time to get everything ready, the announcement, the lists, and invitations."

"That's fine with me," Wilder said.

"Then that's settled. In the morning I'll write and reserve the church." She made a note on a pad she had provided for the purpose. "Now—your family, Wilder. Will they come?"

"I don't know," he said. "I really don't."

"Well, there's one way to find out." She made another note. "We'll send them an invitation."

And so in a few whirlwind days great decisions were made: Catherine bustled off to a photographer, an engagement notice prepared for the newspapers, invitations and announcements ordered, two bridesmaids and their dresses selected. With appropriate anguish a new nightgown, underwear, a going-away dress, a white organdy wedding gown, and a veil were decided upon. Lists of names with proper addresses were compiled. While Wilder's looked pitifully small at first, as he put his mind to it he did recall old friends who could conceivably be called upon now to rally round.

In answer to his careful, hopeful letters, there was joyous news from Cleveland. Not only would Charlie Rodney stand up for his old pal Wiley, but, by golly, just try and keep him away. He'd be there with Mrs. R. (you remember Charlotte —she remembers you!). Leaving the kids behind, Wilder would be glad to hear, but writing old Sam Bean down in Terre Haute to see if he mightn't want to come along. Wilder could not for the life of him recall anyone named Bean but was happy at the prospect he might want to come to the wedding.

By the first week in June the gifts began to arrive—coasters and crystal ash trays and silent butlers too many but a shout of joy each for a pop-up toaster and a casserole and a pale blue blanket and six teaspoons in the Florentine pattern Catherine had chosen.

There was only a hint of disappointment that the *Times* didn't use Catherine's picture on the society page, carried only a small notice of the engagement at the bottom of a column, and that the *Tribune* printed none at all, for that was the day Wilder and Catherine were deciding where to go on their honeymoon.

"An island," Wilder explained in the half spoof he used when he was trying out an idea on her. "It's important we go to an island. Symbolic, you understand, leaving the protection of family and tribe. Cut old ties. Leave old customs, old lovers, old bills. Cross much water. Come to new land. Should be small land so it will not conceal dragons or hostile giants, but land of much beauty, many wonders."

"Count me in, chief," Catherine said. "When does the dugout leave?"

"Well, there are many islands—Coney, Staten. It's a matter of how much water you can afford to put between you and the scene of your past. Now, I have this idea about Britain, about Scotland really. I suppose it was put there by Charlie Rodney when he tried to get me to go along with him and Al Moore the summer before the war. It was a bicycle trip, and I guess I wanted very much to go because I've dreamt about it ever since. I haven't the least idea what Scotland is really like, but it's so vivid to me. A familiar little fishing village with cobbled streets and nets drying on the wharf and cliffs—I'm usually pushing the bike up this road along the cliffs where you can look down to the sea."

"But supposing it isn't like that?"

"I think it is though. Something like that, somewhere. If it isn't, if the real one isn't up to it, I'll go on dreaming about my

Scotland. I would like to see."

"Scotland it is. I'll have kilts and one of those tartan over-seas caps with the ribbons down the back. We'll get a bicycle built for two and I'll loaf and let you do all the pedaling."

And the real disappointment of the day was the discovery in the American Express office on Fifth Avenue that the round-trip fare alone (the most he could hope for was two weeks and they would have to fly) would amount to over fifteen hundred dollars, twice as much as they could afford for the whole trip.

But it was not long before they adjusted to that too, and they left happily reconciled to a ten-day reservation at the Princess Hotel in Bermuda. Bermuda was, after all, an island, an island of extraordinary beauty, and it was small, more ideally suited to cycling than Scotland. What matter if, as something to brag about, it was commonplace? It wouldn't be commonplace for long—not after they got there.

What really set Wilder up that week, what really gave substance to his happiness, were the words of Milton Lazarus.

"Wilder," he said waving him to a chair, "of course, you're welcome to those rooms down at 21 Fifth Avenue. They're no use to us. But I'm damned if I'd want to take my wife there. Bathroom down the hall, no proper kitchen. That's a love nest, not a place for a young man who's getting ahead in the real estate business."

"Catherine doesn't mind. She rather likes it really, and it's one less thing to worry about. It's only temporary, of course. I'll find something better in September."

"Up to you."

"Thank you, sir," Wilder said and got up to leave.

"Hold on a minute. Shut the door, will you, Wilder? There are a couple of other things I've had on my mind." He waited while Wilder did so and took up an attentive position in the side chair. "You've been doing well uptown. I hear nothing but good of you from the superintendents. They're hard to please."

Wilder smiled. "That's a bad sign. I'd better get some enemies."

"Don't try. You'll have them soon enough." He tilted back in his chair. "I'm very happy about you getting married, Wilder. I was beginning to worry a little. What sort of girl is she?"

"Very nice."

He laughed. "Of course she is. If you love her, she is surely nice. There's no doubt of it. I'd like to meet her. Will you bring her in?"

"Of course."

"Maybe you'll bring her out to Mamaroneck for dinner some night. Will you?"

"I'd like that very much."

"Good. We'll arrange it. Now it's also time to think a little of your future, of when the bills come in for all the things a young married couple need to get started. It's such a lot now. Well, we have prepared a little raise, not a great deal, you'll see, but something."

"It couldn't be more appreciated, sir."

Milton Lazarus nodded. "At the meeting this morning we elected you secretary of the company for the next year. It will give you an idea of the over-all function, our planning, the new construction, and it may interest you."

Wilder beamed. "I don't know what to say."

"As a member of the firm, we're obliged to make some stock available to you. It's a hundred dollars a share, and it's paid a pretty good dividend in the last few years. You may want to look into it."

"That's very good of you, Mr. Lazarus."

"Not at all, Wilder. Not good of us at all. It is enlightened self-interest as they say. We wouldn't want to lose you."

"I wondered if I'd be able to buy some stock one day. Of course right at the moment I don't have . . ."

"Oh I understand, Wilder. Right now there are no extra funds around. Well, when there are, the stock will be waiting for you."

True to his word Milton Lazarus did arrange the dinner, and it was riding back in the train from Mamaroneck that Catherine said, "What a dear, sweet little man he is."

"Yes," Wilder replied happily. He was ever prepared to be defensive about him.

"And he's so terribly fond of you," she added.

The thought had never occurred to him, and he reflected pleasantly on it for the balance of their journey into Grand Central.

The weekend of June twenty-ninth proved an unusually hot and sultry one, emptying Philadelphia, Trenton, metropolitan New Jersey, and New York, filling and giving a festive aspect to Sea Girt, the unpretentious Jersey Shore resort where the Massees had summered for a dozen years. It was, as Alma had proposed, an ideal site for the wedding.

Wilder passed his final hours as a bachelor with Charlie and Charlotte Rodney. In spite of a sun which baked them through a light but persistent fog they patrolled the boardwalk, watching a frothy green sea break upon a beach which sprouted a crop of umbrellas in lollipop hues.

As befitted a groom he was apprehensive, peculiarly unhappy and, despite the Rodney's efforts to divert him, very much alone. The hands of his watch were glued at eleven. Yet it ticked. The second hand moved. It agreed with the clock on the pavilion. And in a matter of hours, interminable as they were, he would be a married man.

Here was the very summit of his life, and not only was he failing to enjoy it, he could not even comprehend it. Instead there was a sense of disappointment, a feeling that some essential was missing. He wondered if it was in himself. Perhaps a fear that he might fail? Disappoint? Be ridiculous in the playing of his role? Or was it the absence of his family which, he knew, had been the subject of much conjecture at the Massees' party.

He was still unsure of his mother's plans. She had accepted the wedding but declined Alma's invitation to stay at the Massees' shingled house on Baltimore Boulevard as well as to the party on the eve of the wedding. Millicent had told Wilder on the telephone that they would be at the wedding, that a friend would drive them down on Saturday in plenty of time, but that his father, who had been very tired of late, and Millicent herself, who hadn't been at all well, were not up to much in the way of festivities.

Catherine too had seemed remote—no help—wrapped up as she was in a feminine world that excluded him, laughing with summer friends he did not know, bent on a thousand urgent errands. What a disappointment, what a loneliness it all was, here with these strangers, forcing an old friendship which the occasion demanded.

Small discomforting thoughts plagued him—the fatuousness of his toast to Catherine last night on the Massees' candlelit side porch, the stranger, Sam Bean, who had got drunk and even now was sleeping off the ill effects in the room he

shared with Wilder at the Tremont Hotel, the woman in the
brown dress who had "known Catherine since she was so high,
and, mister, . . . don't you ever get it into your head to mis-
behave." She had pointed an accusing finger at his nose.

Oh it was wrong, all wrong. The world was out of joint and
his head throbbed and his stomach quaked and he wished to
heaven he was elsewhere.

But then when it seemed nothing could help, the hands of
his watch began to move, slowly at first, but accelerating, soon
attaining a dizzy pace. Of a sudden it was three and he was
struggling into flannels and blue coat, and instantly it was
four and Charlie was steering him into position before the
altar in the tiny oven that was the church of St. Uriel The
Archangel, and turning, he saw with pleasure and surprise
his mother, her polite, churchgoing smile on under a dark
brown Queen Victoria hat, his father gripping the top of the
pew, rocking from heel to toe, Lyddie, poker-faced beside
him. And Alma in a flower print, dabbing at her eyes, and
behind a score of strangers in picture hats.

As he tried to mop the perspiration in a manner suitable to
a bridegroom, not a plowhand, he saw to his joy Margaret
Kriendler from the office, then Buddy Lazarus and his wife
Lotte, and Harry Coe and, finally, just coming in the door,
Milton and Grace Lazarus.

Then, to his astonishment he heard the familiar dum-dum-
dee-dum on the shaky little organ, and Catherine was by his
side, with a smile for him, but frightened looking, and he was
murmuring after the minister, his own "I do" a mere croak,
and she was turning back her veil and he was kissing her
chastely, quickly, and they were walking fast down the aisle,
and as the car left the church he saw Joe Massee shaking
hands with Lyddie on the steps and he prayed that his mother

and his father and Lyddie would come on now to the reception at the Stockton, even for just a moment.

They didn't. Nor did it bother him much, for time was still going too fast, and it seemed only seconds were elapsing as he shook strange hands, kissed strange faces, and danced with Catherine and Alma and cut the cake, and then he was driving up the highway in a rented car with Catherine and a bunch of suitcases toward the Holland Tunnel as the world gradually became a real but very different place.

It was in Bermuda, toward the end of the glorious, drowsy ten days at the Princess, that Wilder discovered the miraculous change which the incantations at the church of St. Uriel The Archangel had wrought in his mind and heart.

They sat in the great dining room, still glowing with the sun of Coral Beach, convinced their performance (a yawn over the wine list, a forbearance of the public turtle-dovery common among other guests) was such no one would suspect them of being honeymooners. Here among these appealing comforts a new sense of well-being came to him, a knowledge that all was right with his world, and for that matter had been all along.

He was young, a very young man, not without wisdom, and the future held bright promise— -anything and everything. He liked his job. He could not bear the thought of this brief holiday's end, and yet he was anxious to get back to his desk and the several projects he had left without knowing their outcome.

Passionately and wholly he loved this joyous girl with the great dark eyes, the lovely laughing eyes across the table from him. Looking at her now, the white straps of her dinner dress against the deep tan of her firm young shoulders, knowing in an hour or two she would be close beside him, dark, pale-luminous, all precious in her nakedness, he began to believe that she was really and rightfully his own. Yes, he was as good as any man and luckier than most.

All the evils, the dark specters that had threatened and thwarted him in the past, now magically dissolved in a puff of mirth. His disappointment about college, even the estrangement of his family, no longer seemed tragedies, but simply misfortunes. And you had to expect a certain number of them. They made a man of you. You could even laugh about them if you had someone who understood. And he did.

When on the morning of their departure they turned their bicycles in at the livery (they had come to know these mounts well, their crotchets and graces, and there was a sadness in parting), they told the friendly proprietor they would return the following year. And they meant it too, even though Catherine had a well-grounded suspicion she was already pregnant.

August in New York was oppressively hot, but it made for pleasant weekends in Sea Girt. Catherine would go down early Friday and meet Wilder at the train, and they would go for an evening swim in the bathing suits they had bought at Trimingham's.

Nonetheless, the tiny rooms at 21 Fifth Avenue were a furnace during the day. Catherine reported that at noon the roofing tar outside their window bubbled like boiling fudge. Moreover there wasn't room for the "loot," as she described the roomful of gifts awaiting them in Sea Girt, to say nothing of some odds and ends of furniture Alma had been collecting for them.

Thus when a three-room apartment became available in the same building, Wilder signed the lease and on September first they moved in, swinging the ship model from a beam in the living room ceiling.

In the weeks which followed they gave themselves to decoration, to diligent study of the current household magazines, to a nightly shuffling of paint chips and material samples. They arranged and then rearranged the gifts, the furniture spirited from the Massees. They deliberated upon purchases. They sanded and scraped, painted and varnished, nailed and screwed, fumed and swore at the falling plaster, ohed and ahed with self-admiration at the heart-warming results.

They did very little to the smaller bedroom beyond painting it a cheerful yellow. According to the doctor they needn't expect its occupant until about the first of March. Catherine announced she would get everything yellow. It was a dark room which needed cheering up, and anyway that was the conventional hedge since you didn't know if the occupant's colors were to be pink or blue.

In October Milton Lazarus had further good news for Wilder. They would let him handle the insurance on a good proportion of Lazarus properties. It was the equivalent of a substantial raise.

10.

ON one of the first cold, raw days of the fall, a Monday in early November, Lyddie called Wilder at the office with the news that his mother was ill.

"She's aged terribly in the last few months, Boo," Lyddie told him. "I don't think you'd recognize her. And so tired all the time, just played out. Not like her at all. You know how much energy she's always had. Of course, I thought it was because of you and that she'd snap out of it in time, but she hasn't. And last night she didn't eat any dinner. She complained of a stomach upset and went to bed and about midnight she got these pains in her chest."

"You got the doctor? She's so stubborn about calling him. The doctor's been there?"

"Yes, he's just left. I didn't know whether to call you or not —whether you . . ."

"Of course you should have called me. What did he say? What did the doctor say?"

"She needs lots of rest. He doesn't believe she's in any immediate danger."

"Is her heart all right? It sounds from what you say as though it might be her heart."

"He didn't say anything about that."

"Who is it? Dr. Davis? The old fellow?"

"Yes," she said. "Dr. Davis."

"Is he coming again?"

"He'll try and drop in tonight."

"I'm coming out," Wilder said. "I'll want to talk to him. If he doesn't turn up I'll call him. Is Mother all right now?"

"Yes. She's sleeping. He gave her some tablets."

"Do you need anything?"

"I can't think of anything in particular."

"Are you working?"

"No."

"Well," he said with a sigh, "perhaps that's just as well under the circumstances."

Wilder had never been at his ease with the gnomish Dr. Davis, who had attended the Stones since they had lived in Greenfield. He was a remote man, a man of few words, and these, no matter who was ill, he saved for Millicent.

"No," he told Wilder, jiggling his black bag impatiently, his eye already on the front door, "I don't think it's anything rest and a regular diet won't take care of. I've told your sister all that."

"You're sure it's not her heart?"

"I'm not sure of anything. Any doctor who tells you he's sure of anything is a liar. But her blood pressure's all right and her pulse is normal—for a person her age. A little weak but normal. I'm not saying she didn't have a little stroke here the other night. I'll know more about that. The prescription is the same—rest and regular diet. Good night."

When he had let the doctor out, Wilder went to find Lyddie. She was not in the kitchen, but he paused to take note of the disorder there. On the floor were newspapers, cracked saucers, a grease-caked frying pan. The counter, sink, shelves, the top of the refrigerator, even the seat of a chair, were littered with dirty dishes and silver, empty cans, and bottles. A cat sat beneath the kitchen table, watching him suspiciously.

He discovered Lyddie in the drawing room, huddled in a heavy sweater, slumped into a corner of the settee.

"Lyddie, you can't possibly prepare a meal in a kitchen like that. It's a frightful mess."

She regarded him sourly. "What did the doctor say?"

"He said she must have rest and regular meals and I don't see how she can have either with such a pigpen below her. I'm going up to see Mother now, and when I come down, you and I are going to pitch in and get that place ship-shape. It's no joke now."

"I'm so tired," Lyddie replied. "I've been on the go all day. You've no idea what it's been like here since last night."

"I'm sure it's been unpleasant," Wilder said, starting up the stairs, "but we've got to do something."

Softly Wilder opened the door into his mother's room. His father who was sitting at the dressing table looked up and waved cheerfully. He seemed to Wilder a bit gaunt. Millicent in a lavender bed jacket, her hair neatly brushed, lay back against two pillows, her eyes closed, her face pale and powdery. On the table beside her were a little bell, a bottle of pills, and half a glass of water.

"Is she asleep?" Wilder whispered.

Everett Stone shook his head. "No, Mother's been waiting for you, Wilder."

Millicent's eyes fluttered and opened. Her head turned slowly until she saw him by the door. Then she smiled radiantly. "Wilder. Wilder darling. It's you. You've really come."

"Of course, Mother."

Her weak-looking hand which had been clutching the fold

of sheet reached out to him. "Come give me a kiss and sit here for a moment." She patted the blanket beside her.

He leaned down to kiss her on the cheek and then sat, very gently, on the edge of the bed. "You mustn't tire yourself, Mother."

"It's so good to see you, dear." She touched his hand. "You've no idea what a tonic you are. I'm feeling better already."

"I've had a little chat with Dr. Davis. He says you're to have nothing but rest and plenty of good food at regular hours, and we're going to see that you get it—all of us, aren't we, Father?"

"Exactly," said Everett Stone.

"Oh, you mustn't worry about me," Millicent said. "You just get on about your business. I shall be on the mend in no time."

"Our principal business is you, Mother. To see you well. And that means you're to go to sleep right this instant. If you want anything just give a little ring on your bell. I'll be downstairs for a bit. I'm going to help Lyddie tidy things in the kitchen. You coming along, Father?" He kissed her again, murmured a good night and stood by the door as his father preceded him out of the room.

"Good night," Millicent said. "Will you come again?"

"Any time," Wilder said. "Any time I'm needed."

She frowned, plucked at the sheet. "Not like that," she said. "Not an emergency. Rather just to come and see us. Would you do that for me, Wilder? It would give me such pleasure."

"Of course, Mother."

"Promise?"

"You know I will."

"When?"

"Well, I'm afraid not tomorrow. Catherine and I were planning on going out to dinner tomorrow night."

"Oh, Wilder, I wouldn't think of interfering in your wonderful busy life. You must be having such a gay time."

"Perhaps on Thursday," he said.

"That would be so nice. It's just knowing you haven't forgotten us."

"I'll see," he said. "Now, sleep tight." He closed the door and went down to the kitchen where he found a disconsolate Lyddie leaning against the sink.

"I'm stuck now, aren't I?" she said bitterly. "I'm stuck for good and all."

"No more than ever," he said. "Come on, bear a hand here. Let's get to the dishes." And discovering the dishpan he began to fill it with hot water.

"It's all very well for you to talk. You're out of it."

"You dry," he said, tossing her a dish towel.

For an hour they worked together earnestly, washing and drying, putting things away, listing provisions which Lyddie would buy in the morning, and as they did so Wilder sought some feasible solution for Lyddie and his family.

When at last they had finished and Wilder surveyed their work with some satisfaction, he turned to her and asked, "How would you like to come in and work for us?"

"Doing what?" she said.

"Oh, temporary renting agent. We've got a building going up on Eightieth Street that will be ready for occupancy the first of the year. I might be able to get you a job showing apartments. If you're interested, I'll ask Mr. Lazarus."

"I don't understand. Who's to wait on Mothy? And Father for that matter?"

Wilder set the kitchen clock which was a half hour slow and wound it. "We'll get someone—a housekeeper who'll make Mother her luncheon and tidy the house and have a good meal waiting for you and Father when you get home. There must be some such woman in town."

Lyddie straightened her skirt, looked down at her scuffed moccasins. "I suppose there is."

"If you could find such a woman, how much would you have to pay her?"

"I haven't the least idea, Boo."

"We'd pay you about forty-five a week to start. If a house-keeper were any more I'd make up the difference. What do you say?"

To Wilder's surprise Lyddie said, "I have an idea about someone we might get. It's too late now, but I'll try her in the morning."

"You'll do it?"

Lyddie nodded. "If I can find someone suitable. I'll call you at the office." She gave him a shy, yet flirtatious, glance, and it struck him that she might, after all, have the spunk left.

Wilder's doubts of Lyddie seemed confirmed when he heard nothing from her on the following day, but on Wednesday afternoon he was again surprised and pleased to hear her voice on the phone. "I'm in town, Boo. Do you want me to come in for an interview?"

"You found someone?"

"A Mrs. Bannerman. She's very good with Mother and that's the main thing."

"Lyddie!" Wilder exclaimed. "Good for you. This is wonderful news. Do you want to come in now if I can find someone to talk to you about the job?"

"Actually, I'd prefer tomorrow if that's all right. I want to get some decent clothes. I haven't a thing."

"Yes," he said with enthusiasm, "you'll need some things, won't you? Do you have any money?"

"No."

"You can use my charge at Altman's or Lord & Taylor's."

"I'd rather not."

"All right." He sensed it was something to do with Catherine. "You pick out what you want and call me and I'll come around and pay for it."

"It's just a loan."

He laughed. "Oh, I'm aware of that. And I'll be in an excellent position to garnishee your wages if you're not prompt."

On Thursday, dressed in a new brown dress and stockings and some plain black pumps, she made a favorable if somewhat starchy impression on both Mr. Green and Mr. Lazarus and was hired at fifty dollars a week. She was to commence the following week reporting to the renting office at 37 East Eightieth Street. She needn't appear until ten in the morning but she would be required on alternate Saturdays and Sundays, an arrangement to be worked out with the senior agent.

Keeping his promise to his mother, Wilder rode out to Greenfield with Lyddie on Thursday evening, intending to return to town immediately on seeing her, but Millicent, who seemed improved, had made arrangements for him to stay for dinner.

"You really must, Wilder," she insisted. "Mrs. Bannerman has baked a cake in your honor. She'll be dreadfully disappointed if you don't. She's really very good, Wilder. She rattles on a bit too much but she's a good soul and works like a Trojan."

"The house looks very well, Mother, and so do you."

"I am feeling better. Perhaps it's knowing you were coming

tonight. You *will* stay?"

"All right, I'll give Catherine a ring. She was going to wait dinner for me."

"Surely she won't mind sparing you this once for your family?"

"I expect not."

When he came back from the telephone, he found his mother reading, but she put aside her glasses at once and smiled at him.

"Is that a good enough light for you, Mother? It's not very strong for reading."

"My eyes tire so easily in any light," she said with a sigh. "And yet I so love to keep up with things now that I'm a prisoner here."

"We'll get you a stronger bulb anyway." He sat down beside her and picked up the magazine. It was the *Reader's Digest*.

"Oh Wilder, do finish that one I'd just started—the one about the deaf children. It's really remarkable what they do for them nowadays."

And Wilder read aloud to his mother until the competent Mrs. Bannerman arrived to announce that dinner was ready.

Later that evening Lyddie walked him down to the station. "I was thinking," she said pensively, "how much it meant to Mothy having you here tonight—how sad it will be for her if she doesn't have that to look forward to."

"Lyddie, I can't help it. Look, it's nine thirty. It'll be eleven by the time I get home."

"With Mothy ill? It doesn't seem so much to ask that you come again. Couldn't you? Couldn't you come at some regular interval? She so loved having you read to her tonight."

"But I've Catherine to look after now. You don't seem to

understand that, Lyddie."

"Catherine's not ill."

"We're going to have a baby in March."

"You are?"

"Yes."

"How nice. How fine for you." They had arrived at the station, and under the arc light she appeared to ponder this news sadly. "Life has just begun for you, hasn't it?"

"And for you too. I've been thinking how much this job could mean to you. It could lead to all sorts of interesting things."

But Lyddie did not reply to that. Instead she said, "It needn't be more than one night a week, Boo. And anyway"—a shadow of despair crossed her face and she looked away—"it won't be for long."

"How do you mean?"

"I don't think Mothy's at all well."

Down the track the train's headlight appeared, and a moment later the sound of the puffing locomotive reached them.

"Is there anything I don't know?" Wilder asked.

The pained expression appeared again. She seemed to struggle to answer him but could not bring herself to it.

"Well, come on, Lyddie," Wilder said. "Either you know something or you don't. Here's the train. For God's sake, don't leave me hanging."

"I don't trust Dr. Davis," she said.

"You think he's holding out?"

"It's quite possible."

"Now why on earth would he do that? He might hold out on Mother if there were anything seriously wrong with her—but not on us."

"You know how they've always been."

The locomotive ceased its laboring, and the train arrived, coasting to the depot with only the clacking sound of its wheels.

"It's just a feeling you have about Mother?"

"Yes. A very strong feeling."

He kissed her lightly on the cheek. "So long," he said. "Good luck with the job. If I'm up that way around noon I might blow you to lunch."

"Oh, Boo, that would be lovely," she said, waving. "It's been an eternity."

When he got home Wilder found Catherine in bed. She had been reading Dr. Grantly Dick-Read's *Childbirth Without Fear* and she put it down with some reluctance, keeping a finger in her place, to hear the latest news from Greenfield.

"It's sad to think it required Mother's illness to pry Lyddie out of the house, but, by golly, I'm beginning to think she'll make a go of the job," Wilder told her. "I'm really very happy about it, Catherine. She looked surprisingly well in her new dress and shoes. I was even allowing myself to hope that in time she might get interested . . ." He paused, floundering.

"In men?" Catherine asked, smiling.

"Well, yes. A man."

She laughed. "Why are you so embarrassed about it?"

"I don't know. She's my sister."

Catherine arched an eyebrow at him, then smoothed the covers over the new roundness of her abdomen. "Well, yes, it would be nice, but somehow I don't think I'd count on it."

"She's not so unattractive, Catherine. She used to be a very pretty girl. If we could just get her to do something nice with her hair and to wear a little make-up."

She looked at him doubtfully. "Wilder, you're not proposing I take Lyddie in hand?"

"Well, I did think we might ask her down for dinner some night—after she's through work."

"I doubt she'd come—and as for my putting her hair up and giving her a lesson in the use of the mascara brush, the picture is too funny for words." She re-opened Dr. Dick-Read and glanced at the page she had been reading, then looked back at Wilder. "Supposing she doesn't make a go of the job? What then?"

"We'll be back where we started, that's all."

"Won't it be embarrassing for you? At the office?"

"A little, perhaps."

"What I don't understand is how she'd risk that—a girl with all that pride."

Wilder took one of Catherine's cigarettes from the package on the bed table and smoked it, as he always did, without pleasure, not inhaling, taking a gulp of smoke and expelling it instantly. He watched Catherine, absorbed again in her book.

"Catherine, supposing I were to go out to Greenfield for dinner—one night a week, for a little while. To see that the house is running properly, that Mother's all right, perhaps sit with her a bit. They seem to think that's important to her."

Catherine put down the book. "I'm sure it is."

"Just until she's on her feet."

"It's up to you," Catherine said.

"They haven't long, Mother and Father," he said. "Father's well over sixty and Mother must be near it. I owe them this, I think. After all, you and I have a lifetime before us."

"Yes," Catherine said, watching him. "That's true."

"Would you mind terribly?"

"If it weren't your family I suppose it would be the ponies or the boys or the girls or *something*," she said with a sigh.

"No, I don't mind. Just tell me what night, and I'll go to the movies with Mummy."

"You'll tell me if you do mind?"

She nodded. "Now it's time for body building. Got to get in shape for the main event. Wouldn't hurt you either." And throwing back the covers, she hopped from the bed, stretched out on the floor where she slowly raised her legs and began to move them apart and then together, like a pair of shears.

Christmas Eve was raw and rainy, and Wilder, who had gone to Greenfield to deliver a few gifts, had missed the train back to town and come along on the bus. It was after eleven when he let himself into the apartment, and he was disturbed to find it dark.

The little tree which Catherine had intended to decorate was still bare, the ornaments and strings of lights in a heap beneath it.

"Catherine?" he called. There was no answer.

In a paralysis of alarm it occurred to him there had been some calamity, something about the baby. Horrified, he saw Catherine alone and afraid, appealing to the telephone, the arrival of an ambulance, a siren in the night.

The door to the bedroom was ajar, and flinging it open, he saw to his immense relief that Catherine was in bed, her light out.

"Catherine?" he whispered. There was no answer but her regular breathing, and he concluded she had simply felt exhausted and tumbled in. Now, in her seventh month, she tired easily and gave in quickly to the requests of her body. And so Wilder decorated the tree and wrapped the gifts he had for her, and it wasn't until he too got into bed that he realized she wasn't asleep. She was crying softly.

"Darling." He touched her arm. "What's the matter?"

But she pulled away—wouldn't speak, and he lay still by her side until, presently, she stopped crying and did go to sleep.

Christmas Day was bright and clear, flooding the apartment with a cheerful light, and Wilder brought in the stockings they had filled with funny things from the five-and-ten, and as she opened each one and exclaimed and made jokes over them, Catherine told him with her eyes she was sorry about last night. When, at the toe of her red ski sock she found the tiny box with the gold shell ear clips, she hugged him and laughed for joy and her happiness.

Jimmy arrived a few days earlier than expected—on February twenty-eighth. He announced himself at a little after midnight and sent a frenzied Wilder to the phone for the doctor and Alma, but despite all the commotion, which included an early-morning dash up Fifth Avenue, Jimmy was not to be hurried and entered the world at a leisurely twenty minutes past two in the afternoon.

And Wilder, as he stood admiring him through the plate glass of the Mt. Sinai hospital nursery, felt himself in the presence of the most astonishing of miracles. His *son!* He could not have been given more certain proof that he was part of some benign and marvelous scheme if, in the place of the nurse who displayed his small, scarlet heir, he had seen God Himself in all his celestial majesty.

"Do you want a junior?" Catherine asked him later in the hospital room. "Most men do, I suppose."

Wilder thought for a moment and shook his head. "It's a pardonable conceit on a father's part, I suppose. May even

give a man a nice sense of immortality. But I think I'm op-
posed. He should have a fresh name—without any liens.
One all his own."

"Hooray," cried Catherine. "I was afraid we'd have a Juney
or a Buddy around and I *loathe* them. What'll it be? Marma-
duke? Onderdonck? That's a nice name. There's somebody in
your family with it."

"Something kind of plain," Wilder said. "Everybody always
had trouble with Wilder. They never knew what to call me.
What was the name of your grandfather? The cop that made
mayor?"

"Gustav."

"Gus? No, never do. What else do you have?"

And in the end they took the James from Wilder's side. It
was his paternal grandfather's name and no particular tribute
to him, but it had an agreeable, a new and ringing, sound to
them both. They added the middle name of Massee. James
Massee Stone. Stone, J.M. Old J.M. Jim. Jimmy.

Throughout the early spring it seemed to Wilder that Catherine never left the little yellow nursery. When he came home
from work he would find her there, Alma too as a rule. For
such a tiny thing Jimmy seemed to require the most constant
and careful attention. Every hour he must be fed or changed
or bathed or oiled or powdered, and when he needed nothing
there was opportunity to weigh him, measure him, and to
record the details of his increasing bulk in a light blue volume
with the irritating title, *Our Baby*.

Although he manfully held the swaddled infant, rocked
him a little, talked to him, it was largely for Catherine's and
Alma's benefit. He was disappointed in his own reaction, but
he felt powerless to communicate with his child. While Catherine or Alma could provoke contentment and gurgling laugh-

ter at will, the baby invariably cried when left to him. The sense of wonder at his presence had vanished, and in its place was the knowledge that now he would have to share with him in Catherine's attentions.

Once, as he handed a squalling Jimmy back into Catherine's arms, he had laughed and said, "When he speaks, send the boy to me and I'll instruct him in Greek and the manly art of self-defense, but meanwhile I entrust his care to the ladies."

Yet Wilder was extremely happy with the alteration in his life. He carried a set of after-the-bath photographs which he displayed to Lazarus secretaries and superintendents' wives with traditional pride, and in May was pleased to receive the news that Jimmy's sister (Catherine wanted, and thus assured herself, it would be, a girl) was on the way.

When, in April, the last apartment at 37 East Eightieth Street was rented, Lyddie's job there was over. She had, from all reports, done well. There had even been some compliments for the polite, careful way in which she handled Lazarus affairs there. Milton Lazarus told Wilder they would try and make a place for Lyddie at the office and they did for a week, but without typing, shorthand or bookkeeping there was nothing for her to do. She simply sat, making no effort to acquaint herself with office procedure or personnel, and at the end of the week she went home—and stayed.

Wilder was distressed by this, all the fine progress gone to waste. Although Millicent had made a nearly complete recovery, was now up and about and took her meals at the table, Wilder continued to make his Thursday-evening journeys to Greenfield, with the hope of flattering, bribing, or threatening Lyddie back to New York and the search for another job.

In this he was making no headway at all. She heard his argu-
ments listlessly and promised only that she would "think about
it." Meantime, unable to afford the services of Mrs. Bannerman, Lyddie had dismissed her, and the house was returning
to the squalor in which Mrs. Bannerman had found it.

With the first warm days of June Catherine with Alma's
help packed Jimmy and the essentials of his hygiene off to Sea
Girt for a summer by the sea. Wilder had arranged to take
long weekends instead of a vacation and would stay in the
apartment alone on his nights in town. He found that in the
heat, with nothing to keep him at 21 Fifth Avenue, he would
frequently go to Greenfield on Tuesday as well as the usual
Thursday and on occasion would spend the night and come
in with his father in the morning. He showed them new snapshots of the grandson and nephew they had never seen, told
them of his remarkable feats of strength and ingenuity, and
was pleased to note their growing interest.

But generally these visits distressed him. For one thing the
house was acquiring more cats than he felt a normal comple-
ment. Lyddie, it appeared, was making it her business to pick
up strays. She was seldom without a cat in her arms. She
hugged and stroked them, yet did not permit them the out-of-
doors nor even the run of the house for fear they might escape,
or worse, prey upon birds and mice. In this behavior Wilder
saw the certainty of eccentric old-maidhood and tried vainly
to persuade her to some other course.

Where she had once listened and argued about the sort of
job she should look for and how to go about it, she now stub-
bornly refused to discuss it. Once, when he pressed her, she
burst out at him, "Stop bullying me! If you don't stop I'll go!"
She was literally screaming. "I'll go and leave you all!" It had
been shrill, a tenement voice that carried down the block, and

in the shocked silence which followed they heard the tinkling of their mother's bell.

The Labor Day weekend at Sea Girt was disappointingly cold and rainy and set Catherine to thinking of an early return to town. She decided to go in with Wilder on Tuesday morning and spend the week. She hoped to set the apartment to rights, make a new slipcover for the couch, and shop for some maternity clothes. She would leave Jimmy behind in Alma's care.

Going in on the train she complained of a sore throat, blaming it on their determination to swim the previous afternoon and her folly in sitting on the porch afterward in a wet bathing suit. And the following night, Wednesday, as they walked in the Village, seeking relief from the sudden heat and humidity which had descended on the city, she confessed that the grippy feeling, as she described it, persisted.

She was tempted to return to Sea Girt to escape the heat. She hadn't been able to find anything in the shops and lacked the energy to look further, but she would wait and see how she felt in the morning.

"If I stay," she asked, "must you go to Greenfield tomorrow night?"

"I'm afraid I'd better," he said. "They count on it so."

"But your mother's better?"

"Yes. Much better. It's Lyddie I'm worried about. She does nothing, lets everything go, and Mother has to hustle around and get the meals."

"You mean it's going to go on?" she asked. "It's going to go on and on?"

"For a little while, I'm afraid. I don't know what to do about them."

Catherine said no more, but as they went to bed seemed unhappy. In the morning as she got him breakfast she brooded about her sore throat, which remained, and announced that for fear of infecting Jimmy she would not go to Sea Girt until Friday.

Late in the afternoon (it was four thirty and Wilder was cleaning up his desk preparatory to a prompt departure for Greenfield) Catherine called him.

"I really feel ghastly," she said. "I've never been so hot. Aren't you hot at the office?"

"It's pretty hot all right. It was ninety-six at noon."

"Well, it must be hotter now. And more humid. It's so oppressive it's hard to breathe."

"Why don't you go someplace air-conditioned? Why don't you go to a movie? I'll try and be back around half past eight."

"I don't think I could bear any place cold either. My head's splitting."

"Well," he said with a trace of irritation, "you'd better take an aspirin and lie down for a bit."

"Oh, rats," she said. "Can't you skip Greenfield this once?"

He hesitated, wondering if he could, and saw Miss Russo signaling him from the switchboard. "Not very easily," he said. "Take the aspirin and lie down. I've got a call waiting."

"All right," she said unhappily. "Good-by."

"Good-by."

As Wilder stepped into the crowded elevator at five o'clock he heard Miss Russo's voice behind him. "Mr. Stone, there's a call for you."

Turning, he saw her pointing to the mouthpiece. He was later to recall there had been time. Someone who had got on before him remembered an article left behind, and the operator held the door, time for Wilder to look at his watch, to decide that if he returned to take the call, some tenant's complaint, he would miss the train. He shook his head at Miss Russo and saw her begin to explain that he had just gone down in the elevator.

Arriving at Greenfield, he found Millicent sitting in the shade of the old beech tree in the backyard. She held an empty glass in her hand, and Wilder sat beside her on the wicker settee and heard about how delicious some lemonade had tasted on this hot afternoon.

He had been there for half an hour when he heard the telephone ring. Knowing that Lyddie was somewhere in the house, he did not go to answer it until it had rung several times with a peculiar insistence. As he started for it, Lyddie appeared on the back porch.

"It's for you, Boo," she called.

In the dark hall he picked up the instrument with some presentiment, some forewarning of peril.

"Didn't they tell you I called?" the voice of Joe Massee asked. "I called you twice before."

"No. They must have forgot."

"I'm up at the hospital with Catherine. I'm up at the Presbyterian Hospital on a Hundred and Sixty-eighth Street."

"The hospital? What for? What's the matter? Is it the baby?" Although he was stunned he was not surprised. It was as though it had been revealed to him before.

"No. I don't know what it is. I don't know anything yet. Helpern hasn't got here and these birds won't tell me a thing."

"But why are you at the hospital?" Wilder, sensing now the answer, dreading to know it, fighting it, trying to be calm, heard his own voice, edgy and rising. "She has a little cold, a sore throat. It's just the grippe."

"It got worse. When she couldn't reach you—you'd just left

the office—she got me at home. She said she couldn't get her breath."

"You called the doctor?"

"I did when I got down there. She couldn't breathe. She was heaving her shoulders trying to. And coughing, coughing at the same time, hard, till she was red in the face."

"You got Dr. Helpern? You talked to him?"

"Yes. He said to put her in a taxi and come up to the hospital."

"What is it? What's the matter with her?"

"I don't know. How would I know?"

"Can it be polio?"

"Yes," Joe said. "I guess it can."

"Oh, my God," Wilder murmured. "Oh, my God."

It was nearly dusk, and Wilder stood in the shadows of the dining room awaiting the taxi he had summoned. Through the patched and cobwebbed window screen he saw that Lyddie and his father had joined his mother beneath the old beech tree, and he thought of calling out to them, to tell them he was leaving now, of explaining that Catherine was ill and he had to leave abruptly. He saw his mother holding up the jelly glass, no doubt telling again how delicious she had found the lemonade in the heat. He stood there silently, watching them until he saw the lights stopping in front of the house, and he left without a word, leaving them to make what they would of his disappearance.

The emergency outpatients' waiting room, like all such places, was bare and cheerless. The hard steel chairs were occupied by wilted blear-eyed people, their faces suspicious and hostile. No one read. Magazines lay on the table, twisted and curled by anxious hands. A man held a piece of bloody

gauze to his eye. There was a smell of disinfectant and cigarette butts and human fear.

A veteran nurse sat behind a glass panel, and Wilder was
heading for her when he heard his name and, turning, found
Joe Massee. Squinting up at him, sourly it seemed, his mouth
atwitch, Joe seized Wilder's arm and pulled him down beside
him.

"She's getting oxygen and she's better, much better. Her
color's normal now." Joe touched his own lips. "They were
turning blue—her whole face—lavender—before the oxygen."

"Can I see her?"

"Not now. When Helpern comes out. He's with her now."
He looked at his watch. "He's been with her half an hour. He
should have something to tell us."

"You saw her? Since you spoke to me on the phone?"

"Yes. The intern let me come in with her." He wiped his
mouth with the silk handkerchief from his breast pocket. "She
was scared, you see. I haven't seen her scared since she was
a tiny little girl."

Wilder covered his face with his hands, and he felt Joe's
arm go around him.

"Listen," Joe said. "They're doing everything and this is
one of the greatest hospitals in the world."

"But what? What can they do?"

The door leading into the mysterious labyrinth beyond
swung open, and they looked up eagerly only to see an elderly
man emerging.

"She's breathing better now, with the oxygen. They brought
a little tank on wheels. With a tube taped here." Joe tapped
his upper lip. "And while I was there they put in a catheter.
In her nose."

"Who? Dr. Helpern?"

"No. The intern. The intern that was here when we came. You see she was smothering. She kept saying 'I can't breathe' and they put this in and it was all right. She couldn't swallow. She was filling up—and then with the catheter she was all right."

At eight o'clock David Helpern, the Massees' family physician, came through the doors. He was a pale, round-faced man with brown crinkly hair and a quiet businesslike voice that gave confidence. Wilder stood up when he saw him, looking for some sign.

"You want to see her?" the doctor asked.

"Yes," Wilder said.

"You go ahead," Joe said. "I'm going down to the station to meet Alma."

"Is she going to be all right?" Wilder asked.

Dr. Helpern took a cigarette package from his pocket, offered it to Wilder, who refused. He lit a cigarette and looked into Wilder's eyes. "She's in the respirator. She's breathing well now. We took a lumbar puncture. When I get the results of that I'll know more than I do now—but I still won't be able to tell you if she's going to be all right."

"Is it polio?"

"She's got some of the symptoms."

"All right," Wilder said. "Let me go see her."

In cap, mask, and gown Wilder entered the room where Catherine was and, although he had been expecting it, quailed at the sight of the great metal tank with its ports and dials. There was a cushioned stillness here, the only sound that of the oscillating motor and the bellows which breathed for his wife with a rhythmic, pneumatic sigh.

A nurse, also in a mask, stood at the head of the cylinder,

and she turned, hearing him. "Is it Mr. Stone?"

"Yes."

"Your husband's here, Mrs. Stone." She stepped aside, revealing Catherine's face. It protruded from the tank, high-colored with a collar of damp toweling.

"Hello," he said softly and came close. He looked into her great dark eyes so full of fright, and she smiled. He touched her forehead gently, then her cheek, in lieu of a kiss, found her skin hot.

"Darling," Catherine said. "I'm so sorry." It was a breathy, hollow voice without inflection, scarcely hers at all.

"Don't you worry now," he said. "It's going to be all right. You're going to be fine."

"Am I?" She looked at him eagerly, believing him. "Really?"

"Yes. Of course. You look fine. You've got good color."

"Do I?"

"Yes. How do you feel?"

"Hot. It's hot in—" she gasped, breaking off in midsentence.

"She can only speak when the pressure is positive," the nurse explained.

". . . hot in here." Catherine smiled. "Or down there. Wherever I am."

The nurse wiped her face with a cool towel and replaced the one at her throat.

"I don't think I can move my right arm at all now," she said to the nurse.

"All right," the nurse said. "That's nothing to worry about. That's what we were told to expect now, isn't it?"

The door opened softly and Dr. Helpern entered with an intern.

"She can't move her right arm," the nurse said.

Dr. Helpern touched Wilder's elbow gently. "All right young man. That's enough visiting hour for the moment. You can come back later."

"Catherine," Wilder said. "I'll be right outside. Don't worry."

She had to wait for the positive pressure, and then she said in her hollow voice, "O.K."

They were all three—Wilder, Alma and Joe—in the waiting room when the results of the lumbar puncture came in. The results were positive. Her spinal fluid was under pressure. There were abnormal cells.

"I believe she has bulbar poliomyelitis," Dr. Helpern told them. "It goes to the medulla, the respiratory center in the brain. I can't kid you. Catherine's sick. I can't tell the outcome."

Alma closed her eyes and folded her hands.

"She might die?" Wilder asked.

"Yes, she might. But she needn't. I've given her a sedative and she's sleeping. She'll probably sleep through the night. I suggest you do too."

Wilder returned to the hospital, haggard, at seven in the morning. At eleven he was allowed to see her again for a moment, but she was sleepy under the sedatives and after a flickering smile of acknowledgment she seemed to doze away from him.

When he said to her, "Catherine, I love you. Do you know? Do you know how much I love you?" she slept.

In the afternoon Dr. Helpern acknowledged that her periods of consciousness were getting less, that she was sleeping almost all the time. There was no point in Wilder's going to her. But more alarming was her unsteadiness of pulse. It was fluctuating between sixty and a hundred and twenty.

At a quarter to six Dr. Helpern found Wilder in the waiting room, sat down beside him, and told him his wife was dead.

Wilder nodded. "I tried to tell her. But it was too late. I'm afraid she never knew."

11.

FAINTLY, as though at a great distance, Wilder heard a familiar, beckoning sound. It was the creak of his bedroom door. But consciousness returned slowly, painfully, as he struggled up out of the deep, terrifying mine of his sleep.

Opening his eyes he recognized that he was in his own room in Greenfield. His body was moist, the pajamas sticking to his chest and legs as though he had fever, yet he felt none.

"Wilder?" It was the soft, kindly voice of his mother, and opening his eyes fully now he beheld her at his bedside, cradling in her hands a cup and saucer.

"Yes, Mother?"

"Did you have a nice sleep? It's been several hours. I couldn't bear to wake you."

He yawned, struggled up onto an elbow and smiled at her. "Well, yes. I must have."

"I've brought you the cambric tea."

"Oh thanks, Mother. That looks fine." Taking the cup and saucer, he sipped and nodded appreciatively.

"Feeling better?"

"Oh, much," he said and to his surprise he was. The tea was dispelling the dreams of memory, the bitter taste of old sorrow in his throat, and sending an agreeable warmth through his whole frame. The nap had unquestionably refreshed him. Some small reservoir of energy had filled within him. Not bad. He took another swallow of the tea, and pulling back the covers, he swung up to a sitting position, his toes groping the floor for his slippers.

"Well," he said. "I hope you've all had luncheon."

"No," Millicent said. "It's just ready now—or will be in a moment or so."

Wilder listened for the sound of the lawnmower. "Jimmy?"

"Oh he's trimmed the lawn and got acquainted with Mr. Lounsbury at the chemist's and bought a quart of ice cream and been for a walk—down to the river and the duck pond."

"Has he? I was going to show him the duck pond."

"He's so full of energy," Millicent said, moving toward the door. She stopped, traced the whorls of the bedpost with her stubby fingers. "Wilder, do you suppose he could be brought to call me Grandmother—or some such thing?"

"Yes," Wilder said. "I'll ask him."

"What does he call Mrs. Massee?"

"Mummy—Mom recently."

"I see," Millicent said and pulled the door closed behind her.

Jimmy knocked, put his head in the door.

"Come on in," Wilder called. He was at the bureau tucking a shirttail into his trousers. "I hear you've been all over town."

In the mirror Wilder saw him nod, sit on the straight chair beside the desk, and hook the heels of his scuffed shoes onto its rungs.

The fine-textured brown hair that had been light, nearly blond, as a baby, fringed his ears and grew thick on his neck right to the blue collar of his shirt. It pleased Wilder to recognize the furry, country appearance as a gentlemanly one. His son looked a boy—not one of the shorn little men in gray fedoras and silvery suits he saw accompanying stout mothers into the Radio City Music Hall—and he was grateful to Alma for that.

On the bureau in a green leather easel frame was Catherine's photograph, and Jimmy looked at it furtively, his eyes darting over the lips, eyes, nose, the outmoded hair style and dress. He looked up startled as Wilder spoke.

"Do you like that picture of your mother?"

"It's all right, I guess."

"I've always liked it—the way she's smiling there. She would smile like that before she said something funny." Wilder regarded Catherine's image. "Would you care to have it?"

Jimmy scowled. "What?"

"The picture. Would you like it for your room?"

Jimmy fidgeted uncomfortably, gripped the seat of the chair, and stared at his hands. "Sure. I guess so. Sometime."

Wilder smiled. "You don't have to, you know. I just wondered if you wanted it."

"I haven't got any place for pictures," Jimmy said. "There's junk a mile high all over my desk. It might get knocked off or something." He was silent, watching Wilder as he carefully combed and brushed his hair. "Hey," he said. "Is there one of you? Is there a picture of you?"

"No," Wilder said, "I don't think so. I haven't had a picture taken since the one for my passport. That scared me off."

"Where's that one? Can I see it?"

Wilder began to rummage in the drawer of the desk.

"There's this guy at school that has pictures of his family—his father and mother and sister and even the dog—and they're pasted on this heavy cardboard and cut out and they stand up like—you know, like little soldiers."

"Here," Wilder said, producing the passport. "You'll see what I mean. I'm afraid I won't do for cutouts if that's what you have in mind."

Jimmy turned the visaed pages, fascinated by their curious stamps and jottings. "What's this funny writing?"

"Arabic. That's the language they use in Egypt." He pointed to the lavender stamp. "That's the Sphinx. We never saw it, Harry Coe and I. We meant to, but something happened. The bus broke down as I recall."

Jimmy turned the visa upside down, studying it closely. "Why don't they use regular letters?"

"They might ask the same of us."

Flipping to the first page, Jimmy found his father's photograph. The face was oddly puffy and owl-eyed. It was, as Wilder believed, unflattering.

"Can I have this picture?" Jimmy asked.

Wilder folded the knot of his tie and drew it tight. "Oh Jimmy, it's not a good likeness. It's not a nice picture at all. It's just for identification."

"It's all right."

"But I look like a safecracker off the bulletin board in the post office."

"I want it anyway."

Lifting his jacket from the back of the chair, Wilder gave the collar a whisking with the clothesbrush and slipped into it. "Maybe there's a duplicate someplace. I'll look." Taking the passport from Jimmy, he glanced at the photograph of himself and scowled. "Dear me," he said as he dropped it into the desk drawer and closed it. "I do want to keep the passport intact. We'll need it if we're going off to Europe."

"Really?" Jimmy asked doubtfully. "Do you really mean that about the trip?"

"We'll see," Wilder said. "Come along now. Perhaps they'll give us something to eat." Taking Jimmy's arm, he piloted him toward the hall, but then, recalling another matter, paused. "Oh Jim . . . Mother would be very pleased if you called her Grandmother." Wilder faced his son, smiled at him brightly. "She is, you know. It's quite a legitimate request."

"Grandmother?"

"Or Grandma. Anything you like. Preferably something more affectionate than 'Mrs. Stone.'" Leaning forward, he slipped the knot of Jimmy's tie up so it covered the collar button. "Granny? How's that? No? Granny doesn't fit, does it."

Jimmy tried it gingerly. "Grandma?"

"There you see. It's easy enough." He gave Jim a pat on the back and then opening the door urged him through it to the landing and the stairs beyond. "A little awkward maybe at first, but then it'll seem natural enough."

Arriving in the dining room, Jimmy and Wilder found it empty. The table was laid with a clean though wrinkled cloth and upon it four places were set. There was a lazy susan with some pickles and a cracked jar of brownish sauce. In the center of the table a teapot held a cluster of fresh wildflowers.

"We may as well sit down," Wilder said. "There's no telling how long it will be." He looked at his watch and saw it was quarter after three. Outside it was bright. Through the thick foliage the sun splashed the yellowing net curtains.

"That's a nice job on the lawn," Wilder remarked. "I didn't see any holidays."

"There aren't any holidays," Jimmy said.

"Of course not. I keep forgetting your professional standing. You cut the lawn at Sea Girt now, don't you?"

"For the past two summers."

Wilder pushed the lazy susan slowly around with his finger.

"Well, now. You've been all over Greenfield today. As a visitor from the great city across the Hudson, what do you think of our town?"

Jimmy brightened. "There's a movie theater. I didn't know there was one. They've got *Moon Man* playing."

Wilder looked speculatively at the pantry door. "*Moon Man?* Is that a good picture?"

"It's O.K. It's old but it's O.K. It's about this guy they think is from the moon, only he isn't. He's just dressed up to scare them away from this old house."

"You went quite a distance," Wilder said. "You went all the way to Patterson Avenue."

Jimmy nodded. "And there's a bus terminal over there. A brand-new one. You can get a bus right into New York. Did you know that, Dad?"

Wilder nodded. "They go every hour now. It's faster than the train. But—I still prefer the poky old Erie."

"Why?"

"It's old."

"That's not a good reason."

"Perhaps not. Still—it's a reason. When you get old, you'll find you like some things because they've grown old with you."

"I won't." Jimmy looked at his father unhappily. "Anyway, you're not old."

"I'm glad you feel that way." Wilder stared at the pantry door. "I wonder if we won't both be in our dotage before we get lunch."

"It does take them an awfully long time. Is it going to be something special?"

"I doubt it. I think you'll find it edible. We dare not hope for more."

Jimmy looked out the window. "We'll still have time for

bumming, won't we?"

"We'll see."

Jimmy slumped, tugged at the edge of the tablecloth. "That means no, doesn't it?"

Since it meant something of the sort, Wilder felt a flash of irritation. "No," he said sharply. "Not necessarily." He got up from the table then and went to the pantry door. He pushed it open a crack and called, "Ahoy, in the galley! The crew is starving. What's the news?"

"In a *minute*," Lyddie replied. She sounded absorbed in an experiment whose outcome was still in doubt. "In just a *minute*."

Wilder allowed the door to swing shut, and through it came Lyddie's trilling, girlish laughter. "Keep your shirt on, boys."

They heard Millicent's gentle, admonishing "Oh, *Lyddie*."

Wilder sat down again and emitted a long sigh which was echoed by Jim. Wilder grinned at him.

"We couldn't go now?" Jimmy suggested.

"No. I'm afraid not."

Jimmy played with his spoon, and then, noticing the shape of its bowl, examined it. As he did so Wilder experienced a momentary dizziness as the past and present converged. For an instant he was not sure if this was real or illusion, nor of where he was in time. He watched Jimmy, watched the big dark eyes so absorbed in the spoon's shape, the face, the new face not yet written upon, and beneath it, just beneath its surface, he saw Catherine—for a moment quite clearly, as though she were actually emerging through the body of her son and presently would be at the table, turning to Millicent to say, "I've never seen spoons like these."

A face, Wilder thought, is a palimpsest. Beneath the surface of any face there are a hundred others, stacked like Halloween masks but each varying, shaped by the one beneath, shaping the one above. He thought to look for his own in Jimmy's and was not surprised that it eluded him and that when he looked again for Catherine she had gone.

"It's worn," Wilder said.

Jimmy, puzzled, tried the angle of wear against his plate and looked up at his father. "Like this?"

Wilder nodded. "Now you wouldn't know much about that, about scraping the bottom of a plate, a spoiled young prince like yourself."

Jimmy recognized this for the opening of his father's familiar game, a mild "ragging" about Alma's indulgences. While he sometimes enjoyed it, he wanted none of it now.

Dropping the spoon, he asked "Where shall we go bumming? Chinatown? You said we could go to Chinatown sometime."

Wilder frowned. "I suppose we could go there if you like."

"The trick store? Could we go to the trick store?"

"Well, not both, I'm afraid." He glanced at his watch and saw it was half past three. "We'll be short of time. And Gran will want you to bed early if you're to get a good start for Sea Girt in the morning."

Jimmy nodded soberly and then brightened with an idea. "Hey, why can't you drive down with us?"

Wilder shook his head. He groped for an excuse and found an old but still serviceable one. "I've got some things to do. Some things at the office." He moved uncomfortably in the chair. He was wondering about Bibi Winter. He had a vision of her alone in the apartment and unable to deal sensibly with the crisis she had brought about. He was suddenly anxious to reassure her—to give her spirit whatever support he could spare. He decided to telephone her at the earliest opportunity and make sure she was all right.

"Tomorrow's Sunday," Jimmy said.

"I know. There are some things I must do—some things I've put off." And then, typically, a vision of his desk came to him, and he saw the score of plaguing odds and ends there beneath the castings awaiting disposition. He resolved, as he frequently did on a holiday eve, to "go in first thing in the morning and clean things up." He half believed that he would.

"What time *will* you come down?" Jimmy asked.

"Come down?" Wilder said vaguely, his thoughts still at the office. "Oh, I don't know. Maybe sometime in the early afternoon. If I can get through."

The pantry door opened slowly, elbowed in by Millicent Stone. She placed before Wilder a large platter, in the center of which was a seared pot roast the size of a grapefruit.

Millicent smiled shyly. "I'm dreadfully afraid it may be a bit overdone."

"Well, *I* don't think it's done enough," Lyddie said, appearing in her mother's wake. "Remember the last time. It was raw."

"It looks fine, Mother," Wilder said. "I'm sure it will be." He had risen and now held her chair as she sat down. He noted with displeasure that Jimmy was not observing the convention; instead he was staring apprehensively at the bowl of grayish mashed potatoes which Lyddie had just placed on the table.

Wilder tried to reach him now with a glance (he would not conceivably have spoken a reprimand), but Jimmy was beyond him, absorbed in study of the food on the table. He scarcely spoke throughout the meal, and soon they all fell silent, Wilder watching Jimmy as he ate so sparingly of the roast, only a mouthful, and spurned both the potatoes, which were cold, and the beans, which were burned.

When Hallett, the gray tom, bounded through the door from the hall, leaped onto the mantel and then the sideboard where he crouched, switching his tail and watching them, Wilder saw Jimmy's eyes travel from the watchful cat to the burned roast, saw him sniff, stop chewing, then lay his fork down on the plate. And Wilder laughed aloud.

"What is it, Wilder?" Millicent asked.

"It's all right, Jim," Wilder said, still laughing. "It's pot roast. It's not roast cat."

"Wilder!" Lyddie cried. "What do you mean?"

Jimmy looked at his father, surprised he had read his mind so accurately, and resumed chewing. Nevertheless, he turned down a second helping of ice cream. It was soup by now anyway. He seemed to have no appetite at all.

"Lyddie and I'll tend to the dishes, Jim," Wilder said in getting up from the table. "Why don't you take your grandmother into the drawing room and tell her about your summer plans."

Jimmy, in discovering himself alone with the forbidding figure of his grandmother, was clearly apprehensive. As Millicent arranged herself in the center of the love seat, smoothing the flimsy lavender panels of the old-fashioned dress, he watched her hands. They were constantly in motion as though searching for some small object in the dark. They were white and blue-veined yet bluntly sturdy.

He had no idea what was expected of him—something surely. He looked again at the wispy white hair, the alert eyes, the mouth pulled tight as with a drawstring. He was on guard. With a particular swagger, hands in his pockets, he strode about the drawing room. He peered from the bay window at the empty street, then into the hall, assuring himself that his tweed overcoat and blue school cap with the emblem at its prow were safe there on the piano bench, then into the dining room where he saw that his father had cleared away the last of the dishes.

"Well, Jim," Millicent began, "I hope it isn't too stupid for you here. We're not used to being honored by visits from young gentlemen, but we'll do our best—Lyddie and your father and I—to make you happy with us. Perhaps you'll tell us, will you, if there is anything you'd especially like?"

Jimmy gave her a puzzled look. "Sure," he said. "Oh, sure."

"Lyddie and I have been speaking of fixing up your room. It's at the end of the hall upstairs. Has Lyddie shown you?"

"No."

"Perhaps it's just as well. It's rather a mess at the moment. But next time you come we'll have it tidied up with some fresh curtains and what not. Do you have any preference for color?"

Horrified at the thought of his permanence here, Jimmy shrugged. "No," he said. "I don't care much."

"You don't have a favorite color?"

"I don't know." He shot a desperate glance toward the kitchen. "I guess so."

She waited a moment. "And you're not going to tell me what it is?"

"Sure, I will if you want. Orange. I like orange."

Millicent nodded. "Yes. Orange is a pretty color, isn't it? Well, orange curtains then." Pausing, she gazed at the clock on the mantel. It was stopped, as it had been for many years, at twenty minutes after six. "Your father likes green, you know. Always as a little boy he chose green things. And Everett, blue. Everett always preferred blue. Only blue cravats. Fancy that!" She laughed with delight. "And a bachelor's-button. How he adored them. We used to have a little bed of them in Pueblo, and he would cut one each morning for his lapel. I keep intending to grow some here." From the bodice of her dress she produced a tiny crumpled handkerchief which she squeezed and replaced. "Now you were going to tell me about your plans for the summer. You'll go to Sea Girt, will you?"

Jimmy nodded. "We were supposed to go today. Mummy and I were going to drive down this morning."

"Oh? And you delayed to come and see us?"

"Well—to go bumming with Daddy."

"What?"

"A bumming tour," Jimmy replied, warming promptly to the subject. "It's what we call it. We just go places and walk around. Sometimes to the trick store. Like today we're going to Chinatown."

"I see. Well, we're pleased to be included." She smiled at him wanly. "And when will you and Mrs. Massee go to Sea Girt?"

"Tomorrow."

"Will you find lots of friends there?"

"Oh, sure." Jimmy brightened, finding himself once more on certain ground. "There's the Moore boys and Billy Schuler and Joe Elie—he's a fat guy. And Edgar Hoffman. He got hit in the eye with a BB last summer, and it's still in there. You can see it."

"Goodness!" Millicent cried, genuinely alarmed at the thought. "How dreadful! You must be very careful. Surely Mrs. Massee doesn't permit guns of any sort."

Jimmy, delighted at the effect of this graphic detail upon his grandmother, hitched his pants. "Oh sure. I've got a BB gun." He regarded her squarely. "Of course I don't shoot at people with it. I know how to handle guns. I'm in the Greys you know. I'm a Captain in the Knickerbocker Greys."

Millicent, bewildered by this, said simply, "Dear me." Her hands fumbled about the cushions. "Well," she said at last, "we shall have to find you some friends here. I'm afraid we don't know many young people any more. But we'll give it some thought, Lyddie and I. I do believe Dr. Seton can help."

"Who?"

"Dr. Seton. Our pastor."

Appalled, Jimmy stammered, "Don't bother, Mrs. . . ." — then catching himself in the midst of the forbidden address, paused, and with a blush like fever turned away to the window. "I mean . . . Grandma," he said quietly and then more fervently, "I wouldn't want you to go to any trouble on my account."

Millicent beamed. "It won't be any trouble," she said.

They were both startled to hear Lyddie's voice. Piercing, vibrating with anger, it carried all the way from the kitchen. "When I'm good and ready," she cried. "And all your bullying and nagging doesn't do the least good."

Millicent looked nervously toward the pantry door. "I should like to hear more about Sea Girt, Jim. Do you go bathing?"

"Sure," he replied, and the ensuing silence was again broken by his aunt's voice. "What right have you to criticize me? I can do what I like with the rest of my life. Just as much as you can. I have just as much right to stay here and look after Mother and some poor dumb animals that have been left to starve as you do. . . ."

"What time of day is best for bathing?" Millicent inquired. "Do you go in the morning?"

"Oh, any time. Morning, afternoon, any time but right after

a meal. You're not meant to swim for an hour after a meal. You get cramps and sink."

"Of course." Ordinarily Millicent would have avoided so anatomical a subject, but at the moment it seemed far more inviting than silence. "Only an hour now? It seems to me it used to be two hours. Yes, I'm quite sure that was the rule. You must wait two hours after luncheon before bathing."

"It is my concern," Lyddie shouted. "You're my brother and it pains me to see you degrading yourself. I *won't* be quiet. How can you do this to Mother? She knows. Don't you think for a moment she doesn't."

"Well, now," Millicent went on hastily, "what else is there that you do? Surely you can't bathe the whole day?"

"My bike," Jim said. "I ride my bike."

"Of course you do." Millicent turned to see Wilder fling open the pantry door and stand, looking back into the kitchen. He seemed calm except for his hands which trembled at his side.

"You know, Lyddie," he said evenly. "I rather think I will." He let the door swing closed and came into the drawing room. He glanced at Jimmy, saw that he was bewildered, a little frightened, and took the hand which Millicent held out to him. "Mother, I'm afraid we'll have to be moving along, Jimmy and I. It's gotten quite late."

She put her hand over his. "Oh no, Wilder," she pleaded. "It seems you've only just gotten here."

He smiled at her gently. "I've promised to get Jim back to town at a respectable hour." Withdrawing his hand, he said, "How about it, Jim? Are you nearly ready?"

Jimmy sprang to the hall door. "All ready," he announced. "My coat's just there on the piano stool."

"Well, then . . ." Wilder bent to kiss Millicent, and he felt her pluck beseechingly at his sleeves. Straightening, he smiled at her. "Thank you for the cold treatment, Mother. I'm feeling much better. I do believe I'm on the mend."

"When will you be out again?"

"Soon." He patted her arm. "Very soon."

Millicent glanced at Jimmy, who was fidgeting by the door, anticipating the signal for departure. "Are you going to the shore?"

"Most likely," Wilder replied. He was wondering whether to send Jimmy out to say good-by to Lyddie—if he might find her unequal to the formalities, in tears perhaps—when the pantry door opened and she appeared, flushed and tense.

"Jim?" she called in a shaky voice. "You're not going?"

He looked at his father, who nodded. "Yes," Jim replied. "We have to."

"You're not going without a kiss for your aunt?" Lyddie asked. There was a childish petulance in her voice.

In the silence which followed, Wilder seemed about to speak, but did not. Jimmy marched through the dining room where Lyddie, with a strained, unhappy smile, bent to kiss him. He was frightened by her embrace, which was unexpected. She clutched him convulsively, and he felt the cold moistness of her skin against his own.

"You'll come to see us again?" she asked as he backed away.

"Sure," he said and went quickly into the drawing room where he was dismayed to see his grandmother rising, eying him expectantly.

"Good-by . . . Grandma," he said, and as she leaned forward to accept his kiss he caught a whiff of the sick-sweet smell of age.

It was twenty minutes past four as they left the house and

the air was growing fresh, promising a cool evening. As they walked down the hill Jimmy paced happily at his father's side, trying for the long strides he needed to keep in step.

A stream, Gaddis Creek, wandered through Greenfield, and its course divided the old from the newer, more progressive, part of the town. Wilder and Jim paused on the stone bridge and looked down into the Gaddis' bed where a vigorous current whispered over smoothed pebbles.

"Daddy," Jimmy said. "Are they really going to make that room over for me?"

"They mean to. I expect they'll get as far as hanging a curtain or two. Would you like it? Do you want a room here in Greenfield?"

Jimmy saw something move in the shallows and, thinking it might be a fish, stepped up on the balustrade and leaned over the rail. He decided it was only a shadow. "It'd be dumb," he said. "I wouldn't ever use it."

"You can't tell."

With a defiance that surprised his father, Jimmy said, "I *can* tell. I wouldn't ever use it."

"Supposing I were to move out?"

"But you don't *want* to, do you? You don't like it here."

"I don't mind it." He looked up the hill they had descended. "I might have to, Jim."

"Why?"

Wilder wondered how much he might tell him—what good, what harm there was in sharing with so young a son this confidence. A boy approached on a bicycle and he waited until he had passed. "It's a matter of money, Jim. I don't know that I can afford to keep the little apartment in town any longer."

"Can't you tell Mr. Lazarus you need some more money?"

"No. The trouble's there at the office. They aren't paying

me as much as they used to. They're cutting me down."

Wilder, still in doubt as to the wisdom of this, watched Jimmy for some sign.

"Oh," Jimmy said. He turned to his father with a sobriety that Wilder found reassuring. "Well, if you were here. Sure. A room would be O.K. I could come out and stay sometimes."

Wilder, curiously moved, took Jimmy's arm, and they resumed their way quietly. At his side, Jimmy seemed to have grown. Stealing a glance, Wilder sensed that the moment had not been lost upon Jimmy either. He was walking as though on parade, with Company B straight as an arrow behind him.

To their right now were the modest athletic facilities of the Greenfield High School—some bleachers, a cinder track, goalposts.

"There's the football field," Wilder said. "Did you see that on your travels today?"

"Yes."

"On a Saturday afternoon in the fall you wouldn't know this place. They have a band and a drum majorette and cheerleaders. For the noise you'd think it was the Harvard-Yale game. Perhaps we'll go to one in October. Want to?"

"O.K.," he said without enthusiasm.

Wilder looked up at the school's façade. It was a functional, styleless structure of red brick and freshly painted white trim. "I've been by here once or twice at noon when school's getting out. There are some nice-looking youngsters—some boys and girls your age or a little older. Maybe we can find a way for you to meet some of them."

"It's all taken care of," Jimmy said in a voice edged with disdain that put Wilder in mind of Joe Massee's. "Dr. Seton's fixing me up."

Wilder laughed so that tears came and he regarded Jimmy

solemnly through them, and then he laughed again. "You win," he said, and they swung along together toward Patterson Avenue.

Arriving at the terminal which was, as Jimmy had noted, a recent one, they found that a bus would be leaving for Manhattan at twenty minutes to five, and they sat down on a bench to await it. A bus for Newark arrived, discharged some passengers, and departed. There were people on the street, strolling, looking in at the displays of the drugstore. A car, a battered station wagon, was at the curb, and a woman handed ice cream cones through one of its rear windows. A girl's head emerged. She wore a black beanie with the name of an orchestra leader embroidered on its brim. "Hey," she called to a boy on the sidewalk, "Where's Waldo?" They could not hear the boy's reply, but as the station wagon pulled away, into the stream of traffic, the girl shouted, "Well, have him call me," and her head bobbed inside.

Jimmy, who had been looking on with interest, turned to Wilder. "Maybe they ought to move," he suggested. "Over here. Over to a livelier part of town. Maybe they'd like it better."

Wilder nodded. "It would make sense all right for them to have a little modern house or an apartment that would be easy to heat and to care for. I think it's a fine idea, Jim. It's quite unsound for Mother and Lyddie to live on in that drafty evil-smelling old barn of a place."

"You mean that . . . dark brown smell?"

Wilder smiled. "That's a nice way to put it."

"What makes it smell like that?"

"I'm afraid it's Lyddie's cats. It's cat"—Wilder made a face —"cat mess."

"Doesn't she clean it up?"

"I guess so. Once in a while. But not enough. There're quite a bunch of them."

"Doesn't she smell it? Doesn't, uh . . . Grandma?"

"I suppose. But they're used to it. It just smells like home." He looked at his watch and saw it was twenty-five minutes to five. Getting up from the bench, he peered into the waiting room. "Would you wait here for a jiffy? I'll see if they can spare a timetable."

Several minutes later a brown bus, its destination, NEW YORK CITY—MIDTOWN TERMINAL, in white block letters over the windshield, turned into the nearest bay and with a sigh of compressed air paused and opened its door.

Entering the waiting room, Jimmy saw no sign of his father. A woman and an untidy little girl made for the door. At the counter a display of magazines and candy was surmounted by a fountain of vividly orange drink which sprayed continuously against its plastic dome. From behind this a tired man emerged and said gruffly, "New York bus."

To Jimmy's relief Wilder emerged from the telephone booth. He looked a bit bewildered.

"Daddy, come *on*," Jimmy called. "The bus is leaving."

It was a relatively new bus, and inside it smelled of leatherette and gleamed with chrome plate. Jimmy examined it with satisfaction before turning his attention out the window. There the last of Greenfield's business district—a dentist, an undertaker, a real estate and insurance office, a used car lot festooned with weathered pennants—passed, and they turned onto a highway where the traffic was heavy with trucking and passenger cars. Yet the bus moved rapidly, sometimes swaying with its speed, as the driver maneuvered with admirably superfluous skill through the congestion.

On the throughway crossing the meadows, Jimmy said,

"Why does she want so many cats?"

"I don't know. I suppose it's because she has no other outlet for her affection. People must have that you know. If they can't find some person they will find an animal to care for." Wilder looked at Jimmy who was staring at the Pennsylvania Railroad embankment half a mile away. "Do you understand that, Jimmy?"

He gave a little shrug, an oddly sophisticated gesture, which Wilder took to mean that he did not understand or else he did not care. In either case it was a dismissal, a rejection of Lyddie, and Wilder wondered if it was instinctive or if it might not be Alma's doing, if over the years she had not sowed Jim's heart with seeds of prejudice against Lyddie and his mother. It was natural enough that she should. Even so, he thought, it might be overcome.

Wilder brought his right foot onto his left knee, tightened the lace thoughtfully. "I have an idea you could do so much for them both. They'd accommodate you where they won't me. They're so anxious to please you—have you like them."

Jimmy gazed unhappily out the window. They were swinging in a wide arc, mounting the palisades, and Manhattan appeared suddenly. It seemed no real city at all but a cutout of tissue paper, flimsy spires against the lowering sun, that would flutter off on the next puff of wind.

"I wish they weren't," he said mournfully.

"You don't think you can like them back?"

"They act so nutty . . . oh, you know." Jimmy looked down at the school cap which he held in his hands. "When I was mowing the lawn she was afraid I was going to hurt something."

"Hurt what?"

"I don't know. Things in the grass I guess—bugs, mice,

moles. She made me mow around a molehill. And all that prancing around and singing those phony trills. What does she do that for?"

"She took voice once. In Colorado, when she was . . ." Wilder paused in midsentence, realizing that to Jim Lyddie was no complex of frustrations, of love and ambition gone awry, but simply "nutty" and that it would require more than the minutes which remained to him (a decade more likely) to persuade him otherwise. Then he began to wonder if in the end Jimmy's were not the kinder view, if Lyddie was not beyond eccentricity, if her unhappiness had not brought on a derangement, still minor, but inevitably deepening into real illness.

"Perhaps I make a mistake, pressing her as I do to go in and take a job. I keep thinking if she'd only get out of the house, mix with other people, take up some sort of routine that would draw her out of herself. . . ." He looked at Jimmy, again astonished to find himself confiding, asking advice really. Jimmy was intent, listening. "I'm sorry. I shouldn't unload all my troubles."

"It's all right," Jimmy said.

After a moment Wilder asked "How about Mother? Do you find her 'nutty' too?"

"Well. Not so nutty exactly. Of course she does talk funny. I don't know. She makes me feel I can't get my breath. Like I'm smothering or something."

"Yes," Wilder said. "I see." And in a way he did. He saw for example that his son was, in some respects, no longer a child. Between the tendons at the nape of Jimmy's neck there had once been a recess that Joe Massee had pointed out as ideal to accommodate a collar button. It was barely perceptible now. The once spindly neck that had given Jim a frail look as a little boy was filling out. The chin too was firm. What a wonderful thing, Wilder thought, it is to behold a child, serious-faced, contemplative, as Jimmy was now.

It was as an adult Jimmy had repulsed the siege they had laid to him today. He saw with astonishing clarity Millicent Stone through Jimmy's eyes, and it was not without terror that he viewed her bid for Jimmy's fealty. Whether it was Alma's doing or not, he saw a rightness in Jimmy's suspicion of fixing up "his" room, in the acquiring of young people for his inspection, for he saw now how unlikely it was that Jimmy would have a salutary effect on Greenfield—how likely that any effect would be entirely on Jim.

"You know, I think you're right," Wilder said. They were creeping around the huge hairpin approach to the tunnel, a link in the endless chain of traffic. He patted Jimmy on the arm. "Your instincts, if that's what they are, are in fine order. It's probably not a good idea for you to spend much time in Greenfield."

They were in the tunnel now, moving slowly, tail lights winking red on the tiles as drivers braked. "It's a dangerous place for a young man," Wilder added thoughtfully, and then brightening said, "Listen, call Mother whatever you like. If you can't do the Grandma go back to the Mrs. Stone." He smiled. "I'd prefer something besides 'your mother' though . . . if you can manage it."

Emerging from the tunnel, they were promptly locked in Manhattan traffic. Around them were steep trucks, the nearest stacked with crates of live poultry. Hundreds of chicken heads poked irritably through the slats, seemed to regard them accusingly. A line of boxcars rumbled across a trestle behind them. Overhead a traffic light changed its colors in vain. It seemed they might be here forever.

"What about Bi?" Wilder asked. "You don't find her nutty, do you?"

"No."

"You like her?"

Jimmy was absorbed in the chickens, one in particular that was pecking viciously at its neighbors. "She's O.K."

"Just O.K.?"

Jimmy seemed not to hear.

"If you could arrange things to suit yourself," Wilder asked, "would you see more of Bi—or less?"

"About the same."

"If she were around a lot of the time—would you mind?"

"Yes," he said urgently. "I wouldn't go much for that." But glancing sidewise at his father, he seemed to reconsider and added soberly, "I don't know. I guess I'd get used to it."

And then the bus was moving again, slowly, then swiftly through narrow, choked streets, past dark, windowless warehouses and the Tenth Avenue markets, and then with a last burst of speed into the asphalt honeycomb of the terminal.

"It's too late," Wilder was explaining to a sullen Jimmy. They had paused on Forty-second just west of Eighth while Wilder studied his watch. "It's five thirty or nearly that."

"But you *said* Chinatown. You said we could go."

"It would take us half an hour to just get there. Gran'll be wondering where we are." He saw the baby crossness coming, the whining and wheedling, and knew that any weakness on his part would only encourage it. "No. It's out of the question. We'll do Chinatown some other time."

"You always say that . . . some other time."

"Perhaps we won't then," Wilder said grimly, "if you prefer it that way." They resumed their course across town, and almost at once Wilder was sorry. He was sorry for the disappointment in Jim's face and that the day should end so. He had intended Chinatown and he felt a twinge of guilt about not going.

It seemed important now that things not end badly, that Jimmy be diverted and cheered. Fortuitously he spied a short distance ahead an army surplus cum sporting goods store. Jimmy resisted, his arm unyielding, his feet dragging, but Wilder urged him on toward the shop and presently they stood before the display.

The window dresser had rendered a campsite. There was an olive wall tent, its awning stretched on a pair of birch poles, a hand axe imbedded in a log, a fire (a light bulb hidden in kindling and red cellophane) over which the camper, a fatuously smiling clothing dummy in a lumber jacket cooked a rubber egg in an aluminum skillet.

"That's a dandy tent," Wilder said. "Look, it's got a floor, mosquito netting. How'd you like to go camping with a tent like that?"

Jimmy, who was having difficulty suppressing his interest, said, "Fine."

"As a matter of fact, I've got a tent something like that. It's still in the attic in Greenfield. We'll get it out sometime and put it up."

"You do?" Jimmy looked at his father, the reproach fading from his eyes. "I wish we'd thought of it today."

Wilder nodded in agreement. "You know we'll have to go camping sometime. I used to camp a lot when I was a boy. We'd go on canoe trips." He turned to Jimmy. "Say. The old canoe in Sea Girt. Is it still all right?"

"It's in the garage. It's on saw horses."

"I wonder if it leaks. Do you suppose it would do for us if

we were to go on a canoe trip—you and I?"

"Hey, you know what?" Jimmy chewed his lips with excitement. "We could go tomorrow, maybe. We could go for a little camping trip—just for the day."

"Yes," Wilder said and began to urge him from the window, but Jimmy had rooted to the pavement. "The only trouble is I may not get down early enough." He moved off, letting go of Jimmy's arm, sensing he would follow.

Jimmy reached out and caught Wilder's arm, holding on while he surveyed the adjoining window which held a mountain of camp gear—of packs and blankets, fishing tackle, knives, lanterns and cooking kits. "Then we could go on Monday," he insisted. "Monday's a holiday."

Wilder glanced at his watch. "C'mon, Jim. C'mon now."

"But couldn't we? On Monday?"

"Sure. I guess so. I don't see why not."

They resumed their way across Forty-second Street, Jimmy lagging, looking into windows hopefully, complaining that his father was setting too fast a pace for proper bumming.

They did pause just east of Times Square, where a pitchman had set up the fraudulent game of the dancing dolls. His eye wary for the patrolman, he was dropping the crepe paper figures onto the sidewalk where, inexplicably, they danced a furious jig as though they too knew they had but a moment to perform.

"Only half a dollar." The pitchman held a thin yellow envelope toward Jim and Wilder.

"No thanks," Wilder said, and when the pitchman had turned away, Wilder pointed out the man's confederate, a stoop-shouldered youth who stared morosely at the sparse audience. "Watch his finger," Wilder whispered, and following his father's glance, Jim saw that finger moving in time to the dance and then made out the nearly invisible thread which gave the doll its motion.

As they moved off Jimmy looked over his shoulder and saw a woman buying an envelope. He marveled at the cleverness and the simplicity of the fakery, at the ease with which the gullible were hoodwinked. It was delightful—that he had escaped, that he "knew." He laughed and he looked at his father with admiration and felt one with him. This was more like it. Now this was *bumming*.

They turned uptown on the Avenue of the Americas and at Forty-fourth Street encountered the first of the shops that dealt in souvenirs of the city, practical joke apparatus and sleight-of-hand tricks. Jimmy could stand by the hour before the window of such a store, appraising each item, visualizing the effect of the dribble glass or the ink spot on Alma or some-one at school. And a month ago, in just such a place as this one, Wilder had bought him the vanishing handkerchief, a cylinder with elastic attached which enabled him to make a handkerchief disappear from his fist.

"Look, Dad." Jimmy pointed out Dr. Callini's wand. "It says you can do six tricks with it."

"That's a lot," Wilder said. "C'mon."

Through the door of the shop Jim could see the proprietor idle at the counter. "He's alone in there. Let's get him to show us one of the tricks, Dad. Just one."

"We'd have to buy it."

Jimmy, who saw no harm in that, said, "No, we wouldn't."

"Come on now," Wilder ordered sharply. He was annoyed.

As they proceeded uptown, Jimmy sulked. The disappoint-ment on his face was, if anything, plainer than before. Wilder read it, the rebuke for depriving him of Dr. Callini's wand, of Chinatown, the suspicion that answered his vague promises.

He saw this and deplored it and then for the moment dismissed it. Or rather it was crowded from his mind.

He turned Jimmy into the RCA building arcade, and in walking through it they hesitated a moment before the window of a cutlery-and-gadget shop where Jimmy was hypnotized by a bright red campers' lantern. It was a rectangular box with a black pistol grip and large, plated reflector. A poster claimed for it a quarter-mile range and showed in four drawings dramatic scenes of its usefulness.

"Dad, look! Look at that lantern."

"Yes. It is a beauty."

"With a quarter-mile range. Wow! How far is that? That's all the way to Fifth Avenue, isn't it?"

"I guess so. Something like that."

"Couldn't we get it?" Jimmy pleaded fervently. "For when we go camping?"

Wilder urged him on. "We'll think about it—when we're ready to go camping."

"It might not be here then." Jimmy dragged behind. "They might have sold it."

"I guess we'll have to take that chance," Wilder said and started him toward the revolving door.

Out in Rockefeller Plaza there were spring flowers, banks of red and white tulips recently set out in the broad stone tubs, and overhead the flags of a score of nations snapped in the fresh breeze. It was altogether a handsome sight.

"Well, look who's here!" Wilder said and pointed out Bibi Winter, who sat alone by a pool, reading. With Jimmy still lagging he approached her and raising his hat said, "Excuse me, Miss, but we're strangers in town. Could you direct us to a nice clean place where we could have a cup of tea?"

Bibi, looking up from her pocket-sized magazine, gasped,

"Jimmy! Wilder! Whatever in the *world?*"

"We're on a bumming tour," Wilder explained, "just sort of moseying around looking at things."

"We saw this camping lantern in the RCA building there," Jimmy said. "It has a quarter-mile beam. If it was nighttime we could light up Saks with it. Right from here. You want to see it, Bibi?"

"I'd love to see it."

"What about a cup of tea?" Wilder proposed. "I was quite serious about that."

Bibi gave Jimmy a conspiratorial smile that seemed to say she wasn't forgetting the lantern, and then to Wilder she said, "All right, what about the Café Français down there? That's clean."

Wilder looked unhappy.

"Oh, it's not expensive just for tea. There's a limit to what they can charge for a cup of tea."

It was not a popular hour, and descending the broad steps to the sunken promenade they found only a few tables occupied. There were some foreign officers in light blue airline uniforms, and there was a party of ladies who might have been schoolteachers from upstate. But when the tea came it was hot and good, and the cinnamon toast, wrapped handsomely in a napkin, was inviting. To Wilder's surprise he found it pleasant here, with the shadows creeping up the sandstone above, a brilliant sun still gilding the spires of St. Patrick's, the inconstant breeze flirting with the fringe of the umbrella, sometimes bringing them the finest spray from the great fountain beneath splendid Prometheus, and around them the sound of splashing.

"Isn't it a wonderful thing—the sight and sound of falling water. I wonder why it's so lovely to the ear." Wilder addressed them both. "What are the associations? What does it make you think of?"

"It makes me thirsty," Bibi said and blandly poured herself more tea.

Wilder laughed. "Jimmy?"

"A canoe."

Wilder looked at the fountain. "Down the rapids? Are you going canoeing in a waterfall?"

"In the inlet. Up at the head there. In the reeds where it's hard to find where the stream goes."

Wilder smiled. "Now come on. That's not a fountain association. That was there already. 'Fess up. What does the fountain make you think of?"

"A canoe," he persisted.

"All right, have it your way. Where are you going in it? Up to the old mill?"

"Coming back. We're trying to get home and I'm up in the front."

"The bow."

"The bow, then. We're paddling as hard as we can, but it doesn't do any good because we're lost in the tall reeds, and it's getting darker all the time."

Wilder smiled. "Ahh, *now* I see. Now I understand the association."

"I don't," Bibi said.

"We need a lantern, don't we, Jim?" Wilder laughed. "A red lantern with a quarter-mile beam."

"Daddy, can I *please?*"

"I'm sure you've got lanterns by the dozen in Sea Girt."

"No, we don't. Not a red one. Not one like that."

Wilder said sharply, "Now, Jimmy, don't. Don't act like a baby."

"I'm not." There was a whine in his voice that was certain to exasperate Wilder. "I'm not acting like a baby."

"Come on now." Opening her purse, Bibi glanced at herself critically in its mirror but made no adjustments. "Let's go take a look at it. I want to see what all the fuss is about."

Wilder made a sign to the waiter for a check. "It's just a lantern. Just a red lantern."

"It isn't just a lantern," Jimmy said with new hope. "It's . . . Bibi, wait'll you *see*." And as they left the café he ran ahead of them, dancing up the steps, turning back to make sure they followed, urging them onward.

When they came at last to the cutlery shop and stood all three looking through the window at the lantern. Bibi said, "Well, I see what you mean. It is a lovely lantern. How much is it, do you suppose?"

"Seven dollars," Jimmy said soberly. "It says so there on the card."

"Well," she said. "That's high for a lantern . . . but it is a beaut. I'll buy it for you."

"Whoopee!" Jimmy took his cap off and put it back on his head several times.

"Now, Bi, that's silly," Wilder said. "You mustn't do that."

"But I want to, Wilder."

"Daddy, *please*."

From his breast pocket Wilder produced a handkerchief which he unfurled and waved overhead. "You win. *I'll* buy the lantern. Come on."

Riding uptown on the D train Jimmy sat between Wilder and Bibi, the box containing the lantern open on his lap. He stroked the slippery-smooth red enamel, the shining plated handle and reflector, and from time to time he took the lantern out, and aiming it carefully brought the quarter-mile beam to bear on a section of the floor. It made a gleaming white disc there in the dirt and Jimmy was happy. He felt that he and this bright light would never part.

"We could have taken a taxi," Bibi was saying to Wilder. "It would have come to about the same thing. A dime more, maybe."

"Yes," Wilder replied, "or I could have hired a car and chauffeur. They're quite reasonable now—ten dollars or so an hour. It mightn't have come to much more than the taxi."

Bibi didn't answer. She stared grimly down at her immaculate white gloves, rubbing the seams together, until they got to Columbus Circle.

It was seven o'clock and nearly dark as they walked up Central Park West. Some children came out of the park, calling to one another piercingly, their roller skates clattering on the pavement. Under a canopy a man in dinner clothes was getting into a cab, and a fat woman with a hard face walked her tiny dog.

As they approached Alma's building Wilder found himself thinking of Joe Massee. He wondered where he was and thought of the last time he had seen him. It was in the summer of 1948, about a year after Catherine had died. Joe had asked him to come by The Players.

Wilder had heard from Alma that Joe was planning to leave her, and he arrived with the most fragile of hopes he might prevent it.

But Joe had said, "No lectures please. I don't feel like any lectures."

"But it's senseless, Joe. It's destructive to all of us, to Alma, of course, and most of all to you."

Joe had smiled and said, "I'm in love. I'm in love with a girl half my age. Younger. She's twenty-seven. Of course, I'm a fool.

It doesn't matter. I've always been a fool. I'm alive when I'm with this girl. Everything is intense. There's pleasure and pain in every minute. That's the way I like it. Understand?" He took the cigar out of his mouth and tipped the ash into the brass tray. "If you want to know what it's like when you get to my age—I'm nearly sixty—I'll tell you. I can still satisfy a woman." He looked at Wilder. "I wish you the same."

"Thanks."

"When I don't have this girl to look forward to, the day is dead before it starts. I don't want to get up and I turn to torturing my wife. I love her and I don't like to do that. She doesn't understand that, that I can love her and still make her life miserable and go to bed with Jackie. Very few women understand that. Maybe you don't either."

"Yes, I think I do."

"Good. You want a drink?"

"Yes."

Wilder watched Joe signal the bartender to bring Wilder a whisky to match his own. "Are you going to marry her?"

"I don't know."

"You don't see it as a permanent thing?"

"I don't see anything as permanent. Do you?"

Wilder watched Joe for a moment, and then he smiled and said, "You know something? You're not only irresponsible, you're crazy. And you know something else? I envy you, Joe. I really do."

"Good." Joe raised his glass. "I'm glad," he said and drank to Wilder's health.

Arriving at the entrance to 312, Alma's apartment house, Jimmy said to Wilder, "Aren't you coming up?"

"No. We've got to be getting along."

Jimmy pointed the light across the street, shined it into the trees. "Hey, look at that. I bet it will go twice as far." In swinging the beam uptown, it fell upon the hood and windshield of a passing taxicab.

"Look out, now," Wilder said. "You'll blind somebody with that thing. You could cause an accident."

"Could I? No kidding?"

"Come on. Gran'll think we're lost." He looked at his watch. "Good Lord, it's after seven. Move along now. You've got to help get ready for an early start in the morning. Hop to it."

"O.K." Jimmy pecked dutifully at Bibi's proffered, perfumed cheek and shook hands with his father. "Don't forget you're coming down early tomorrow. As early as you can."

Bibi looked quickly at Wilder, unable to contain her surprise and displeasure. "You're going to Sea Girt tomorrow?"

Wilder frowned. "I'll try to, Jim. I'll do the best I can. I do have some things to tend to."

"I'll get the canoe out. I'll make sure it's O.K., that it doesn't leak or anything."

Wilder turned him, headed him for the entrance. "That's a good idea. Now off you go."

With his hand on the door Jimmy turned, and they all waved. "See you tomorrow," he called and disappeared within.

Wilder and Bibi crossed the avenue and walked slowly, silently, along the edge of the park, looking over the low stone parapet where the young trees and shrubbery were shading to purple and black. Despite the moving belts of traffic and the strands of milky bubbles of light that crisscrossed it, the park now, as night fell, was forbidding, a dark well of fear here in the heart of the city.

"You're not going to Sea Girt tomorrow, are you, Wilder?"

"I don't know. Perhaps. I've half promised Jim. You saw."

"But on the phone you said you hadn't made plans."

"I haven't."

They walked along and it seemed to each that all the world had stopped. The noise and sights of the city receded leaving them alone in space and time, in a void where the only sound was the click of Bibi's heels on the pavement.

At the corner of Sixty-third Street she seized his arm. In the greenish glare of the street lamp her face was shadowed and ghostly.

"Have you decided?" she asked. "About us? Please don't hold out on me. I couldn't stand it. Tell me now."

"I haven't decided anything."

She sighed deeply. It was in truth a sigh of relief, but it seemed to Wilder one of exasperation with him. "All right," she said. "But you mustn't go off and leave me to wonder. Not for two whole days. I'd go wild. I really would, Wilder. I think I'd go right out of my mind."

Wilder took her arm and they recrossed Central Park West and walked another block downtown.

"Are you hungry?" she asked.

"Not especially. We had a late luncheon in Greenfield."

"Well, let's go home," she said. "We'll have a drink and I'll make you an omelette while we decide where to go tomorrow."

"Go? Are we going somewhere?"

"I've got to get out of this filthy city. All day I've felt in prison. I want to breathe some fresh air and see a tree or a bit of ocean."

"For the day? You want to go someplace for the day?"

"Overnight."

"This is the middle of the holiday weekend, Bi."

"There's always someplace. You know places at the shore."

"The shore?" Wilder paused on the curb, waiting for the light to change.

"Now you're going to put me off," Bibi said, her voice ragged. "You're so exasperating, Wilder. You've made up your mind that you aren't even going to try." The light changed and they crossed the street. "Haven't you?"

"No. I haven't made up my mind to anything."

"You won't try. I know. You never do. Nothing's worth the effort to you. You just drift along like an old log in the river. It's what makes you miserable—and everybody around you."

"Would you tell me how I can expect to be any less miserable in some crowded place at the shore shelling out twenty-five dollars for a couple of rooms?"

"Not you. It's me that would be less miserable. I want us to be together someplace. I want to be with you. Can't you understand that?" Without waiting for an answer she turned into a doorway. He saw her searching in her purse for a handkerchief, then heard her soft, heartbroken sobbing.

12.

AS Jimmy had learned, the first taste of any delight was the sweetest, and Sea Girt was no exception. All in an hour he had rediscovered summer. Wiggling open the drawers (he had forgotten how they stuck) he had found and donned summer uniform—khaki shorts, a faded blue polo shirt, sneakers. From the sleeping porch he smelled the pines, watched their feathery tips stir in the fresh-washed sunlight. The world was close here. In the stillness he heard the chirping of the awning pulley below, the thwang of the back door, the hillyer-hillyer of a bluejay and, away off, the burst and sigh of surf. All about him some sight or sound or smell beckoned.

Thundering down the stairs, he found Alma in the kitchen instructing a slim colored girl from Manasquan in the stowing of provisions.

"Did you bring everything out of the car?" she asked him.

"No. I think there's more. Some blankets and stuff."

"The blankets are for your father's bed. Violet'll be going upstairs in a few minutes."

Jimmy nodded vacantly, passed through the kitchen and onto the back porch.

"Where are you going?"

"The garage. I want to see if my bike's all right."

"Don't be long." She looked at the clock in the panel of the range. "The train gets in at ten after three."

"I'll be back in plenty of time." He let himself out the back door.

He noticed how the hollies had bushed out into this path which, he thought, he could run blindfolded, and how the new fall of needles were bright gold on the dark ones beneath.

The bike rested on its handlebars and he righted it, rolled it carefully out into the driveway, and pumped up the tires. Returning the pump to the workbench, he saw the canoe, and he pushed open the other two garage doors to examine its bottom. The paint, he saw, was flaking in places and there was a spot near the bow where the canvas was bare, but it wasn't too bad. Poking his head underneath, he saw that the paddles were there, resting on the thwarts. He passed his arm through the cobwebs and shuddered as they clung to his skin.

As he carried the blankets into the house he wondered if he could persuade Alma and Violet to one end of the canoe and if between the three of them they could get it out into the light.

At the depot a half-dozen cars were parked alongside Alma's green 1956 Chevrolet, and she chatted with a neighbor while Jimmy stood lookout at the trackside.

It was a long train, eight coaches, and as it arrived Jimmy tried to catch a first glimpse of his father—in the vestibule perhaps, behind the conductor, valise in hand, waving, or through a window, a silhouette moving down the aisle.

"Do you see him?" Alma asked joining Jimmy.

"No. Not yet."

The train stopped and the passengers alighted—a woman and two children from the first car, an elderly man, two colored women, a soldier, from the cars opposite, three men carrying hand luggage from the rear cars. Jimmy inspected them hopefully, rising on his toes, ready to run, but none of them, he saw, was Wilder. They were already turning toward other cars, embracing other children, other women.

He looked forward along the platform, then back again. No, no one else. The brakeman raised his hand in signal, climbed aboard and the wheels began to turn.

"Well," Alma said. "I guess your father missed this one."

"I guess he did." They walked back to the car and when they got in he asked "How soon is the next one?"

Alma took the timetable from her purse and adjusting her glasses studied it carefully. "Well," she said, "there's a Jersey Central at quarter past four."

"He'll be on that."

Alma started the car. "If not, there's another Penn train at quarter to six."

When they got home Alma consented to help with the canoe and conscripted Violet. Together, they managed to get it onto the wheelbarrow, out into the driveway alongside the rose of Sharon bushes, and back onto the sawhorses which had supported it. There, Jimmy examined the worn spot, found the canvas was not broken, and decided some paint could do it no harm. He loosened up a brush and thinned some green paint they had bought for the porch glider. He painted a neat square over the worn patch. When he had finished it was time to go and meet the quarter-past-four train.

Wilder was not on it, and returning home once more, Alma suggested Jimmy take his bike and go look for some of his friends.

As he rose off the saddle and let his weight carry the pedal down, the bike surged forward with a familiar crunch of tires in the gravel. He felt a new power in his arms and legs, a sense of great things in store now, and tomorrow and all summer long.

At the bathing pavilion he paused, one foot on the wooden steps, and frowned at a new sign with a list of recent ordinances about bathing and cycling. The sun was low and the boardwalk cast a long shadow in the sand. It looked cold on the beach, but a cluster of sweatered and shorted teen-age girls lay sprawled on blankets, still occupied with the browning of their skins.

Some older boys gathered around a convertible whose identity (it looked mostly Ford) had been disguised by body-shop improvisations. Jimmy knew two of them by name but did not risk the possible snub involved in greeting them. He proceeded south along the sidewalk and up Philadelphia Boulevard to the Elies' but no one was home.

He went west then, along Third Avenue to Baltimore Boulevard and the Schulers', where he found Bill sitting on the grass watching a new puppy. Although they were good friends and had not seen one another since early September they wasted no time on greeting or reporting on the winter just past but turned instead to thoughts of the present.

"Dad and I are going on a canoe trip tomorrow," Jim said.

"Your dad down?"

"He's coming."

"When?"

"Quarter to six. Say, I've got to be home by five thirty." He started up the steps to look at the clock in the kitchen.

"The time?" Bill made a display of his wrist watch.

"Hey, where'd you get that?"

"My birthday." He demonstrated the stop watch hand. "It's like Dad's, only smaller."

Jimmy sat down beside Bill, and they turned their attention to the puppy who was chewing unenthusiastically on a child's baseball bat, watching them hopefully for some activity.

"I've got this lantern Dad bought me yesterday. It's pretty good. It's got a quarter-mile beam."

"I'll come over tomorrow and see it."

"You better come early. We'll be going on this canoe trip."

"Where you going in the canoe?"

"Up the inlet. Maybe as far as the Old Mill if we can get there. You think we can get up that far?"

"You can't in a rowboat. We got stuck up there in the marsh last summer."

"You can go places in a canoe you can't in a rowboat. A canoe is better for exploring—and camping." He picked up a stick and threw it a few feet away, but the puppy only eyed it speculatively. "This trip, it's a sort of a trial run for a camping trip we might be taking."

"No kidding."

Jimmy nodded and had another look at Bill's watch. "I gotta go," he said rising. "I don't want to be late." And he left impressively. A bare leg flying across the saddle, he made a wide sweep out the drive and into the street.

Alma decided not to meet the train that arrived at seven twenty. She sat with her grandson on the front porch and as darkness fell heard the clink of china and silver as Violet set the table within.

"But he did say he was coming?" Alma asked.

"Well I *think* so." Jimmy was sprawled in a fan-backed wicker chair, his chin on his chest, his legs wide apart. "I mean he said he'd try to get down early. He had some stuff to do at the office."

"It looks to me as if he isn't coming," Alma said. "He probably got tied up with something or other and forgot to call."

"Yes. I guess that's it." He sat up a little for a car was coming down the street. He saw the headlights approaching, thought the car was slowing, thought it might be a taxi. But it passed, went by steadily, and soon it was quiet again, and there was a sound of a breeze stirring in the pine boughs and from across the street a radio playing.

Alma arose and went to the door. "Violet," she called. "There'll just be the two of us for dinner. Mr. Stone's not coming."

"Yes, ma'am," Violet replied, and Alma sat down, slowly gathering up her knitting, giving Violet time to clear away Wilder's place.

They heard footsteps half a block away, and they both sat very still, listening. It was nearly dark and they couldn't see who it was, but the tread was firm and it was coming from the right direction, from the station. If it was Wilder, if it was any-one coming in, there would be a hesitation as he turned and then the different sound of his shoes on the winding gravel path as he came through the privet hedge and toward them.

Jimmy listened so attentively that it seemed the man did hesitate. He was sure he did hear the first step upon the gravel —so sure that for a while, for the time it took the stranger to walk the length of the hedge, for the sound of his footsteps to begin to fade, he refused to believe that the man was not his father.

"Supper's ready," Violet said shyly from the door.

"All right." Alma got up from the glider, and turning on the porch light found its globe cradled the remains of a score of last year's insects. "We'll have to get after that in the morn-ing," she said to Violet.

"Yes, ma'am."

Turning at the door which Violet held open for her, Alma saw that Jimmy had not moved. "Come on, Jimmy. Supper's on the table."

"I don't want any."

"Of course you do. You mustn't let it get you down, darling. Maybe he'll come tomorrow."

He shook his head.

"Well, anyway, I don't want to eat supper all by myself."

And after a moment he rose from the chair and followed her slowly into the house.

13.

THE DAY began inauspiciously under a cold fog that during the night had crept in off the sea. Along the Jersey shore golfers, swimmers, picnickers, sun bathers peered dourly at this ghostly flotilla adrift in the streets and predicted it would burn off promptly—but by nine o'clock it had become a thin drizzle.

Jimmy took little comfort from Alma's observation that it was just as well his father hadn't come down to this dreary weather; nevertheless, when Billy Schuler turned up at ten to see the lantern, Jimmy explained it was the weather that had postponed the canoeing and his father's visit until the following weekend.

When Jimmy was alone he put the lantern back on his bureau and laid himself down on the bed that Violet had made up for Wilder. Alma found him there a few moments later. He seemed to be asleep, but he rolled over when she spoke his name.

"It's stopped raining," she said. "Aren't you going out?"

He turned his head to look out and saw that although the needles were still dripping the air was clear.

"No. Not now. Later maybe. I might go over to the Elies'." He rolled back away from her, as though he intended going to sleep.

"Are you all right?" she asked. "Do you feel all right?"

"Sure. I feel fine."

Alma's hand reached out automatically, and as it touched his forehead, he pushed it away with a quick, savage thrust.

"Jimmy!" Alma cried.

"Just leave me alone. Don't touch me."

Alma stood by the bed for several minutes. They were both still, and in the quiet they heard a sigh of fresh wind and the sprinkling of rain it blew onto the roof of the sleeping porch.

"I've got to get some things," Alma said. "I need some things from the drugstore. I'd forgotten. I cleaned out the medicine cabinet in the fall. Do you want to come?"

"No."

"I was thinking we could go for a little drive. We could see what's at the movies. If there's something good we might go tonight."

He didn't answer, and Alma left him then and went down to the desk in the living room where she had been compiling her shopping list, and presently she heard him coming downstairs accelerating as he came and she smiled briefly with her victory.

Alma was a fair if fitful driver, but Jimmy, a perfectionist in such matters, was unable to withhold occasional criticism.

"You're riding the clutch again," he pointed out as she turned the green Chevrolet into Ocean Avenue.

She took this as a favorable sign and, instead of being cross as she sometimes was, moved her foot quickly from the pedal and said "Why, so I am. Thanks, honey."

For a holiday there was not much traffic, but Alma drove slowly to observe this familiar landscape, on the alert for innovations. There was a for-sale sign on the Borden cottage, and although the Bordens were the barest of acquaintances, the thought that they had gone away distressed her. It crossed her mind that they might have bought another house. But it was Borden's health more likely—or rather his lack of it. He had been ailing she recalled.

But farther down the street, and as though to comfort her, some potted geraniums appeared. They were in freshly painted white tubs so well remembered from previous seasons and signified the return of a family named Pilcher. And there was Mr. Fritz, the plumber, returning to his truck for a wrench and the same baker's boy as last summer (Harry, was it?) and some children's bathing suits on a line. These things cheered her and led her to believe the ravages of the winter had not been as great as she feared.

To Jim, change and the lack of it were equally acceptable. A new house going up at the foot of Beacon Boulevard would require immediate investigation. There was untold promise for a scavenger in the piles of scrap surrounding it. At the Inlet Garage they had changed the brand of gasoline, and there were shiny new pumps and an electric sign, but the compressed-air hose had not been altered.

Crossing the bridge, he looked seaward and saw the inlet was closed. A continuous shelf of sand stretched across its mouth—from Sea Girt light to the Spring Lake fishing pier. The sky was still overcast, but here in this widening expanse of sea and sand and dune it seemed bright, and overhead the sun was beginning to make itself felt, drying out the oppressive humidity.

Looking to the west, through Alma's window he beheld the main body of Wreck Pond. There was the mucky black southern shore where, if his father had come, they might now be launching the canoe. A mile beyond he could make out the narrowing channel as it meandered through the marsh, disappearing under the railroad bridge and into the scrub and piny woodlands to the west.

Coming into Spring Lake he could see some guests on the porch of the Allaire. Ladies were in the majority. They were rocking and reading and looking out at the weather prospects. He saw the flag flying from the peak of the Monmouth, a long blue streamer with the name spelled out in white letters. It folded and unfolded lazily against the gray sky.

Alma found a parking place in front of Hills', and they looked eagerly to see what was at the Ritz. To their disappointment it was *Careless Love* with Sheree North, and the stills in the lobby were not encouraging.

"We'll see what's at the Community," Alma said.

While she ordered the toilet articles Jimmy wandered among the tables, looking through their glass lids at displays of cosmetics, and when Alma came with her package wrapped neatly in lavender paper, he said, "Can I have a cone?"

"It's nearly eleven. It'll spoil your lunch."

"Please."

"All right." She dug into her purse for change.

Outside they paused to look at the sky again. What had been a thick, still blanket was now stirring, seeming to creep westward. Across the street a girl in white shorts emerged from the Monmouth's tennis house. She too glanced up at the sky, then peeled the cover from her racket and hit a ball against the bang board.

Alma turned onto the Ocean Drive, and they moved slowly past the long, sweeping porches of the Monmouth and the Essex and Sussex, where guests were sitting and strolling, standing in groups to chat. The lawn, freshly cut, was a carpet sloping gently to the sea. On the beach a man in hip boots was surf-casting, and some children stood nearby looking into his basket. And here and there along the boardwalk couples in raincoats promenaded.

At the Bath and Tennis Club an optimistic beach boy was setting out an umbrella, shaking the rain out of it, stretching it, jabbing its point deep in the sand, and rocking it back and forth to secure it.

"I'd like to have you join the Bath and Tennis Club sometime," Alma observed. "Would you like to?"

He recalled she had said this before in passing here and licked a drip off the outside of the cone. "Sure, I guess so."

"It would be a good place to learn to play tennis. If you want to learn to play tennis. Do you?"

"Sure. I don't mind."

She looked at him crossly. "Well, you'll have to be more enthusiastic than that."

He shrugged and looked at the cone. "I'd like to learn how to play tennis. What do you want me to do? Jump through the roof or something?"

Alma took a last glance at the awnings over the terrace where they sometimes had dances, at the enclosed pool with its high diving board, at the courts where they had the matches in midsummer. "And you might meet some nice people there, too—some young people you'd like. I don't know." She looked at him speculatively and found him absorbed in the cone. "Well. We'll see. Maybe next year. We'll look into it."

"Yes," he said. "That's a good idea."

Although she had intended to turn inland to the center of Spring Lake, Alma continued along the shore, past the familiar landmarks of the Sunday drive, the awesome banks and hedges that hid the Chesebrough and Roebling houses and thence across the bridge, out of propriety, into the sudden blowziness of Belmar. Belmar was all weathered bathhouses and gaudy boarding houses elbowing each other for a place near the shore.

Here there were people in bathing suits. Some brave ones were in the water. Others, in sweat shirts, passed a football on the beach, and the boardwalk stands were already clustered with customers gripping pop bottles and paper plates.

At Avon, Alma turned inland along a street where the houses were named "Ma-Jo" and "Dunrovin" and "Snuggery" and (though it had long ceased to amuse her, Alma continued to point it out to visitors) "Mortgage Manor."

Then having come this far, she turned right, went farther up the coast, past Bradley Beach, the forbidding, gloomy gates to Ocean Grove, and on into the city of Asbury Park. Here the weather was discouraging no one. In the lagoon tiny electric boats chuffed around an oval course while apprehensive children gripped their steering gear.

From the skee-ball parlors and the auction rooms and the carousel and the candy counters, where mechanical arms pulled and stretched at lime-colored salt water taffy, came a ringing of bells and a midway hum of voices that was momentarily cheering.

"Hey," Jimmy said pointing to a billboard. "It's *Submarine.* They've got *Submarine* at the Mayfair."

"Oh dear. Do you really want to see that?"

"Yes."

"Are you sure we didn't see it? Isn't that the one where the destroyer runs into them and they're down on the bottom for such a long time?"

"No-o-o," he said. "That's an old one. My gosh that was *U-Boat* with Brian Donlevy."

"Well, it seems to me if you've seen one submarine picture you've seen them all."

"But, Mom, this is an *atomic* submarine."

"Well," she sighed. "If that's *really* the one you want to see . . ."

"It is." Jimmy smiled, satisfied with a job well done, as the Chevrolet's nose turned toward Sea Girt and a luncheon for which the cone had not lessened his interest.

There was no question about it now. The sun was certainly burning its way through the overcast. Its dull reflection was appearing in shop windows and upon the polished surfaces of the cars of which there was suddenly an annoying prevalence. The noon hour and the sun's promise had brought out the motorists in force. Laden with picnic baskets and beach balls and the brightest expectations, the holiday makers were on the road.

Noting it was nearly twelve thirty, that she was still creeping and stopping through the business districts, Alma grew impatient and in Bradley Beach took a left turn. She headed back toward the shore road, which she recalled as free of traffic, hoping it would prove the quicker route home.

The street into which she had turned was called Surf Avenue, and it was lined with vaguely familiar private houses. They were all large, four-square, with wide porches and fresh awnings, and they managed to look like so many houseboats drawn up at a wharf.

At the foot of the street Alma paused and looking into Ocean Drive was disappointed to find a continuous stream of cars, moving slowly just as on the back road.

"Oh dear," she said. "I do hope Violet has the sense to take the chicken out of the oven."

As they waited for a break in the line of traffic, Jimmy saw the sign hanging from a cedar post. It was cut from plywood in the likeness of a bird in flight, and it read *Sea Gull Inn*.

A path, lined with clamshells, led to a tan Victorian house which one entered by a heavy, oval-windowed front door.

On the porch was a high-backed rattan settee. It was painted green and it had orange cushions, and sitting in one end of it, holding in his lap a bathing suit rolled in a towel, was his father.

"Hey," Jimmy said, sitting up. "That's Dad. Up there on the porch."

Alma glanced. "No, it isn't." She put the car into gear and turned into the line of traffic. As the Sea Gull Inn passed from his view Jimmy was still craning backward, staring at its porch.

"But it *was*, Mom. It was Dad and Bibi Winter. They were there on the porch."

"It wasn't," Alma replied. "I saw the man you meant. He looked like your father a little, but it wasn't."

Jimmy stared at Alma and saw that she was gripping the wheel as though the car might at any moment leap out of control and glaring at the crawling traffic ahead with a curious fierceness.

And then, all in an instant, the sun came out, dispelling the thin clouds that remained, turning a gray world into a bright one, sending the holiday hordes scurrying across the Chevy's path to the pure white sand and the glistening blue sea. He slumped down in his seat, and neither of them spoke for the rest of the journey home.

From the bottom of the stairs Alma called to say that luncheon was now on the table, and in answer there was a pounding. She called again. There was no reply, and she went up to find Jimmy on the sleeping porch. There was a hammer in his hand, the utility hammer that was kept in the kitchen drawer. He was on his knees. His small face, so delicate of feature, seemed strangely coarse—his lips drawn in over his teeth, flattening the tiny nose. His eyes were wide and dry. Spread out before him were the bits of glass and metal that had been his lantern.

"Come on, Jim," Alma said. "Lunch is ready."

14.

WILDER STONE paused in front of Alma's house. He waved to a man across the street who stood admiring a bed of cannas. He noted the evenness of Alma's privet hedge and guessed she had had its initial trim done by a professional before turning it over for the balance of the season to Jimmy's well-intentioned shears.

He turned into the gravel path and started up toward the house. Through the trees he could see the car parked in the clearing near the garage. It was a quarter to seven and although still daylight the sun was gone, and the thick growth of pine and cedar trees which surrounded the house cast long dark shadows onto the porch. He couldn't be sure there was anyone there.

He whistled—four notes descending—the gook whistle from his own school days. He had taught it to Jim and they used it sometimes to find one another in a crowd. There was no answer, but seeing Jim's bike leaning against a tree, he whistled again. He heard the screen door close.

"Hello?" he called. "Jimmy? Gran?" He continued up the path and stopped with one foot on the bottom step, discovering that there was indeed someone on the porch. Alma Massee sat on the glider, rocking it gently with her heel. She smoothed a pair of Jimmy's socks in which she had been making repairs and looked up at him, squinting somewhat as though she didn't recognize him.

"Well," he said, "well, Gran." Normally he would have bent to place a kiss on her cheek, but he had received the warning and instead sat down in the wicker chair across from her.

"I'm sorry I didn't make it yesterday."

Alma stopped her rocking. "Yes. So were we."

"I got"—he shrugged as though to say it couldn't be helped —"involved."

"I know."

He raised his eyebrows questioningly. Alma rolled the socks into a ball and dropped them into the sewing basket at her side. She closed its lid with a firm snap.

"I thought it better to come along now."

"Than not at all?"

"Yes."

Alma frowned. "I don't know."

Within he saw Violet turn on the light over the dining room table and spread a light blue cloth. He suspected he would shortly be urged to stay for supper and then to spend the night, which would inevitably get him to the office late in the morning. Then it crossed his mind that even now, come to apologize for the scarcity of hours in a day, days in a weekend, the hands of the clock were pushing him on, not even letting him get the words out. He stole a glance at his watch. "Where's Jim?"

"I don't know."

"His bike's there. He can't be far."

"No. I suppose not."

Wilder peered out front, back toward the garage, up to the

sleeping porch, and then whistled again, the four notes. There was stillness.

"He must have wandered off somewhere." Wilder stood up, walked to the end of the porch, and leaning on the rail, whistled again, toward the wood at the back of the house.

"Wilder, he was here with me." She indicated the chair Wilder had just left. "When you came, when he saw you coming up the path, he went inside the house."

"Oh? Is it as bad as that? My tardiness?"

"Don't be smart. If I thought you were being smart now I'd . . ." With her clenched fist she struck the cushion beside her.

"I'm not being smart, Gran."

"He saw you. We were coming back from Asbury a little after noon. It was a freak thing. The traffic was heavy on the back road, and I came down to the shore road through Bradley Beach. He saw you there on the porch of that place with . . . what's-her-name."

Wilder was silent for a moment. "Aw, dammit," he said miserably. "Dammit to hell."

He sat down again in the wicker chair, hoping she would tell him what he must do, but she was concentrating on the slender tops of the tall cedars and seemed disinclined to advice.

"I'll go find him," Wilder said, and rising, walked to the screen door. At the foot of the stairs he whistled the four notes. "Jim?"

There was no answer and he went up. At the landing he turned on the hall light. The bathroom was empty. He went into the room which had once been Catherine's and which he generally used when he came. He saw that the red gingham bedspread was mussed. The room opened onto the sleeping porch, which was dark now with its awnings down.

"Jim?"

Something gleamed in the little tin wastebasket. He stepped to the threshold of the porch and looked out. He saw the two beds, one Jimmy's, empty, the table, the chairs, the toy chest. Looking back into the basket he saw that what gleamed was a twisted reflector. He picked it up, turned it over, and seeing the metal, the broken glass beneath, recognized it. He dropped it back with a clatter.

He stepped out onto the porch, and on the north side where there was no awning he looked out through the screening. He recalled that at one time you could see the garage roof from here, but now the trees were too tall. He could see the clearing though. He could see the car and something beyond which he could not at first identify. The canoe—of course. Remorse turned his stomach, weakened him. He sagged onto the cot and sat staring into the shadows across the porch, his chin cupped in his hands.

To his astonishment he found that he was looking directly at his son. He was crouched against the wall, almost hidden by the bed and toy chest.

"Jim!" Wilder said. "Jim!" His mind searched for words, for the right words, for some apology, some explanation that might atone, that would begin to repair the damage he had done. No words came. His own forlorn despair choked him. He arose unsteadily and took a step toward his boy.

Jim, seeing his father's approach, leaped up, came toward him with a strange expression. Wilder had only a glimpse but it was to remain with him always. Jimmy's eyes were gleaming.

Ducking his father's outstretched hands, Jimmy ran hard

around the end of his bed and through his father's room. Dumfounded, Wilder heard him going down the stairs two at a time, heard Alma call, "Jimmy, what is it? Where are you going?", heard the slam of the back door.

He saw him then, a streak of white shirt and dark hair running through the trees below, and Wilder followed. Alma, on the front porch, was calling with mounting anxiety, "Jimmy! Jimmy!" and then, finding on the table the little cowbell she used to call him to meals, she rang it.

"Excuse me," Wilder said to Violet as he went through the kitchen and out the back door. He went straight toward the garage, and coming into the clearing, saw him standing there behind the canoe. "Jim, listen . . ."

Jimmy put a foot up on the hull of the canoe and shoving with all his might pushed it off the sawhorses so that it landed right side up in the gravel with a clatter of floorboards. He started down the driveway, running.

"Jimmy! Come back!"

But Jimmy did not stop. Reaching the sidewalk, he paused, looked to the right, heard the sound of Alma's bell, then turned left and disappeared.

Now alarmed, Wilder started down the drive. At the sidewalk he could see Jimmy still running, heading toward the beach, and Wilder pursued at a trot. But it was dusk now, and beneath the trees that shaded the walk, he promptly lost sight of him.

On reaching the foot of the street, Wilder stood, not sure which way to turn. In these last moments of daylight, cars, mostly of recent model, were passing and repassing the pavilion in a leisurely, automotive promenade. The summer residents were displaying their vehicular finery and observing their neighbors'. Some youngsters leaned against the rail, just looking too. A block to the north the boardwalk ended abruptly, and there small children played a listless game.

Wilder crossed the street and peered into the pavilion's refreshment shop. At the counter there were children of Jimmy's age, turning the pages of comic books, sucking on purple ices, and he was tempted to ask if anyone had seen Jimmy Stone. He did not. On the benches facing the sea there were older people—the gnomish manager of the bathhouses, some proper-looking ladies in pastels and white pumps, and a man in a wheel chair.

The boardwalk was a broad avenue stretching southward, spanning the dunes, passing under the brows of the beachfront cottages, a few of which were still proudly Gothic. It led all the way to the Stockton Hotel at the far end of the beach. Wilder set off along it, walking briskly, looking ahead for some sign of his son.

There were many children. They perched on the rail and stared at the strollers, looking for lovers to ridicule, or they sat on the benches with their parents, looking out at the graceful heads of surf that rose up and rushed into the shore, gleaming in the last light.

As Wilder proceeded, the lamps came on, and realizing it would be dark in ten minutes, he began to jog along, his footsteps resounding hollowly on the planks. He had covered half a mile or so, and the people had thinned out. He slowed to a walk, wondering if it wouldn't be wisest to turn back, to go home where, sooner or later, Jimmy would have to appear. But then he saw a child sitting alone on a bench. As he drew closer he saw that it was his own. Wilder walked by to be sure and then returned, placing his hands on the backrest.

Jimmy, who had been staring out to sea, his feet on the rail, his chin on his folded arms, was startled. Leaping to his feet, he shied away.

"Jimmy, don't go," Wilder said gently. "I want to talk to you."

Jimmy turned and ran.

"Wait! Please wait!" He started off again, fast this time, determined to overtake him. Ahead, he saw Jimmy turn and run down a flight of steps onto the beach itself and disappear underfoot.

Beneath the boardwalk it was already night. The huge pilings stood giantlike in the gloom. It was a chill cave here, and although the tide did not come this high, now it was damp here. It smelled of soggy newsprint and darkness and the sourish flotsam of the Atlantic.

"Jimmy?" Wilder called.

He saw something move—a white sleeve, perhaps, or a bare knee—and he went that way, southward, until he found him, sitting, his back to a piling, his arms folded about his knees.

Wilder sat down quietly nearby, and after a bit he said, "I'm sorry about yesterday. If I could do yesterday again I'd do it differently. But I can't. That's an unfortunate thing that once you do a thing you can't do it over, no matter how much you want to. But I can promise you that next weekend I'll come down on Friday. I'll come down early Friday."

There was no answer. From above came the sound of heels echoing on the planks, a couple walking, now in step, now out, now approaching, now fading away. Wilder looked up, saw pencil stripes of lamp light filtering through the blackness. Then there was the soft thudding of a child running. It stopped and all was quiet.

On hands and knees he moved toward Jimmy, sitting so still

there five feet away, and when he was beside him, Wilder knelt. He reached out to touch his son's shoulder, and at that instant got a handful of sand in his face. It was flung with such violence that he fell back spitting it from his mouth, blinking it from his eyes, and yet he was on his feet instantly with a cry of shock and fury. Jimmy had sprung away and once more was escaping, into the darkness, deeper under the walk. Leaping forward, he threw himself at the boy and catching him about the knees brought him down into the cold sand with a thud.

They lay there for a moment, both panting, and then Wilder reached out, and taking firm hold of Jimmy's wrist, sat up.

"Now look here. No more nonsense. Do you understand?"

Jimmy didn't move from the sand, and Wilder gave his arm a yank. "I said, do you understand?"

Jimmy sat up. Wilder saw him nod grudgingly. Keeping his grip on Jimmy's wrist, Wilder led him out from under the boardwalk, and they trudged slowly through the sand to the steps. Pausing, Wilder sat down on the lowest, pulling Jimmy with him.

"Isn't that good enough?" he asked. "If I promise you I'll come down next Friday and we can spend all day Saturday and all day Sunday doing whatever you like? We can go in the canoe, or anything. You're the boss."

Jimmy didn't answer, and they sat quietly, Wilder still gripping Jimmy's arm, afraid to release it for fear he'd lose him again. Quite suddenly night had fallen. On the blue-black sea there were lights of fishermen returning to the Manasquan and Barnegat, and far out a steamer moved slowly southward along the rim. The moon had not yet put in its appearance, but there were stars in profusion and they lit the sky.

"We'll have more time than we would have this weekend."

There was no answer.

"If that isn't good enough, you tell me what is. I'll do it."

Jimmy tried to pull his arm from his father's grip. "Let go," he said.

"You won't run away again?"

"Let go."

Wilder released his arm, watched, ready to spring after him if he fled. But Jimmy did not. He leaned sideways, away from his father, on an elbow, and dug the toe of his sneaker into the sand.

They sat in silence for several minutes, and then Jimmy spoke. "But you said you were coming down." Fraying with emotion, Jimmy's voice had risen rather musically, quavering on the final word.

Wilder hadn't promised. He had carefully avoided that, but he realized now it didn't matter, and so he said, "I know. I'm sorry." He thought somehow to explain but found he could not. Jimmy knew. He knew the essentials, and nothing Wilder could say would alter that.

"You know that I care about you more than anything in this world," Wilder said. "I wouldn't do anything to hurt you. I'd rather cut off an arm."

"But you said you were coming down." It was a plaintive chorus.

"And next week? I'm coming down next week. Doesn't that help?"

"You won't come."

"I will. I'll come next week."

"I don't care."

"You don't care if I come or not?"

"No. I don't care if you never come again."

These words, said so softly they were nearly inaudible and

which for several minutes Wilder's mind would not accept, sank in his heart. In vain he told himself it was hurt that had spoken, not Jim at all. Still he felt forlornness grow, a ball of ice in his belly. He saw with a sudden clarity that of all his failures he had, until this moment, been blind to the most agonizing.

What *had* he done? What had he *not* done? How? Where had he failed Jimmy? The answer was automatic. He had rehearsed it so many times. After all I *do* what I can. There's Greenfield. Lord knows, with Lyddie such a worry—and Mother . . . And my business, such as it is . . . Surely it's through inattention, through concern about these other things, that I'm falling apart as a breadwinner. If I'm not that, I'm nothing. And, say what you will, I've got my own life to live. A man must have a little cheer and comfort—and that too must be paid for. Each day they ask more of me, he thought, and each day I have less to give.

Looking into the night sky, he beheld the dazzling galaxy, blurry here and there with a film of cloud. He had the extraordinary feeling he was on the point of laughter, for the futility of everything he had ever done or failed to do in all his life was plain—not just crushingly, but now, confronting the universe, ludicrously so. How little it, how little he, how little anything mattered. He scooped up some sand and let it sift through his fingers. He folded his hands as though about to pray, and although he did not, he closed his eyes and dropped his head and wished that he could.

Wilder, startled at the sound of footsteps on the boardwalk, opened his eyes. He looked sideways with the chilling expectation he might find himself alone. But no, Jimmy was still there, leaning on his elbow, his head drooping. And he took some comfort from this. That he had stayed, for whatever reason, seemed the only agreeable development of an appalling day.

Immediately he had the converse of the vision of futility he had had moments earlier. It *did* matter. With a timid and suspect first light of joy he saw that here upon this plank of his and Jimmy's it did matter. "Above everything else," he said aloud.

"Are you talking to me?" Jimmy asked.

"Yes. Yes, I am. I was wondering if you'd want to go away. On a trip I mean. Would you want to leave Sea Girt and go on a trip?"

Jimmy's face was expressionless in the lamplight. "What kind of a trip?"

"Just you and I." Wilder, surprised at this developing thought, was tense with enthusiasm. "We could go for a month or two. Perhaps more if it's not too expensive. Maybe we could take the camping trip we spoke of. If that's too much camping, and maybe it is for a couple of tenderfeet, we could go on that steamer we saw going down the harbor on Saturday. Or a plane. We might go to Scotland."

Wilder waited vainly for Jimmy's answer. "You don't want to go?"

Jimmy sniffed. "When? When the cows come home?"

"Now." Wilder nodded slowly. "As soon as we can get off. It'll take some planning, of course. I'll have to get some money and arrange to leave my job. We'll have to decide where to go, and get the tickets. And we'll have to prepare Cran. Her whole life revolves around you, you know. We can't just suddenly . . ."

He saw Jimmy turn away. "But I do mean now. I'll start tomorrow. I'll reserve some space for us. I can't promise. I'll not risk promising you anything. But give me a month." He

stood up and held out a hand. "C'mon. We'll go home and
ask Gran if she can spare you. That's the first thing."

Jimmy, still full of suspicion, looked up at his father. He
got up, put his hands in his pockets, and followed him slowly
up the steps.

15.

PERVERSELY, this working day began as all that the holiday should have been. Coming through the arcade of Pennsylvania Railroad Station, and out into the bright bustle of Seventh Avenue, Wilder paused to read a thermometer and found it was already 75. Girls in print dresses with newly pink skin and armfuls of lilac hurried by him toward their offices, and he thought how pretty they looked. The city itself was inviting, seemingly rested after the weekend. The black asphalt, still dripping from a recent wash, was immaculate.

Although he had had but a few hours' sleep, he too was deeply refreshed. With long strides he set off eastward along Thirty-second Street. The feeling of rebirth had buoyed him all the way up from the shore. The familiar landscape of the Amboys, which had so often depressed him, was today a feast —the sky so bright, the earth so rich and black, the square-roofed railroad houses, for all their neglect and bloomers on the line, picturesque. What fascinating errand led the man to labor up the fire escape with the awkward bundle? The little girl to run so fast?

Throughout the night he had been filling with purpose. He had lain awake on the sleeping porch, looking out at the stars, feeling new vigor, feeling that the heart beat strong in his chest, that the flesh was firm, that he *was* a young man, that all things were possible. It was only to know that you wanted something. And hearing Jim's breathing a few feet away, a regular, soft sighing, he did know, and the fear was gone.

For a reason not at first clear to him, Harry Coe was much in his thoughts. His mocking eyes haunted Wilder's new hopes and made them suspect—until at last he saw that Harry was the symbol of his weakness, and he resolved to begin this day by confronting him, by accusing him of the plot against him. "I know about Gordon," he would say. "I know that you put him up to it. And I hope I'll be able to return the favor."

He would shirk nothing today. Not Bibi Winter. He felt that at last he could act decisively with Bibi, that before the day was out the relation of their lives would be resolved.

He would see Milton Lazarus and request a leave of absence. Then he would turn to the details. He would arrange for the transfer of available funds to his checking account. He had two savings accounts and some "E" bonds he would cash in.

Finally, on his way home, he would stop in at Cook's or American Express and find someone with whom he could discuss the trip itself. Scotland? He would keep an open mind. Perhaps the weather would be bad there. He'd want a rough idea of the expense and if, in this brisk tourist season, a boat were possible. Jimmy, he felt, would like the boat trip.

Emerging from the dark canyon of Thirty-second Street, Wilder turned down Fourth Avenue and into the lobby of 430. Here he waited with a squad of office workers until the door opened and the cross elevator man, Leo, emerged glowering at his new passengers.

Wilder waited for the others to board, and as he was about to step on, he felt the tap of a newspaper at his elbow. Turning, he found Harry Coe in a new straw hat. A knowing smile was tucked in the corner of his mouth. The short, velvety chin was heavily lotioned. It was an ornate and powerful scent.

"Have a nice weekend, Wilder?" Placing a hand on Wilder's shoulder, Harry shepherded him into the car. "Where'd you go? The shore? You seem to have a little burn there."

Wilder, feeling a first qualm of nervousness, a stage fright for the ordeal which lay before him, murmured, "Yes." It was inaudible. He stared at the annunciator.

"You say you went to the shore? I didn't hear you."

"Yes," Wilder repeated. He looked hopefully at Leo, who remained in the lobby awaiting additional passengers.

"Have a good time?"

"All right." Wilder's voice trembled, and he cleared his throat. "Harry, I want to talk to you."

"What about? Shoot."

"When we get upstairs."

Harry yawned. "We had a grand time. Stayed with friends up in Ardsley. We played some golf on Sunday and yesterday morning when it was raining. . . . You get any rain down there on the shore yesterday?"

"Fog. There was heavy fog in the morning. It cleared up in the afternoon."

"We had a little rain in the morning." Harry brightened. "We played Scrabble. They had this sixteen-year-old daughter. A knockout of a girl she was. I'm surprised that a girl sixteen years old wouldn't know any better. I mean where's she been keeping herself? In this game—you know Scrabble?"

Wilder nodded.

"You spell out words with letters. Well she spelled out . . ." Here Harry looked around the cab and, discovering three women in the back, leaned close to Wilder's ear and whispered hoarsely. Someone behind snickered, and as Leo entered the car and started them aloft, Wilder found himself laughing weakly to accommodate Harry Coe.

Stepping off on the seventh floor, Wilder was stricken with the thought that he was not going to be able to do it, that the habit of a decade was too strong, that he had played a passive role too long, that a hard shell of relationship had formed between them and it could not now be altered. He approached the appalling conclusion that, in spite of his will to do so, he was unable to tell Harry Coe off.

In passing the reception window he failed to tip his hat to Helen Russo and did not hear her call him to take his message. It was Harry who brought him the slip bearing the familiar legend: "Mrs. Newbold called, wants you to call her immediately," the *immediately* underlined three times.

"What was it?" Harry asked, carefully placing his new hat on the rack, pausing for an instant to admire it. "What did you want to talk about?"

Wilder stood at his desk, still fingering the message Harry had handed him, feeling a fine perspiration on his brow. His shirt was damp and chill with it. He shuddered and sat down.

"Nothing," he said quietly. "It was nothing."

What *held* his tongue? What strings of habit sewed it down? What fear of unpleasantness paralyzed it? What old despair sapped his new purpose? He uttered a deep sigh. It was now clear. He no longer had even the illusion of a will.

And what of Bi? Would it be the same with her—the same drifting into the familiar channel? To his growing horror he saw that it would. There would be no change for him. He could not bring about the crises of his plan. He could not face Bibi with his decision—nor even the thought of relinquishing her. When he saw her, he would be stalling again, giving her just enough encouragement to keep her from quitting him. And if just enough encouragement were to mean next week-end, he would disappoint Jimmy again.

And requesting a leave of absence? That now seemed equally impractical. Milton Lazarus wouldn't give it to him. Or worse, he would, for it would prove just the opportunity to rid himself of Wilder. No, no. If he went away now, Harry would have what was left of his job by September.

And the new purpose of the night? The resolve? The promise?

It was a dream. The fancy of a madman. How could he have so deluded himself?

Here—he felt the surface of the golden oak, touched the pile of invoices, looked through the window into the grimy courtyard at the rusting fire escape, the sooty bricks of the Martha Washington's rear wall—was reality.

He opened the drawer of the desk and taking out the bank books, looked at the columns, the deposits and withdrawals of a dozen years. He felt the stealthy warmth induced by these figures beneath his name. They were not large sums, but they were enough to lend a bit of substance, a little dignity—and a protection too, anchor to windward. And it had been his intention in the night, even as he came up on the train, to give these fine black columns of himself for a few months' holiday. Then it had seemed an act of courage. Now it was so clearly folly—the frivolity that would drain the last strength from him—that would leave him an impotent, a resourceless old man.

What had bewitched him in the night? How could he have been so bent on destroying himself? What had possessed him to the very threshold of 430 Fourth Avenue, until Harry Coe, like a hypnotist awakening his subject, tapped him with the tip of his *Herald Tribune*?

It must have been fatigue, a wooziness from having lain awake through the night, a delirium, a result of the terrible business of Jimmy's running from him.

Once again he heard the clatter of the canoe as it struck the gravel, saw Jimmy running fast down the drive, running from him along the boardwalk.

Wilder slipped his hand into the pocket of his jacket, and there he found along its bottom seam a thin welt of sand. Bringing up a pinch, he let it fall on the desk blotter. He looked at the coarse grains closely, saw a black grain, some gray, brown, yellow and pure white ones and some clear as glass. He brought up another pinch and then another. He searched his pockets and his trouser cuffs, and when he was through, he had a puddle of sand as large as a quarter in the middle of his desk. Thoughtfully he pushed it into a hill, flattened it, pushed it into a hill again. Then, with a curious haste, he fumbled in the drawer for an envelope and, finding it, swept the sand into it. He licked the envelope, sealed it, and with a stub pencil printed across its face SEA GIRT BEACH 6/1/59. He put the envelope in his pocket and rose from his chair. Harry Coe glanced up. Wilder felt the knot of his tie, gave the points of his vest a downward snap, and walked toward Milton Lazarus' office.

"Come in, Wilder." Milton Lazarus looked up from his desk. "Be with you in a moment." He initialed some expense sheets and gave them to the waiting Miss Kelly. "Do the long letter first," he said to her. "I want to get that in the mail this morning."

She nodded and went to her own desk. Milton Lazarus picked up a phone message, then turned his attention to Wilder. He frowned, anticipating further unpleasantness. "A tenant, a Mrs. Newbold at 67 East Eighty-fourth Street, has been trying to reach me. I'm told it's about the painters." He squinted over the steel rims of his spectacles. "Can't you deal with that?"

"Yes," Wilder said, chewing at his lip. "I'll get to her directly. I . . . I've been putting her off. Some other things. I'll do it right away."

"Good." Milton Lazarus handed him the message. "You take care of it." He looked impatiently at the correspondence on his desk. "Was there something. . . ?"

Wilder shifted uneasily on his feet. "Yes," he said. "There was."

"All right." He swung around in the tall-backed blue chair that dwarfed him. This morning his nervous energy seemed a petulance. "What is it, Wilder?"

Wilder folded the telephone message and put it in his pocket. "I want to go on a long vacation," he said. "I want to take Jimmy on a trip."

Milton Lazarus folded his hands across his stomach and smiled. "Well, you know my views on vacation trips. I haven't been on a vacation for, let me see, it's over ten years." He grimaced, scratched his chin, as though the recollection amused, yet still pained him. "Grace wanted to go to Florida." He shook his head. "Never again. There was nothing for a man like me to do. I don't play golf. I don't play bridge. I don't like to drink to excess, and I don't like to do nothing. I've got to have something to occupy my mind. In the end I found old Glover down there, Jerome Glover. We sat in the lobby and talked about business for four hours, and it made me so anxious for this desk I packed up and flew home. I left Grace and Anne behind." He chuckled and leaned forward. "I think anybody who goes on a trip for pleasure is out of his mind—but that's your affair."

"Well, not entirely." Wilder sat down. "It concerns the company too. I'd like to make it a long trip. Europe, I think. A trip without any definite limit. I don't want to have to come back until we're both tired of it—or each other. On the other hand, I don't want to be sticking it out if it doesn't work."

"How long is a long trip? A matter of weeks?"

"Months."

"You'd keep your boy out of school in the fall?"

Wilder shrugged. "Maybe we'll find someplace abroad where he could do a term or two. It wouldn't do him any harm I think. Anyway I don't want to feel I have to get back in September."

Milton Lazarus pulled a long face. "Let me tell you, Wilder, I have yet to see anyone get any real benefit from a holiday. It's escape. People wish to escape from themselves, from what they are. They can't, of course." He waved toward the outer office. "Look at these girls going off to the Catskills full of hope. You see them. They come back disappointed and poorer. Every time."

"Perhaps you're right. I don't know. But it's become clear to me I haven't been all the father I might. I want to correct that as best I can."

They were silent, and then Milton Lazarus said, "Your purpose in going is . . ." he searched for the word, ". . . wistful. Bound to fail."

Wilder was, to his surprise, angry. "I don't believe that."

Milton Lazarus pushed with his foot against the desk and swiveled around so that he could look down Twenty-ninth Street toward the river. "A father and son are not good company. A father and daughter, perhaps. There are times when I have been good friends with Anne—but not with Buddy. I have never been friends, you know, pals"—he smiled—"buddies, with Buddy. That's all right. It's not important that we be pals."

"I don't think that's necessarily true, Milton," Wilder replied to his own continuing astonishment. "I think a father and son can be close—at a certain age, when the son is getting to be a man and before the father is . . . too old a crock."

Milton Lazarus did not reply to this, though he seemed to be thinking it over. There was a burst from Miss Kelly's typewriter, and Wilder looked over at her desk, wondering if she had been listening, if this held any interest for her.

"A boy doesn't travel well," Milton continued. "A boy is similar to an old man like me. He will soon be homesick for his friends, for his grandmother." He took off his eyeglasses, folded them on the desk, and leaned his head against the leather upholstery. "I see you in some Midlands hotel where you have come from the ruins of the old castle or the museum where you were bored and exhausted and cheated on top of it. You're not the museum type, Wilder, no more than I."

"Then I'll learn to be."

Milton flapped a hand at Wilder. "And when the day's sight-seeing is over, it will be his natural inclination to go off with people of his own age. And for you the same. You will see some attractive woman, perhaps." He shook his head. "You will be drawn apart—not together. It will make you both unhappy. You'll be back in a couple of weeks having simply spent a lot of money."

"Now I want to go for still another reason."

"What's that?"

"To prove you wrong."

Milton Lazarus reached for his glasses. He examined the lenses, and finding them satisfactory, put them on.

"Can you afford such a trip?" he asked.

"Not without sacrifice."

"Well, there you are. And your job—that you were so concerned about on Friday? You'd be willing to let that go?"

"I was hoping you'd agree to keep it open for me."

Milton Lazarus held out his hands hopelessly. "How can I, Wilder? Be reasonable. We can't leave your job open for a couple of months—or worse, indefinitely. Nor can we ask a qualified man to take over on those terms. Surely you can see that."

"Yes," Wilder said. "I can." He nodded slowly, digesting it. "Perhaps that's best. Yes. I'm sure it is."

"Of course it is. You'll see." He was already turning back to the matters on his desk with an air of having set to rights one of the day's untidinesses.

"No," Wilder said. "I mean it the other way around. I'm going to quit. I'm giving you notice now, effective the last day of the month. Do you want a letter?"

Milton Lazarus raised his eyebrows, pushed forward his lower lip.

"Yes. I'll get you a letter." Wilder hopped up from the chair and made for the door.

At the water cooler he stopped for a drink. His throat was dry, and he swallowed gratefully and drew a second cup. To his joy he could feel the determination inside him like a rock. It was glorious. Looking for Margaret Kriendler (she was not at her desk) his eyes roamed the office, saw its staff bent to their tasks, Krauss's familiar gleaming scalp, Miss Fell's fleshy back in purple net, Miss Saur's gray hair, gone nearly white now, cut so short and gracelessly in a style that had taken her fancy twenty years ago. He was smitten with affection for them all. He had the desire to pass down the ranks of desks, embracing their occupants, or to cry out and tell them that he loved them. Instead he drank the water at a draught and, crumpling the cup, threw it at a wastebasket six feet away and took an enormous satisfaction from its going squarely in.

Milton Lazarus appeared in the door of his office and, seeing Wilder, walked toward him. From a foot away he peered up at him, puzzled. He took a cup, filled it, and drank thoughtfully.

"All right," he said. "We'll keep the job for you. We'll keep the job until September fourteenth."

"Thanks. You needn't."

He shook his head. "You won't want that much time, anyway. You'll be back long before that if I'm any judge."

"We'll see."

"I'll speak to the bookkeeper. You speak to Harry."

"Harry?"

"Ask him to take charge of your buildings while you're gone. He could go on vacation in October. He could accommodate somebody else for a change."

Dazed, Wilder watched Milton Lazarus' brisk return to his office. "I'll be damned," he said aloud, and the wonder was at himself.

Returning to his desk, Wilder found Harry with the *Tribune* still spread before him. He was reading the television column.

"I've got some news for you," Wilder said.

Harry did not look up. "Oh? What news?"

"It can wait a bit."

"Why wait? Do it now."

"I've got to go uptown." He sat down on the edge of his desk, and taking up the phone, he asked for an outside line. He dialed a number, and waiting for it to answer, he said to Harry, "Busy for lunch?"

Harry looked up and shook his head.

"I'll tell you then." He looked at his watch and saw it was not quite ten. "I'll be back by noon."

Harry looked at him curiously. "O.K. What's it all about?"

On the phone a voice said, "Sophie. Good morning."

"Good morning," Wilder said. "Miss Winter, please."

Wilder seldom called her from his desk, and Harry smiled at the mention of her name, for it seemed to him a reassuring evidence of Wilder's corruption.

"Hello?" It was Bibi Winter's voice on the phone.

"Bi?" Wilder said. "I'm coming uptown. I wonder if you could slip out and meet me for a cup of coffee?"

"Now?" she asked crossly.

"In about half an hour. Ten thirty."

"I can't, Wilder. I have an appointment. I have someone coming in at ten thirty."

"Could you get someone else to take it?"

"Not very easily. Can't it wait? Can't it wait until lunchtime?"

"I've got a lunch date."

"Until this evening?"

"No."

"Oh . . ." she said. "All right. I'll get someone. Where do we meet?"

"In the coffee shop across from you. The place with the eggs in the window."

"Murray's," she said.

At this midmorning hour Murray's Chicken Coop was becalmed. A girl in a translucent uniform which displayed her unremarkable underwear was preparing a tower of cream-cheese-and-jelly sandwiches against the noontime demand. Half a dozen leisurely coffee drinkers were at the serpentine counter. Wilder took a seat, saving the one alongside with his hat. In the mirror he glimpsed himself and touched his chin. He recalled that it had been six o'clock in the morning when he had shaved. Sea Girt. It seemed a year ago. His beard should have been to his collar. He could feel, yet he couldn't see the stubble. Actually, he thought, he looked pretty well. There was no sign of the fatigue. He appeared rather flushed. He was surprised and cheered by his reflection.

He stirred his coffee and realized he had given no thought to how he was going to put it to Bi. He had rehearsed nothing. But the determination was tangible inside him. That was enough.

Nevertheless, seeing her on the opposite curb, pausing to let a taxi pass, then coming across, skipping between two parked cars and through the glass door toward him, he felt a quickening, a little fright, a doubt—and then the sinking feeling of wanting her.

"Hello," she said. She laid her linen purse on the counter, and her eyes searched his for an instant. Then she sat beside him and touched his hand. She unbuttoned the pumpkin cardigan which she wore over a green cotton dress. "Warm," she said. "It's warm in here."

"Coffee?" the waitress asked.

"Very dark," Bibi said. "Just a tiny little bit of cream."

They watched her pour the coffee and with exaggerated care add a few drops of cream. In sampling it Bibi sipped cautiously, pursing her lips as in a kiss.

"Is it all right?" Wilder asked.

"Fine." She glanced in the mirror and touched her hair.

"Do you want something else? Some pastry?"

She looked at him coquettishly over the rim of her cup. "No."

"I think I'll have another cup." He signaled the waitress. "You're sure?"

"I'm sure." In his eyes she had seen the desire for her. It was, she thought, the sign she had been awaiting, and she smiled. A feeling of relief swept over her. "Who are you having lunch with?"

"Harry."

"Coe? Detestable Harry?" She laughed. "You stood me up for him?"

Wilder nodded. "I've got to break him some news, and I don't think he'll be pleased. He was planning on going away in August. Now he's to take my job for the summer."

"Why?" she asked. "Why is he taking your job for the summer?"

Wilder took a sip of his coffee, then another. "Because I'm going away. I'm taking Jimmy on a trip."

Bibi sat up straight on the stool, cocked her head. "*You? You're* going away?" He was stirring his coffee, staring into it unhappily, and she felt he had withdrawn. But surely this was some whimsy on his part, or she had misunderstood him. He meant they. He was taking her. "Jimmy? What do you mean? I don't get it."

In the mirror Wilder saw Bibi and himself, side by side, flanked by other patrons absorbed in their own conversations, their papers. Could it be, he wondered, that this was the end here among these strangers?

It occurred to him then that they were in transit, he and Bibi Winter, that they had been sharing a seat in some public vehicle and become so absorbed in one another that they had

had the illusion they were alone and private. But now, arriving unexpectedly at the terminal, they found it had been crowded all along with other travelers, unfamiliar people. And now they became part of that crowd once again—pushing and jostling on to their separate destinations. Looking once more at the strange faces, he felt a crushing sadness.

He addressed her in the mirror. "They saw us, Bi," he said gently. "Alma and Jimmy drove by the inn while we were on the porch. When I went to Sea Girt last night he ran away. He ran away from me."

They were both silent for a moment until at last Bibi looked into her cup and found it empty. "You know, I think I will have some more coffee," she said.

When the fresh cup arrived, she took a sip from it and said, "Well, you know it isn't so awful. It sounds awful, but it's just the way it happened. I mean it isn't that he didn't know about us. Jimmy knows there's a relationship between us, and naturally he's jealous of it. As a child he wouldn't want to share you with . . . anyone, least of all with someone like me where there's no . . . formal relationship. You know I've always said that if we were married Jimmy would accept our . . . our love for one another, perfectly easily. Kids do."

"Maybe."

"You see, he was acting like a kid. I mean, that's the child, the spoiled child wanting everything. And Alma *has* spoiled him. She *has* brought him up to think the world revolves around him. Being an only child, and that just intensified by Alma's giving him his every wish. In a way I think the experience of seeing us there, the growing knowledge that he can't have everything, and he can't have all of everybody, is good. I mean that's the way people grow up. Well, isn't it?"

"I don't know. I suppose it's one of the ways."

"What did you expect to gain by a trip? Was it just to make up to him for yesterday? To clear your conscience of that?"

Wilder wadded up his paper napkin and dropped it into his empty cup. "To behave like a father instead of letting Alma do it."

"Alma. Good Lord, Cousin Alma'd die without Jimmy. Have you thought of how miserable she'd be if you took him away?"

"Yes."

"For how long?"

"A couple of months."

"Oh, Wilder, you couldn't. What would she do?"

"She's thinking about it."

Bibi's eyes widened and then, without a sound, she began to cry. The waitress noticed and watched with mild interest as Bibi fumbled in her purse for a handkerchief. "And me?" she whispered. "What about me?"

He didn't reply.

"Have you thought about me, for God's sake?"

"Yes."

"What?" Her voice, growing sharp, coarsening, pained him. "That I'll sit here twiddling my thumbs and counting the days? Telling Emil Braun that I'll let him know when you get back?"

He smiled unhappily. "As a matter of fact, something of the sort keeps occurring to me."

"Well, let it unoccur. It's no good."

"I know. I know it's no good." He turned to her and looked at her, his eyes full of love. "It's just that I can't bear the thought of . . . not seeing you. I'm going to miss you terribly."

"That isn't true," she said. Reaching into her purse, she took out a cigarette and a match book. Her hand shook as she brought the lighted match to the cigarette, and it went out.

She handed the matches to Wilder, and he went about the firing of her cigarette with great concentration, as though all their happiness depended on it.

She blew out a puff of smoke and said, "You're lying, Wilder. You don't really give a damn about me."

Wilder let the match burn, and then when it had almost reached his fingers, waved it out. "It's on the tip of my tongue to hold out some hope that when I come back . . . to ask you to put him off until I do get back. It's because I do give a damn about you that I'm not going to do that. It would only lead to more unhappiness for you."

Bibi rubbed the cigarette out in the saucer and turned her eyes upon him. She said with some ferocity, "Balls!"

Wilder's face burned as though she had slapped him. He was shocked, not by the crudity itself, but he hadn't believed her capable of it. Here, to his anguish, she was becoming the stranger, before his eyes.

Hopping from the stool, Bibi Winter snatched up her purse, started toward the door, but paused, and turning back to him, she said "You're your Momma's." People nearby turned to watch. "You'll never be anyone else's." She fumbled with the buttons of the sweater, clutching it in her fist as she backed away. "Not Jimmy's or mine or anybody else's—just your Momma's boy." Then she was gone, running down the aisle, out the door, into the street. Wilder looked into the mirror and saw that the others had already gone back to their papers, their conversations.

"More coffee?" the waitress asked.

"No. No, thank you," he said, and after a moment Wilder picked up the checks and started slowly toward the cashier.

At the Petit Coin, the little restaurant on Twenty-sixth Street, Wilder and Harry Coe had to wait in the crowded vestibule for a table, and when at last they were seated, it was in one of the alcoves. There were four of these along the wall, trysting places for hand holding, the sharing of secrets. Wilder would have much preferred a place in the open for this interview with Harry. Silently they ignored the dessert dishes of their predecessors and tried to catch the attention of the waitress, who looked more distraught, wearier, than when she had last attended them.

"Why do we come to this place?" Harry asked. "You're the one that always steers us in here."

Wilder, who had been thinking of Bibi Winter, wondering if she was with Emil Braun now in some uptown restaurant, if she was accepting him, frowned, trying to recall what Harry had said.

"Because it's cheap, I guess."

"There are plenty of places you can get a ninety-five-cent lunch in this neighborhood."

"Not such a good one." He looked toward the kitchen and saw in the corridor layers of blue haze. "The French can't really cook a poor dish."

"They try," Harry said. "They really try in here."

And then the waitress came, gathering the dirty dishes onto her tray, taking their order impatiently.

"Wine?" Harry asked him.

"No," Wilder said. "I don't want any wine."

"Well, that's upright of you." He put the little wine card back behind the salt and pepper shakers and dismissed the waitress with a shake of his head. He licked his thin lips as though he anticipated an argument to which he was fully equal. "Now, what's up?"

Wilder looked down at the stained tablecloth and began to brush the breadcrumbs together.

"Am I meant to guess?" Harry asked. "Is it a game?"

"When are you planning your vacation?" Wilder asked. "Is it August?"

Harry nodded. "The first two weeks. We're going to drive up to Maine, maybe on into Nova Scotia. I've never been up that way."

Wilder scraped the pile of breadcrumbs into the ashtray. "You couldn't be persuaded to go in the fall?"

"The fall? Why the fall?"

"I want you to take my buildings for the summer. I'm going away."

Harry made a distasteful face. "No. I don't want to go up there in the fall. It's probably as cold as a witch's twitch up there in the fall. Anyway the whole point is getting out of New York in August." The waitress passed with an order of filet of sole, and he craned to see if he had made the right selection in the lamb. "All summer? You're going away for all summer? How are you going to arrange that?"

"With your help, I hope. I'm taking a leave of absence until September fourteenth. No pay. But I'll need somebody, somebody who knows and somebody I can trust, to look after things while I'm gone."

Harry watched him for a moment, thinking, and then shook his head. "I'd like to help you out, Wilder. You know that. But Bernice has been counting on this. She's been down to the AAA and got the maps and figured out where we'll stay and all that . . . no, I couldn't change it now. Why do you want to go off for such a long time? What are you up to?" A smile was starting in the corner of his mouth.

Wilder raised a spoon of sugar from the bowl and poured it back slowly. "Actually, I've spoken to Mr. Lazarus about it. He's given his approval."

"To what?"

"To your looking after my buildings while I'm away."

Harry pulled at his nose. Picking up his knife, he drummed with its point and slapped it down again with a bang.

"Now, I don't like that, Wilder. I don't like that a damn bit. I don't like having things done behind my back."

"I'll remember that," Wilder said.

"Is that what you had in mind coming up in the elevator?"

"No," Wilder said. "That was something else."

"Well, you might have come to me first."

"I didn't suggest it. It didn't even occur to me. Mr. Lazarus did."

The waitress set before them the thick white plates, each with its slice of lamb, and Wilder watched Harry take up his knife and fork and begin to eat vigorously, as though the dish required his punishment.

"Well, now it's my inning," he said, "I'm back to see Milton the minute we've finished here."

"Harry," Wilder said, "I'm taking Jimmy to Europe. It's important to me. If necessary, I'll quit. Still I can't afford to throw away the only job I know. I want you to keep it for me. If I don't come back—and I may not—it's yours."

Harry cut a piece of his meat. Mute, chewing thoughtfully, he stared at the wall over Wilder's head, and Wilder presumed he was confronting Milton Lazarus with the injustice done him.

"I have still another problem," Wilder went on. "Someone's got to keep an eye on Mother and Lyddie while I'm away. The Edison turns off the electricity on them every now and again. I don't know anyone to ask but you."

Wilder took up his fork to find his luncheon already cold.

Across the table it looked as though Harry had not heard a word. He was busy mopping up the gravy with a crust of bread.

"I'm not much on pleading," Wilder said. "You know that. But I do want you to do this for me."

"Why me?" Harry asked. "Why not Buddy Lazarus? He can manage your buildings. So can Murray. Why don't they take their vacations in the fall?"

Wilder turned his water glass slowly. "Because you're my friend. At least, that's the assumption."

"What do you mean by that?"

"Are you my friend?"

"I always thought so." Harry leaned against the bench. "What is this? I have to junk my vacation and do your work for you to qualify as a friend?"

"If you're not my friend, I have none," Wilder said. "And that's possible. Yes, that's very possible. I was just thinking that we *have* been friends, very close friends, you and I, and somewhere along the line I've spoiled it. I'm the one to blame." He looked at Harry, who returned his gaze evenly. "I sometimes wonder about my own capacity for friendship—if I have any at all. You know, even as a boy I wasn't much good at it. Catherine had it, of course. She had it to spare. We had begun to see a lot of people—the Hinmans, Charlie Freeman, Phil and Sue Coles." He shrugged. "I haven't any notion what's become of them. When Catherine died I went about it deliberately, cutting free of them."

From the center of the restaurant there was a crash, and both men looked to see the waitress glance toward the cashier and then, with a sigh, kneel to gather up the shattered crockery.

"Yes," Harry said, drawing Wilder's attention back to themselves. "I know that. It was natural after what you'd been through."

"It was selfishness. Not that I could have helped it if I'd wanted. I'd shriveled up. I wasn't generating enough energy —not even enough to accept kindness."

Harry nodded. "I know what you mean. God knows, Bernice and I have talked about it. You know we've tried time and time again to—"

"Yes," Wilder interrupted, "you have. That's what I mean. It's not you that's failed. It's me." He sighed. "In any case, what's left is something hollow. The empty shell of it." He looked up. "Don't you think?"

Harry shifted uncomfortably. "Maybe. Maybe not. I don't know if it's the kind of thing you can put your finger on."

"No? Perhaps. But I'm going to try. I think it will be good for both of us if we can put a finger on it. You see, it's occurred to me that I am so anxious to preserve that shell, even the semblance of your friendship"—he looked straight across the table into Harry's eyes—"that I don't want to admit you arranged the Gordon business."

Harry wiped his mouth carefully, kneaded the napkin into a ball and put it beside his plate. "The Gordon business?"

Leaning back, Wilder hooked his thumbs into the bottom pockets of his vest. "I'm told that you've had George Gordon in the office, that you took him in to meet Milton Lazarus."

"Well, I did. Yes, I did." Harry said quickly. "But good Lord, Wilder, I had no idea he was going to . . ." Hunching his shoulders, he tugged at the collar of his jacket. "All I did was introduce . . . For a long time George had been saying how he'd like to meet Milton. Now, there's no harm in that, is there? I didn't see how I could refuse. Do you? I mean he could have called up himself, and Milton would have seen him. But I assure you, Wilder, I had no idea . . ." He broke off, reddening with fresh indignation. "Listen, are you accusing me? Do you think there was some kind of a deal?"

Wilder shook his head. "No. As a matter of fact that hadn't even occurred to me. I'm that simple-minded. Was there?"

"Now listen, Wilder. You're beginning to make me mad. If you think I'd sell you out . . . if you really think I could . . ."

Wilder nodded. "Of course you could."

"My God, Wilder." He drew a wallet from his hip, and snatching two dollars from it, threw them scornfully across the table. "I don't have to sit here and be insulted by you."

"I haven't finished. Sit down a minute."

Harry hesitated, slowly sat down on the edge of the seat.

"Why shouldn't you take some small pleasure in my misfortunes?" Wilder smiled. "That's the competitive spirit."

"Well, I don't," Harry said. "For your information, I don't. My God, Wilder. What kind of a guy do you take me for? You've had a pretty rough time of it. I know that, and I've done what I can to try and make it easier."

"Yes, you have. Nevertheless, your course is through me, over me, over my dead body." He raised his hand to suppress Harry's protest. "I've fallen in your path and let you down." He nodded, thinking it over. "I'm afraid the friend who grows weak is as much at fault as the one who takes advantage of it. Whatever your role in the Gordon business, it's as much my fault as yours, Harry. I bear no grudge." Leaning back in the seat, he shoved his legs out straight under the table and thrust his hands deep in his pants pockets. He beamed. "Listen. It's good to tell you that. Thanks. It is a fine feeling to have you know that I know about the one hundred and one little treacheries you have committed against me in the last

year—of getting the handyman fired up at Seventy-ninth
Street, of reporting all that mess about Gunderson to Murray.
You have no idea how marvelous it is to get that off my chest."
Wilder laughed. "A grand and glorious feeling. Here," he
cried, sighting the waitress miraculously empty-handed,
"could you bring us a bottle of wine? A bottle of that Al-
maden? We have got something to celebrate in here."

When the wine came, they drank it from heavy, opaque
glasses—Wilder, exuberantly, as he expanded the list of
Harry's perfidies, Harry moodily, protesting at first, floundering wretchedly in the corner, where at last he collapsed into
silence.

Seeing him suddenly as pitiable, Wilder relented and
turned to his plans for the trip until slowly, cautiously Harry
revived to make a suggestion about the itinerary. The lakes,
he had heard, were the thing to see and, he thought, no more
than a day's journey from London.

When the two men left the restaurant and walked slowly
west toward Fourth, Wilder was again recalling the walks
with Harry, how they would move silently along these city
pavements and feel no need to speak. At the corner Wilder
said, "I'm going uptown." He nodded toward the subway
kiosk at Twenty-eighth Street. "Will you tell Miss Russo? I'll
be up at 67 East Eighty-fourth if anyone wants me—8B, Mrs.
Newbold's apartment."

Harry nodded. "O.K." He turned toward the window of an
office supplier and studied a rotary card index. "Look, don't
worry about your going away. I'll take care of everything.
What the hell, I'll do it. I've been thinking it over, and I'd
just as soon go in October. That's a pretty month, with the
foliage turning and all."

"Thanks," Wilder said. "I was pretty sure you would."

Harry looked up at him. "You were?"

Wilder nodded and reached for Harry's hand.

On the Twenty-eighth Street subway platform he leaned out and looked down the tracks and saw the headlights of the local train just coming into the station at Twenty-third Street. He looked at his reflection in the mirror of a gum dispenser and decided he looked all right, the fatigue still not showing, the beard still not dark. And he thought again of Bibi Winter. With an acute stab of desolateness he realized he would not be seeing her tonight. As darkness fell upon the city and men and women walked fast along the pavements, hurrying to their light and their love, he would be alone. In the little apartment in Tudor City his hand would move toward the phone. He would be thinking of Bi. She was a habit not easily broken.

The train came into the station, and Wilder stepped aboard. As the doors slid closed and he began to move swiftly uptown, he pulled the slip from his pocket that had Mrs. Newbold's name on it. Looking at it, he found to his joy he was anticipating the interview. The blue in Mrs. Newbold's dining room. He was sure she was going to be happy with it.